FORGOTTEN REALMS®

R·A·SALVATORE

THE LONE DROW

THE HUNTER'S BLADES TRILOGY

Wizards OF THE COAST®

The Hunter's Blades Trilogy, Book II
THE LONE DROW

©2003 Wizards of the Coast, Inc.

Distributed in the United States by Holtzbrinck Publishing. Distributed in Canada by Fenn Ltd.

Distributed to the hobby, toy, and comic trade in the United States and Canada by regional distributors.

Distributed worldwide by Wizards of the Coast, Inc. and regional distributors.

Printed in the U.S.A.

Cover art by Todd Lockwood
First Printing: October 2003
Library of Congress Catalog Card Number: 2003100830

9 8 7 6 5 4 3 2 1

US ISBN: 0-7869-3012-8
UK ISBN: 0-7869-3013-6
620-17986-001-EN

U.S., CANADA,
ASIA, PACIFIC, & LATIN AMERICA
Wizards of the Coast, Inc.
P.O. Box 707
Renton, WA 98057-0707
+1-800-324-6496

EUROPEAN HEADQUARTERS
Wizards of the Coast, Belgium
T Hofveld 6d
1702 Groot-Bijgaarden
Belgium
+322-467-3360

Visit our web site at **www.wizards.com**

ALSO BY R.A. SALVATORE

DEMONWARS SERIES
The Demon Awakens
The Demon Spirit
The Demon Apostle
Mortalis
Ascendance
Transcendence
Immortalis

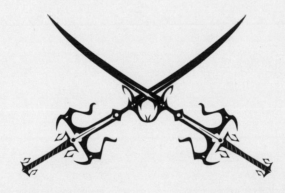

"The three mists, Obould Many-Arrows," Tsinka Shrinrill shrieked, her eyes wide, eyeballs rolling about insanely. She was in her communion as she addressed the orc king and the others, lost somewhere between the real world and the land of the gods, so she claimed. "The three mists define your kingdom beneath the Spine of the World: the long line of the Surbrin River, giving her vapors to the morning air; the fetid smoke of the Trollmoors reaching up to your call; the spiritual essence of your long-dead ancestors, the haunting of Fell Pass. This is your time, King Obould Many-Arrows, and this will be your domain!"

The orc shaman ended her proclamation by throwing up her arms and howling, and those many other mouths of Gruumsh One-Eye, god of orcs, followed her lead, similarly shrieking, raising their arms, and turning circles as they paced a wider circuit around the orc king and the ruined wooden statue of their beloved god.

The ruined *hollow* statue used by their enemies, the insult to the image of Gruumsh. The defiling of their god.

Urlgen Threefist, Obould's son and heir to the throne, looked on with a mixture of amazement, trepidation, and gratitude. He had never liked Tsinka—one of the minor, if more colorful shamans of the Many-Arrows tribe—and he knew that she was speaking largely along the lines scripted by Obould himself. He scanned the area, noting the sea of snarling orcs, all angry and frustrated, mouths wide, teeth yellow and green, sharpened and broken. He looked at the bloodshot and jaundiced eyes, all glancing this way and that with excitement and fear. He watched the continual jostling and shoving, and he noted the many hurled insults, which were often answered by hurled missiles. Warriors all, angry and bitter— as were all the orcs of the Spine of the World—living in dank caves while the other races enjoyed the comforts of their respective cities and societies. They were all anxious, as Urlgen was anxious, pointy tongues licking torn lips. Would Obould reshape the fate and miserable existence of the orcs of the North?

Urlgen had led the charge against the human town that had been known as Shallows, and he had found a great victory there. The tower of the powerful wizard, long a thorn in the side of the orcs, was toppled, and the mighty wizard was dead, along with most of his townsfolk and a fair number of dwarves, including, they all believed, King Bruenor Battlehammer himself, the ruler of Mithral Hall.

But many others had escaped Urlgen's assault, using that blasphemous statue. Upon seeing the great and towering idol, most of Urlgen's orc forces had properly prostrated themselves before it, paying homage to the image of their merciless god. It had all been a ruse, though, and the statue had opened, revealing a small force of fierce dwarves who had massacred many of the unsuspecting orcs and sent the rest fleeing for the mountains. And so there had been an escape by those remaining defenders of the dying town, and the fleeing refugees had met up with another dwarf contingent—estimates put their number at four hundred or so. Those combined forces had fended off Urlgen's chasing army.

The orc commander had lost many.

Thus, when Obould had arrived on the scene, Urlgen had expected to be berated and probably even beaten for his failure, and indeed, his vicious father's immediate responses had been along those very lines.

But then, to the surprise of them all, the reports of potential reinforcements had come filtering in. Many other tribes had begun to crawl out of the Spine of the World. In reflecting on that startling moment, Urlgen still marveled at his father's quick-thinking response. Obould had ordered the battlefield sealed, the southern marches of the area cleared of signs of any passage whatsoever. The goal was to make it seem as if none had escaped Shallows—Obould understood that the control of information to the newcomers would be critical. To that effect, he had put Urlgen to work instructing his many warriors, telling them that none of their enemies had escaped, warning them against believing anything other than that.

And the orc tribes from the deep holes of the Spine of the World had come running to Obould's side. Orc chieftains had placed valuable gifts at Obould's feet and had begged him to accept their fealty. The pilgrimages had been led by the shamans, so they all said. With their wicked deception, the dwarves had angered Gruumsh, and so many of Gruumsh's priestly followers had sent their respective tribes to the side of Obould, who would lead the way to vengeance. Obould, who had slain King Bruenor Battlehammer, would make the dwarves pay dearly for their sacrilege.

For Urlgen, of course, it had all come as a great relief. He was taller than his father, but not nearly strong enough to openly challenge the mighty orc leader. Add to Obould's great strength and skill his wondrously crafted, ridged and spiked black battle mail, and that greatsword of his, which could burst into flame with but a thought, and no one, not even overly proud Urlgen, would even think of offering challenge for control of the tribe.

Urlgen didn't have to worry about that, though. The shamans, led by the gyrating priestess, were promising Obould so many of his dreams and desires and were praising him for a great victory at Shallows—a victory that had been achieved by his honored son. Obould looked at Urlgen more than once as the ceremony continued, and his toothy smile was wide. It wasn't that vicious smile that promised how greatly he would enjoy torturing someone. Obould was pleased with Urlgen, pleased with all of it.

King Bruenor Battlehammer was dead, after all, and the dwarves were in flight. And even though the orcs had lost nearly a thousand warriors at Shallows, their numbers had since swollen several times over. More were coming, too, climbing into the sunlight (many for perhaps the first time in their lives), blinking away the sting of the brightness, and moving along the mountain trails to the south, to the call of the shamans, to the call of Gruumsh, to the call of King Obould Many-Arrows.

"I will have my kingdom," Obould proclaimed when the shamans had finished their dance and their keening. "And once I am done with the land inside the mountains and the three mists, we will strike out against those who encircle us and oppose us. I will have Citadel Felbarr!" he cried, and a thousand orcs cheered.

"I will send the dwarves fleeing to Adbar, where I will seal them in their filthy holes!" Obould went on, leaping around and running along the front ranks of the gathered, and a thousand orcs cheered.

"I will shake the ground of Mirabar to the west!" Obould cried, and the cheers multiplied.

"I will make Silverymoon herself tremble at the mention of my name!"

That brought the greatest cheers of all, and the vocal Tsinka grabbed the great orc roughly and kissed him, offering herself to him, offering to him Gruumsh's blessing in the highest possible terms.

Obould swept her up with one powerful arm, crushing her close to his side, and the cheering intensified yet again.

Urlgen wasn't cheering, but he was surely smiling as he watched Obould carry the priestess up the ramp to the defiled statue of Gruumsh. He was thinking how much greater his inheritance would soon become.

After all, Obould wouldn't live forever.

And if it seemed that he might, Urlgen was confident that he would find a way to correct that situation.

PART ONE EMOTIONAL ANARCHY

I did everything right.

Every step of my journey out of Menzoberranzan was guided by my inner map of right and wrong, of community and selflessness. Even on those occasions when I failed, as everyone must, my missteps were of judgment or simple frailty and were not in disregard of my conscience. For in there, I know, reside the higher principles and tenets that move us all closer to our chosen gods, closer to our definitions, hopes, and understandings of paradise.

I did not abandon my conscience, but it, I fear, has deceived me.

I did everything right.

Yet Ellifain is dead, and my long-ago rescue of her is a mockery.

I did everything right.

And I watched Bruenor fall, and I expect that those others I loved, that everything I loved, fell with him.

Is there a divine entity out there somewhere, laughing at my foolishness?

Is there even a divine entity out there, anywhere?

Or was it all a lie, and worse, a self-deception?

Often have I considered community, and the betterment of the individual within the context of the betterment of the whole. This was the guiding principle of my existence, the realization that forced me from Menzoberranzan. And now, in this time of pain, I have come to understand—or perhaps it is just that now I have forced myself to admit—that my belief was also something much more personal. How ironic that in my declaration of community, I was in effect and in fact feeding my own desperate need to belong to something larger than myself.

In privately declaring and reinforcing the righteousness of my beliefs, I was doing no differently from those who flock before the preacher's pulpit. I was seeking comfort and guidance, only I was looking for the needed answers within, whereas so many others seek them without.

By that understanding, I did everything right. And yet, I cannot dismiss the growing realization, the growing trepidation, the growing terror, that I, ultimately, was wrong.

For what is the point if Ellifain is dead, and if she existed in such turmoil through all the short years of her life? For what is the point if I and my friends followed our hearts and trusted in our swords, only for me to watch them die beneath the rubble of a collapsing tower?

If I have been right all along, then where is justice, and where is the reciprocation of a grateful god?

Even in asking that question, I see the hubris that has so infected me. Even in asking that question, I see the machinations of my soul laid bare. I cannot help but ask, am I any different than my kin? In technique, surely, but in effect? For in declaring community and dedication, did I not truly seek exactly the same things as the priestesses I left behind in Menzoberranzan? Did I, like they, not seek eternal life and higher standing among my peers?

As the foundation of Withegroo's tower swayed and toppled, so too have the illusions that have guided my steps.

I was trained to be a warrior. Were it not for my skill with my scimitars, I expect I would be a smaller player in the world around me, less respected and less accepted. That training and talent are all that I have left now; it is the foundation upon which I intend to build this new chapter in the curious and winding road that is the life of Drizzt Do'Urden. It is the extension of my rage that I will turn loose upon the wretched creatures that have so shattered all that I held dear. It is the expression of what I have lost: Ellifain, Bruenor, Wulfgar, Regis, Catti-brie, and, in effect, Drizzt Do'Urden.

These scimitars, Icingdeath and Twinkle by name, become my definition of myself now, and Guenhwyvar again is my only companion. I trust in both, and in nothing else.

—Drizzt Do'Urden

1

ANGER'S REMINDER

Drizzt didn't like to think of it as a shrine. Propped on a forked stick, the one-horned helmet of Bruenor Battlehammer dominated the small hollow that the dark elf had taken as his home. The helm was set right before the cliff face that served as the hollow's rear wall, in the only place within the natural shelter that got any sunlight at all.

Drizzt wanted it that way. He wanted to see the helmet. He wanted never to forget. And it wasn't just Bruenor he was determined to remember, and not just his other friends.

Most of all, Drizzt wanted to remember who had done that horrible thing to him and to his world.

He had to fall to his belly to crawl between the two fallen boulders and into the hollow, and even then the going was slow and tight. Drizzt didn't care; he actually preferred it that way. The total lack of comforts, the almost animalistic nature of his existence, was good for him, was cathartic, and even more than that, was yet another reminder to him of what he had to become, of whom he had to be if he wanted to survive. No more was he Drizzt Do'Urden of Icewind Dale, friend to Bruenor and Catti-brie, Wulfgar and Regis. No more was he Drizzt Do'Urden, the ranger trained by Montolio deBrouchee in the ways of nature and the spirit of Mielikki. He was once again that lone drow who had wandered out of Menzoberranzan. He was once again that refugee from the city of dark elves, who had forsaken the ways of the priestesses who had so wronged him and who had murdered his father.

He was the Hunter, the instinctual creature who had defeated the fell ways of the Underdark, and who would repay the orc hordes for the death of his dearest friends.

He was the Hunter, who sealed his mind against all but survival, who put aside the emotional pain of the loss of Ellifain.

Drizzt knelt before the sacred totem one afternoon, watching the splay of sunlight on the tilted helmet. Bruenor had lost one of the horns on it years and years past, long before Drizzt had come into his life. The dwarf had never replaced the horn, he had told Drizzt, because it was a reminder to him always to keep his head low.

Delicate fingers moved up and felt the rough edge of that broken horn. Drizzt could still catch the smell of Bruenor on the leather band of the helm, as if the dwarf was squatting in the dark hollow beside him. As if they had just returned from another brutal battle, breathing heavy, laughing hard, and lathered in sweat.

The drow closed his eyes and saw again that last desperate image of Bruenor. He saw Withegroo's white tower, flames leaping up its side, a lone dwarf rushing around on top, calling orders to the bitter end. He saw the tower lean and tumble, and watched the dwarf disappear into the crumbling blocks.

He closed his eyes all the tighter to hold back the tears. He had to defeat them, had to push them far, far away. The warrior he had become had no place for such emotions. Drizzt opened his eyes and looked again at the helmet, drawing strength in his anger. He followed the line of a sunbeam to the recess behind the staked headgear, to see his own discarded boots.

Like the weak and debilitating emotion of grief, he didn't need them anymore.

Drizzt fell to his belly and slithered out through the small opening between the boulders, moving into the late afternoon sunlight. He jumped to his feet almost immediately after sliding clear and put his nose up to the wind. He glanced all around, his keen eyes searching every shadow and every play of the sunlight, his bare feet feeling the cool ground beneath him. With a cursory glance all around, the Hunter sprinted off for higher ground.

He came out on the side of a mountain just as the sun disappeared behind the western horizon, and there he waited, scouting the region as the shadows lengthened and twilight fell.

Finally, the light of a campfire glittered in the distance.

Drizzt's hand went instinctively to the onyx figurine in his belt pouch. He didn't take it forth and summon Guenhwyvar, though. Not that night.

His vision grew even more acute as the night deepened around him, and Drizzt ran off, silent as the shadows, elusive as a feather on a windy autumn day. He wasn't constricted by the mountain trails, for he was too nimble to be slowed by boulder tumbles and broken ground. He wove through trees easily, and so stealthily that many of the forest animals, even wary deer, never heard or noted his approach, never knew he had passed unless a shift in the wind brought his scent to them.

At one point, he came to a small river, but he leaped from wet stone to wet stone in such perfect balance that even their water-splashed sides did little to trip him up.

He had lost sight of the fire almost as soon as he came down from the mountain spur, but he had taken his bearings from up there and he knew where to run, as if anger itself was guiding his long and sure strides.

Across a small dell and around a thick copse of trees, the drow caught sight of the campfire once more, and he was close enough to see the silhouettes of the forms moving around it. They were orcs, he knew at once, from their height and broad shoulders and their slightly hunched manner of moving. A couple were arguing—no surprise there—and Drizzt knew enough of their guttural language to understand their dispute to be over which would keep watch. Clearly, neither wanted the duty, nor thought it anything more than an inconvenience.

The drow crouched behind some brush not far away and a wicked grin grew across his face. Their watch was indeed inconsequential, he thought, for alert or not, they would not take note of him.

They would not see the Hunter.

The brutish sentry dropped his spear across a big stone, interlocked his fingers, and inverted his hands. His knuckles cracked more loudly than snapping branches.

"Always Bellig," he griped, glancing back at the campfire and the many forms gathered around it, some resting, others tearing at scraps of putrid food. "Bellig keeps watch. You sleep. You eat. Always Bellig keeps watch."

He continued to grumble and complain, and he continued to look back at the encampment for a long while.

Finally, he turned back—to see facial features chiseled from ebony, to see a shock of white hair, and to see eyes, those eyes! Purple eyes! Flaming eyes!

Bellig instinctively reached for his spear—or started to, until he saw the flash of a gleaming blade to the left and the right. Then he tried to bring his arms in close to block instead, but he was far too slow to catch up to the dark elf's scimitars.

He tried to scream out, but by that point, the curved blades had cut two deep lines, severing his windpipe.

Bellig clutched at those mortal wounds and the swords came back, then back again, and again.

The dying orc turned as if to run to his comrades, but the scimitars struck again, at his legs, their fine edges easily parting muscle and tendon.

Bellig felt a hand grab him as he fell, guiding him down quietly to the ground. He was still alive, though he had no way to draw breath. He was still alive, though his lifeblood deepened in a dark red pool around him.

His killer moved off, silently.

"*Arsh*, get yourself quiet over there, stupid Bellig," Oonta called from under the boughs of a wide-spreading elm not far to the side of the campsite. "Me and Figgle is talking!"

"Him's a big mouth," Figgle the Ugly agreed.

With his nose missing, one lip torn away, and green-gray teeth all twisted and tusky, Figgle was a garish one even by orc standards. He had bent too close to a particularly nasty worg in his youth and had paid the price.

"Me gonna kill him soon," Oonta remarked, drawing a crooked smile from his sentry companion.

A spear soared in, striking the tree between them and sticking fast.

"Bellig!" Oonta cried as he and Figgle stumbled aside. "Me gonna kill you sooner!"

With a growl, Oonta reached for the quivering spear, as Figgle wagged his head in agreement.

"Leave it," came a voice, speaking basic Orcish but too melodic in tone to belong to an orc.

Both sentries froze and turned around to look in the direction from whence the spear had come. There stood a slender and graceful figure, black hands on hips, dark cape fluttering out in the night wind behind him.

"You will not need it," the dark elf explained.

"Huh?" both orcs said together.

"Whatcha seeing?" asked a third sentry, Oonta's cousin Broos. He came in from the side, to Oonta and Figgle's left, the dark elf's right. He looked to the two and followed their frozen gazes back to the drow, and he, too, froze in place. "Who that be?"

"A friend," the dark elf said.

"Friend of Oonta's?" Oonta asked, poking himself in the chest.

"A friend of those you murdered in the town with the tower," the dark elf explained, and before the orcs could even truly register those telling words, the dark elf's scimitars appeared in his hands.

He might have reached for them so quickly and fluidly that the orcs hadn't followed the movement, but to them, all three, it simply seemed as if the weapons had appeared there.

Broos looked to Oonta and Figgle for clarification and asked, "Huh?"

And the dark form rushed past him.

And he was dead.

The dark elf came in hard for the orc duo. Oonta yanked the spear free, while Figgle drew out a pair of small blades, one with a forked, duel tip, the other greatly curving.

Oonta deftly brought the spear in an overhand spin, its tip coming over and down hard to block the charging drow.

But the drow slid down below that dipping spear, skidding right in between the orcs. Oonta fumbled with the spear as Figgle brought his two weapons down hard.

But the drow wasn't there, for he had leaped straight up, rising in the air between the orcs. Both skilled orc warriors altered their weapons wonderfully, coming in hard at either side of the nimble creature.

Those scimitars were there, though, one intercepting the spear, the other neatly picking off Figgle's strikes with a quick double parry. And even as the dark elf's blades blocked the attack, the dark elf's feet kicked out, one behind, one ahead, both scoring direct and stunning hits on orc faces.

Figgle fell back, snapping his blades back and forth before him to ward off any attacks while he was so disoriented and dazed. Oonta similarly retreated, brandishing the spear in the air before him. They regained their senses together and found themselves staring at nothing but each other.

"Huh?" Oonta asked, for the drow was not to be seen.

Figgle jerked suddenly and the tip of a curving scimitar erupted from the center of his chest. It disappeared almost immediately, the dark elf coming around the orc's side, his second scimitar taking out the creature's throat as he passed.

Wanting no part of such an enemy, Oonta threw the spear, turned, and fled, running flat out for the main encampment and crying out in fear. Orcs leaped up all around the terrified Oonta, spilling their foul foods—raw and rotting meat, mostly—and scrambling for weapons.

"What'd you do?" one cried.

"Who got the killing?" yelled another.

"Drow elf! Drow elf!" Oonta cried. "Drow elf kilt Figgle and Broos! Drow elf kilt Bellig!"

Drizzt allowed the fleeing orc to escape back within the lighted area of the camp proper and used the distraction of the bellowing brute to get into the shadows of a large tree right on the encampment's perimeter. He slid his scimitars away as he did a quick scan, counting more than a dozen of the creatures.

Hand over hand, the drow went up the tree, listening to Oonta's recounting of the three Drizzt had slain.

"Drow elf?" came more than one curious echo, and one of them mentioned Donnia, a name that Drizzt had heard before.

Drizzt moved out to the edge of one branch, some fifteen feet up from the ground and almost directly over the gathering of orcs. Their eyes were turning outward, to the shadows of the surrounding trees, compelled by Oonta's tale. Unseen above them, Drizzt reached inside himself, to those hereditary powers of the drow, the innate magic of the race, and he brought forth a globe of impenetrable darkness in the midst of the orc group, right atop the fire that marked the center of the encampment. Down went the drow, leaping from branch to branch, his bare feet feeling every touch and keeping him in perfect balance, his enchanted, speed-enhancing anklets allowing him to quickstep whenever necessary to keep his feet precisely under his weight.

He hit the ground running, toward the darkness globe, and those orcs outside of it who noted the ebon-skinned figure gave a shout and charged at him, one launching a spear.

Drizzt ran right past that awkward missile—he believed that he could have harmlessly caught it if he had so desired. He greeted the first orc staggering out of the globe with another of his innate magical abilities, summoning purplish-blue flames to outline the creature's form. The flame didn't burn at the flesh, but made marking target areas so much easier for the skilled drow, who, in truth, didn't need the help.

They also distracted the orc, with the fairly stupid creature looking down at its flaming limbs and crying out in fear. It looked back up Drizzt's way just in time to see the flash of a scimitar.

Another orc emerged right behind it and the drow never slowed, sliding down low beneath the orc's defensively whipping club and deftly twisting his scimitar around the creature's leg, severing its hamstring. By the time the howling orc hit the ground, Drizzt the Hunter was inside the darkness globe.

He moved purely on instinct, his muscles and movements reacting to the noises around him and to his tactile sensations. Without even consciously registering it, the Hunter knew from the warmth of the ground against his bare feet where the fire was located, and every time he felt the touch of some orc bumbling around beside him, his scimitars moved fast and furious, turning and striking even as he rushed past.

At one point, he didn't even feel an orc, didn't even hear an orc, but his sense of smell told him that one was beside him. A short slash of Twinkle brought a shriek and a crash as the creature went down.

Again without any conscious counting, Drizzt the Hunter knew when he would be crossing through to the other side of the darkness globe. Somehow, within him, he had registered and measured his every step.

He came out fast, in perfect balance, his eyes immediately focusing on the quartet of orcs rushing at him, his warrior's instincts drawing a line of attack to which he was already reacting.

He went ahead and down, meeting the thrust of a spear with a blinding double parry, one blade following the other. Either of Drizzt's fine scimitars could have shorn through the crude spear, but he didn't press the first through and he turned the second to the flat of the blade when he struck. Let the spear remain intact; it didn't matter after his second blade, moving right to left across his chest, knocked the weapon up high.

For Drizzt's feet moved ahead in a sudden blur bringing him past the off-balance orc, and Twinkle took it in the throat.

Drizzt continued without slowing, every step rotating him left just a bit, so that as he approached the second orc, he turned and pivoted completely, Twinkle again leading the way with a sidelong slash that caught the orc's extended sword arm across the wrist and sent its weapon flying. Following that slash as he completed the circuit, his second scimitar, Icingdeath, came in fast and hard, taking the creature in the ribs.

And the Hunter was already past.

He went down low, under a swinging club, and leaped up high over a thrusting spear, planting his feet on the weapon shaft as he descended, taking the weapon down under his weight. Across went Twinkle, but the orc ducked. Hardly slowing, Drizzt flipped the scimitar into an end-over-end spin, then caught the blade with a reverse grip and thrust it out behind him, catching the surprised club-wielder right in the chest as it charged at his back.

At the same time, the drow's other hand worked independently, Icingdeath slashing the spear-wielding orc's upraised, blocking arm once, twice, and a third time. Extracting Twinkle, Drizzt skipped to the side, and the dying orc stumbled forward past him, tangling with the second, who was clutching at his thrashed arm.

The Hunter was already gone, rushing out to the side in a direct charge at a pair of orcs who were working in apparent coordination. Drizzt went down to his knees in a skid and the orcs reacted, turning spear and sword down low. As soon as his knees hit the ground, though, the drow threw himself into a forward roll, tucking his shoulder and coming right around to his feet, where he pushed off with all his strength, leaping and continuing his turn. He went past and over the surprised pair, who hardly registered the move.

Drizzt landed lightly, still in perfect balance, and came around to the left with Twinkle leading in a slash that had the turning orcs stumbling even more. His weapons out wide to their respective sides, Drizzt reversed Twinkle's flow and brought Icingdeath across the other way, the weapons crossing precisely between the orcs, following through as wide as the drow could reach. A turn of his arms put his hands atop the weapons, and he reversed into a double backhand.

Neither orc had even managed to get its weapon around enough to block either strike. Both orcs tumbled, hit both ways by both blades.

The Hunter was already gone.

Orcs scrambled all around, understanding that they could not stand against that dark foe. None held ground before Drizzt as he rushed back the way he had come, cleaving the head of the orc with the torn arm, then dashing back into the globe of darkness, where he heard at least one of the brutes hiding, cowering on the ground. Again he fell into the world of his other senses, feeling the heat, hearing every sound. His weapons engaged one orc before him; he heard a second shifting and crouching to the side.

A quick side step brought him to the fire, and the cooking pot set on a tripod. He kicked out the far leg and rushed back the other way.

In the blackness of his magical globe, the one orc standing before him couldn't see his smile as the other orc, boiling broth falling all over it, began to howl and scramble.

The orc before him attacked wildly and cried for help. The Hunter could feel the wind from its furious swings.

Measuring the flow of one such over-swing, the Hunter had little trouble in sliding in behind.

He went out of the globe once more, leaving the orc spinning down to the ground, mortally wounded.

A quick run around the globe told Drizzt that only two orcs remained in the camp, one squirming on the ground, its lifeblood pouring out, the other howling and rolling to alleviate the burn from the hot stew.

The slash of scimitars, perfectly placed, ended the movements of both.

And the Hunter went out into the night in pursuit, to finish the task.

Poor Oonta fell against the side of a tree, gasping for breath. He waved away his companion as the orc implored him to keep running. They had put more than a mile of ground between them and the encampment.

"We got to!"

"*You* got to!" Oonta argued between gasps.

Oonta had crawled out of the Spine of the World on the orders of his tribe's shaman, to join in the glory of King Obould, to do war with those who had defaced the image of Gruumsh on a battlefield not far from that spot.

Oonta had come out to fight dwarves, not drow!

His companion grabbed him again and tried to pull him along, but Oonta slapped his hand away. Oonta lowered his head and continued to fight for his breath.

"Do take your time," came a voice behind them, speaking broken Orcish—and with a melodic tone that no orc could mimic.

"We got to go!" Oonta's companion argued, turning to face the speaker.

Oonta, knowing the source of those words, knowing that he was dead, didn't even look up.

"We can talk," he heard his companion implore the dark elf, and he heard, too, his companion's weapon drop to the ground.

"I can," the dark elf replied, and a devilish, diamond-edged scimitar came across, cleanly cutting out the orc's throat. "But I doubt you'll find a voice."

In response, the orc gasped and gurgled.

And fell.

Oonta stood up straight but still did not turn to face the deadly adversary. He moved against a tree and held his hands out defenselessly, hoping the death-blow would fall quickly.

He felt the drow's hot breath on the side of his neck, felt the tip of one blade against his back, the other against the back of his neck.

"You find the leader of this army," the drow told him. "You tell him that I will come to call, and very soon. You tell him that I will kill him."

A flick of that top scimitar took Oonta's right ear—the orc growled and grimaced, but he was disciplined and smart enough to not flee and to not turn around.

"You tell him," the voice said in his ear. "You tell them all."

Oonta started to respond, to assure the deadly attacker that he would do exactly that.

But the Hunter was already gone.

GRIT AND GUTS

The dozen dirty and road-weary dwarves rumbled along at a great pace, leaping cracks in the weather-beaten stone and dodging the many juts of rock and ancient boulders. They worked together, despite their obvious fears, and if one stumbled, two others were right there to prop him up and usher him on his way.

Behind them came the orc horde, more than two hundred of the hooting and howling, slobbering creatures. They rattled their weapons and shook their raised fists. Every now and then, one threw a spear at the fleeing dwarves, which inevitably missed its mark. The orcs weren't gaining ground, but neither were they losing any, and their hunger for catching the dwarves was no less than the terrified dwarves' apparent desperation to get away. Unlike with the dwarves, though, if one of the orcs stumbled, its companions were not there to help it along its way. Indeed, if a stumbling orc impeded the progress of a companion, it risked getting bowled over, kicked, or even stabbed. Thus, the orc line had stretched somewhat, but those in the lead remained barely a dozen running strides behind the last of the fleeing dwarves.

The dwarves moved along an ascending stretch of fairly open ground, bordered on their right, the west, by a great mountain spur, but with more open ground to their left. They continued to scream and run on, seeming beyond terror, but if the orcs had been more attuned to their progress and less focused on the catch and kill, they might have noticed that the dwarves seemed to be moving with singular purpose and direction even though so many choices were available to them.

As one, the dwarves came out from the shadows of the mountain spur and swerved between a pair of wide-spaced boulders. The pursuing orcs hardly registered the significance of those great rocks, for the two boulders were really the beginning of a channel along the stony ground, wide enough for three orcs to run abreast. To the vicious creatures, the channel meant only that the dwarves couldn't scatter. And so focused were the orcs that they didn't recognize the presence of side cubbies along both sides of that channel, cunningly hidden by stones, and with dwarf eyes peering out.

The lead orcs were long into the channel, with more than half the orc force past the entry stones, when the first dwarves burst forth from the side walls, picks, hammers, axes, and swords slashing away. Some, notably the Gutbuster Brigade led by Thibbledorf Pwent, the toughest and dirtiest dwarves in all of Clan Battlehammer, carried no weapons beyond their head spikes, ridged armor, and spiked gauntlets. They gleefully charged forth into the middle of the orc rush, leaping onto the closest enemies and thrashing wildly. Some of those same orcs had been caught by surprise by that very same group only a tenday earlier, outside the destroyed town of Shallows. Unlike then, though, the orcs did not turn wholesale and run, but took up the fight.

Even so, the dwarves were better armored and better equipped to battle in the tight area of the rocky channel. They had shaped the ground to their liking, with their strategies already laid out, and they quickly gained an upper hand. Those at the front end, who had come out closest to the entry to the channel, quickly set a defense. Their escape rocks had been cleverly cut to all but seal the channel behind them, buying them the time they needed to finish off those orcs in immediate contact and be ready for those slipping past the barricade.

The twelve fleeing decoys, of course, spun back at once into a singular force, stopping the rush of the lead orcs cold. And those dwarves in the middle of the melee worked in unison, each supporting the other, so that even those who fell to an orc blow were not slaughtered while they squirmed on the ground.

Conversely, those orcs who fell, fell alone and died alone.

"Yer boys did well, Torgar," said a tall, broad dwarf with wild orange hair and a beard that would have tickled his toes had he not tucked it into his belt.

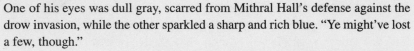

One of his eyes was dull gray, scarred from Mithral Hall's defense against the drow invasion, while the other sparkled a sharp and rich blue. "Ye might've lost a few, though."

"Ain't no better way to die than to die fightin' for yer kin," replied Torgar Hammerstriker, the strong leader of the more than four hundred dwarves who had recently emigrated from Mirabar, incensed by Marchion Elastul's shoddy treatment of King Bruenor Battlehammer—ill treatment that had extended to all of the Mirabarran dwarves who dared to welcome their distant relative when he had passed through the city.

Torgar stroked his own long, black beard as he watched the distant fighting. That most curious creature, Pikel Bouldershoulder, had joined in the fray, using his strange druidic magic to work the stones at the entrance area of the channel, sealing off the rest of the pursuit.

That was obviously going to be a very temporary respite, though, for the orcs were not overly stupid, and many of the potential reinforcements had already begun their backtracking to routes that would bring them up alongside the melee.

"Mithral Hall will not forget your help here this day," the old, tall dwarf assured Torgar.

Torgar Hammerstriker accepted the compliment with a quiet nod, not even turning to face the speaker, for he didn't want the war leader of Clan Battlehammer—Banak Brawnanvil by name—to see how touched he was. Torgar understood that the moment would follow him for the rest of his days, even if he lived another few hundred years. His trepidation at walking away from his ancestral home of Mirabar had only increased when hundreds of his kin, led by his dear old friend Shingles McRuff, had forced Marchion Elastul to release him and had then followed him out of Mirabar, with not one looking back. Torgar had known in his heart that he was doing the right thing for himself, but for all?

He knew then, though, and a great contentment washed over him. He and his kin had come upon the remnants of King Bruenor's overwhelmed force, fleeing the killing ground of Shallows. Torgar and his friends had held the rear guard all the way back to the defensible point on the northern slopes of the mountains just north of Keeper's Dale and the entrance to Mithral Hall. During their flight back to Bruenor's lines, the dwarves had found several skirmishes with pursuing orcs, and even one that included a few of the orcs unusual frost giant allies. Staying the course and battling without complaint, they had, of course, received many thanks from their fellow dwarves of Mithral Hall and from Bruenor's two adopted human children, Wulfgar and Catti-brie, and his halfling friend, Regis.

Bruenor himself had been, and still was, far too injured to say anything at all.

But those moments had only been a prelude, Torgar understood. With General Dagnabbit dead and Bruenor incapacitated and near death, the dwarves of Mithral Hall had called upon one of their oldest and most seasoned veterans to take the lead.

Banak Brawnanvil had answered that call. And how telling that Banak had asked Torgar for some runners to spring his trap upon some of the closest of the approaching orc hordes. Torgar knew there and then that he had done right in leading the Mirabarran dwarves to Mithral Hall. He knew there and then that he and his Delzoun dwarf kin had truly become part of Clan Battlehammer.

"Signal them running," Banak turned and said to the cleric Rockbottom, the dwarf credited with keeping Bruenor alive in the subchambers of the destroyed wizard's tower in Shallows through those long hours before help had arrived.

Rockbottom waggled his gnarled fingers and uttered a prayer to Moradin. He brought forth a shower of multicolored lights, little wisps of fire that didn't burn anything but that surely got the attention of those dwarves stationed near to the channel.

Almost immediately, Torgar's boys, Pwent's Gutbusters, the other fighters, and the brothers Bouldershoulder came scrambling over the sides of the channel, along prescribed routes, leaving not a dwarf behind, not even the few who had been sorely, perhaps even mortally, wounded.

And another of Pikel's modifications—a huge boulder almost perfectly rounded by the druid's stoneshaping magic—rumbled out of concealment from behind a tumble of stones near the mountain spur. A trio of strong dwarves maneuvered it with long, heavy poles, bending their shoulders to get it past bits of rough ground, and even up one small ascent. Other dwarves ran out of hiding near the top of the channel, helping their kin to guide the boulder so that it dropped into the back end of the channel, where a steeper incline had been constructed to usher it on its way.

The rumbling, rolling boulder shook the ground for great distances, and the remaining orcs in the channel issued a communal scream and fell all over each other in retreat. Some were knocked to the ground, then flattened as the boulder tumbled past. Others were thrown down by their terrified kin in the hopes that their bodies would slow the rolling stone.

In the end, when the boulder at last smashed against the channel-ending barricades, it had killed just a few of the orcs. Up higher on the slope, Banak, Torgar, and the others nodded contentedly, for they understood that the effect had been much greater than the actual damage inflicted upon their enemies.

"The first part of warfare is to defeat yer enemies' hearts," Banak quietly remarked, and to that end, their little ruse had worked quite well.

Banak offered both Torgar and Rockbottom a wink of his torn eye, then he reached out and patted the immigrant from Mirabar on the shoulder.

"I hear yer friend Shingles's done a bit of aboveground fighting," Banak offered. "Along with yerself."

"Mirabar is a city both above and below the stone," Torgar answered.

"Well, me and me kin ain't so familiar with doing battle up above," Banak answered. "I'll be looking to ye two, and to Ivan Bouldershoulder there, for yer advice."

Torgar happily nodded his agreement.

———— ⊹ ————

The dwarves had just begun to reconstitute their defensive lines along the high ground just south of the channel when Wulfgar and Catti-brie came running in to join Banak and the other leaders.

"We've been out to the east," Catti-brie breathlessly explained. A half foot taller than the tallest dwarves, though not nearly as solidly built, the young human did not seem out of place among them. Her face was wide but still delicate; her auburn hair was thick and rich and hanging below her shoulders. Her blue eyes were large even by human standards, certainly much more so than the eyes of a typical dwarf, which seemed always squinting and always peeking out from under a furrowed and heavily haired brow. Despite her feminine beauty, there was a toughness about the woman, who was raised by Bruenor Battlehammer, a pragmatism and solidity that allowed her to hold her own even among the finest of the dwarf warriors.

"Then ye missed a good bit o' the fun," said an enthusiastic Rockbottom, and his declaration was met with cheers and lifted mugs dripping of foamy ale.

"Oo oi!" agreed Pikel Bouldershoulder, his white teeth shining out between his green beard and mustache.

"We caught 'em in the channel, just as we planned," Banak Brawnanvil explained, his tone much more sober and grim than the others. "We got a few kills and sent more'n a few runnin' . . ."

His voice trailed off in the face of Catti-brie's emphatic waves.

"You used yer decoys to catch their decoys," the woman explained, and she swept her arm out to the east. "A great force marches against us, moving south to flank us."

"A great force is just north of us," Banak argued. "We seen it. How many stinking orcs are there?"

"More than you have dwarves to battle them, many times over," explained the giant Wulfgar, his expression stern, his crystal blue eyes narrowed. More than a foot taller than his human companion, Wulfgar, son of Beornegar, towered over the dwarves. He was slender at the waist, wiry, and agile, but his torso thickened to more than a dwarf's proportions at his broad chest. His arms were the girth of a strong dwarf's leg, his jaw firm and square. Those features of course brought respect from the tough, bearded folk, but in truth, it was the light in Wulfgar's eyes, a warrior's clarity, that elicited the most respect, and so when he continued, they all listened carefully. "If you battle them on two flanks, as you surely will should you stay here, they will overrun you."

"Bah!" snorted Rockbottom. "One dwarf's worth five o' the stinkers!"

Wulfgar turned to regard the confident cleric, and didn't blink.

"That many?" Banak asked.

"And more," said Catti-brie.

"Get 'em up and get 'em moving," Banak instructed Torgar. "Straight run to the south, to the highest ground we can find."

"That'll put us on the edge of the cliff overlooking Keeper's Dale," Rockbottom argued.

"Defensible ground," Banak agreed, shrugging off the dwarf's concerns.

"But with nowhere to run," Rockbottom reasoned. "We'll be putting a good and steep killing ground afore our feet, to be sure."

"And the flanking force will not be able to continue far enough south to strike at us," Banak added.

"But if we're to lose the ground, then we've got nowhere to run," Rockbottom reiterated. "Ye're puttin' our backs to the wall."

"Not to the wall, but to the cliff," Torgar Hammerstriker interjected. "Me and me boys'll get right on that, setting enough drop ropes to bring the whole of us to the dale floor in short order."

"It's three hunnerd feet to the dale," Rockbottom argued.

Torgar shrugged as if that hardly mattered.

"Whatever you're to do, it would be best if you were doing it fast," Catti-brie put in.

"And what're ye thinking we should be doing?" Banak replied. "Ye seen the orc forces—are ye not thinking we can make a stand against them?"

"I fear that we might be wise to go to the edge of Keeper's Dale and

23

beyond," said Wulfgar, and Catti-brie nodded, in apparent agreement with him. "And all the way to Mithral Hall."

"That many orcs?" asked another visitor to Mithral Hall who had been caught up in the battle, the yellow-bearded Ivan Bouldershoulder, Pikel's tougher and more conventional brother. The dwarf pushed his way through his fellows to move close to the leaders.

"That many orcs," Catti-brie assured him. "But we cannot be going all the way into Mithral Hall. Not yet. Bruenor's the king of more than Mithral Hall now. He went to Shallows because his duty took him there, and so ours tells us that we cannot be running all the way into our hole."

"Too many'll die if we do," Banak agreed. "To the highest ground, then, and let the dogs come on. We'll send them running, don't ye doubt!"

"Oo oi!" Pikel cheered.

All the other dwarves looked at the curious little Pikel, a green-haired and green-bearded creature who pulled his beard back over his ears and braided it into his hair, which ran more than halfway down his back. He was rounder than his tough brother, seeming more gentle, and while Ivan, like most dwarves, wore a patchwork of tough and bulky leather and metal armor, Pikel wore a simple robe, light green in color. And where the other dwarves wore heavy boots, protection from a forge's sparks and embers, and good for stomping orcs, Pikel wore open-toed sandals. Still, there was something about the easygoing Pikel, who had certainly shown his usefulness. The idol that had gotten the rescuers close to Shallows had been his idea and fashioned by his own hand, and in the ensuing battles, he had always been there, with magic devilish to his enemies and comforting to his allies. One by one, the other dwarves offered him a smile appreciative of his enthusiasm.

For with the arrival of Wulfgar and Catti-brie and the grim news from the east, their own enthusiasm had inevitably begun to wane.

The dwarves broke camp in short order, and not a moment too soon, for barely had they moved up and over the next of the many ridgelines when the orc force to the north started its charge and the flanking force from the east began to sweep in.

Nearly a thousand dwarves rambled across the stones, legs churning tirelessly to propel them up the sloping ground of the mountainside. They crossed the three thousand foot elevation, then four thousand, and still they ran on and held their formation tight and strong. Now taller mountains rose on the east, eliminating any possible flanking maneuver by the orcs, though the force behind them continued its pursuit. The dwarves moved more than a mile up and were gasping for breath with every stride, but still those strides did not slow.

Finally Banak's leading charges came in sight of the last expanse, and to the lip of the cliff overlooking Keeper's Dale, the abrupt ending of the slope where it seemed as if the stone had just been torn asunder. Spreading out below them, fully the three hundred feet down that Rockbottom had described, lay Keeper's Dale, the wide valley that marked the western approach to Mithral Hall. A mist hung in the air that morning, creeping around the many stone pillars that rose from the nearly barren ground.

With discipline so typical of the sturdy dwarves, the warriors went to work sorting out their lines and constructing defensive positions, some building walls with loose stone, others finding larger boulders that could be rolled back upon their enemies, and still others marking all the best vantage points and defensive positions and determining ways they might link those positions to maximum effect. Torgar, meanwhile, brought forth his best engineers—and there were many fine ones among the dwarves of Mirabar—and he presented them with the problem at hand: the quick transport of the entire dwarf force to the floor of Keeper's Dale, should a retreat be necessary.

More than a hundred of Mirabar's finest began exploring the length of the cliff face, checking the strength of the stone and seeking the easiest routes, including ledges where the descending dwarves might pause and switch to lower ropes. Within short order, the first ropes were set, and Torgar's engineers slid down to find a proper resting ground where they might set the next relays. It would take four separate lengths at the lower points and at least five at the higher, and that daunting prospect would have turned away many in despair.

But not dwarves. Not the stubborn folk who might spend years digging a tunnel only to find no precious ore at its end. Not the hearty and brave folk who put hammer to spike in unexplored regions of the deepest holes, not even knowing if any ensuing sparks might set off an explosion of dangerous gasses. Not the communal folk who would knock each other over in trying to get to kin in need. To the dwarves who formed King Bruenor's northern line of defense, those of Mithral Hall and Mirabar alike, their common pre-surname of Delzoun was more than a familial bond, it was a call to honor and duty.

One of the descending engineers got caught on a jag of stone, and in trying to extricate himself, slipped from the rope and tumbled from the cliff, plummeting more than two hundred feet to his death. All the others paused and offered a quick prayer to Moradin, then went back to their necessary work.

Tred McKnuckles tucked his yellow beard into his belt, hoisted his over-stuffed pack onto his shoulders, and turned to the tunnel leading west out of Mithral Hall.

"Well, ye coming?" he asked his companion, a fellow refugee from Citadel Felbarr.

Nikwillig assumed a pensive pose and stared off absently into the dark tunnel.

"No, don't think that I be," came the surprising answer.

"Ye going daft on me?" Tred asked. "Ye're knowin' as well as meself's knowin' that Obould Many-Arrows's got his grubby fingers in this, somewhere and somehow. That dog's still barking and still bitin'! And ye're knowing as well as meself's knowing that if Obould's involved, he's got his eyes looking back to Felbarr! That's the real prize he's wanting, don't ye doubt!"

"I ain't for doubting none o' that," Nikwillig answered. "King Emerus's got to hear the tales."

"Then ye're going."

"I ain't going. Not now. These Battlehammers saved yer hairy bum, and me own as well. Here's the place where there's orcs to crush, and so I'm stayin' to crush some orcs. Right beside them Battlehammers."

Tred considered Nikwillig's posture as much as his words. Nikwillig had always been a bit of a thinker, as far as dwarves went, and had often been a bit unconventional in his thinking. But this reasoning against returning to Citadel Felbarr, with so much at stake, struck Tred as beyond even Nikwillig's occasional eccentricity.

"Think for yerself, Tred," Nikwillig remarked, as if he had read his companion's puzzled mind. "Any runners to Felbarr'll do, and ye know it."

"And ye think any runners'll be bringing King Emerus out o' Citadel Felbarr to our aid if we're needin' it? And ye're thinking that any runners'll convince King Emerus to send word to Citadel Adbar and rally the Iron Guard of King Harbromm?"

Nikwillig shrugged and said, "Orcs're charging out o' the north and the Battlehammers are fighting them hard—and two o' Felbarr's own, Tred and Nikwillig, are standing strong beside Bruenor's boys. If anything's to get King Emerus up and hopping, it's knowin' that yerself and meself've decided this fight's worth fighting. Might be that we're making a bigger and louder call to King Emerus Warcrown by staying put and putting our shoulders in Bruenor's line."

Tred stared long and hard at the other dwarf, his thoughts trying to catch up with Nikwillig's surprising words. He really didn't want to leave Mithral Hall. Bruenor had charged headlong into danger to help Tred and Nikwillig avenge those human settlers who'd died trying to help the two wayward dwarves and to avenge Tred and Nikwillig's dead kin from Felbarr, including Tred's own little brother.

The yellow-bearded dwarf gave a sigh as he looked back over his shoulder, at the dark upper-Underdark tunnel that wound off to the west.

"Might that we should go find the runt, Regis, then," he offered. "Might that he'll find one to get to King Emerus with all the news."

"And we're back out with Bruenor's human kids and Torgar's boys," said Nikwillig, not backing down from his eager stance one bit.

Tred's expression shifted from curious to admiring as he looked over Nikwillig. Never before had he known that particular dwarf to be so eager for battle.

To tough Tred's thinking, the timing for Nikwillig's apparent change of heart couldn't have been better. The yellow-bearded dwarf's resigned look became a wide smile, and he dropped the heavy pack off his shoulder.

"I would ask of your thoughts, but I see no need," Wulfgar remarked, walking up to join Catti-brie.

She stood to the side of the scrambling dwarves, looking down the slope—not at the massing orcs, Wulfgar had noted, but to the wild lands beyond them. Catti-brie brushed back her thick mane of hair and turned to regard the man, her blue eyes, much darker and richer in hue than Wulfgar's crystalline orbs, studying him intently.

"I, too, wonder where he is," the barbarian explained. "He is not dead—of that I am certain."

"How can you be?"

"Because I know Drizzt," Wulfgar replied, and he managed a smile for the woman's sake.

"All of us would've perished had not Pwent come out," Catti-brie reminded him.

"We were trapped and surrounded," Wulfgar countered. "Drizzt is neither, nor can he easily be. He is alive yet, I know."

Catti-brie returned the big man's smile and took his hand in her own.

"I'm knowing it, too," she admitted. "Only if because I'm sure that me heart would've felt the break if he'd fallen."

"No less than my own," Wulfgar whispered.

"But he'll not return to us soon," Catti-brie went on. "And I'm not think-ing that we're wanting him to. In here, he's another fighter in a line of fighters—the best o' the bunch, no doubt—but out there. . . ."

"Out there, he will bring terrible grief to our enemies," Wulfgar agreed. "Though it pains me to think that he is alone."

"He's got the cat. He's not alone."

It was Catti-brie's turn to offer a reassuring smile to her companion. Wulfgar clenched her hand tighter and nodded his agreement.

"I'll be needin' the two o' ye to hold the right flank," came a gruff voice to the side, turning the pair to see Banak Brawnanvil, the cleric Rockbottom, and a pair of other dwarves marching their way. "Them orcs're coming," the dwarf warlord asserted. "They're thinking to hit us quick, afore we dig in, and we got to hold 'em."

Both humans nodded grimly.

Banak turned to one of the other dwarves and ordered, "Ye go and sit with Torgar's engineers. Tell 'em to block their ears from the battle sounds and keep to their work. And as soon as they get some ropes all the way to the dale floor, ye get yerself down 'em."

"B-but . . ." the dwarf sputtered in protest.

He shook his head and wagged his hands, as if Banak had just condemned him. Banak reached up and slapped his hand over the other dwarf's mouth, silencing him.

"Yer own mission's the toughest and most important of all," the warlord explained. "We'll be up here smacking orcs, and what dwarf's not loving that work? For yerself, ye got to get to Regis and tell the little one we're needing a thousand more—two thousand if he can spare 'em from the tunnels."

"Ye're thinking to bring a thousand more up the ropes to strengthen our position?" Catti-brie asked doubtfully, for it seemed that they really had nowhere to put the extra warriors.

Wulfgar cast her a sidelong glance, noting how her accent had moved back toward the Dwarvish with the addition of Banak's group.

"Nah, we're enough to hold here for now," Banak explained. He let go of the other dwarf, who was standing patiently, though he was beginning to turn a shade of blue from Banak's strong grasp. "We got to, and so we will. But this orc we're fighting's smart. Too smart."

"You're thinking that our enemy will send a force around that mountain spur to the west," Wulfgar reasoned, and Banak nodded.

"More o' them stinking orcs get into Keeper's Dale afore us, and we're done for," the dwarf leader replied. "They won't even be needing to come up for us, then. They can just hold us here until we fall down starving." Banak fixed the appointed messenger with a grim stare and added, "Ye go and ye tell Regis, or whoever's running things inside now, to send all he can spare and more into the dale, to set a force in the western end. Nothing's to come in that way, ye hear me?"

The messenger dwarf suddenly seemed much less reluctant to leave. He stood straight and puffed out his strong chest, nodding his assurances to them all.

Even as he sprinted away for the cliff face, a cry went up at the center of the dwarven line that the orc charge was on.

"Ye get back to Torgar's engineers," Banak instructed Rockbottom. "Ye keep 'em working through the fight, and ye don't let 'em stop unless them orcs kill us all and come to the cliff to get 'em!"

With a determined nod, Rockbottom ran off.

"And ye two hold this end o' the line, for all our lives," Banak asked.

Catti-brie slid her deadly bow, Taulmaril the Heartseeker, from off her shoulder. She pulled an arrow from her quiver and set it in place. Beside her, Wulfgar slapped the mighty warhammer Aegis-fang across his open palm.

As Banak and the remaining dwarf wandered off along the assembling line of defense, the two humans turned to each other, offered a nod of support, then turned all the way around—

—to see the dark swarm coming fast up the rocky mountain slope.

BONES AND STONES

King Obould Many-Arrows at once recognized the danger of this latest report filtering in from the mountains to the east of his current position. Resisting his initial urge to crush the head of the wretched goblin messenger, the huge orc king stretched the fingers of one hand, then balled them into a tight fist and brought that fist up before his tusked mouth in his most typical posture, seeming a mix between contemplation and seething rage.

Which was pretty much the constant emotional struggle within the orc leader.

Despite the disastrous end to the siege at Shallows, when the filthy dwarves had snuck onto the field of battle within the hollowed out statue of Gruumsh One-Eye, the war was proceeding beautifully. The news of King Bruenor's demise had brought dozens of new tribes scurrying out of their holes to Obould's side and had even quieted the troublesome Gerti Orelsdottr and her superior-minded frost giants. Obould's son, Urlgen, had the dwarves on the run—to the edge of Mithral Hall already, judging from the last reports.

Then came reports that some enemy force was out there, behind Obould's lines. An encampment of orcs had been thrashed, with most slaughtered and the others scattered back to their mountain holes. Obould understood well the demeanor of his race, and he knew that morale was everything at that crucial moment—and usually throughout an entire campaign. The orcs were far more

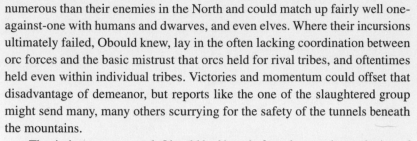

numerous than their enemies in the North and could match up fairly well one-against-one with humans and dwarves, and even elves. Where their incursions ultimately failed, Obould knew, lay in the often lacking coordination between orc forces and the basic mistrust that orcs held for rival tribes, and oftentimes held even within individual tribes. Victories and momentum could offset that disadvantage of demeanor, but reports like the one of the slaughtered group might send many, many others scurrying for the safety of the tunnels beneath the mountains.

The timing was not good. Obould had heard of another coming gathering of the shamans of several fairly large tribes, and he feared that they might try to abort his invasion before it had really begun. At the very least, a joined negative voice of two-dozen shamans would greatly deplete the orc king's reinforcements.

One thing at a time, Obould scolded himself, and he considered more carefully the goblin messenger's words. He had to find out what was going on, and quickly. Fortunately, there was one in his encampment at the time who might prove of great help.

Dismissing both the goblin and his attendants, Obould moved to the southern edge of the large camp, to a lone figure that he had kept waiting far too long.

"Greetings, Donnia Soldou," he said to the drow female.

She turned to regard him—she had sensed his approach long before he had spoken, he knew—peering at him under the low-pulled hood of her magical *piwafwi*, her red-tinged eyes smiling as widely and wickedly as her tight grin.

"You have claimed a great prize, I hear," she remarked, and she shifted a bit, allowing her white hair to slip down over one of her eyes.

Mysterious and alluring, always so.

"One of many to come," Obould insisted. "Urlgen is chasing the dwarves back into their hole, and who will defend the towns of the land?"

"One victory at a time?" Donnia asked. "I had thought you more ambitious."

"We cannot run wildly into Mithral Hall to be slaughtered," Obould countered. "Did not your own people try such a tactic?"

Donnia merely laughed aloud at the intended insult, for it had not been "her" people at all. The drow of Menzoberranzan had attacked Mithral Hall, to disastrous results, but that was hardly the care of Donnia Soldou, who was not of, and not fond of, the City of Spiders.

"You have heard of the slaughter at the camp of the Tribe of Many Teeth?" Obould asked.

"A formidable opponent—or several—found them, yes," Donnia replied. "Ad'non has already started for the site."

"Lead me there," Obould instructed, his words obviously surprising Donnia. "I will witness this for myself."

"If you bring too many of your warriors, you will inadvertently spread the news of the slaughter," Donnia reasoned. "Is that your intent?"

"You and I will go," Obould explained. "No others."

"And if these enemies that massacred the Tribe of Many Teeth are about? You risk much."

"If these enemies are about and they attack Obould, then *they* risk much," Obould growled back at her, eliciting a smile, one that showed Donnia's pearly white teeth in such a stark contrast to the ebon hue of her skin.

"Very well then," she agreed. "Let us go and see what we might learn of our secretive foe."

The site of the slaughter was not so far away, and Donnia and Obould came upon the scene later that same day to find not only Ad'non Kareese, but Donnia's other two drow companions, Kaer'lic Suun Wett and Tos'un Armgo, already moving around the place.

"A couple of attackers, and no more," Ad'non explained to the newcomers. "We have heard of a pair of pegasus-riding elves in the region, and it is our guess that they perpetrated this slaughter."

As Ad'non spoke those words, his hands worked the silent hand code of the drow, something that Donnia, but not Obould, could understand.

This was the work of a drow elf, Ad'non quickly flashed.

Donnia needed to know nothing more, for she and her companions were aware that King Bruenor of Mithral Hall kept company with a most unusual dark elf, a rogue who had abandoned the ways of the Spider Queen and of his dark kin. Apparently, Drizzt Do'Urden had escaped Shallows, as they had suspected from the stories told by Gerti's frost giants, and apparently, he had not returned to Mithral Hall.

"Elves," King Obould echoed distastefully, and the word became a long drawn-out growl, with the powerful orc bringing his clenched fist up before him once again.

"They should not be so difficult to find if they are flying around on winged horses," Donnia Soldou assured Obould.

The orc king continued to utter a low and seething growl, his red-veined eyes glancing about the horizon as if he expected the pegasi riders to come swooping down upon them.

"Pass this off to the other leaders as an isolated attack," Ad'non suggested to the orc. "Donnia and I will ensure that Gerti does not become overly concerned."

"Turn fear into encouragement," Donnia added. "Offer a great bounty for the head of those who did this. That alone will place all the other tribes at the ready as they make their way to your main forces."

"Most of all, the fact that this was a small group attacking by ambush, as it certainly seems to be, lessens the danger to others," Ad'non went on. "These orcs were not vigilant, and so they were killed. That has always been the way, has it not?"

Obould's growl gradually decreased, and he offered an assenting nod to his drow advisors. He moved off then to inspect the campsite and the dead orcs, and the drow pair joined their two companions and did likewise.

No surface elf, Ad'non's fingers flashed to his three drow companions, though Kaer'lic Suun Wett wasn't paying attention and actually drifted away from the group, moving outside the camp. *The wounds are sweeping and slashing in nature, not the stabs of an elf. Nor were any killed by arrows, and those surface elves who went against the giants north of Shallows fought them with bows from on high.*

Tos'un Armgo moved around the bodies, bending low and examining them the most carefully of all.

"Drizzt Do'Urden," he whispered to the other three, and as Obould moved back toward him, he silently flashed, *Drizzt favors the scimitar.*

Kaer'lic returned soon after Obould, the plump priestess's fingers signing, *Cat prints outside the perimeter.*

Drizzt Do'Urden, Tos'un signaled again.

From a ridge to the northeast, Urlgen Threefist watched the great dark mass of orcs sweeping up the ascent. He had the dwarves pinned against the cliff and wanted nothing more than to push them into oblivion. Urlgen respected the toughness and work ethic of dwarves enough to understand that their defenses would strengthen by the hour if he let them sit up there. However, his own force was hardly prepared for such an attack; no reinforcements of giants had even caught up to the orc hordes yet, and many of those in the ranks were very new to the crusade and probably still confused about their order of battle and the hierarchy of leadership.

Urlgen's forces would strengthen in number, in weapons, and in tactics soon enough, but so too would the dwarves' defenses.

Weighing both and still stinging from the unexpected breakout at Shallows, the orc leader had sent the waves ahead. At the very least, he figured, the attacks would keep the dwarves from digging in even deeper.

Still, the orc leader grimaced when the leading edge of his rolling masses neared the lip of the ascent, for the dwarves leaped out in fury and fell over them from on high. Thrown rocks and rolling boulders led the way, along with those same devastating, streaking silvery arrows that had so stung Urlgen's forces at Shallows. Urlgen knew that orcs were dying by the dozen. As panic overcame many of those who survived the initial barrage, their disorientation and terror made the dwarves' countercharge all the more effective, allowing the vicious bearded folk to slice into the humanoid lines.

Those orcs turning in retreat only hindered the reinforcing back ranks from getting into the fray, and the confusion opened even more opportunities for the aggressive dwarves.

And still those arrows reached out, and in conjunction with that archer, a towering figure on the eastern end of the dwarf position swept orcs away with impunity.

"What we gonna do?" a skinny orc asked Urlgen, the creature running up and hopping all around frantically. "What we gonna do?"

Another of the gang leaders came rushing over.

"What we gonna do?" he parroted.

And a third charged over, shouting, "What we gonna do?"

Urlgen continued to watch the wild battle up the rocky slope. Dwarves were falling, but most who did were landing on the bodies of many orcs. Melee was fully joined, and Urlgen's orcs seemed no closer to forming into any acceptable formations, while the dwarves had grouped neatly into two defensive squares flanking a spearheading wedge. As that wedge charged forward, its wide base smoothly linked with the corners of each square, and those squares pivoted perfectly. One line of each square broke free to link up fully with the wedge, thus turning it into a defensive square, while the flanking dwarves reconfigured their ranks into more offensive formations.

To Urlgen, their movements were a thing a beauty, exhibiting the very same discipline that he and his father had tried hard to instill in their orc hordes. Given the one-sided slaughter, though, his soldiers obviously had a long way to go.

So mesmerized was Urlgen with the paradelike maneuvers of the seasoned dwarves that for many moments he hardly noticed the three orc commanders dancing around him and shouting, "What we gonna do?"

Finally their questions registered once more, as did the realization that the dwarves were turning the battle into a clear rout.

"Retreat!" Urlgen ordered. "Brings them back! Brings them all back until Gerti's giants get here."

Over the next few minutes, watching the relay of the order and the response to it, it occurred to Urlgen that his soldiers were much better at retreating than they were at charging.

They left many behind in their run back down the stones—stones that were slippery with blood. Scores lay dead or dying, screaming and groaning, until the closest dwarves walked over and shut them up forever with a heavy blow to the head.

But there were dead dwarves among those reddened stones, and orcs, by nature, hardly cared for their own losses. Urlgen nodded his acceptance. His forces would grow and grow, and he meant to keep throwing them at the dwarves until exhaustion killed them if the orcs could not. The orc leader knew what lay over the ridge behind the dwarves.

He knew he had them cornered. Either many more dwarves were going to have to pour out of Mithral Hall and take a roundabout route east or west to try to rescue that group, or the dwarves there were going to have to abandon their defensive position and break out on their own. Either way, Urlgen's lead strike force would have more than fulfilled Obould's vision for them.

Either way, Urlgen's stature among the swelling band of orcs would greatly increase.

"We know it was Drizzt Do'Urden, yet we tell Obould that surface elves were the cause," Tos'un Armgo said to his three drow companions as they retired to a comfortable cave to digest the latest developments.

"Thus leading Obould to even greater hatred for the surface elves," Donnia replied, her lips curling up in a delicious smile, one side of it almost reaching the cascading layers of white hair that crossed diagonally down her sculpted black face.

"He needs little urging in that direction," Kaer'lic remarked.

"More important, we delay Obould from believing that there are drow elves working against him," said Ad'non Kareese.

"He knows of Drizzt already, to some degree," Kaer'lic reasoned.

"Yes, but perhaps we can alleviate the problem of the rogue before it swells to proportions that enrage Obould against us," said Ad'non. "He does seem to think in terms of race, and not individuals."

"As does Gerti," said Kaer'lic. "As do we all."

"Except for Drizzt and his friends, it would seem," Tos'un said, the simple and obvious statement making them all gape.

The four drow rested back for just a moment, each looking to the others, but if there was any significant philosophical epiphany coming to the group, it was quickly buried under the weight of pragmatism and the needs of the present.

"You believe that we should do something to eliminate the threat of Drizzt Do'Urden?" Kaer'lic asked Ad'non. "You consider him to be our problem?"

"I consider that he could grow to become our problem," Ad'non corrected. "The advantages of eliminating him might prove great."

"So thought Menzoberranzan," Tos'un Armgo reminded. "I doubt the city has recovered fully from that folly."

"Menzoberranzan fought more than Drizzt Do'Urden," Donnia put in. "Would not Lady Lolth desire the demise of the rogue?"

As she asked the question, Donnia turned to Kaer'lic, the priestess of the group, and both Ad'non and Tos'un followed her lead. Kaer'lic was shaking her head to greet those inquisitive stares.

"Drizzt Do'Urden is not our problem," said Kaer'lic, "and we would do well to stay as far from his scimitars as possible. Sound reasoning is always Lady Lolth's greatest demand of us, and I would no more wish to leap into battle against Drizzt Do'Urden than I would to lead Obould's charge into Mithral Hall. That is not why we instigated all of this. You remember our desires and our plan, do you not? My enjoyment, such as it is, will not end at the tip of one of Drizzt Do'Urden's scimitars."

"And if he seeks us out?" asked Donnia.

"He will not, if he knows nothing about us," Kaer'lic replied. "That is the better course. My favorite war is one I watch from afar."

Donnia's sour expression as she turned to Ad'non was not hard to discern. Nor was Ad'non's responding disappointment.

But Kaer'lic had an ally, and a most emphatic one.

"I agree," Tos'un offered. "Since his days in Menzoberranzan, Drizzt Do'Urden has been nothing but a difficult and often fatal problem to those who have tried to go against him. In my wanderings of the upper Underdark after the disaster with Mithral Hall, I heard various and scattered tales about the repercussions within Menzoberranzan. Apparently, soon after my city's attack on

Mithral Hall, Drizzt returned to Menzoberranzan, was captured by House Baenre, and was placed in their dungeons."

Astonished expressions followed that tidbit, for the mighty and ruthless House Baenre was well known to drow across the Underdark.

"And yet, he has returned to his friends, leaving catastrophe in his wake," Tos'un went on. "He is almost a cruel joke of Lady Lolth, I fear, an instrument of chaos cloaked in traitorous garb. More than one in Menzoberranzan has remarked on his belief that Drizzt Do'Urden is secretly guided by the Lady of Chaos for her pleasure."

"If we served any other goddess, your words would be blasphemous," Kaer'lic replied, and she gave a chuckle at the supreme irony of it all.

"You cannot believe . . ." Donnia started to argue.

"I do not have to believe," Tos'un interrupted. "Drizzt Do'Urden is either much more formidable than we understand, or he is very lucky, or he is god-blessed. In any of those cases, I have no desire to hunt him down."

"Agreed," said Kaer'lic.

Donnia and Ad'non looked to each other once more, but merely shrugged.

"It's a fine game, this," Banak Brawnanvil said to Rockbottom, who stood beside him as he directed the formations of his forces. "Except that so many wind up dead."

"More orcs than dwarves," Rockbottom pointed out.

"Not enough of one and too many o' the other. Look at them. Fighting with fury, taking their hits without complaint, willing to die if that's the choice o' the gods this day."

"They're warriors," Rockbottom reminded. "Dwarf warriors. That's meaning something."

"Course it is," Banak agreed. "Something."

"Yer plan's got them orcs on the run," Rockbottom observed.

"Not any plan of me own," the dwarf leader argued. "Was that Bouldershoulder brother's idea—the sane one, I mean—along with the help of Torgar of Mirabar. We found ourselfs some fine friends, I'm thinking."

Rockbottom nodded and continued to watch the beautifully choreographed display of teamwork, the three interlocking formations rolling down the slope and sweeping orcs before them.

"A child of some race or another will come here in a few hundred years,"

Banak remarked a short time later. He wasn't even watching the fighting anymore, but was more focused on the bodies splayed across the stones. "He'll see the whitened bones of them fighting for this piece of high ground. They'll be mistaken for rocks, mostly, but soon enough, one might be recognized for what it is, and of course that will show this to be the site of a great battle. Will those people far in the future understand what we did here? Or why we did it? Will they know our cause, or the difference of our cause to that o' the invading orcs?"

Rockbottom stared long and hard at Banak Brawnanvil. The tall and strong dwarf had been an imposing figure among the dwarves of Clan Battlehammer for centuries, though he usually kept himself to the side of the glory, and rarely offered his strategies for battle unless pressed by Bruenor or Dagna, or one of the other formal commanders. The other side of Banak, though, was what really separated him from others of the clan. He had a different way of looking at the world, and always seemed to be viewing current events in the context with which they might be seen by some future historian.

A shriek to the right had them both looking that way, to see the superb coordination and harmony of Wulfgar and Catti-brie as they held fast the flank. Orcs came up at them haphazardly, and many fell to the woman's deadly bow and her unending supply of arrows. Those that managed to escape sudden death at the end of a missile likely soon wished they had been hit, for they wound up before the great barbarian Wulfgar and his devastating hammer, the magnificent Aegis-fang, crafted by Bruenor Battlehammer himself. Even as Banak and Rockbottom focused on the pair, Wulfgar smashed one orc so hard atop its head that its skull simply exploded, showering the barbarian and those other orcs scrambling in with blood and brains.

An arrow whistled past Wulfgar to take down a second orc, and a great sweep of Aegis-fang had the remaining two stumbling, one falling to the ground, the other dancing out wide.

Catti-brie got the second one; a chop of Aegis-fang finished the one on the ground.

"Them two are making tales that'll live through the centuries," Rockbottom remarked.

"To some point," said Banak, "then they will fade."

Rockbottom looked at him curiously, surprised by his glum attitude.

"On his way home," Banak explained, "King Bruenor marched through Fell Pass."

Rockbottom nodded his understanding, for he had been on that caravan.

"Find any bones there?" Banak asked.

"More than ye can count," the cleric replied.

"Ye think that any of them fighting that long-ago battle in Fell Pass stood above the others, in bravery and might?"

Rockbottom considered the question for just a moment, before offering a shrug and an agreeing nod.

"Ye know their names?" Banak asked. "Ye know who they were and what they were about? Ye know how many orcs and other monsters they killed in that battle? Ye know how many held the head of a friend as he died?"

The point hit Rockbottom hard. He looked back to the main battle, where the dwarves were routing the orcs and sending them running.

"No pursuit down the slope!" Banak ordered.

"We've got them scared witless," Rockbottom quietly advised.

"They're witless anyway," said the dwarf warlord. "They only came on to draw us from our preparations. That preparation's not to wait while we chase a ragtag band around the mountains. We bring our boys all back and get back to work. This was a skirmish. The big fight's yet to come."

Banak looked back over his shoulder to the cliff area, and hoped that the engineers had not slowed in their work with the rope ladders to the floor of Keeper's Dale.

"Just a skirmish," he reiterated even as the fighting diminished and many of the dwarves began to turn their precise formations back toward his position.

He saw the dead and wounded lying around the blood-soaked stones.

He thought of the bones that would soon enough litter that ground, as thick and as quiet as rocks.

THE SELECTION PROCESS

His trail always seemed to lead him back to that spot. For Drizzt Do'Urden, the devastated rubble of Shallows served as his inspiration, his catalyst to allow the Hunter to fill his spirit with hunger for the hunt. He moved around the broken tower and ruined walls, but rarely did he go to the south of the town. It had taken him several days to muster the nerve to venture past the ruined idol of the foul orc god. As he had feared, he had found no sign of escaping survivors.

Drizzt soon started to visit that place for different purposes. On every return, he hoped he might find some orcs milling around the strewn dead, seeking loot perhaps.

Drizzt thought it would be fitting for him to slaughter orcs in the shadow of the devastation that was Shallows.

He thought he had found his opportunity upon his approach that afternoon. Guenhwyvar, beside him, was clearly on edge, a sure sign that monsters were about, and Drizzt noted the movements of some creatures around the ruins as he moved along the high ground across the ravine north of the town—the same high ground from which the giants had bombarded Shallows as a prelude to the orc assault.

As soon as he got a clear view of the ruins, though, Drizzt understood that he would not be doing any battle there that day. There were indeed orcs in Shallows—thousands of orcs—several tribes of the wretches encamped around the shattered remains of that great wooden statue south of the town's ruined southern wall.

Beside him, Guenhwyvar lowered her ears and issued a long and low growl.

That brought a smile to the dark elf's face—the first smile that had found its way there in a long time.

"I know, Guen," he said, and he reached over and riffled the cat's ear. "Hold patience. We will find our time."

Guenhwyvar looked at him and slowly blinked, then tilted her head so he could scratch a favored spot along her neck. The growling stopped.

Drizzt's smile did not. He continued to scratch the cat, but continued, too, to look across the ravine, to the ruins of Shallows, to the hordes of orcs. He replayed his memories over and over, recalling it all so vividly; he would not let himself forget.

The image of Bruenor tumbling in the tower ruins. The image of giants heaving their great boulders across the ravine at his friends. The image of the orc hordes overrunning the town. None of it had been asked for. None of it deserved.

But it would be paid back, Drizzt knew.

In full.

***

"King Obould knows of this travesty?" asked Arganth Snarrl, the wide-eyed, wild-eyed shaman of the orc tribe that bore his surname. With his bright-colored feathered headdress and tooth necklace (with specimens from a variety of creatures) that reached below his waist, Arganth was among the most distinctive and colorful of the dozen shamans congregated around the ruined Gruumsh idol, and with his shrieking, almost birdlike voice, he was also the loudest.

"Does he understand, does he? Does he? Does he?" the shaman asked, hopping from one of his colleagues to the next in rapid succession. "I do not think he does! No, no, because if he does, then he does not place this . . . this . . . this, blasphemy in proper order! More important than all his conquests, this is!"

"Unless his conquests are being delivered in the name of Gruumsh," shaman Achtel Gnarlfingers remarked, the interruption stopping Arganth in his tracks.

Achtel's dress was not as large and attention-grabbing as Arganth's, but it was equally colorful, with a rich red traveling cloak, complete with hood, and a bright yellow sash crossing shoulder to hip and around her waist. She carried a skull-headed scepter, heavily enchanted to serve as a formidable weapon, from

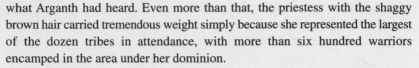

what Arganth had heard. Even more than that, the priestess with the shaggy brown hair carried tremendous weight simply because she represented the largest of the dozen tribes in attendance, with more than six hundred warriors encamped in the area under her dominion.

The colorful priest stared wide-eyed at Achtel, who did not back down at all.

"Which Obould does do," Arganth insisted.

"We march for the glory of Gruumsh," another of the group agreed. "The One-Eye desires the defeat of the dwarves!"

That brought a cheer from all around, except for Arganth, who stood there staring at Achtel. Gradually, all eyes focused on the trembling figure with the feathered headdress.

"Not enough," Achtel insisted. "King Obould Many-Arrows marches for the glory of King Obould Many-Arrows."

Gasps came back at him.

"That is our way," Arganth quickly added, seeing the dangerously rising dissent and the sudden scowling of dangerous Achtel. "That is always our way, and a good way it is. But now, with the blasphemy of this idol, we must join the two, Obould and Gruumsh! Their glory must be made as one!"

The other eleven shamans neither cheered nor jeered, but simply stood there, staring at the volatile shaman of Snarrl.

"Each tribe?" one began tentatively, shaking his head.

The orc tribes had come to Obould's call—especially after hearing of the fall of King Bruenor Battlehammer, who had long been a reviled figure—but the armies remained, first and foremost, individual tribes.

Arganth Snarrl leaped up before the speaker, his yellow-hued eyes so wide that they seemed as if they would just roll from their sockets.

"No more!" he yelled, and he jumped wildly all about, facing each of the others in turn. "No more! Tribes are second. Gruumsh is first!"

"Gruumsh!" a couple of the others yelled together.

"And Gruumsh is Obould?" Achtel calmly asked, seeming to measure every movement and word carefully—more so than any of the others in attendance, certainly.

"Gruumsh is Obould!" Arganth proclaimed. "Soon to be, yes!"

He ended in a gesticulating, leaping and wildly shaking dance around the ruined idol of his god-figure, the hollowed statue the dwarves had used as a ruse to get amidst Obould's forces. With imminent victory in their grasp, overrunning Shallows, the ultimate, despicable deception of the wretched dwarves had salvaged some escape from what should have been a complete slaughter.

To use the orc god-figure for such treachery was beyond the bounds of decency in the eyes of those dozen shamans, the religious leaders of the more than three thousand orcs of their respective tribes.

"Gruumsh is Obould!" Arganth began to chant as he danced, and each shaman in turn took up the cry as he or she fell into line behind the wildly gesticulating, outrageously dressed character.

Except for Achtel. The thoughtful and more sedentary orc stepped back from the evocative dance and observed the movements of her fellow shamans, her doubts fairly obviously displayed upon her orc features.

All the others knew of her feelings on the matter and of her hesitation in counseling her chieftain to lead her tribe out of its secure home to join in the fight against the powerful dwarves. Until then, none had dared to question her in that decision.

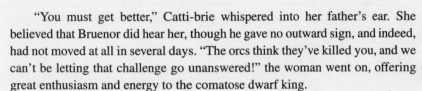

"You must get better," Catti-brie whispered into her father's ear. She believed that Bruenor did hear her, though he gave no outward sign, and indeed, had not moved at all in several days. "The orcs think they've killed you, and we can't be letting that challenge go unanswered!" the woman went on, offering great enthusiasm and energy to the comatose dwarf king.

Catti-brie squeezed Bruenor's hand as she spoke, and for a moment, she thought he squeezed back.

Or she imagined it.

She gave a great sigh, then, and looked to her bow, which was leaning up against the far wall of the candlelit room. She would have to be out again soon, she knew, for the fighting up on the cliff would surely begin anew.

"I think he hears you," came a voice from behind Catti-brie, and she managed a smile as she turned to regard her friend Regis.

Truly, the halfling looked the part of the battered warrior, with one arm slung tight against his chest and wrapped with heavy bandages. That arm had fended the snapping maw of a great worg, and Regis had paid a heavy price.

Catti-brie rolled up from her father's side to give the halfling a well-deserved hug.

"The clerics haven't healed it yet?" she asked, eyeing his arm.

"They've done quite a bit, actually," Regis answered in a chipper tone, and to show his optimism, he managed to wriggle his bluish fingers. "They would have long ago finished their work on it, but there are too many others who need their healing spells and salves more than I. It's not so bad."

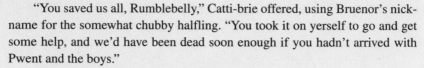

"You saved us all, Rumblebelly," Catti-brie offered, using Bruenor's nickname for the somewhat chubby halfling. "You took it on yerself to go and get some help, and we'd have been dead soon enough if you hadn't arrived with Pwent and the boys."

Regis just shrugged and even blushed a bit.

"How do we fare up on the mountain?" he asked.

"Fair," Catti-brie answered. "The orcs chased us right to the edge, but we got more than a few in a trap, and when they came on in full, we sent them running. Ye should see the work of Banak Brawnanvil, Ivan Bouldershoulder, and Torgar Hammerstriker of Mirabar. They had the dwarves turning squares and wedges every which way and had the orcs scratching their heads in confusion right up until they got run over."

Regis managed a wide smile and even a little chuckle, but it died quickly as he looked past Catti-brie to the resting Bruenor.

"How is he this day?"

Catti-brie looked back at her father and could only offer a shrug in reply.

"The priests do not think he'll come out of it," Regis told her, and she nodded for she had of course heard the very same from them.

"But I think he will," Regis went on. "Though he'll be a long time on the mend, even still."

"He'll come back to us," Catti-brie assured her little friend.

"We need him," Regis said, his voice barely a whisper. "All of Mithral Hall needs King Bruenor."

"Bah, but that's no attitude to be takin' at this tough time," came a voice from out in the hallway, and the pair turned to see a bedraggled old dwarf come striding in.

They recognized the dwarf at once as General Dagna, one of Bruenor's most trusted commanders and the father of Dagnabbit, who had fallen at Shallows. The two friends glanced at each other and winced, then offered sympathetic looks to the dwarf who had lost his valiant son.

"He died well," Dagna remarked, obviously understanding their intent. "No dwarf can ask for more than that."

"He died brilliantly," Catti-brie agreed. "Shaking his fist at the orcs and the giants. And how many felt the bite of his anger before he fell?"

Dagna nodded, his expression solemn.

"Banak's got the army out on the mountain?" he asked a moment later, changing both his tone and the grim subject with a burst of sudden energy.

"He's got it well in hand," Catti-brie answered. "And he's found some fine

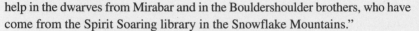

help in the dwarves from Mirabar and in the Bouldershoulder brothers, who have come from the Spirit Soaring library in the Snowflake Mountains."

Dagna nodded and mumbled, "Good, good."

"We'll hold up there," Cattie-brie said.

"Ye best," said Dagna. "I've got more than I can handle in securing the tunnels. We're not to let our enemies walk in through the Underdark while they're distracting us up above."

Catti-brie stepped back and looked to Regis for support. She had expected that, somewhat, for when Banak's couriers had come in with requests that a second force be sent forth from Mithral Hall to secure the western end of Keeper's Dale, their reception had been less than warm. Clearly there was a battle brewing about whether to fall back to Mithral Hall and hold the fort or to go out and meet the surface challenge of the orc hordes.

"They're getting their ropes down to the dale so that Banak can get them all out o' there?" Dagna asked.

"They've several rope ladders to the valley floor already," Catti-brie answered. "And Warlord Banak's ordered many more. Torgar's engineers are putting the climbs together nonstop. But Banak's not thinking to come down anytime soon. If we can assure him that Keeper's Dale is secure behind him, he'll stay up on that mountain until the orcs find a way to push him off."

Dagna grumbled something unintelligible under his breath, and though Catti-brie and Regis couldn't make it out, it was fairly obvious that the crusty old warrior dwarf wasn't thrilled with that prospect.

"We've got the right three directing the forces out there," Catti-brie assured him.

"True enough," Dagna admitted. "I sent Banak Brawnanvil out there meself, and I knowed there'd be none better among all the ranks o' Clan Battlehammer."

"Then give him the support he needs to hold that ground."

Dagna looked long and hard at Catti-brie, then shook his head. "Choice ain't me own to make," he replied. "Clerics asked me to direct the defense o' the tunnels, and so I am. They're not asking me to steward Bruenor's crown."

As he finished, he glanced over at Regis, and Catti-brie followed his gaze to her little friend, who suddenly seemed embarrassed.

"What do ye know?" the woman quietly asked the halfling.

"I-I told them it sh-should be you," Regis stammered. "Or Wulfgar, if not you."

Catti-brie turned her confused expression over Dagna, then back to the halfling.

"Yourself?" she asked Regis. "Are ye telling me that you've been asked to serve as Steward of Mithral Hall?"

"He has," Dagna answered. "And meself's the one who nominated him. With all me respect, good lady, for yerself and yer stepbrother, we're all thinking that none knew Bruenor's thoughts better than Regis here."

Catti-brie's expression as she turned back to regard Regis was more amused than angry. She lifted her head just a bit so that she could peek over the low collar of the halfling's shirt, looking toward a certain ruby pendant the halfling always wore. The implications of her questioning stare were clear enough and almost as obvious as if Catti-brie had just asked the halfling aloud if he had used his ruby pendant to "persuade" some of those deciding upon the matter of who should be steward in Bruenor's absence.

Regis's sudden gulp was even louder.

"You've got the word as king, then?" Catti-brie asked.

"He's got the primary vote," Dagna corrected. "The king's over there, lest ye're forgetting."

The crusty old dwarf pointed his chin Bruenor's way.

"Over there, and soon enough to join us again," Catti-brie agreed. "Until then, Steward Regis it is."

From somewhere down the hall came a call for Dagna, and the old dwarf gave a few "bahs" and excused himself, which was exactly what Catti-brie wanted, for she needed to have a few words in private with a certain little halfling.

"I-I've done nothing untoward," Regis stammered as soon as he was alone with Catti-brie, and the way the blood drained from the halfling's face showed that he understood her every concern.

"No one said you did."

"They asked me to serve Bruenor," Regis went on unsteadily. "How could I say no to that? You and Wulfgar will stay out and about, and who knows when Drizzt will return?"

"The dwarves wouldn't follow any of us three, anyway," Catti-brie agreed. "They'll take to a halfling, though. And everyone knows that Bruenor took Regis into his confidence all the way back from Icewind Dale. A good choice, I'd say, in Steward Regis. I've no doubt that you'll do what's best for Mithral Hall, and that's the point, after all."

Regis seemed to steady a bit, and even managed a smile.

"And what's good for Mithral Hall right now is for Steward Regis to get a thousand more dwarves out and in position to defend Keeper's Dale in the western edge," Catti-brie said. "And another two hundred running supplies, Mithral Hall to Keeper's Dale, and Mithral Hall to Warlord Banak and the force up on the mountain."

"We haven't got that many to spare!" Regis protested. "We're maintaining two groups outside the mines already, with those holding defense along the Surbrin in the east."

"Then bring that second group in and close the eastern gate," Catti-brie reasoned. "We know we're in for a fight up on the mountain, and if the orcs get around us into Keeper's Dale, Banak's to lose his whole force."

"If the orcs float down the Surbrin . . ." Regis started to warn.

"Then one well-positioned scout will see them," Catti-brie answered. "They'll be moving near to striking distance of some of our allies then as well."

Regis considered the logic for a short while, then nodded his agreement.

"I'll bring most of them in," the halfling said, "and send out the force through Keeper's Dale. Do we really need a thousand in the west? That many?"

"Five hundred at the least, by Banak's estimation," Catti-brie explained. "Though if they're left alone for a bit and can get the defenses up and in place, then we can cut that number considerably."

Regis nodded.

"But I'll not deplete the defenses of the mines," he said. "If the orcs are striking aboveground, then we can expect trouble below as well. Bruenor's got a responsibility to the folks of the land around, I agree, but his first duty is to Mithral Hall."

Catti-brie glanced past Regis, to the very still form of her beloved adoptive father.

She managed a wistful smile as she whispered, "Agreed."

The black foot came down softly, toes touching the dirt and stone, weight shifting gradually, ever so gradually, to allow for continued perfect balance and complete silence. A shift brought the next foot out in front, to repeat the stealthy stride.

He moved through the largest of the dozen separate encampments around the field of Shallows, slipping in and out of the predawn shadows with the skill that only a drow warrior—and only the best of the drow warriors—could possibly attain. He moved within a few strides of one group of oblivious orcs as they argued over something that didn't concern him in the least.

He slipped to the side of a tent then went in and silently through it, passing right between a pair of snoring orcs. Using a fine-edged scimitar, he cut a slice in the back flap, and quiet as a slight breeze, the dark elf moved back out.

Normally, he would have paused to slaughter those sleeping two, but Drizzt Do'Urden had something else in mind, something that he didn't want to compromise for lesser trophies.

For there sat a larger and more decorated tent in the distance, its deerskin flaps covered in sigils and murals representing the orc god. A trio of heavily armed guards paced around its entryway. There lay the leader of the tribe, Drizzt reasoned, and that tribe was the largest by far of those assembled.

The Hunter moved along, light-stepping and quick-stepping, always in balance, always at the ready, scimitars drawn and moving in harmony with his body as he strode and rolled, dipping back and stepping forward suddenly. It would not do for him to merely hold the weapons at his sides, he knew, for he wore the enchanted bracers around his ankles, speeding his stride, and in crossing so rapidly past so many cubbies and blind corners, the drow had to be ready to strike with precision in an instant. So the curving blades did a dance around him as his legs propelled him across the encampment, inexorably toward that large, decorated tent.

Within the cover of a lean-to just across from the large tent's entrance and its three orc guards, Drizzt slid his scimitars away. He had to be fast and precise, and he had to pick his moment carefully.

He looked around, waiting for another group of orcs to walk farther away.

Satisfied that he had a few moments alone, he casually rested his hands on the pommels of his belted weapons and strode across the way, smiling and with an unthreatening posture.

The orc guards, though, tensed immediately, one clutching his weapon more tightly, another even ordering Drizzt to stop.

The drow did halt, and locked the image of them into his sensibilities, noting their exact placement, counting the number of strides that would bring him before them, one after another.

The orc in the middle kept on talking, ordering, and questioning, and Drizzt just held his ground, smiling.

Just as one of the other orcs turned as if to move into the great tent, the drow reached into his innate magical powers and dropped a globe of darkness upon the trio. Even as he summoned it, Drizzt was moving, hands and feet. His scimitars appeared in his hands before he had taken two strides, and he was into the darkness before the orcs even realized that the world had suddenly gone black.

Drizzt veered left first, still holding fast to the image of the three and confident that none had begun to move.

Twinkle came across at neck height, turning an intended cry for help into a gurgle.

A spin had both blades cutting down the second guard and a sudden forward rush out of that spin propelled the drow straight into the third, again with his blades finding the mark. He bowled over that third orc, the creature falling right through the tent flap, and Drizzt stepping in right across it, exiting the area of darkness.

Several startled faces looked back at him, including that of a red-cloaked female shaman.

Unfortunately, she was across the room.

Not slowing in the least, Drizzt rushed the closest orc, severing its upraised, blocking arm and quick-stepping past it while thrusting his other scimitar into its belly.

A table was set between Drizzt and the next in line on that right-hand side of the tent. The orc fell behind the table, using it to slow the drow's progress— or thinking to, for Drizzt went over it as if it wasn't even there. His foot came up to kick aside the small stool the orc thrust his way.

As that orc fell to the slashing blades, the Hunter spun around, bringing both his weapons across defensively, one following the other, and the first turned the tip of a flying spear while the second knocked the clumsily-thrown missile completely aside.

But the other orcs were organizing and setting their defenses, and the shaman was casting a spell.

Drizzt called upon his innate magical abilities yet again, but paused enough to mouth, *"olacka acka eento."*—a bit of arcane-sounding gibberish.

He even tossed one of his blades into the air and waggled his fingers dramatically to heighten the ruse. The shaman took the bait, and where the room had been in a ruckus and growing louder, suddenly all was silent.

Completely and magically silent, as the shaman predictably used the most efficient spell in her clerical arsenal to prevent attacks of wizardry.

That spell didn't prevent Drizzt's innate magic, though, and so the shaman was suddenly covered in purplish-glowing flames that outlined her form clearly, making her an easier target.

Drizzt didn't stop there, bringing forth another globe of impenetrable darkness right before the orc warriors who were even then bearing down upon him.

He summoned a second globe for good measure, to ensure that the whole

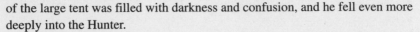

of the large tent was filled with darkness and confusion, and he fell even more deeply into the Hunter.

He couldn't hear a thing and couldn't see a thing, and so he played by touch and instinct alone. He went into a spinning dance, his blades whipping all around him, setting a defense, and every so often he came out of it with one blade or the other stabbing forward powerfully or bringing it in a sudden and wide slashing sweep.

And whenever he sensed the presence of an orc in close quarters—the smell of the creature, the hot breath, or a slight brush—he struck fast and hard, scimitars coming to bear with deadly accuracy, finding holes in any offered defense simply because Drizzt knew the height of his opponents and understood their typical offered posture, defensive or attacking.

He worked his way straight across the room, then back toward the center tent pole, using that as a pivot.

He would have been surprised, had he not been in that primal and reactive mode, when a spell burst forth, countering his darkness with magical light.

Orcs were all around him, and all surprised—except for the shaman, who stood at the back wall of the tent, her eyes glowing fiercely, her body still outlined in the drow's faerie fire, her fingers waggling in yet another casting.

Those surprised orcs closest to Drizzt's right fell fast and fell hard, and the drow spun back to the left to meet the advance of some others, his weapons rolling over and over furiously, slapping away defenses, stinging arms and hands, and driving the entire remaining quartet of warriors back.

He slowed suddenly, feeling as if his arms were leaden, as a wave of magical energy flowed through him. He knew the spell instinctively, one that could paralyze, and had he not been within the hold of the Hunter at that time, where instinct and primal fury built for him a wall of defense, his life would have swiftly ended.

As it was, the drow's defenses became sluggish for a moment, so much so that a club came in from the side and smacked him hard in the ribs.

Very hard, but the Hunter felt no pain.

A globe of darkness engulfed him again, and he went right at the attacker, accepting a second hit, much less intense, and returning it with a trio of quick stabs and a slash, and any of the four attacks could have alone laid the orc low.

The enchantment of magical silence expired or was dismissed, and the Hunter's ears perked up immediately, registering the movements of those orcs nearby and hearing, too, the incantation of the troublesome shaman. He brought his scimitars into sudden crossing diagonal slashes before him, winding them around in a loop to continue the rolling movements, then used that to get between a pair of orcs. On one downward roll, the drow used his building momentum to leap forward and out, turning a complete somersault and landing lightly on his feet in a short run out of the darkness.

Right behind him came a burst of sharp sound, as if the air itself exploded, and the drow fell into a stagger and nearly went to the floor.

And if that spell had done that much to him, Drizzt could well understand its effect on the orcs behind him!

He caught himself, pivoted, and went right back into the darkness, blades slashing wildly. He hit nothing, for as he had expected, the orcs were down, but he really didn't want to hit anything. Rather, he stopped short and cut a right angle to his left, then burst out of the darkness once more, right in front of the shaman, who was waggling her fingers yet again.

Twinkle took those fingers.

Icingdeath took her head.

Hearing a tremendous commotion back the other way, the Hunter ran right past the falling shaman to the wall of the tent. His fine blades slashed down, and he squeezed through.

He ran off across the encampment, and orcs scrambled to get out of his way even as the screams continued to grow from the main tent behind him. He picked his path carefully, running from shadow to shadow at full bent.

Soon he was running clear, his enchanted anklets speeding him on his way to the rougher ground to the east and north of the town.

He had killed only a handful of orcs, but Drizzt was certain that he had brought great distress to his enemies that day.

5

THE WIDER WORLD

Shoudra Stargleam moved back toward the light of her campfire. The woman, the Sceptrana of Mirabar and a fairly adept wizard as well, had gone out to search for some roots and mushrooms to use as components for a new spell she was researching. In the verdant land south of Fell Pass, she had found exactly what she was looking for, in great abundance, and so her arms were full, wrapped around the rolled up side of her dress.

She was about to call out to her traveling companion to bring her a sack when she caught sight of him—and all that came out of her mouth was a giggle. For the little gnome cut quite a figure as he sat huddled before the fire, rubbing his hands before him. He had his cloak tight around him, the hood up and pulled far forward.

But not forward enough to hide Nanfoodle's most prominent feature, his long and crooked snout.

"If you lean in much closer, you will burn the hair out of your nose," Shoudra managed to say as she moved into the perimeter of fallen logs they had set around the fire.

"A chill wind tonight," the gnome replied.

"Unseasonably so," Shoudra agreed, for it was still summer, though fall was fast approaching.

"Which'll of course, only adds to the misery of the open road," Nanfoodle muttered.

Shoudra giggled again and took a seat opposite him. She started to unroll the side of her stuffed dress but paused when she caught the gnome staring at her shapely leg. She thought it perfectly ridiculous, of course; Shoudra was a statuesque woman, which made her leg alone taller than little Nanfoodle. She held the pose anyway, and even turned her leg just a bit to give Nanfoodle a better view, and watched his jaw drop open.

Eventually, the gnome glanced up enough to see Shoudra staring at him, an amused smile on her beautiful face.

Nanfoodle blinked repeatedly and cleared his throat, shuffling around as if he had misplaced something. Watching his every move, Shoudra unrolled her skirt and guided the roots and mushrooms gently to the ground.

"Do you find the road so miserable, truly?" she asked a few moments later, as she began separating the various components by type and size. "Do you not find it invigorating?"

Nanfoodle crossed his arms before him and huddled closer to the fire.

"Invigorating?" he echoed incredulously.

"Have you no sense of adventure then, my good Nanfoodle?" Shoudra asked. "Have you become so tame from your years and years in front of beakers and solutions that you've forgotten the thrill of roasting a goblin with a fireball?"

Nanfoodle fixed her with a curious stare.

"The Nanfoodle I met those years ago in Baldur's Gate could weave a spell or two, if I remember correctly," Shoudra remarked.

"Nothing as crude as a fireball, surely!" the gnome protested with a dismissive wave of his little hand. "Bah, a fireball! Next you will recount your glory at bringing forth a bolt of lightning. No, no, Shoudra. I prefer the magic of the mind to the blast and burn of elemental forces."

"Ah, yes," Shoudra replied. "Of course. I should have better recognized the link between illusion magic and alchemy."

How Nanfoodle's eyes widened at that! He had been hired by Marchion Elastul of Mirabar, Shoudra's superior, to bring his alchemical brilliance to the aid of their inferior ore in their trade war against Mithral Hall. Many times had he suffered the dry wit of Shoudra Stargleam on those occasions when he had to report his progress to the marchion, for alchemy was an imprecise and trial-and-error science. Unfortunately for Nanfoodle, his efforts in Mirabar had been almost exclusively of the error variety.

Something that Shoudra rarely failed to point out.

"What do you imply?" the gnome asked evenly.

Shoudra laughed and went back to separating her mushrooms.

"You do not believe in alchemy at all, do you?"

"Have I ever made a secret of that?"

"Yet, were you not the one who gave my name to Marchion Elastul?" Nanfoodle asked. "I was under the impression that he had learned of my growing reputation from none other than Shoudra Stargleam."

"I have no use for alchemy," Shoudra explained. "I never said that I have no use for, nor care for, Nanfoodle Buswilligan."

After a moment of quiet, the woman glanced up to see Nanfoodle staring at her curiously.

"If Marchion Elastul was so determined to throw his coin away on fool's gold, then why not have some of it go to Nanfoodle, at least?" Shoudra explained with a wry grin.

The alchemist nodded, but his perplexed expression showed her that he really didn't seem to know whether to thank her or berate her.

She liked it that way.

"We eat the food and yet our load increases," the gnome remarked, staring sourly at Shoudra's growing component collection.

"Our load?" came the sarcastic response. "A single mushroom would seem to be a load for poor little Nanfoodle." She ended by playfully throwing a small white-capped mushroom across the fire. Nanfoodle's hand came up to block it, but he merely deflected the item, which bounced from his hand to thump against his long nose, drawing yet another laugh from Shoudra.

Scowling and muttering under his breath, Nanfoodle deliberately reached down and picked up the missile, then regarded it for a moment, still muttering, before throwing it back.

Shoudra had her defenses set, her hands up in front of her, except that not one, but a half dozen identical mushrooms suddenly flew her way.

"Well done!" she congratulated as the real missile bounced off her forehead, the illusionary ones flying right through her, and she laughed all the louder.

"One should be careful not to raise the ire of Nanfoodle," the gnome boasted, and he puffed out his chest, which almost tightened his small cloak around him.

"I have a few here we can use to dress our dinner," the woman remarked, and she held up both hands full of mushrooms and various roots. "If you eat enough—and that has never seemed to be a problem for you!—our load will lighten."

Nanfoodle started to offer a reply, but the sound of hoofbeats stopped him short and turned both him and Shoudra to regard the road that passed just south of their camp.

"The rider has seen our fire!" the gnome said with alarm.

He fell back to the shadows, seeming to retreat even more under his cloak, and he began chanting and waggling his fingers almost immediately.

Shoudra watched the gnome with some amusement, but then focused on the road. She wasn't overly afraid, for she was a seasoned adventurer and could stand her ground with weapon and with spell.

But then everything seemed to go out of focus, as if some enchantment had engulfed the camp, and Shoudra gave a slight cry and started to dive aside.

Started to, for she quickly enough realized that the spell was not the work of an enemy, but of Nanfoodle. She glared at the gnome, who just looked at her from under the cowl of his hood, grinning from ear to ear. He placed a finger over his lips, bidding her to silence.

Up bounded the horse, a large and muscular bay stallion, bearing a tall human rider in a weather-beaten gray cloak. The man pulled his mount up short, then dismounted with practiced ease. He walked before the horse and patted the dust from his cloak, then bowed politely—bowed to a tree a couple of feet to the side of Nanfoodle.

The rider seemed to be of middle age, perhaps forty years, but was in fine physical shape, and his hair was still mostly black, with a bit of gray showing at the edges. He wore a broadsword on his left hip and a dagger on his right, and he had his right hand resting on that smaller weapon as he approached, in a position that seemed one of convenience to the untrained eye. To a seasoned adventurer like Shoudra, though, the man's posture was one of readiness. She could tell from the angle of his settled right arm that he could bring his hand around in an instant, drawing forth and launching the dagger in a single fluid movement.

"Well met, good gnome," the tall man said to the tree, and Shoudra had to fight hard to stop from giggling.

She looked to Nanfoodle, who was grinning even wider and more emphatically trying to silence her. The little one began waggling his fingers once more.

"I am Galen Firth of Nesmé," the man introduced himself.

"And I am Nanfoodle, principal alchemist of the Marchion of Mirabar," the tree answered through the power of the illusionist gnome's spell. "Pray tell us, good sir, your business in these parts. You are a long way from home."

"As are you," Galen commented.

"Indeed, but it was our camp which was violated," Nanfoodle's chosen tree replied.

Galen bowed again.

"Grim news from Nesmé," he remarked. "The bog blokes and the trolls have marched upon us. Our situation is grim—I do not know if my people hold on even as we speak."

"We can turn fast for Mirabar!" came a voice from the side, Shoudra's voice, and the woman moved toward Galen.

His gig up, Nanfoodle waggled his fingers and dispelled the grand illusion, leaving Galen Firth to blink repeatedly as he tried to get his bearings.

"I am the Sceptrana of Mirabar," Shoudra explained when Galen focused on her at last. "Let us turn for Mirabar immediately, that I can persuade Marchion Elastul to rouse the guard to your aid."

"Riders are well on their way to your Marchion," Galen explained, and he continued to blink and look around. "My course is Mithral Hall and the court of King Bruenor Battlehammer."

The man finally focused on the real Nanfoodle, looking from the gnome to the area of illusion, as if he was still trying to figure out what had just happened, and why he was talking to and bowing before a tree.

"Mithral Hall is our destination as well," came Nanfoodle's voice from the back of the camp, and the gnome came forward under Galen's scrutinizing glare. "Forgive the misdirection illusion that greeted you, good rider of Nesmé. One cannot be too careful, after all."

"Indeed," said Galen. "Especially where illusionists are concerned."

Nanfoodle grinned and bowed.

"Your horse shines with sweat," Shoudra remarked. "He cannot run much farther this night. Come, share our evening meal with us and tell us your tale of Nesmé more completely. We will accompany you with all haste to find King Bruenor, and I will add what weight I can to the urgency of your cause."

"That is most generous, Sceptrana," Galen replied.

He moved to the side and tethered his horse.

"This is not good," Nanfoodle whispered to Shoudra while they were alone by the fire.

"I only hope the Marchion is more sympathetic to Nesmé's plight than he has shown toward outsiders of late," Shoudra replied.

"King Bruenor will send aid," Nanfoodle reasoned, and Galen Firth, heading into the camp by then, heard him.

"I can only hope that King Bruenor's memory is short concerning slights," Galen admitted, drawing curious looks from both.

"He came through the region of Nesmé some years ago," the newcomer explained as he took an offered seat on a log beside the fire. "I fear that my patrol did not treat him very well." He gave a little sigh and lowered his eyes, but then quickly added, "It was not King Bruenor who instilled our doubts and fear, but his traveling companion, a drow elf."

"Drizzt Do'Urden," Shoudra remarked. "Yes, I expect that the company Bruenor keeps is off-putting to many people."

"I am hoping that the dwarf will see beyond our past indiscretion," said Galen, "and recognize that it is in his best interests to bolster Nesmé in her time of need."

"From all that we know of King Bruenor, we would expect no less," Nanfoodle put in, and Shoudra nodded her agreement.

Galen Firth nodded as well, but his expression held grim.

The night deepened around them, and given Galen's news of Nesmé, the darkness seemed all the more intimidating.

"A big well-done for yer friend Rumblebelly," Banak Brawnanvil said to Catti-brie as he and a group of others looked over the rope-strewn cliff facing down into Keeper's Dale, to see a substantial dwarf force moving east-to-west across the valley.

"He's one to count on," Catti-brie remarked.

"Oo oi!" Pikel Bouldershoulder seconded.

"Well, I feel better knowing the dale's secure behind us," Ivan Bouldershoulder joined in. "But I'm still thinking that the ridge to the west is a problem in the making."

All eyes turned to the north and west as Ivan reminded them, to view that one long mountain spur, the only higher ground in the region that seemed at all accessible.

"The orcs have been hunting beside giants," Ivan added. "They might be thinking to put a few o' them up there."

"Giants couldn't reach us from up there," Banak answered, the same reply he had offered earlier in their strategy discussions. "Long way off."

"Still a good place for them to hold," Ivan countered. "Even if they just put a few scouts up there, it will give them a fine view of the entire battlefield."

"It is good ground," agreed Torgar Hammerstriker.

"Yer scouts get back from the ridge yet?" Banak asked.

"It's clear so far," Torgar reported. "Me boys said the place is full of tunnels. Quite a network, as far as they could tell. They're guessing that some would lead up to the high ground."

"Probably," said Ivan.

"Let me take a hunnerd," Torgar offered. "I'll go and hold those tunnels."

"And if they find out ye're there?" Banak asked. "Them orcs might come on ye in full. I'm not for losing a hundred!"

"Ye won't," Torgar assured him. "There's an entry into the tunnels way back near to the Keeper's Dale cliff, just down to the west o' here. We'll get in fast and get out faster, if need be."

Banak looked to Ivan for some answers, then to Catti-brie and Wulfgar.

"Catti-brie and I will move to the tunnel entrance and serve as liaison," Wulfgar offered.

Banak looked back out over his current defenses. They had turned the orcs back twice, though the second assault had been nowhere as determined as the first. The orc leader had simply come on again with his forces to disrupt the work of the dwarves, Banak understood, and he was quite a bit impressed by the unusual display of tactics.

Still, that second assault had done little to disrupt the dwarves' preparations, for Banak's warriors had repelled it with ease, and with many never stopping the rock chopping and stone piling. The battlefield was nearly shaped, with solid walls of piled stones forcing any orc charge into a bottleneck. Given that and the fact that the engineers were done with their initial rope work along the cliff face, Banak knew that he could spare a hundred dwarves, even two hundred, without compromising his position.

For if the orcs came on, a large number of the dwarves would have to simply stand behind their fighting kin, missing all the fun.

"Take half of yer own and sweep those tunnels clear," Banak instructed Torgar. "And get a good look at what's to the north once ye get up atop them rocks, will ye?"

"I'll paint ye a picture," Torgar said with a wide grin.

"Hee hee hee," said Pikel.

"And if they come against ye with too much, ye get yerself and yer boys out o' there," Banak instructed. "I don't want to be telling King Bruenor that I lost all his new recruits before they even got themselves into his halls!"

"Ye're not to be losing Torgar and the boys from Mirabar to a bunch of smelly orcs!" Torgar insisted.

"Even if they bring a hundred giants beside them!" agreed Shingles McRuff, the old and grizzled dwarf standing beside Torgar.

Shingles gave a wink at Banak, then dropped a friendly hand hard onto Torgar's shoulder. Torgar's look told all the onlookers that the two were good old friends indeed. In fact, Shingles had been a friend of Torgar's family long before Torgar had seen his first sunrise over Mirabar, and that was centuries gone by.

When the Marchion of Mirabar had treated Torgar so shabbily, blaming him for the warm reception some of Mirabar's dwarves had given to Bruenor, Shingles had been the first to Torgar's side, and had, in fact, been the one to organize the exodus that had taken more than four hundred of Mirabar's finest dwarves out of the city and onto the road to Mithral Hall.

And there they were, a long way from their old home but with their new home in sight across Keeper's Dale. Before they had ever gotten near to Mithral Hall, they had chanced upon the caravan fleeing the disaster of Shallows with the wounded King Bruenor. Torgar, Shingles, and the Mirabarran dwarves had fought a rearguard for that caravan and had performed brilliantly.

Even with all the fighting, even with the orc hordes pressing down upon them, not one of the Mirabarran dwarves had shown the slightest inclination to turn back to their old city in the west.

Not one.

And soon after Torgar's meeting with Banak, with the potentially dangerous duty offered before them, not one backed away from volunteering to spearhead the push into the tunnels of the mountain spur.

Torgar left it to Shingles to pick the half who would accompany him.

The expressions on the faces of the three guests showed that the leader sitting on Mithral Hall's throne before them was not exactly who or what they had expected.

But Regis did not shrink away in the face of those obvious doubts.

"I am the Steward of Mithral Hall," he explained, "serving in the name and interests of King Bruenor."

"And where is your king?" asked Galen Firth, his tone a bit abrupt and impatient.

"Recovering from grievous wounds," Regis admitted, and how he hoped his description was correct. "He was on the front end of the fighting you heard when you were escorted across Keeper's Dale."

Galen started to respond again, but Regis came forward and put on as stern an expression as he could muster with his cherubic features.

"I have heard rumors as to whom you three are," said the halfling, "who

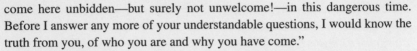

come here unbidden—but surely not unwelcome!—in this dangerous time. Before I answer any more of your understandable questions, I would know the truth from you, of who you are and why you have come."

"I am Galen Firth of the Riders of Nesmé," said Galen, and his mention of the riders brought a hint of a scowl to the halfling's face. "Come to bid King Bruenor to send aid to my besieged town. For the trolls have arisen out of their moors. We are sorely pressed!"

Regis brought a hand up to rub his chin, and he glanced to the Battlehammer dwarves standing a bit off to the side. They were a long way from Nesmé; could he dare to send any of Bruenor's clan so far and into such exposure? He offered Galen a nod, for he had nothing more to give just then.

"And you are the Sceptrana of Mirabar," Regis remarked, turning from Galen to Shoudra. "Such was told to me, and I recognize you in any case from my recent visit to your town."

"Your scrimshaw has become quite a novelty in Mirabar, good Steward Regis," Shoudra said politely, and she bowed low. "Shoudra Stargleam at the service of Mithral Hall. This is my assistant, Nanfoodle Buswilligan."

"At the service of Mithral Hall?" Regis echoed. "Or come to check on your wayward dwarves?"

The gnome at Shoudra's side bristled, but the sceptrana merely smiled all the wider.

"I pray that Torgar fares well," she replied, and if she was bothered at all by the emigration of Torgar and his band of dwarves, neither her tone nor her expression showed it.

"But you have not come to join him," said Regis.

Shoudra chuckled at the seemingly absurd notion and said, "I do not agree with Torgar's choice, nor with those who accompanied him away from Mirabar, but it was I who convinced Marchion Elastul that he must allow the dwarves to leave, if that was their decision. It was a sad day in Mirabar when Torgar Hammerstriker and his kin departed."

"When they came to Mithral Hall," Regis reminded. "And Mithral Hall has accepted them as brothers, a bond forged in battle from the day we first met up with Torgar in the mountains and valleys north of here. They are of Clan Battlehammer now. You know this?"

"I do, and though it pains me greatly, I accept it," Shoudra finished with another bow.

"Then why have you come?"

"I beg of your pardon, Steward Regis," Galen Firth interrupted, "but I have not come to witness an argument over the disposition of purposefully misplaced dwarves. My town is besieged, my business urgent." Some of the dwarves at the side of the room began to mutter and shift uneasily as Galen's voice steadily rose in ire. "Could you not continue your discussion with Sceptrana Shoudra at a later time?"

Regis paused and stared at the tall man for a long time.

"I have heard your request," the halfling said, "and deeply regret the situation in Nesmé. I too have some experience with the foul creatures of the Trollmoors, having come through that place in our search to find and reclaim Mithral Hall."

He fixed Galen with a look that told the man in no uncertain terms that he remembered well the shabby treatment the Riders of Nesmé had offered to Bruenor and the Companions of the Hall on that long-ago occasion.

"But you cannot expect me to throw wide the gates of Mithral Hall and empty the place of warriors with a horde of orcs and giants pressing us across the northland," Regis went on, and he gave a glance at the dwarves and took comfort in their assenting nods. "Your situation and request will be discussed at length, and in short order, but before I adjourn this meeting I wish to have all the facts open before me concerning the disposition of all of Mithral Hall's guests, that I might bring all options to the council."

"Decisive action is necessary!" Galen argued.

"And I have not the power to give you that which you desire!" Regis yelled right back. He came forward out of the throne and stood upon the dais, which allowed him to almost look the tall man in the eye. "I am not King Bruenor. I am not the king of anything. I am a steward, an advisor. I will discuss your situation in detail with the dwarves who better understand what Mithral Hall could or could not do to aid Nesmé in her time of need, particularly when we, too, are in a time of need."

"Then my business now, at this meeting, is at its end?" Galen asked, not blinking as he matched Regis's stare.

"It is."

"I will take my leave, then," said Galen. "Am I to presume that Mithral Hall will offer me a place of respite, at least?"

That last "at least" had Regis narrowing his brown eyes.

"Of course," he said, though his jaw hardly moved to let the words escape.

The halfling turned to the side and nodded. A pair of dwarves moved up to flank Galen. The man gave a bow that was more curt than polite and moved off, his heavy boots emphatically thumping against the stone floor.

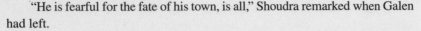

"He is fearful for the fate of his town, is all," Shoudra remarked when Galen had left.

"True enough," Regis agreed. "And I certainly understand his fears and impatience. But the folk of Clan Battlehammer do not consider Nesmé to be much of a friend, I fear, for Nesmé has never shown much friendship to the folk of Mithral Hall. When we came looking for the Hall those many years ago, we encountered a group of the Riders of Nesmé just outside of the Trollmoors. They were in dire straits, under assault by a band of bog blokes. Bruenor didn't hesitate to go to their rescue—neither did Wulfgar, nor Drizzt. We saved their lives, I believe, and were soundly rebuffed in return."

"Because of the drow elf," Shoudra said.

"True enough," Regis sighed. He gave a little shrug as he settled back in his chair. "That in itself wasn't such a problem. It has happened often and will again."

His obvious reference to the treatment the caravan out of Icewind Dale had received at Mirabar's gate, where Drizzt Do'Urden had not been allowed entrance, had the woman and the gnome looking to each other with a bit of embarrassment.

"After the reclamation of Mithral Hall, Settlestone was rebuilt," the halfling went on. "By Uthgardt warriors, not dwarves."

"I remember Berkthgar the Bold and his people," said Shoudra.

"The community was promising early on," said Regis. "We were all hopeful that the barbarians from Icewind Dale would flourish here. But while they maintained a close relationship with Mithral Hall, their primary goods—furs—were of little use to the dwarves who lived underground, where the temperature remains nearly constant. If Nesmé, the closest neighbor of Berkthgar's people, had welcomed them with trade, Settlestone might still thrive today. Instead, it is just another abandoned ruin along the mountain pass."

"The people of Nesmé lead a difficult existence," Shoudra remarked. "They suffer on the very edge of the dangerous moors, in nearly constant battle. They have learned through tragic experience that they must rely upon themselves most of all, oftentimes only upon themselves. Not a family in Nesmé has not known the tragedy of loss. Most have witnessed at least one of their loved ones being carried off by horrid trolls."

"It's all true," Regis admitted. "And I do understand. But I could not pledge any help to Galen. Not now. Not with Bruenor lying near death and the orcs pressing us to our gates."

"Offer him a sanctuary, then," Shoudra suggested. "Tell him that if his people are overrun, they should turn to Mithral Hall, where they will find friendship, comfort, and shelter."

Regis was nodding before she ever finished, for that was exactly along the lines he had been thinking.

"Perhaps we might find some spare warriors to return with him to Nesmé, as well," the halfling said. He paused for a moment, then gave a little snort. "Here I am, begging advice from a visitor. A fine steward am I!"

Shoudra started to reply, but Nanfoodle cut in, "The finest leaders are those who listen more than they talk."

That brought a smile to Shoudra and to Regis, but the halfling asked, "Does that show wisdom? Or trepidation?"

"For one whose actions greatly affect others, they are one and the same," Nanfoodle insisted.

Regis pondered that remark, and took some comfort in it. However, the finest leader Regis had ever known was none other than Bruenor Battlehammer, and if the dwarf was ever unsure of a decision, even the boldest of decisions, he surely had never shown it.

THE RECKLESS ONE

"He is sure to get himself killed," Tarathiel whispered to Innovindil as the two lithe and small figures lay on a flat overhang, looking down at the returning Drizzt Do'Urden. The drow was clearly limping and favoring his right hip.

"His determination borders on foolishness," Innovindil replied. She looked at her companion. Their eyes were quite similar in color—rich blue—but looked very different in their respective faces, for while Innovindil's hair was golden, Tarathiel's was as black as a raven's wing. "Never have I seen one so singularly . . . angry."

The elf pair had been keeping an eye on Drizzt ever since the sacking of Shallows. In that fight, when Drizzt had been across the ravine distracting the giant bombardiers, Tarathiel and Innovindil had flown in to his aid. Up high on their pegasi, Sunset and Sunrise, the elves believed that Drizzt had seen them, though he had made no move to find them subsequent to that one incident.

Not so with the elves. Both were skilled trackers, and Tarathiel had found Drizzt again soon after the fateful fight—mostly by following the trail of dead orcs the drow was leaving in his wake. In the two tendays since Shallows's fall, Drizzt had struck at orc camps and patrols nearly every day. The latest attack, against one of the great tribes that had recently arrived on the scene at Shallows, showed that he was growing bolder—dangerously so.

Still, he was winning, and to Tarathiel and Innovindil, that was an admirable thing.

"He lost friends at Shallows," Tarathiel reminded her. "The orcs claim that Bruenor Battlehammer fell there."

Innovindil looked down at the drow warrior. He had undressed then and was cleaning his latest wound—one of many—in a small brook near to his meager shelter of piled boulders.

"He is not one I would desire as an enemy," she whispered.

Tarathiel turned to her as he considered her words, and the implication they clearly held for another of the clan. As soon as they had heard that Bruenor Battlehammer was returning to Mithral Hall, with Drizzt Do'Urden beside him, Tarathiel and Innovindil had welcomed the chance to meet with Drizzt. For one of their own, poor lost Ellifain, had gone off after the drow, seeking revenge for a dark elf raid that had occurred decades before, when Ellifain had been just an infant. Ellifain's entire family had been slaughtered in that terrible raid, and Drizzt Do'Urden had been among the raiders.

But Drizzt had not partaken of that slaughter, the elves knew, and in fact, had saved Ellifain by splashing her with her own mother's blood and hiding her beneath her mother's corpse. To Tarathiel and Innovindil, and all the other elves of the Moonwood, Drizzt Do'Urden was more hero than villain, but poor Ellifain had never been able to get past her grief, had never been able to view the noble drow ranger as anything more than a lie.

Despite all their efforts to educate and calm Ellifain, she had gone off from the Moonwood a couple of years previous in search of her revenge. Tarathiel and Innovindil had tracked her and chased her, determined to stop her, but the trail had gone stone cold in Silverymoon.

Drizzt was back in the area, though, and very much alive. What might that bode for Ellifain?

Innovindil had thought to go right down and speak with Drizzt about that very thing when first they'd located him, but Tarathiel, after observing the drow for a short while, had advised against that course. From all appearances, Drizzt Do'Urden seemed to Tarathiel to be an unknown entity, a wild card, a creature existing purely within his rage and survival instincts.

He wasn't even wearing boots as he set out each day across the unforgiving stony ground, and on the two occasions in which Tarathiel had witnessed Drizzt in battle, the drow seemed something beyond a conscious and cautious warrior. Tarathiel had seen Drizzt taking hits without a flinch and had seen him lop the heads from enemies without the slightest hesitation or expression of regret.

In many ways, the drow reminded him of that Moonwood friend he had recently lost, that young elf maiden so full of anger that she was blind to anything else in all the world.

"We must speak with him before he is slain," Tarathiel said suddenly.

His callous words, spoken so matter-of-factly, turned Innovindil's surprised look his way. For the tone of Tarathiel's words made it clear that he considered the outcome, that Drizzt would be slain, an inevitability. Tarathiel felt the intensity of her gaze and returned her concern with a simple shrug.

"Is his quest murderous or suicidal?" Tarathiel asked. "Or both, perhaps?"

"Then perhaps we should dissuade him of this course."

Tarathiel gave a little laugh and looked back to the distant Drizzt, who had stopped washing by then and had moved into a slow and steady series of stretching and balancing movements, focusing most of his movements on his wounded right hip. Stretching out the bruise, likely.

"He might know of Ellifain," Innovindil went on.

"And if he has faced Ellifain and defeated her, then what will he make of us two when we walk in upon him?"

"You are not a complete stranger to Drizzt Do'Urden," Innovindil argued. "Did he not convince you of his goodness those years ago when he crossed through the Moonwood? Did not the goddess Mielikki grant him a visit by her unicorn before your very eyes?"

It was all true, of course, but somehow in looking at that angry creature exercising below him, Tarathiel couldn't help but feel that it was not the same Drizzt Do'Urden he had once met.

His balance held perfectly, with not a tremor of muscle or sudden shift of his planted left foot. Slowly, Drizzt let his horizontally extended right leg flow through its full range of motion, front to back and back to front. He kept it up high, stretching his hamstring and other muscles as he worked through the tightening sensation within his right hip.

It truly surprised him to realize how hard he had been struck in that last fight, and he feared that he might have a broken bone.

Gradually, as the drow worked through his range of motion, his fears lessened. He found no impediment to his movement other than the ache and realized no overly sharp pains.

Drizzt had survived another encounter intact, fortunately so, and if any

second-guesses about his decision to go into that large camp flitted through his thoughts, they were quickly dismissed by the drow's imagining of the scene he had left behind. He had delivered a blow to the orcs that would not be soon forgotten.

But it was not enough, the Hunter knew.

Not nearly enough.

Drizzt looked up at the midmorning sky and calculated when he might bring Guenhwyvar back to his side. The panther needed her rest on the Astral Plane, but she would be ready to resume her hunt soon, Drizzt knew, and the thought brought a wicked grin to his ebon-skinned face.

The orcs might be scrambling to find him, and if they were, he and Guenhwyvar would surely find a few wayward creatures to slaughter.

Drizzt's attention shifted quickly from that pleasant thought to consider the two elves who were up on the flat rock watching him.

Yes, the Hunter knew of them, for in that state, Drizzt was too attuned to his environment to miss even that stealthy pair. He didn't know who they might be, but given his last, tragic encounter with a surface elf, he wasn't pleased by the possibilities.

"It was drow!" the orc protested, as vigorously as he dared. "I seen drow!"

Arganth Snarrl leaped over to stand before the insistent orc, the shaman's huge tooth necklace swinging around wildly, and even slapping across the face of the upstart.

"You seen drow?" the shaman asked.

"I just told you!" the orc protested.

Arganth ignored the reply and spun around to regard the other shamans, all gathered at the scene of Achtel's demise.

"Did Ad'non Kareese do this?" one of the other shamans asked, his brutish face full of outrage.

Arganth searched about for some answer, not wanting to reduce the drama of the murder—a mystery that the volatile shaman desired to exploit for his own ends. Achtel, after all, had been the sole quiet opposition among the gathered shamans to Arganth's insistence that King Obould should be viewed as one with Gruumsh. Not willing to relinquish the independence of her powerful tribe, Achtel had privately questioned some of the other shamans concerning the wisdom of Arganth's unification desires.

Achtel wasn't just dead, he seemed to have been singled out. For Arganth, the answer was obvious: Achtel's impudence had angered Gruumsh One-Eye, whose vengeance had been swift and uncompromising. Of course, Arganth was also wise enough to recognize that if the other shamans somehow connected Obould's drow friends to the murder of Achtel, then they might come to suspect some nefarious organization, working to persuade through terror—which was, after all, the orc way.

"Not Ad'non," the orc witness dared to put in. "It was the . . . one."

The suddenly husky tone of his voice as he uttered that peculiar phrase told the others exactly of whom he was speaking. Word had been filtering throughout the ranks of all the orcs and giants who had come out of their mountain holes that a lone drow, an ally of dead King Bruenor, was working behind their lines, and to deadly effect.

"The Drizzit," Arganth said in low and threatening tones. "Gruumsh has used our enemy against our enemy."

"Achtel was our enemy?" asked one of the other shamans.

"Achtel denied the joining of his spirit to King Obould's body," Arganth explained. "It is clear before us. This sign cannot be denied!"

Murmurs erupted all around him as soon as he widened the investigation to encompass his political aspirations, but most of those murmuring orcs were also nodding their agreement.

"Obould is Gruumsh!" Arganth dared to declare.

Not a protesting word came back at him.

"He wastes little time," Innovindil said to Tarathiel when she caught up to him around the backside of a copse of trees on the mountain slopes overlooking the region where Drizzt Do'Urden had taken up his shelter.

"Is he out again already?" Tarathiel asked, and he looked up at the sky, confirming that it was still a couple of hours to sunset. "I would have thought he would need to rest his hip."

"He brought in the panther," Innovindil explained.

Tarathiel nodded and looked again at the sky, his blue eyes glowing in the light.

"I fear he has erred," said the elf. "His hip is more injured than he realizes—if the wound upsets his balance. . . ."

Innovindil drew forth her slender sword and shrugged. She turned toward the path that would put them on the trail of the dark elf.

"Perhaps I should follow alone," Tarathiel offered. "On Sunrise, and high above the hunting cat."

Innovindil stared at him hard.

"Sunset is not yet ready to carry you," Tarathiel reasoned. "Soon, perhaps, but not yet."

Innovindil had little to offer in the way of an argument to that. In the fight with the giants north of Shallows, her pegasus had been struck in the wing, causing a deep bruise and laceration. Sunset seemed well on the mend, for pegasi were resilient creatures, but Tarathiel's assessment was correct, she knew, and she would not dare ask the mount to climb into the sky, particularly not with her added weight.

But she had no intention of being excluded.

"What a fine target you will make in the afternoon sky," she said. "Or perhaps you will still be airborne when the sun does set, leaving your steed blind and soaring about the mountain spurs."

"I only fear that we might encounter the panther as it moves about Drizzt," Tarathiel explained. "I have little desire for a battle with that creature!"

"It will not come to that if we are cautious," Innovindil insisted.

She motioned toward the path. Tarathiel was by her side in a moment, and the two rushed off, their footfalls silent, their senses trained. Soon enough, they had the trail of Drizzt and Guenhwyvar.

The orcs were so thick about the region that Drizzt and Guenhwyvar had already found a band of them with the sun still hanging in the western sky.

"Gerti says," one of the creatures complained, scooping a bucket in the cold waters of a fast-rushing mountain spring. "Gerti says!"

"How do we know what Gerti says, and what them giants says Gerti says?" another bitched, and he too sloshed a bucket through the water.

"Gerti talks too much," a third chimed in.

"Gerti," Drizzt whispered to Guenhwyvar. "A giant?"

The intelligent panther, seeming to understand every word, lowered her ears flat to her head. Thinking it wise to better assess the strength of the group, Drizzt motioned for Guenhwyvar to circle off to the right, while he went left. Sure enough, within a couple of minutes time, the drow found a frost giant, reclining on the river stones around a bend, head back to bask in the late afternoon sun. Her heavy boots sat on the bank, one upright, the other bent over in half, and her huge cleaver rested there as well. Oblivious to all the world she seemed as she splashed her bare feet in the icy water.

Drizzt spotted Guenhwyvar across the river and motioned to her, then to the relaxing giantess.

The Hunter went back over the rocks to the spot around the bend where the handful of orcs were still at work—they seemed to be filling a wide and shallow pit. A fire burned nearby, with rocks piled all around. Every now and then, an orc would kick one of those heated stones into the watery shallow.

"A bathtub?" Drizzt whispered under his breath.

The drow dismissed the thought as unimportant and narrowed his focus to the task at hand. He subconsciously rubbed his wounded hip as he surveyed the lay of the land, taking note of possible escape routes, for the orcs more than for himself, and searching among the up-and-down terrain to try to guess if other orc bands might be in the immediate area.

A growl from beyond the bend, followed by a scream of surprise, ended that search and sent the Hunter leaping from the stones and sprinting toward the orcs. As one the pig-faced creatures howled, tossing buckets aside.

One sprinted out to the right, along the river, but Drizzt, his feet sped by the enchanted anklets, caught it quickly and sliced it down. He turned fast—and nearly stumbled as a sharp pain rolled out from his hip—and charged back toward the main group.

The closest pair lifted spears to slow his charge, but he skidded down to his knees before them, then came up fast as they adjusted the angle of their weapons. Two fast strides had Drizzt rushing out to the left, and a pair of spears came slashing across that way to fend.

Except that the Hunter had already reversed his direction back to the right and had started down low for just an instant, just long enough to bring the two spears into a second dip as the orcs tried to reverse their momentum.

Drizzt leaped up and forward, double-kicking left and right, hitting one orc squarely in the face and clipping the other's forearm as it let go of its spear and moved to block. The Hunter came down lightly on one pointed foot—and again came a wave of pain from that hip. He turned immediately into a spin, scimitars flying out wide.

Both orcs fell away, lines of bright red appearing on each.

The Hunter ran past, into the next orc in line. A twist, a turn, a feint, then a second, had the orc turning every which way as the drow ran right past it. A flip of the wrist and reversed stab took the confused creature in the spine. On

Drizzt went, not even slowing as a tremendous roar came from around the bend, followed by the splashing of the running giantess.

She came around the bend, stumbling across the many large, slick river stones, her hands up by her face, trying to pull the stubborn panther free.

The Hunter dispatched another orc with a double-thrust low that had the creature leaping back, then stumbling forward in the inevitable overbalance. The drow followed with a pair of twisting uppercuts, one right behind the other, that took the creature about the face and neck. Before the dying orc even fell, the Hunter had turned, focusing on the giantess.

He saw Guenhwyvar finally come away from the behemoth's torn face, go up in the air over the staggering giantess's head, then go flying away. He heard the plaintive, wounded roar and felt, for just a moment, the panther's agony.

But he was the Hunter, not Drizzt, and he didn't move immediately for the figurine to dismiss the pained cat back to the Astral Plane and her peace. Instead, scimitars high, he took the opening on the horribly wounded and obviously blinded giantess, rushing in and stabbing her hard about the belly and back, running around to keep her turning. Always one step ahead of her, the Hunter scored again and again, and when the stubborn giantess finally went down to her knees in the river, he took up the attacks even more ferociously, finding her neck with every strike.

Blood flew wildly, inciting nothing but an even deeper rage within the Hunter. He bashed and slashed with abandon, even as the giantess fell face down into the water. His surroundings didn't matter to him. He saw the fall of Elli-fain at the end of one scimitar, saw Bruenor ride that burning tower down to the ground. And he fought those images with all his heart and soul, battered them away by cracking one blade after another against the giantess's thick skull. She became the focus of all that rage; for those few seconds of pure intensity, Drizzt Do'Urden broke free of his turmoil.

The wail of broken Guenhwyvar brought him from his frenzy, though, and shot through his heart with a stab of profound guilt. The panther lay on the river's far bank, struggling to get clear of the water's incessant pull with her shaking front paws, while her rear haunches lay limp and twisted, her pelvic area shattered by the giantess's strong grip.

Behind her came another group of orcs, spears raised and some already throwing for the panther.

"Go home, Guen," Drizzt called softly, lifting the onyx figurine from his belt pouch. He knew that she would heal well on the Astral Plane, knew that no injuries Guenhwyvar received on this plane of existence could ever truly harm her.

Still, she felt pain, a searing agony that rode her wail to Drizzt's heart.

A spear soared in for her, the shot true.

But it passed through as the panther faded and became a swirling gray mist drifting away and dissipating to nothingness.

The orcs shifted direction, coming fast for the drow standing midstream. He hardly registered them at first, still hearing Guenhwyvar's cry, still feeling the weight of her pain.

He glanced up at the closing orcs and tried to use that pain to shift back to his rage, to let free the Hunter once more. Behind him, he heard more of the brutes.

He raised his scimitars; in glancing around, he understood just how badly he was outnumbered. Too badly, likely.

The Hunter merely smiled—

—then charged through a rain of flying spears, his scimitars slashing before him to take the missiles from the sky. He dodged and turned, his senses falling so keenly into the sounds around him that he knew without looking when one of the spears from behind would catch him and he was able to react, a quick turn in perfect balance, to parry it aside.

He went out of the river along a run of five slick stones, his bare feet not slipping an inch on any of the sure-footed strides. He hit the rocky and sandy bank in a dead run, then threw himself aside into a sudden roll, and back up and forward, and to the side once more.

Through the orc ranks he went, scimitars cutting the way. His hands worked in a blur as his feet stepped forward and sideways, toes ahead, toes turned, every step sure and fast, his weight shifting effortlessly to stay over his pumping legs.

His momentum only gradually began to falter; he kept up the run for a long, long while. But at every turn, the orcs were there, pressing back at him, swinging clubs and swords, stabbing spears. Twinkle and Icingdeath rang repeatedly against metal and wood, taking blades high or low, or pushing them out wide so that Drizzt could step through.

But the orcs weren't stupid creatures, nor were they cowardly. They took their losses but kept their formations, groups working in concert to lock down every possible escape route the rogue drow might find.

Finally, the exhausted drow found himself in a shallow dell, over a sandy bluff twenty feet away from the river. Ringed by orcs, but with not a one within striking distance, he fell into a defensive stance, scimitars ready to intercept any forthcoming missile.

One of the orcs barked a command at him, a word that he thought meant "surrender." That one would die first, the Hunter decided. His feet shifted under him. Orcs all around feigned a charge or a throw but held back to their tight ranks.

The Hunter wanted them to move first, to present him an opening.

They would not.

The Hunter dashed out to the side, against the orc line, weapons working in a blaze. But the orcs held firm, their defenses tight and coordinated.

Again he went at them and again was repulsed.

They were gaining confidence, he realized from their wide, toothy smiles, and he knew, too, that their confidence was well founded. There were too many. His rage had carried him to a place beyond his abilities.

If only they would break the circle!

A commotion to the side had him spinning, weapons coming up to block. The orcs weren't coming his way, though, and many from that side weren't even looking at him any longer. He watched in shared confusion with them as their back ranks scrambled and fell, as orcs shoved orcs aside frantically.

The wave cut right through the perimeter, and a pair of slender forms emerged into the dell before the Hunter. Dressed in white tunics and tan breeches, with forest green cloaks flying behind them, the two were joined, forearm to forearm as they came in, and each used the other to heighten his or her balance as they moved in a whirlwind of a sword dance. Long and thick hair, black and yellow, flew out behind as they crossed around each other repeatedly, always maintaining the slightest contact, each altering the attack angles independently but in perfect harmony with the movements and choices of the other.

One went around and down low, and the orcs closest responded accordingly—except that the leading elf (and they were indeed surface elves, Drizzt recognized) simply rotated along past them, while his partner came in hard and high, above the set defenses. Orcs screamed and orcs fell, and more orcs tried to press in.

They fell, too.

The Hunter forced himself free of the amazing spectacle, a dance as graceful and perfect as anything he had ever before witnessed. He purposely put his back to the spinning pair, refusing to be distracted, and he charged into the nearest orcs, who suddenly and quite understandably seemed more intent upon running away

He caught a few and slew them, and many more went howling in flight across the trails. The threat gone, and the battle won. He turned to face his unknown allies, offering a salute to them with one scimitar.

The male of the group, breathing heavily but wearing an easy smile, similarly saluted with his bloody sword.

And he nearly knocked the drow over with a simple statement, "Well met again, Drizzt Do'Urden."

BEYOND THE
BOUNDS OF TIME

"I have heard of your citadel," Nanfoodle said to Nikwillig.

The gnome was wandering the grounds outside of Mithral Hall's western gate when he came upon his fellow visitor to the Battlehammer stronghold sitting on a flat stone in Keeper's Dale. They could hear the fighting up above them in the north.

"Me kinsman Tred's up there now," Nikwillig remarked.

"You fear for him," reasoned the gnome.

"For Tred?" came the laughing response. "Nah, never that. Nikwillig's the name here, little one, and who might yerself be?"

"Nanfoodle Buswilligan at your service, good dwarf," the gnome answered with a polite bow. "A visitor to Mithral Hall, as are you."

"Ye come from Silverymoon?"

"Mirabar," Nanfoodle answered. "I serve as Marchion Elastul's Principal Alchemist."

"Alchemist?" Nikwillig echoed, and his tone clearly showed that he didn't hold much faith in that particular art. "Well, what's an alchemist doing out on the wider roads?"

That question set off warning bells in Nanfoodle's head and reminded him that perhaps he should not be so forthcoming, given his true mission. Certainly Torgar and the others from Mirabar knew the truth of his position in that city, but why make the information so readily available?

"Better that yer marchion sent a war advisor, I'm thinking," the dwarf added.

"Ah, but we did not know that Mithral Hall was at war," Nanfoodle answered, and coincidentally, at that moment, horns blew up above, followed by the rousing cheers of another dwarf charge. "I came with the sceptrana, following the exodus of many of Mirabar's dwarves."

"I heard about that," Nikwillig replied. He turned to the cliff behind him and nodded. "Torgar and his boys're up there now, from what I'm hearing."

"Doing Mirabar proud, though they are not of Mirabar any longer."

"Ye come to coax them back, did ye?"

Nanfoodle shook his head.

"To check on them," said the gnome. "Too see that their journey went well and that their reception here was appropriate. There are bridges to be rebuilt—animosity serves neither Mirabar nor Mithral Hall."

How Nanfoodle wished that he could believe in those words as he spoke them!

"Ah," Nikwillig mumbled. "Well, no worry then. No better hosts in all the world than King Bruenor and his kin, unless of course one goes to Citadel Felbarr and the court of King Emerus Warcrown."

"They have treated you and your friend well?"

"How do ye think King Bruenor got himself knocked silly?" Nikwillig said. "He was hunting the band of orcs and giants that hit me and Tred. We paid them back, too, we did, though in the end too many of the stinking orcs came onto the field. Aye . . . no better friend than Bruenor Battlehammer."

"How will your king react to this attack?" Nanfoodle asked, genuinely curious.

The gnome had always recognized the bond between dwarves—and had been among the loudest voices warning Marchion Elastul and his advisors that he might be erring greatly in his treatment of Torgar Hammerstriker. It touched Nanfoodle to hear this dwarf of Citadel Felbarr, the closest dwarven stronghold to Mithral Hall and certainly a trading rival, speaking so highly of Bruenor and his kin.

The gnome glanced up the tall cliff, thinking that Tred was up there battling, risking his life for a kingdom that was not his own. And that Torgar was up there, and Shingles McRuff as well, no doubt fighting with all the fury they would muster in defending Mirabar herself.

Nanfoodle began to ask another question, but the dwarf perked up suddenly and looked past him. Nikwillig hopped down and pushed past the gnome to intercept a dwarf wearing long robes.

"What of King Bruenor then?" Nikwillig asked. "Ye been with him?"

The dwarf, young in appearance but looking quite weary and worn, straightened his shoulders and his robes and tucked his brown beard into the belt sash.

"Hello once again, Nikwillig of Citadel Felbarr," he said.

"This is me new friend, Nanfoodle," Nikwillig introduced, pulling the gnome forward.

"Of Mirabar, yes," the dwarf replied, and he gave Nanfoodle's small hand a solid grasp and shake. "Cordio Muffinhead at yer service."

"Priest of Moradin," the gnome observed, and Cordio bowed deeply.

"And yes, I've just come from the side of King Bruenor, where yet again today, meself and several others have exhausted our magical energies on his behalf."

"To gain?" Nikwillig asked.

"So we were thinking," the despondent cleric replied. "King Bruenor uttered some words earlier, and we thought he'd found his way back to us. But he was calling to his father and his father's father, warning them of the shadow."

"The shadow?" Nanfoodle asked.

"The shadow dragon, perhaps," Cordio added.

"King Bruenor was seeing in the past," Nikwillig explained. "Far in the past, before Clan Battlehammer got chased away from Mithral Hall, to wander and settle in Icewind Dale."

"Where I was born," Cordio said. "I never knew Mithral Hall until King Bruenor took it back. What a fight that was, I tell ye! I was there all the way, fighting right beside Dagnabbit, finest young warrior in all the clan."

"Dagnabbit fell at Shallows," Nikwillig explained to Nanfoodle, and the gnome offered a deferential nod at Cordio.

"Lost me a good friend that dark day," Cordio admitted. "But he died fighting orcs—no dwarf could ever be wanting a better way to go."

Cordio turned around and stepped away from the flat stone. Many other dwarves were in the area, ferrying supplies—both up the rope ladders to Banak Brawnanvil and his boys and out to the west where a force was digging in for the defense of Keeper's Dale. Other dwarves coming back from the wall in the north ferried the wounded and dead.

"Been a long and bloody history in these lands," Cordio remarked. "Lots o' dead dwarves."

"More dead orcs," Nanfoodle reminded. "And more dead goblins."

That brought a grin to the weary cleric, and Nikwillig clapped Cordio warmly on the shoulder.

"The most dwarves o' Mithral Hall that ever died in one place at one time, died right about where ye're sitting," Cordio explained to Nanfoodle.

"In the fight with the drow?" Nikwillig asked.

"Nah," answered the cleric. "Long before that. Way back afore me father's father's father's time. Way back when Gandalug was just a boy."

That news brought wide eyes from both of Cordio's listeners. Gandalug Battlehammer had become quite a legend in Mirabar and Citadel Felbarr, and everywhere else in the North. He had been the proud and revered King of Mithral Hall centuries before, but he had been magically imprisoned and wound up in the clutches of Matron Mother Baenre of Menzoberranzan. When the drow had come against Mithral Hall a decade before, Bruenor had slain Baenre and had freed Gandalug. And Bruenor had returned to Icewind Dale, which had been his home for centuries, giving Mithral Hall back to his returned ancestor.

"Gandalug told me so much of them old days," Cordio Muffinhead went on, and his gray eyes seemed to look off in the distance, across space and time. "He oft walked with me out here in Keeper's Dale. The dale wasn't a valley in his childhood, but this whole place . . ." He paused and swept his short arms out to encompass the whole of the rocky dale. "This whole place was the grand entryway of Mithral Hall, and what a foyer it was! With great towers. . . ." He laughed and pointed to some of the closer obelisks that so dotted the floor of Keeper's Dale. "Every one o' them was covered in carvings, ye know. Grand carvings. Battles of old, even the finding of Mithral Hall. Ye can't see 'em now—wind's taken them and scattered them to the bounds o' time.

"Like the dead, ye know? Scattered and gone when we're not remembering them anymore." Cordio gave a helpless little chuckle and added, "I'm not thinking to let Gandalug or Dagnabbit go that way for a bit!"

Nanfoodle sat quietly, staring at that most unusual dwarf and at the effect his words were obviously having on Nikwillig. Their bond struck the gnome profoundly. As thick as a dwarven handshake, it seemed, or as a mug of the mead the dwarves passed off as holy water.

Nikwillig inquired as to what could have so caused the complete destruction of an area as large as Keeper's Dale, and in looking around, what most struck Nanfoodle was the lack of rubble and broken stones.

"Flight o' dragons?" Nikwillig asked, and Nanfoodle answered "No" even before Cordio could.

Both dwarves looked at the gnome.

"Ye've heard the story?" Cordio asked.

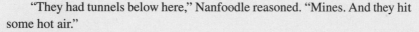

"They had tunnels below here," Nanfoodle reasoned. "Mines. And they hit some hot air."

He didn't have to explain to either of the dwarves, who had spent years and years working in tunnels, about the dangers and potential catastrophe of "hot air," or natural gas deposits. Any dwarf would babble on for hours about the dangers of their tunnels or the deeper Underdark, of goblins and displacer beasts, of drow and shadow dragons. Few spoke openly about hot air, though, for it was a killer they could not smash with a hammer or chop with an axe.

Nanfoodle could only imagine the height of catastrophe that had shaped Keeper's Dale. It must have been quite a flow of hot air to get up there so completely and in so short a span of time as to go undetected until it was too late. The gnome could imagine those last frantic moments—perhaps the dwarves had at last detected the invisible killer. And the explosion, a clean puff of fiery orange and the grating of stone being torn apart. The area all around Keeper's Dale was littered with boulders. Nanfoodle had a better idea of what had put them there.

"No mines below Keeper's Dale now," Cordio Muffinhead remarked. "We shut them down centuries ago. Sealed them good!"

Nanfoodle nodded his agreement. Before going out there, he had wandered around the great Undercity of Mithral Hall, with the lines of forges and the many entryways for carts filled with ore coming in from all the working mines. There were many maps down there, old and new, and in recalling some of them, it seemed to Nanfoodle indeed that the western gate to Mithral Hall was the westernmost point below, as well as above.

Their thoughts were interrupted then by renewed shouts and sounds of battle from up on the cliff to the north. Cordio Muffinhead glanced that way and gave a great sigh.

"I must go and take my rest," he remarked. "My powers will be needed all too soon, I fear."

"Damn orcs," muttered Nikwillig.

Nanfoodle eyed the Felbarr dwarf for a long while, then meandered back to the gate and into Mithral Hall. He headed for the Undercity and the maps, wanting to view them again in light of Cordio's tale.

Regis was surprised to see Torgar Hammerstriker awaiting an audience later that day.

"Well met, Steward," the dwarf from Mirabar greeted with a low bow.

"The battle goes well?"

Torgar gave a shrug and replied, "Orcs ain't really throwing much our way. They're more thinking to knock down our defenses and stop us from digging in too deep, is me own guess."

"While they bring up allies," Regis reasoned and Torgar nodded.

"Group o' giants been seen moving this way."

"I'm surprised that you've come down then."

"Just for a bit," said Torgar. "Just to see yerself in private. I'm moving me Mirabar dwarfs off to Banak's left flank when darkness falls. We're to hold the tunnels beneath the mountain spur."

"We've protected the backside, the western end of Keeper's Dale, as much as we can," Regis explained. "Every dwarf but the necessary workers in Mithral Hall are out on the fronts now, but I couldn't send too many out. We have reports of trouble in Nesmé, not too far to the southwest, and there are tunnels connecting to our mines from there."

"Protect the hall at all costs," Torgar agreed. "Them who're outside will run back in, if they're needing to."

Regis replied with a warm smile, for he was truly glad to hear even more approval of his decisions. This mantle of steward weighed heavily upon him, even though he realized that the true leaders of Mithral Hall in Bruenor's absence, the toughened Battlehammer dwarves, wouldn't let him do anything they didn't agree with.

"And I come down here to talk to yerself about protecting yer hall," Torgar went on. "Ye've got more visitors from Mirabar, so's been told to me."

"The sceptrana herself, and a gnome companion," Regis confirmed.

"Good enough folk, mostly," said Torgar. "But keep yer head that Mirabar's in desperate straits now that me and so many o' me kin've walked away. Nanfoodle's a clever one, and Shoudra's got some powerful magic at her disposal."

"You believe they were sent here to do more than check up on your welcome?"

"I'm not for knowing," Torgar admitted. "But when I heard from Catti-brie that they'd come in, first thing I thinked was that them two are worth watchin'."

"From afar," Regis agreed, and Torgar nodded again.

"Whatever ye're thinking is best, Steward Regis," he said, and the halfling could hardly hold back from wincing at the open recitation of his title. "I just figured it'd be best for me to come to yerself direct and let ye know me feelings."

"And it is appreciated, Torgar," Regis quickly replied. "More than you can understand. You and your boys from Mirabar have already proven yourselves as friends of the hall, and I expect that Bruenor will have more than a little to say to you all when he awakens. He does like to personally greet the newest members of his clan, after all."

Regis knew that he had worded that perfectly when he saw the smile beam out from Torgar's hairy face. The dwarf nodded and bowed, then moved off, leaving Regis with his warning.

What to do about Shoudra and Nanfoodle? the halfling wondered. Regis had been taken by their warmth and openness in his meeting with them, and certainly, they seemed to be reasonable enough folks. But the Steward of Mithral Hall could not ignore the possibility of mischief, not when such mischief could prove absolutely disastrous for Clan Battlehammer.

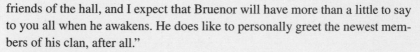

"You understand that you did not come down here alone," Shoudra Stargleam remarked to Nanfoodle when she caught up to the gnome along the floor of the Undercity.

Hammers rang out all around them and smoke filled the uncomfortably warm air, for every furnace was fully stoked, every anvil engaged. To the side, great whetstones spun unceasingly, weapon after weapon running across them, honing the fine edges so that they could be delivered back to the forces engaged with the orcs.

"They are unobtrusive enough," the gnome replied, referring to the dwarf pair who had quietly shadowed his every movement through the tunnels. Nanfoodle wiped the sweat from his face, then pulled off his red robe and began to cross it over his forearm. Noting the soot that had already settled upon the fine garment, the gnome crinkled his long nose, brushed the robe, then reversed it back to its weathered brown. "Could we expect anything else?"

"Of course not," Shoudra agreed. "And I do not complain of our treatment here, certainly. Steward Regis is a fine host. But if we are to carry out our designs, we might need a bit of deceptive magic. Easily enough accomplished."

The sceptrana narrowed her gaze as she scrutinized Nanfoodle's sour expression.

With a shrug, the gnome continued on his way, Shoudra falling into step beside him.

"Why here?" she asked. "Would we not have a better opportunity in the lower transfer rooms, where the separated ore awaits delivery?"

Still the sour expression, and Nanfoodle noticeably increased his pace.

"Or have you perhaps forgotten why we ventured here to Mithral Hall?" Shoudra asked bluntly.

"I have forgotten nothing," Nanfoodle snapped back.

"Second thoughts, then?"

"Have you noted the treatment Mithral Hall has afforded Torgar and the others?"

"Regis needs the warriors," Shoudra replied. "Torgar was a convenient addition."

Nanfoodle stopped and stared hard at her.

The sceptrana smiled helplessly back. Of course the gnome was right, she knew. Torgar and the other dwarves of Mirabar were helping the cause, and in a vital role, and it was just that vital role that proved Nanfoodle's point. Bruenor's clan had taken the Mirabarran dwarves at their word and on their honor, without question. Especially in such dangerous times, that was no small thing.

"You have made a friend in the other visitor to Mithral Hall, I have heard," she remarked as Nanfoodle started on his way once more.

"Nikwillig of Citadel Felbarr—a place that is as much a rival to Mithral Hall as is Mirabar, surely," the gnome explained. "Have you heard his tale?"

"You will tell me that Bruenor fell avenging him," Shoudra predicted, for she had indeed.

They came up to a large wood and stone table then, its front side holding a rack of pigeon holes and each with a rolled parchment inside. Nanfoodle bent low, reading the descriptions, then he pulled forth a map and unrolled it on the sloping tabletop. A quick perusal brought a frustrated sigh, and the gnome bent low again, seeking a second map.

"None are better at shaping an axe blade, but one would think that these dwarves would know how to label a simple map!" he complained.

Shoudra put her hand on his shoulder, drawing his attention.

"We are being observed, you understand," she said.

"Of course."

"Then what are you doing?"

Nanfoodle drew out the second map and stood straight, spreading it over the first one before him.

"Trying to determine how I might aid in the cause of Clan Battlehammer," the gnome said matter-of-factly.

Shoudra's hand slapped down on the center of the map.

"Bruenor fought for the dwarves of Felbarr," the gnome responded.

"Bruenor himself! Fighting for a rival. Would Marchion Elastul think of such a thing?"

"Is it our place to judge?"

"Is it not?"

Shoudra glared at her diminutive companion—or tried to, for in truth, she had a hard task in defending their mission. They had come to use Nanfoodle's alchemical potions to secretly ruin a great deal of Mithral Hall's ore, that Clan Battlehammer would produce a batch of inferior works—perhaps enough to weaken Mithral Hall's reputation with the merchants of the North, thus affording Mirabar an upper hand in the trade war.

"How petty are we two, Shoudra?" Nanfoodle quietly asked. "The marchion pays me well, 'tis true, but how am I to ignore that which I see about me? These dwarves follow a course of justice, first and foremost. They welcomed Torgar and the wayward pair from Felbarr with open hearts."

"Dwarf to dwarf," came the skeptical reply.

"And dwarf to gnome, and dwarf to sceptrana," Nanfoodle countered. "Consider our welcome here compared to that which Elastul afforded King Bruenor."

"You are beginning to sound a bit too much like Torgar Hammerstriker," the tall and beautiful woman remarked.

"You did not disagree with Torgar."

"Not with his greeting of King Bruenor, no," Shoudra admitted. "But with his abandonment of Mirabar? I do indeed disagree, Nanfoodle. I am glad of our reception, do not doubt, and I harbor no ill will toward Bruenor and his clan, but I am first and foremost the Sceptrana of Mirabar, and there remains my first loyalty."

"Do not ask me to poison their metal," Nanfoodle pleaded. "Not now . . . I beg you."

Shoudra stared at him for a few moments, then backed away, removing her hand from the map.

"No, of course not," she agreed, and Nanfoodle gave a great sigh of relief. "Our actions would do more than wound them in trade, but would likely cost the lives of many now engaged with the foul orcs. Clearly Elastul would agree with our decision to abort the mission . . . for now."

Nanfoodle nodded and smiled, but his expression told Shoudra clearly that he, like her, did not believe that last statement in the least. Shoudra knew—and it truly pained her to know—that Marchion Elastul would insist on attacking the ore even more aggressively if he thought it might bring even greater catastrophe upon Mithral Hall.

"So tell me what you are looking for, and what you plan to do?" she asked the gnome, and she peered at the map over his shoulder, recognizing it at once as the westernmost reaches of Mithral Hall, the gate at Keeper's Dale and the tunnels below.

"I do not yet know," Nanfoodle admitted. "But I will see what I can see and try to find a way to use my expertise to the benefit of the cause."

"Seeking a better offer from King Bruenor?" Shoudra asked with a wry grin.

Nanfoodle started to protest, until he noted her expression.

"I have been here but a couple of days and already I feel as if Mithral Hall is more my home than Mirabar ever was," he admitted.

Shoudra didn't argue the point. She wasn't quite as enamored of the place, for the whole of it was below ground, but she certainly understood the gnome's feelings.

"You should study beside me," Nanfoodle said, turning his attention back to the map. "Your skills with magic could prove of great value to Clan Battlehammer in this dark time."

Again, despite herself, Shoudra didn't argue the point.

Exhausted and with several new wounds to attend, Catti-brie was barely back into Mithral Hall that night when she heard the commotion of the clerics rushing to her father's side. The woman dropped her cloak, her bow, and even her sword belt right there in the hallway and sprinted off to the room, to find her father's bed surrounded by a handful of priests and Pikel Bouldershoulder. All of them were chanting, praying, and one by one they placed their hands gently on Bruenor's chest and released their healing magic.

Halfway through the process, Bruenor actually moved a bit and even coughed, but then he settled quickly back into his completely sedentary state.

Cordio Muffinhead and Stumpet Rakingclaw, the two highest ranking clerics, took a moment to examine Bruenor, then looked around and nodded with satisfaction. They had staved off another potential disaster, had once again brought Bruenor back from the very brink of death.

Catti-brie spent more time looking at the priests then, than at her resting father. Several leaned on the edge of Bruenor's bed, obviously spent, and though they had performed another apparent miracle, not a one of them seemed overly pleased—not even the perpetually happy Pikel.

They began to filter out then, moving past Cathi-brie, most of them patting her on the shoulder as they passed.

"Every day we come to him. . . ." Cordio Muffinhead remarked when he and Catti-brie were alone in the room.

Catti-brie moved to her father's side and knelt by the bed. She took his hand in her own and squeezed it to her breast. How cool he felt, as if the energy of his life had diminished to almost nothingness. She gave a cursory glance around the room, to the many candles and the warm furnishings, trying to remind herself that this was a very different place than the cramped, dark, and wet tunnels beneath the ruins of Withegroo's crumbled tower in Shallows. Surely it was more comfortably furnished and ventilated, and gently lit, but to Catti-brie, it didn't seem all that different. The focus of the young woman could not be the furnishings, nor the light, but on, always on, the central figure that lay so very still in the middle of the room.

In looking at him at that moment, Catti-brie was reminded of another friend lying close to death. Back in the west, along the Sword Coast, she and the others had found Drizzt in such a state, lying mortally wounded on one side of the room with Le'lorinel—Ellifain—that most tragic of elves, similarly slashed on the other. Drizzt had begged her to save Ellifain instead of him, to use the one magical potion available to them to heal the elf's wounds and not his own.

Bruenor had been the one to dismiss that thought out of hand, and so Drizzt had survived. Still, Catti-brie and the others had been given a difficult choice at that moment, and they had acted for their own personal needs and for the greater good—fortunately, the two had seemed congruous.

But what about now? Were their personal, perhaps even selfish, desires making them all follow a course that was not for the greater good?

The heroics of the clerics were keeping Bruenor alive—if what he was now could even be considered alive. Every day, often more than once, they had to rush in and put forth their greatest healing efforts just to bring him back to that comatose state of near-death.

"Should we just let ye go?" the woman asked Bruenor quietly.

"What was that ye say?" asked Cordio, hustling over beside her.

Catti-brie looked up at the dwarf, studied his concerned expression, and smiled and said, "Not a thing, Cordio. Was just calling to my father."

She looked back at Bruenor's grayish face and added, "But he's not hearing me."

"He knows ye're here," the dwarf whispered, and he put his hands on the back of the woman's shoulders, offering her his strength.

"Does he? I'm not thinking it so," Catti-brie replied. "Might that that's the problem. Have ye lost all of your heart and hope?" she asked Bruenor. "Are you thinking me dead, and Wulfgar and Regis and Drizzt all dead? The orcs won at Shallows, from what you know, didn't they?"

She stared at Bruenor a moment longer, then looked up at Cordio, and his expression was all the agreement she needed.

"Is he all right?" came a call from the door, and the two looked to see Regis come running into the room, Wulfgar close behind.

Cordio assured them that Bruenor was fine, then took his leave, but not before bowing low to Catti-brie's side and offering her a kiss on the cheek.

"Keep talking to him, then," the dwarf whispered.

Catti-brie squeezed Bruenor's hand all the tighter and focused all of her senses on that hand, seeking some return grasp, some tiny hint that Bruenor felt her presence.

Nothing. Just the cool, seemingly inanimate skin.

The woman took a deep breath, gave another squeeze, then forced herself back to her feet and turned around to regard her friends.

"We've got some choices we're needing to make," she said, holding her voice steady with great determination.

Wulfgar looked at her curiously, but Regis, more familiar with all that was going on within the hall, offered a loud sigh.

"The priests grow more and more frustrated," he said.

"And they're needed elsewhere, as much as here," Catti-brie made herself admit, though every word stung her profoundly. She looked back at poor Bruenor, his breath coming so shallow that she couldn't even see the rise and fall of his chest. "We have wounded with injuries that can be tended."

"Do you believe they will leave their king?' Wulfgar asked, with a hint of anger edging his tone. "Bruenor *is* Mithral Hall. He brought his clan back here and brought them back to prominence. They owe him all of their efforts and more."

"And do you think Bruenor would want that?" Regis asked before Catti-brie could reply. "If he knew that others were suffering, perhaps even dying, because so many priests were stuck here time after time, holding him alive when he had so little life left in him, he would not be pleased."

"How can you speak such words?" Wulfgar shouted back. "After all that Bruenor has—"

"None of us love him less than yourself," Catti-brie interrupted. She moved right up to Wulfgar and pushed his pointing, accusing fingers aside, battling with him for a moment before wrapping her arms around him and pulling him close. "Not me, and not Rumblebelly."

She finished by hugging Wulfgar even tighter, and he didn't resist.

"None of us can serve in his stead," Regis remarked. "I am Steward of Mithral Hall, but that is only because I speak for Bruenor. I cannot speak without Bruenor—not to Clan Battlehammer."

"Nor can I, and not Wulfgar nor Drizzt," Catti-brie agreed, finally letting go and stepping back from the overwhelmed barbarian. "Only a dwarf can serve as King of Mithral Hall, but I'm thinking that we three, as Bruenor's family and friends, will have a large say in who succeeds him. We owe it to Bruenor to choose well."

"It would have been Dagnabbit, I think," said Regis.

"His father, then?" Catti-brie asked, and though she had incited it, she could hardly believe that they were discussing such grim business.

Regis shook his head and replied, "Dagna wouldn't take it . . . as he refused the stewardship. We should speak with him, of course, but he's shown little interest."

"Then who?" asked Wulfgar.

"Cordio Muffinhead has been an amazing leader among the dwarves in the hall," Regis remarked. "He has organized the defense of the lower tunnels brilliantly, as well as putting all of the priests into balanced shifts to handle the wounded and Bruenor."

"But Cordio's not a Battlehammer," Catti-brie reminded them. "And never has a priest led Mithral Hall."

"The Brawnanvil's are the closest cousins of Bruenor," said Wulfgar. "And surely none has distinguished himself any greater than Banak in the fighting outside the hall."

The other two thought on that for a moment, then each nodded their agreement.

"Banak, then," said Regis. "If he survives the war with the orcs."

"And if . . ." Catti-brie started to add, but the words caught in her throat, and she turned back to regard Bruenor.

They would recommend Banak as the new King of Mithral Hall, but only, of course, after her father, the dear old dwarf who had taken her in as an orphaned child and raised her with dignity and hope, had passed on from the world of flesh and blood.

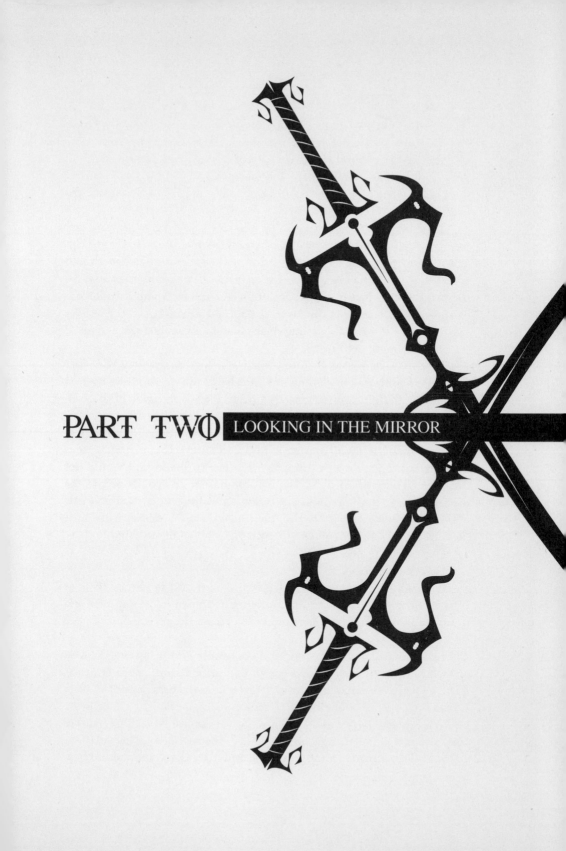

PART TWO LOOKING IN THE MIRROR

I erred, as I knew I would. Rationally, in those moments when I have been able to slip away from my anger, I have known for some time that my actions have bordered on recklessness, and that I would find my end out here on the mountain slopes.

Is that what I have desired all along, since the fall of Shallows? Do I seek the end of pain at the end of a spear?

There is so much more to this orc assault than we believed when first we encountered the two wayward and wounded dwarves from Citadel Felbarr. The orcs have found organization and cooperation, at least to an extent that they save their sharpened swords for a common enemy. All the North is threatened, surely, especially Mithral Hall, and I would not be surprised to learn that the dwarves have already buttoned themselves up inside their dark halls, sealing their great doors against the assault of the overwhelming orc hordes.

Perhaps it is that realization, that these hordes threaten the place that for so long was my home, that so drives me on to strike against the raiders. Perhaps my actions are bringing some measure of discomfort to the invaders, and some level of assistance to the dwarves.

Or is that line of thinking merely justification? Can I admit that possibility to myself at least? Because in my heart I know that even if the orcs had retreated back to their holes after the fall of Shallows, I would not have turned back for Mithral Hall. I would have followed the orcs to the darkest places, scimitars high and ready, Guenhwyvar crouched beside me. I would have struck hard at them, as I do now, taking what little pleasure seems left in my life in the warmth of spilling orc blood.

How I hate them.

Or is it even them?

It is all too confusing to me. I strike hard and in my mind I see Bruenor atop the burning tower, tumbling to his death. I strike hard and in my mind I see Ellifain falling wounded across the room, slumping to her death.

I strike hard, and if I am lucky, I see nothing—nothing but the blur of the moment. As my instincts engulf my rational mind, I am at peace.

And yet, as those immediate needs retreat, as the orcs flee or fall dead, I often find unintended and unwelcome consequences.

What pain I have caused Guenhwyvar these last days! The panther comes to my call unerringly and fights as I instruct and as her instincts guide. I ask her to go against great foes, and there is no complaint. I hear her wounded cry as she writhes in the grip of a giant, but there is no accusation toward me buried within that wail. And when I call upon her again, after her rest in the Astral Plane, she is there, by my side, not judging, uncomplaining.

It is as it was in the Underdark those days after I walked out of Menzoberranzan. She is my only contact to the humanity within me, the only window on my heart and soul. I know that I should be rid of her now, that I should hand her over to one more worthy, for I have no hope that I will survive this ordeal. How great it wounds me to think of the figurine that summons Guenhwyvar, the link to the astral spirit of the panther, in the clutches of an orc.

And yet, I find that I cannot make that trip to Mithral Hall to turn over the panther to the dwarves. I cannot walk this road without her, and it is a road I am unable to turn from.

I am weak, perhaps, or I am a fool. Whichever the case, I am not yet ready to stop this war I wage; I am not yet ready to abandon the warmth of spilled orc blood. These beasts have brought this pain upon me, and I will repay them a thousand thousand times over, until my scimitars slip from my weakened grasp and I fall dying to the stone.

I can only hope that Guenhwyvar has gone beyond the compulsion of the magic figurine, that she has found some free will against its pressure. I believe that she has, and that if an orc pries the figurine from my dead body and somehow discovers how to use it, he will bring to his side the instrument of his death.

That is my hope at least.

Perhaps it is another lie, another justification.

Perhaps I am lost in a web of such soft lies too deep to sift through.

I know only the pain of memory and the pleasure of the hunt. I will take that pleasure, to the end.

—Drizzt Do'Urden

POSTURING

Drizzt stared hard at the elf who had just spoken his name. A flicker of recognition teased the drow, but it was nothing tangible, nothing he could hold onto.

"We have some salves that might help with your wound," the elf offered.

He took a step forward—and Drizzt backed away an equal step.

The elf stopped his approach and held up his hands.

"It has been many years," said the elf. "I am pleased to see that you are well."

Drizzt couldn't completely suppress his wince at the irony of that statement, for he felt anything but "well." The reference that he had met the elf before had his thoughts shifting away from that, however, as he tried hard to place the speaker. He had known few surface elves in his years out of the Underdark. Not many were in Ten-Towns, though Drizzt hadn't been close to many of the folk of the towns, anyway, preferring to spend his hours with the dwarves or out on the open tundra.

As soon as he thought of Ellifain, though, that poor troubled elf who had pursued him to the end of the world, and to the end of her life, Drizzt made the connection.

"You are of the Moonwood," he said.

The elf glanced at his female companion, bowed, and said "Tarathiel, at your service."

It all came flooding back to Drizzt then. Years before, on his journey back to the Underdark, he had traveled through the Moonwood and had met up with the clan of Ellifain. This elf, Tarathiel, had led him away, had even allowed him to ride on of the elf clan's fine horses for a bit. Their meeting had been brief and to the point, but they had left with mutual respect and a bit of trust.

"Forgive my poor memory," Drizzt replied.

He wanted to express his gratitude for Tarathiel's former generosity and to thank the pair for coming to his aid in the recent fight, but he stopped. Drizzt found that he simply did not want to begin that conversation. Did the pair know of Ellifain's pursuit of him and attack upon him? Could he tell them about Ellifain's fate, slain at the end of the very scimitars Drizzt even then held at his sides?

"Well met again, Tarathiel," Drizzt said, somewhat curtly.

"And Innovindil," Tarathiel remarked, motioning to his beautiful and deadly partner.

Drizzt offered her a somewhat stiff bow.

"The orcs are fast returning," Innovindil remarked, for she alone had been looking around during the brief exchange. "Let us go somewhere that we might better speak of the past, and of the present danger that engulfs this region."

The two started off and motioned for Drizzt to hurry to keep up, but the drow did not.

"We cannot give our enemies a single target of pursuit," Drizzt said. "Perhaps our paths will meet again."

He gave another bow, slid his scimitars away, and rushed off in the opposite direction.

Tarathiel started after Drizzt and started to call out, but Innovindil caught him by the arm.

"Let him go," Innovindil whispered. "He is not ready to speak with us."

"I would know about Ellifain," Tarathiel protested.

"He knows of us now," Innovindil explained. "He will seek us out when he is ready."

"He should be warned of Ellifain at least."

Innovindil shrugged as if it didn't matter.

"Is she anywhere about?" she asked. "And if so, will her pursuit of Drizzt Do'Urden overrule all sensibility? The land is thick with more immediate enemies."

Tarathiel continued to look after the departing drow and still leaned that way, but he didn't pull away from Innovindil's insistent hold.

"He will seek us out, and soon enough," Innovindil promised.

"You sound as if you know him," Tarathiel remarked.

He turned to regard his companion, to find that she, too, was staring off in the direction of the departing drow.

Innovindil slowly nodded.

"Perhaps," she replied.

Urlgen Threefist watched the latest wave of his shock troops, goblins mostly, charging up the sloping stone ground, throwing themselves with abandon at the dwarven defenses. The orc leader ignored the sudden shift from battle cry to wail of agony, focusing his attention on the defenders of the high ground.

The dwarves moved with great precision, but their lines wove a bit more slowly now, the orc leader believed, as if their legs were growing weary. Urlgen's lip curled back from his tusked mouth in a wicked smile. They should be tired, he knew, for he would allow them no rest. By day, he hit them with his orc forces and by night, his goblin shock troops. Even in those hours of retreat and regroup, the dwarves could not rest, for their defenses were not fully in place.

Flashes to the right side of the dwarven line, ahead to Urlgen's left, drew the tall orc's attention. Once again the dwarves had anchored their line with a marvelous pair of warriors, a huge human, strong as a giant, and an archer woman whose magical bow had devastated the extreme of Urlgen's left flank on every attack. They were two of Shallows's survivors, Urlgen knew, for he remembered well those silvery lines of death—the shining magical arrows—and the barbarian who had inspired terror among his ranks back at the doomed town. The great warrior had held the center of Shallows's wall single-handedly, scattering the attackers with impunity. His fists struck as hard as iron weapons, and that hammer of his had swept orcs from the wall two or three at a time.

Urlgen noted that fewer of the goblins seemed anxious to come in from that angle. His force was more constricted toward the center and right.

But still that magical bow fired off shot after shot, and Urlgen had no doubt that the barbarian warrior would find enemies to slaughter.

Soon enough, the assault stalled, and the disorganized and overwhelmed goblins came running back down the stony slope. Perhaps as a sign of their growing exhaustion, the dwarves did not pursue nearly as far as on the previous attacks, and Urlgen took faith that he was wearing them down.

That notion had the tall orc looking back over his shoulder, back to the wide lands north of his position. Reports had come in of the great gathering of orc tribes. His father's ranks were swelling. But where were they?

Urlgen was torn about the implications of that question. On the one hand, he understood that he simply didn't have the numbers at his disposal to dislodge the dwarves, and so he wanted those hordes to come forth and help him to push the ugly creatures right off the cliff face and back into their filthy hole at Mithral Hall. But on the other hand, Urlgen wasn't overly thrilled at the prospect of being rescued by his arrogant father, and even less by the thought of Gerti Orelsdottr coming in with the large remaining force of her giants and devastating the dwarves before him.

Perhaps it would be better if things continued as they were, for more warriors were filtering into Urlgen's force every day. Despite the hundreds of orcs and goblins dead on the mountain slope, Urlgen's army was actually larger than when he had first cornered the dwarves.

He couldn't risk a straight-out charge to push the dwarves off.

But attrition was on his side.

<hr />

She started to draw her bow, but the creature was too close. Always ready to improvise, Catti-brie just flipped the weapon in her hand, bringing it up high before her where she caught it by the end in both hands and swept it out, swatting the pesky goblin across the face.

The goblin stumbled backward but was hardly felled by the blow. At last seeing an apparent opening in the defenses of that terrible pair, it and its companions howled and charged the woman.

But Catti-brie had dropped her bow and drawn out Khazid'hea, and the sentient, fine-edged blade felt eager in her hands. She met the goblin charge with one of her own, slashing across, then stabbing ahead, once and again. Khazid'hea, nicknamed Cutter, lived up to its reputation, slicing through anything the goblins put in it way: spears, a feeble wooden shield, and more than one arm.

The goblin press continued forward, more out of momentum than any eagerness to engage the warrior, but Catti-brie did not back down. A backhand severed a spear tip before the thrusting weapon got close; a turn down had the overbalancing creature throwing its feet out behind it, but a sudden reverse brought Khazid'hea straight up, slicing the goblin's face in half.

Well done! the sword telepathically communicated.

"Glad to be of such service," Catti-brie muttered.

She forced the sword across, then slid out to the side, sensing a presence coming fast for her back.

With perfect timing, Wulfgar rushed past her and headlong into the front of the charging goblin group. Hardly slowing, he ran over the first two in line, kicking them aside as he passed, and swept another couple from out before him with mighty Aegis-fang. It was his turn to pause, and he did so, bringing his hammer around and up high so that Catti-brie could charge past under his upraised arms, Cutter stabbing repeatedly.

Within a matter of a few moments, the goblins understood their doom, and those closest to the powerful pair fell all over each other and trampled down those behind them in their frenzy to get away.

All the goblins were running then, from one end to the other along the dwarven line. Wulfgar gave pursuit, catching one by the back of the neck in one hand. With a growl, the barbarian put the creature up high, and when it tried to resist, when it tried to swing its club out behind at the man, Wulfgar gave it such a vicious shake that its lips flapped loudly and its body jerked wildly, so much so that its club went flying away. Then the goblin followed, as Wulfgar threw it high and far, and over the lip of the small ravine that marked the end of the dwarven line.

The barbarian turned around to see Catti-brie leveling Taulmaril, and he walked back to join the woman as she put a few shots out among the retreating goblins.

"My damned sword's complaining," Catti-brie said to him. "Wants to be out, fighting and killing enemies." She gave a chortle. "Killing enemies and friends alike, for all Cutter's caring!"

"I fear that it will get all that it desires and more," Wulfgar replied.

"The wretches don't even care that we're slaughtering them," said Catti-brie. "They're coming up here for no better reason than to keep us tired, and we're killing them one atop the next."

"And in the end, they will have this ridge," Wulfgar remarked.

He put his arm on Catti-brie's shoulder as he glanced back, drawing the woman's gaze with his own.

The dwarves were already clearing their wounded, loading them onto stretchers lashed to the rope ladders and sending them down the cliff face using blocks-and-tackle. Only the most grievously wounded of the dwarves were going, of course, since the tough warriors weren't easily to be taken out of battle, but still, more than a few went over the cliff, sliding down to waiting hands in Keeper's Dale.

Other dwarves who were leaving the battlefield had been lined up off to the side, and there was no hurry to evacuate that group, for they were beyond the help of any priests.

"With the enchanted quiver, I can keep shooting Heartseeker day and night," Catti-brie observed. "I'll not run short of arrows. Not like Banak's charges, though, for his line's to thin and thin. We'll be getting no help from below, for they're working hard to secure the lower halls and tunnels, the eastern gate, and Keeper's Dale."

"He would do well to have a quiver like yours," Wulfgar agreed, "only one that produces dwarf warriors instead of magical arrows."

Catti-brie barely managed a smile at the quip, and in looking at Wulfgar, she knew that he hadn't meant the statement humorously, anyway.

Already the stubborn dwarves were back to their other work, building the defensive positions and walls, but it seemed to Catti-brie that the hammers swung a bit more slowly.

The orcs and goblins were wearing them down.

The monsters didn't care for their dead.

⚔

He came to the lip of the huge boulder silently, on bare feet and with an easy and balanced stride. Drizzt went down to his belly to peer over and spotted the cave opening almost immediately.

As he lay there watching, the female elf walked into sight, leading a pegasus. The great steed had one wing tied up tight against its side, but that was no effort to hobble the winged horse, Drizzt knew, but rather some sort of sling. The creature's discomfort seemed minimal, though.

As Drizzt continued to watch, the sun sliding to the horizon behind him, the female elf began to brush the glistening white coat of the pegasus, and she began to sing softly, her voice carrying sweetly to Drizzt's ears.

It all seemed so . . . normal. So warm and quiet.

The other pegasus came into view then, and Drizzt ducked back a little bit as Tarathiel flew the creature down across the way, beyond his partner. As soon as the steed's hooves touched stone, Tarathiel dismounted with a graceful movement, putting his left leg over the saddle to the right before him, then turning sidesaddle and simply rolling over into a backward somersault. He landed in easy balance and moved to join his companion—who promptly tossed him a brush so that he could groom his mount.

Drizzt watched the pair for a bit longer with a mixture of bitterness and hope. For in them, he saw the promise of Ellifain, saw who she might have become, who she *should* have become. The unfairness of it all had the drow clenching his hands at his sides, had him gnashing his teeth, had him wanting nothing more than to run off right then and find more enemies to destroy.

The sun dipped lower and twilight descended over the land. Side by side, the two elves led their winged horses into the cave.

Drizzt rolled onto his back, marking the first twinkling stars of the evening. He rubbed his hands across his face and thought again of Ellifain, and thought again of Bruenor.

And he wondered once more what it was all about, what worth all the sacrifice had been, what value was to be found in his adherence to his moral codes. He knew that he should go right off for Mithral Hall, to find out which of his friends, if any, had survived the orc victory at Shallows.

But he could not bring himself to do that. Not now.

He knew, then, that he should crawl off his rock and go and speak with those elves, with Ellifain's people, to explain her end and express his sorrow.

But the thought of telling Tarathiel such grim news froze him where he lay.

He saw again the tower falling, saw again the death of his dearest friend.

The saddest day of Drizzt's life played out so clearly and began to pull him down into the darkness of despair. He rose from the boulder, then, and rushed off into the deepening gloom, running the mile or so to his own tiny cave shelter, and there he sat for a long while, holding the one-horned helmet he had retrieved from the ruins.

The sadness deepened as he turned that helmet in his hands. He felt the blackness rising up around him, grabbing at him, and he knew that it would swallow him and destroy him.

And so Drizzt used the only weapon he possessed against such despair. He wanted to bring in Guenhwyvar, but he could not, for the panther had not rested long enough, given the wounds the giant had inflicted.

And so the Hunter went out alone into the dark of night to kill some enemies.

9

WITH GRUUMSH WATCHING

King Obould built a wall of tough guards all around him as he made his way through the vast encampment at the ruins of Shallows. The great orc was tentative that day, for the ripples emanating from the murder of Achtel were still flowing out among the gathering and Obould had to wonder if that backlash would turn some of the tribes against him and his cause. The reactions of the orcs guarding the region's perimeter had been promising, at least, with several falling flat before Obould and groveling, which was always welcomed, and all the others bowing low and staying there, averting their eyes to the ground whenever they reverently answered the great orc king's questions. As one, the sentries had directed Obould to seek out Arganth Snarrl.

The spectacular shaman was not difficult to locate. With his wild clothing and feathered headdress, the cloak he had proffered from dead Achtel, and his continual gyrations, Arganth commanded the attention of all around him. Any trepidation Obould held that the charismatic shaman might pose some rivalry to him were dispelled almost immediately when he came in sight of the shaman. The shaman caught sight of Obould and fell flat to his face as completely and as surely as if he had been felled by a giant-thrown boulder.

"Obould Many-Arrows!" Arganth shrieked, and it was obvious that the shaman was literally crying with joy. "Obould! Obould! Obould!"

Around Arganth, all the other orcs similarly prostrated themselves and took up the glorious cry.

Obould looked to his personal guards curiously and returned their shrugs with a suddenly superior look. Yes, he was enjoying it! Perhaps, he mused, he should demand more from those closest around him. . . .

"Are you Snarrl? Arganth Snarrl?" the king asked, moving up to tower over the still gyrating, facedown shaman.

"Obould speaks to me!" Arganth cried out. "The blessings of Gruumsh upon me!"

"Get up!" King Obould demanded.

When Arganth hesitated, he reached down, grabbed the shaman by the scruff of his neck and jerked him to his feet.

"We have awaited your arrival, great one," Arganth said at once, and he averted his eyes.

Obould, falling back off balance a bit, realizing then that such apparent overblown fealty could be naught but a prelude to an assassination, grabbed the shaman's chin and forced him to look up.

"We two will speak," he declared.

Arganth seemed to calm then, finally. His red-streaked eyes glanced around at the other prone orcs, then settled back to meet Obould's imposing stare.

"In my tent, great one?" he asked hopefully.

Obould released him and motioned for him to lead the way. He also motioned for his guards to stay on alert and to stay very close.

Arganth seemed a completely different creature when he and Obould were out of sight of the rest of the orcs.

"It is good that you have come, King Obould Many-Arrows," the shaman said, still holding a measure of reverence in his tone, but also an apparent inner strength—something that had been lacking outside. "The tribes are anxious now and ready to kill."

"You had a . . . problem," Obould remarked.

"Achtel did not believe, and so Achtel was murdered," said Arganth.

"Believe?"

"That Obould is Gruumsh and Gruumsh is Obould," Arganth boldly stated.

That put the orc king back on his heels. He narrowed his dark eyes and furrowed his prominent brow.

"I have seen this to be true," Arganth explained. "King Obould is great. King Obould was always great. King Obould is greater now, because the One-Eye will be one with him."

Obould's expression did not lose its aura of obvious skepticism.

"What sacrilege was done here by the dwarves!" Arganth exclaimed. "To use the idol!"

Obould nodded, beginning to catch on.

"They defiled and desecrated Gruumsh, and the One-Eye is not pleased!" Arganth proclaimed, his voice rising and beginning to crack into a high-pitched squeal. "The One-Eye will exact vengeance upon them all! He will crush them beneath his boot! He will cleave them with his greatsword! He will chew out their throats and leave them gasping in the dirt!"

Obould continued to stare and even brought his hand up in a wave to try to calm the increasingly animated shaman.

"His boot," Arganth explained, pointing to Obould's feet. "His greatsword," the shaman went on, pointing to the massive weapon strapped across Obould's strong back. "Obould is the tool of Gruumsh. Obould is Gruumsh. Gruumsh is Obould! I have seen this!"

Obould's large and ugly head tilted as he scrutinized the shaman, seeking even the slightest clue that Arganth was taunting him.

"Achtel did not accept this truth," Arganth went on. "Gruumsh did not protect her when the angry drow arrived. The others, they all accept and know that Obould is Gruumsh, I have done this for you, my king . . . my god."

The great orc king's suspicious look melted into a wide and wicked grin.

"And what does Arganth want in return for his service to Obould?"

"Dwarf heads!" the shaman cried without the slightest hesitation. "They must die. All of them! King Obould will do this."

"Yes," Obould mused. "Yes."

"Will you accept the blessings of Gruumsh, delivered through the hand of Arganth and the other gathered shamans?" the orc priest asked, and he seemed to shrink down a bit lower as he dared ask anything of Obould, his gaze locked on the floor.

"What blessings?"

"You are great, Obould!" Arganth shrieked in terror, though there was no overt accusation in Obould's questioning tone.

"Yes, Obould is great," Obould replied. "What blessings?"

Arganth's bloodshot eyes sparkled as he answered, "To Obould we give the strength of the bull and the quickness of the cat. To Obould we give great power. Gruumsh will grant this. I have seen it."

"Such spells are not uncommon," Obould answered sharply. "I would demand no less from—"

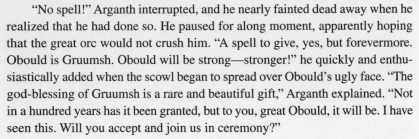

"No spell!" Arganth interrupted, and he nearly fainted dead away when he realized that he had done so. He paused for along moment, apparently hoping that the great orc would not crush him. "A spell to give, yes, but forevermore. Obould is Gruumsh. Obould will be strong—stronger!" he quickly and enthusiastically added when the scowl began to spread over Obould's ugly face. "The god-blessing of Gruumsh is a rare and beautiful gift," Arganth explained. "Not in a hundred years has it been granted, but to you, great Obould, it will be. I have seen this. Will you accept and join us in ceremony?"

Obould stared long and hard at the shaman, having no idea what he might be referring to. He had never heard of any "god-blessing of Gruumsh" before. But he could tell that Arganth was afraid and full of sincere respect. The priests had always favored Obould before. Why should they not when he made every conquest with his obligatory dedication to the great One-Eye?

"Obould will accept," he told Arganth, and the shaman nearly did a back flip in his excitement.

Obould was quick to sober him, grabbing him by the collar and lifting him easily right from the ground, then pulling him in close so that he could smell the king's hot breath.

"If I am disappointed, Arganth, I will stake you to a wall and I will eat you, starting at your fingers and working my way up your arm."

Arganth nearly fainted dead away again, for it was often rumored that Obould had done just that to other orcs on several occasions.

"Do not disappoint me."

The shaman's response might have been a "yes," or might have been a "no." It didn't really matter to Obould, for the mere tone of it, a simple and pitiful squeak, confirmed all the orc king needed to know.

"Am I doing them honor?" Drizzt asked Guenhwyvar.

He sat on the boulder that formed half of his new home, rolling the one-horned helmet of Bruenor over in his delicate fingers. Guenhwyvar lay beside him, right up against him, staring out over the mountainous terrain. The wind blew strongly in their faces that evening and carried a bit of a chill

"I know that I escape my pain when we are in battle," the drow went on.

His gaze drifted past the helmet to the distant mountains. He was speaking more to himself than to the cat, as if Guenhwyvar was really a conduit to his own conscience.

Which of course, she had always been.

"As I focus on the task at hand, I forget the loss—it is a moment of freedom. And I know that our work here is important to the dwarves of Mithral Hall. If we keep the orcs off-balance, if we make them fear to come out of their mountain holes, the press against our friends should lessen."

It all made perfect sense of course, but to Drizzt, the words still sounded somewhat shallow, somewhat of a rationalization. For he knew beneath the surface that he should not have stayed out there, not immediately, that despite the obvious signs that none had escaped, he should have gone straightaway from Shallows to Mithral Hall. He should have gone for his own sensibilities, to confirm whether or not any of his dear friends had escaped the onslaught, and he should have gone for the sake of the surviving dwarves of Clan Battlehammer, to bear witness to the fall of their king and to coordinate his subsequent movements with their own defenses.

The drow dismissed his guilt with a long sigh. Likely the dwarves had buttoned up the hall behind their great doors of iron and stone. The orcs would bring great turmoil to the North, no doubt, particularly to the myriad little towns that dotted the land, but Drizzt doubted that the humanoids would pose much of a real threat to Mithral Hall itself, even with the loss of King Bruenor. The dark elves of Menzoberranzan had attempted to wage such a war, after all, and with far greater resources and greater access through the many Underdark tunnels, and they had failed miserably. Bruenor's people were a resilient and organized force, indeed.

"I miss them, Guenhwyvar," the drow whispered, and the panther perked up at the resumption of talk, turning her wide face and soft eyes over her friend. "Of course I knew this could happen—we all knew it. In fact, I expected it. Too many narrow escapes and too many lucky breaks. It had to end, and in this type of a fall. But I always figured that I would be the first to fall, not the last, that the others would witness my demise, and not I, theirs."

He closed his eyes and saw again the fall of Bruenor, that terrible image burned indelibly into his mind. And again he saw the fall of Ellifain, and in many ways, that faraway battle wounded him even more deeply. For the fall of Bruenor brought him personal pain, but it was in accordance with those principles that had so guided Drizzt for all of his life. To die in defense of friend and community was not so bad a thing, he believed, and while the disaster at Shallows wounded his heart, the disaster along the Sword Coast, in the lair of Sheila Kree, wounded more, wounded the very foundation of his beliefs. Every memory of the fall of Ellifain brought Drizzt back to that terrible day in his

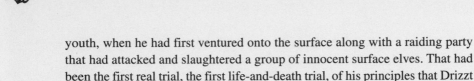

youth, when he had first ventured onto the surface along with a raiding party that had attacked and slaughtered a group of innocent surface elves. That had been the first real trial, the first life-and-death trial, of his principles that Drizzt Do'Urden had ever faced. That fateful night so long ago, his first night under the stars, had changed Drizzt's perceptions indelibly. That fateful night had indeed been the beginning of the end of his existence in Menzoberranzan, the moment when Drizzt Do'Urden had truly come to see the evil of his people, an evil beyond redemption, beyond tolerance, beyond anything Drizzt could hope to combat.

Zaknafein had nearly killed him for that wretched surface raid, until he had learned that Drizzt had not really partaken of the killings and had even deceived his companions and the Spider Queen herself by allowing the elf child to live.

How it had pained Drizzt those years before, when he had ventured through the Moonwood to happen upon Ellifain and her people, only to find the grown elf child out of her mind with rage and so obviously distorted.

And in the battle along the Sword Coast, for him to inadvertently slay her!

On so many levels, it seemed to Drizzt that Ellifain's death had mocked his principles and had made so much of his life, not a lie, but a fool's errand.

The drow rubbed his hands over his face, then dropped one atop Guenhwyvar, who had lain her head upon his leg by then, and was breathing slowly and rhythmically. Drizzt enjoyed those moments with Guenhwyvar, when they were not engaged in battle, when they could just rest and enjoy the temporary peace and the mountain breezes. The instincts of the Hunter understood that he should dismiss the cat, to allow her to rest in her Astral home. For she would be needed more desperately when orcs and giants were about.

But Drizzt, and not the Hunter, so torn and internally battling at that moment, could not listen to that pragmatic alter ego.

He closed his eyes and thought of his friends—and not of their fall. He saw again the uncomplicated Regis on the banks of Maer Dualdon, his fishing line stretched out to the dark waters before him. He knew that the hook wasn't baited, and that the line was nothing more than an excuse to simply relax.

He saw again Bruenor, grumping about the caves surrounding Kelvin's Cairn, shouting orders and banging his fists—and all the while winking at Drizzt to let him know that the gruff facade was just that.

He saw again the young boy that was Wulfgar, growing under the tutelage of both Drizzt and Bruenor. He remembered the fight in the verbeeg lair, when he and Wulfgar had charged in headlong against a complex full of powerful ene-

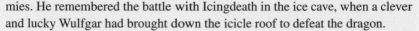

mies. He remembered the battle with Icingdeath in the ice cave, when a clever and lucky Wulfgar had brought down the icicle roof to defeat the dragon.

He saw again Catti-brie, the young girl who had first greeted him on the slopes of Kelvin's Cairn. The young woman who had first shown him the truth of his life on the surface, in a faraway southern desert. The woman who had stayed beside him, through all his doubts and all his fears, through all his mistakes and all his triumphs. When he had foolishly returned to Menzoberranzan in an effort to free his friends of the shackles of his legacy, Catti-brie had braved the Underdark to rescue him from the drow and from himself. She was his conscience and always told him when she thought he was wrong, but more than that, she was his friend and never really judged him. With a gentle touch, she could take away the shivers of doubt and fear. With a glance from those enticing blue eyes, she could look into his soul and see the truth of his emotions, busting any facade he might have painted upon his face. With a kiss on his cheek, she could remind him that he had his friends around him, always and evermore, and that in light of those friends, nothing could truly wound him.

In light of those friends. . . .

That last thought had Drizzt's head slumping to his hands, had his breath coming in shorter, forced gasps, and had his shoulders bobbing with sobs. He felt himself sinking into a grief beyond anything he had ever known, felt himself falling into a dark and empty pit, where he was helpless.

Always and evermore? Ellifain? Were those the lies of Drizzt Do'Urden's life?

He saw Zaknafein fall into the acid. He saw Withegroo's tower, that awful tower, crumble to dust and flames.

He fell deeper, and he knew only one way to climb out of that pit.

"Come, Guenhwyvar," the Hunter said to the panther.

He rose on steady legs, and with steady hands, he drew forth his scimitars. The Hunter's eyes scanned the distance, moving below the twinkling stars and their invitation to painful introspection to the flickers of campfires and the promise of battle.

The promise of revenge.

Against the orcs.

Against the lies.

Against the pain.

Thousands of orcs gathered around the broken statue of Gruumsh One-Eye one dark night, staying respectfully back as they had been instructed by their respective spiritual leaders. They whispered among themselves and bullied for position that they might witness the miraculous event. Those scuffles were kept to a minimum, though, for the shamans had promised that any who distracted the proceedings would be offered as sacrifice to Gruumsh. To back up their threat, the shamans had more than a dozen unfortunate orcs already in custody, allegedly for crimes committed out on the battlefield.

Gerti Orelsdottr was there that night as well, along with nearly a hundred of her frost giant kin. She kept her enclave even farther back from the statue, wanting to witness the supposed miracle that had the orcs in such a state of frenzy, but not wanting to give it too much credence by the weight of her immediate presence.

"Detached amusement," she had instructed her kin. "Watch it with little outward concern and detached amusement."

Another two sets of eyes were also witnessing the event. Kaer'lic Suun Wett and Tos'un Armgo at first remained near to Gerti's group—and indeed had met with the frost giantess earlier in the evening—but soon they inched closer, the drow cleric in particular wanting to get a better view.

The call for silence went out from those shamans near to the statue, and those orcs who did not immediately obey were quickly warned, usually at the end of a spear tip and often with a painful prod, by the many soldiers of Obould who were scattered throughout the throng.

Many shamans, Tos'un communicated to Kaer'lic, using the silent drow language of intricate hand movements.

A great communal spell, Kaer'lic explained. *It is not so uncommon a thing among the drow, but rarely have I heard of the lesser races employing such a tactic. Perhaps this ceremony is as important as the orcs have hinted.*

Their powers are not great! Tos'un argued, emphatically grabbing his thumb at the end of his statement.

Individually, no, Kaer'lic agreed. *But do not underestimate the power of shamans joined. Nor the power of the orc god. Gruumsh has heard their call, perhaps.*

Kaer'lic smiled as she noted Tos'un shift uncomfortably, his hands sliding near to the twin weapons he had sheathed on his hips.

Kaer'lic was not nearly as concerned. She knew Obould's designs, and she understood that those designs were not so different from her own or those of her companions or those of Gerti. This would not be a ceremony that turned the orcs against their allies, she was certain.

Her thoughts were cut short as a figure dramatically appeared atop the ruined idol of the orc god. Wearing dead Achtel's red robes and his typical ceremonial headdress, Arganth Snarrl leaped up to the highest point on the broken statue and thrust his arms up high, a burning torch in each hand, flames dancing in the night wind. His face was painted in reds and whites and a dozen toothy bracelets dangled from each arm.

He gave a sudden shrill cry and thrust his arms even higher, and two dozen other torches soon flared to life, in a ring around the statue.

Kaer'lic carefully eyed the holders of these lower torches, shamans all, and painted and decorated garishly to an orc. The drow had never seen so many orc shamans in one place, and given the typical stupidity of the brutish race, she was surprised that so many were even clever enough to assume that mantle!

Up on the statue, Arganth began to slowly turn around. In response, those shamans on the ground began to move slowly around the perimeter of the statue, each turning small circles within the march around the larger circle. Gradually Arganth began to increase the pace of his turn, and those below similarly began to move faster, both in their own circles and in their larger march. That march became more animated with each step, becoming more of a dance. Torches bobbed and swayed erratically.

It went on for many minutes, the shamans not seeming to tire in the least— and that alone told perceptive Kaer'lic that there was some magic afoot. The drow priestess narrowed her eyes and began scrutinizing more closely.

Finally, Arganth stopped all of a sudden, and those below stopped at precisely the same moment, simply freezing in place.

Kaer'lic sucked in her breath—only a heightened state of communion could have so coordinated that movement. With the synchronicity of a practiced dance team—which of course they were not, for the shamans were not even of the same tribes, for the most part, and hadn't even known each other for more than a few days—the group swayed and rotated, gradually coming to stand straight, torches held high and steady.

And Obould appeared. As one, the crowd, including Kaer'lic and her drow associate, including Gerti and her hundred giants, gasped.

The orc king was naked, his muscular frame painted in bright colors, red and white and yellow. His eyes had been lined in white, exaggerating them so that it seemed to every onlooker as if Obould was scrutinizing him specifically, and the crowd reflexively shrank back.

As she collected her wits about her, Kaer'lic realized how extraordinary the ceremony truly was, for Obould was not wearing his magnificent masterwork armor. The orc king had allowed himself to be vulnerable, though he hardly appeared helpless. His torso rippled with every stride, and his limbs seemed almost as if his muscles were stretched too tightly, the sinewy cords standing taut and straight. In many ways, the powerful orc seemed every bit as imposing as if he had been fully armed and armored. His face contorted as his mouth stretched in a wide and threatening growl, as his intensity heightened so that it seemed as if his mortal coil could not contain it.

Up above, Arganth dropped one torch to the horizontal, then swept it before him. The first orc prisoner was dragged out before Obould and forced to his knees by the escorting guard.

The creature whined pitifully, but its squeals were quickly drowned out by the shamans, who began chanting the name of their god. That chant moved outward, to encompass the front ranks of the crowd, and continued to spread back through all the gathering until thousands of orc voices joined in the call to Gruumsh. So hypnotic was it that even Kaer'lic caught herself mouthing the name. The drow glanced around nervously, hoping that Tos'un had not seen, then she smiled to see him similarly whispering to the orc god. She gave him a sharp elbow to remind him of who he was.

Kaer'lic looked back to the spectacle just as Arganth shrieked and brought his two torches in a fast and definitive cross before him, and the crowd went suddenly silent. Looking down to Obould, Kaer'lic saw that he had produced a great blade from somewhere. He slowly raised it high above his head. With a cry, he brought it flashing down, lopping the head from the kneeling orc.

The crowd roared.

The second orc prisoner was dragged in and brought to his knees beside the decapitated corpse of the first.

And so it went, the process of chanting and beheading repeated through the ten prisoners, and each execution brought a greater cry for the glory of Gruumsh than the previous.

And each made Obould seem to stand just a bit taller and stronger, his powerful chest swelling more tightly beneath his stretched skin.

When the killings were finished, the shamans began their circular dance once more, and all the crowd took up the chant to the great One-Eye.

And another creature was brought forth, a great bull, its legs hobbled by strong chords. The orc soldiers surrounding the creature prodded it with their spears and gave it no leeway whatsoever, marching it before their magnificent king.

Obould stared hard at the bull for a long while, the two seeming to fall into some sort of a mutual trance. The orc king grasped the bull by the horns, the two standing motionless, just staring.

Arganth came down from on high, and all the shamans moved around him and surrounded the bull. They began their spellcasting in unison, invoking the name of Gruumsh with every sentence, seeking the blessings of their god.

Kaer'lic recognized enough of the words to know the general spell, an invocation that, temporarily, greatly increased the strength of the recipient. There was a different twist to that one, though, the drow understood, for its intensity was so great that she could feel the magical tingling even from a distance.

A series of weird, multicolored lights, green and yellow and pink, began to flow around the bull and Obould. More and more of the lights began to emanate from the bull, it seemed. Those lights ran forward to engulf and immerse themselves in the orc king. Each one seemed to take a bit of strength from the animal, and soon it stood on trembling legs, and each one seemed to make Obould just a bit more formidable

It ended, and only then did Kaer'lic even recognize that during the process, the bindings had been cut away from the bull, so that the only thing holding it was Obould, one hand grasped upon each horn.

All fell silent, a great hush of anticipation quieting the crowd.

Obould and the creature stared at each other as the moments slipped by. With sudden strength and speed, the orc king brought his hands around, twisting the bull's head upside down. Reversing his grips, the orc king completed the circuit, bringing the poor creature's head around a full three hundred and sixty degrees.

Obould held that pose for a long moment, still staring at the bull. He let go, and the bull fell over.

Obould thrust his arms to the sky and cried out, "Gruumsh!"

A wave of energy rolled out from him across the stunned and silent crowd.

It took Kaer'lic a moment to realize that she had been knocked to her knees, that all around her were similarly kneeling. She glanced back at the frost giants, to see them on their knees as well, and none of them, particularly Gerti, looking overly pleased by that fact.

Again the shamans went into their wild dance around the broken statue, and not a one in the crowd dared to rise, though every voice immediately joined in the chanting.

It stopped again, abruptly.

A second creature was brought forth, a great mountain cat, held around the neck by long noose poles. The creature growled as it neared Obould, but the orc king didn't shy from it at all. He even bent forward, then fell to all fours, staring the cat in the eye.

The attendants loosened their nooses and removed the poles, freeing the beast.

The stare went on, as did the anticipating hush. The cat leaped forward, snapping and roaring, claws raking, and Obould caught it in his hands.

The great cat's claws couldn't dig in against Obould's flesh.

The great cat's teeth could find no hold.

Obould rose up to his full height and easily brought the squirming, thrashing cat up high above his head.

The orc king held that pose for a long moment, then called out again to Gruumsh and began to move about, his feet gaining speed with every stride, his balance holding perfect with every turn and every leap. He stopped in the middle of the frenzied movement and gave a great and sudden twist. The cat cried out, then fell silent and limp. Obould tossed its lifeless body to the ground beside the dead bull.

The crowd began to roar. The shamans began to sing and to dance, their circle bringing them around the orc king and the dead prisoners and animals.

Arganth moved inside the ring, then he ordered the culmination of the dance. The leading shaman began to sway rhythmically, whispering an incantation that Kaer'lic could not hear.

The ten headless orcs stood up and marched in silent procession to form two ranks behind Obould.

Again Arganth fell into his spellcasting, and suddenly, both the bull and the mountain cat sprang up, very much alive.

Very much alive!

The confused and frightened creatures leaped about and ran off into the night. The orcs cheered, and Obould stood very calm.

Kaer'lic could hardly draw her breath. The animation of the corpses did not seem like such a tremendous feat—certainly nothing she had expected from an orc shaman, but nothing too great in magical power—but the resurrection of the animals! How was that possible, coming from an orc?

And Kaer'lic knew, and Kaer'lic understood. Gruumsh had attended the ceremony, in spirit at least. The orc cry to their god had been answered, and the One-Eye's blessing had been instilled in Obould.

Kaer'lic saw that clearly in scrutinizing the calm orc king. She could feel the gravity of him, even from afar, could recognize the added, supernatural strength and speed that had been placed within his powerful frame.

The dwarves had erred, and badly, she knew. Their ruse in using the image of Gruumsh to so deceive his minions had brought upon them the wrath of the orc god—in the form of King Obould Many-Arrows.

Suddenly, Kaer'lic Sun Wett was very much afraid. Suddenly, she knew, the balance of power among those united in battling the dwarves had shifted.

And not for the better.

10

WHEN THE TUTORED
STEPS FORTH

"It was impressive," Kaer'lic Suun Wett somberly admitted.

Beside her, Tos'un scoffed, and across from her, both Donnia and Ad'non sat very still, their mouths agape.

"They are mere orcs," said the castoff of House Barrison Del'Armgo. "It was all illusion, all emotion."

For a moment, it seemed as if Kaer'lic would reach over and smack Tos'un, for her face grew very tight, her muscles very taut.

"Of course," Donnia agreed with a dismissive chuckle. "The mood, the throng—the ceremony was amplified by the intensity of the—"

"Silence!" Kaer'lic demanded, so forcefully that both Donnia and Ad'non slipped hands quietly to their respective weapons. "If we underestimate Obould now, it could prove disastrous. This shaman, Arganth of tribe Snarrl . . . he was inspired. Divinely inspired."

"That is quite a claim," Ad'non quietly remarked.

"It is something I have witnessed before, in a ceremony in which several yochlol appeared," Kaer'lic assured him. "I recognized it for what it was: divine inspiration." She turned to Tos'un. "Are you normally so easily deceived that you can now convince yourself that you did not see what you did indeed see?"

"I understand the trick of the mood," Tos'un hesitantly replied.

"The bull's head was twisted right around," Kaer'lic scolded him and reinforced to the others. "The creature was dead, then it was not, and this sort of resurrection is simply beyond the powers of orc shamans."

"Normally so, yes," said Ad'non. "Perhaps it is Arganth whom we should not underestimate."

Shaking her head with every word, Kaer'lic replied, "Arganth is indeed worthy, relative to his heritage. He is frenetic in his devotion to Gruumsh and handled the coincidental death of Achtel quite cleverly. But if he was possessed of priestly powers sufficient to resurrect the two dead animals, then he could have overwhelmed Achtel and her doubts long before her untimely death. He did not do that—did not even attempt to do it."

"You believe Achtel's death a fortunate coincidence?" Donnia asked.

"She was killed by Drizzt Do'Urden," answered Kaer'lic. "There can be no doubt. He was witnessed, right down to his scimitars. He slew her and rampaged through the camp and off into the night. I would doubt him to be an instrument of Gruumsh. But Arganth played it that way to the dimwitted orcs, much to his credit and much to his success."

"And now we know that Drizzt has allied with the surface elves," Tos'un remarked.

"To what extent?" asked Donnia, who, despite the reports of the fight at the river, was not so convinced.

"That is secondary," Kaer'lic pointedly reminded. "Drizzt Do'Urden is not our concern!"

"You keep saying that," Ad'non interrupted.

"Because it seems as if you do not understand it," the priestess replied. "Drizzt is not our problem, nor are we his unless he learns of our existence. He is Obould's problem and Gerti's problem, and we would do well to let them handle him. Particularly now that Obould has been gifted by Gruumsh."

A couple of snorts accompanied that claim from the still-doubting duo across from Kaer'lic.

"Underestimate him at your peril now," Kaer'lic replied to those scoffs. "He is stronger—visibly so—and he is possessed of great quickness. Even Tos'un, who believes he was tricked, cannot deny these things. Obould is far more formidable."

Tos'un reluctantly nodded his agreement.

"Obould was always formidable," Ad'non replied. "Even before this ceremony, I had little desire to wage battle with him openly. And surely none of us wishes to do battle with Gerti Orelsdottr. But did the shamans make the orc king brighter and more clever? I hardly think so!"

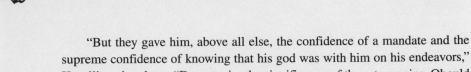

"But they gave him, above all else, the confidence of a mandate and the supreme confidence of knowing that his god was with him on his endeavors," Kaer'lic pointed out. "Do not miss the significance of these two gains. Obould will be possessed of no insecurity now, of no inner doubts that we might exploit to our wishes. He walks with confidence, with strength, and with surety. He will look more carefully at our every word that contradicts his instincts, and even more carefully at our suggestions that run tangentially to his previously decided course. He is a stronger and swifter running current now, one that will be more difficult to deflect along our desired course."

The doubting smirks became scowls, and quickly so.

"But I believe that we have already set the river's course in proper flow," Kaer'lic went on. "We need not manipulate Obould any longer, for he is determined to execute the very war we desired—and now he seems more able to do it."

"We become detached and amused onlookers?" Tos'un asked.

Kaer'lic shrugged and replied, "Not such a bad fate."

Across the way, Donnia and Ad'non exchanged doubting glances, and Ad'non shook his head.

"There is still the matter of Gerti," he reasoned. "And this ceremony for Obould will likely put the giantess even more on her guard. Seeing the growth of Obould might bring cohesion to the orc tribes, but it will likely instill grave doubts in Gerti. For all the power you believe the orc king has gained, he will need Gerti's giants to seal the dwarves back in their holes and ravage the countryside."

"Then we must make certain that Gerti continues to follow Obould," said Tos'un.

The other three turned somewhat sour looks upon him, silently berating him for his lack of understanding. He took their expressions with proper humility. He was the youngest of the group, after all, and by far the least experienced in such matters.

"No, not follow," Donnia corrected. "We need to make her continue to travel the course beside him and to make sure that he still understands that he is walking beside her, and not leading her."

The others nodded; it was a subtle distinction, but a very important one.

Ad'non and Donnia went out as soon as the sun had set, exiting the deep cave the group had taken as their temporary residence, not too far to the east of the ruins of Shallows. The two dark elves blinked repeatedly as they came to the surface, for though no moon was up, the relative light of the surface night remained at first uncomfortable.

Donnia looked out to the east, beyond the steep slopes and cliffs, to see the Surbrin winding its way south, starlight sparkles dancing around the rushing waters. Beyond that lay the darkness of the Moonwood, Donnia knew, where more elves resided. As far as the four drow knew, only a couple had involved themselves in the affairs of Obould since the orc king, at the drow's bidding, had not yet crossed the Surbrin with any substantial numbers.

"Perhaps they will come forth from their forest home," Ad'non said to Donnia, reading her mind and her desires.

The male drow grinned wickedly and gave a low laugh.

They both hoped that the elves would come forth in force, Donnia knew. Obould could handle a small clan, and how sweet it would be to see some faeries lying dead at orc feet. Or even better—dare she even hope?—to have faeries taken as prisoners and handed over to Donnia and her band for their pleasures.

"Kaer'lic's continuing fear of Drizzt is disturbing," Ad'non remarked.

"Tos'un names the rogue as formidable."

"Indeed, and I do not doubt our Menzoberranyr friend at all in that regard," said Ad'non. "Still. . . ."

"Kaer'lic seems more fearful of everything lately," Donnia agreed. "She verily trembled when she spoke of Obould. A mere orc!"

"Perhaps she has been away from our people for too long. Perhaps she needs to revisit the Underdark—back to Ched Nasad, possibly, or even Menzoberranzan, if Tos'un can smooth our way in."

"Where we would be homeless rogues until one matron mother or another saw fit to offer us shelter—in exchange for slavish fealty," Donnia said sourly, and Ad'non could only shrug at that distinct possibility.

"Kaer'lic would not be pleased if she knew our intent this night," Donnia remarked a moment later.

Again Ad'non shrugged and said, "I answer not to Kaer'lic Suun Wett."

"Even if her reasoning is sound?"

Ad'non paused and considered the words for a long while.

"But we are not seeking Drizzt Do'Urden in any case," he said at length.

It was true enough, if only technically so. The pair had made up their minds to investigate the troubles Obould's rear lines had been experiencing over the past couple of tendays. Of course they knew that Drizzt Do'Urden was central to those troubles, but it was not he who had lured the two drow out of their deep holes—both because of Kaer'lic's reasoning and Tos'un's warnings, and because, as far as Donnia and Ad'non were concerned, there was better prey to hunt.

A pair of surface elves, seen by Gerti's giants riding winged horses—wouldn't those mounts be fine trophies!

Within the hour, the pair were at the scene of the last assault, near to the smaller river within the mountains. Orc bodies still littered the ground, for no one had bothered to bury them. Following the path of the massacre, the two soon had Drizzt's route of battle discerned, and the bodies of many orcs in a circle around one point showed them where the two surface elves had joined the fray.

More than a score dead, and only three blades engaged, Donnia flashed with silent hand signals, taking care to hold her silence.

Most felled by Drizzt, no doubt, before the other two even arrived, came Ad'non's answer.

They tarried around the battleground for quite a while, trying to learn as much as they could, both from the pattern of the dead to the types of wounds, about the fighting styles of those engaged. More than once, Donnia flashed to Ad'non a signal revealing her admiration for the sword work, and more than once, Ad'non agreed. And, with the night almost half over, the pair went out from the immediate area, working about the perimeter and beyond for some sign of passage.

To their surprise and delight, they found a trail easily enough and knew from the footprints and the bent blades of grass that it had been made by at least two of the three enemies.

The surface elves, Ad'non flashed. *I would have expected them to better cover their tracks.*

Unless they were not making the trail for the orcs, Donnia reasoned. *Few orcs could follow these subtle signs, I expect, though to our trained eyes they seem obvious.*

To our trained eyes and to those of Drizzt Do'Urden, perhaps? asked Ad'non's fingers.

Donnia grinned and bent low to study one particular stretch of brush. Yes, it made perfect sense to her. The trail seemed obvious to the keen eyes and tracking skills of the trained dark elves, but surely it was nothing that any orcs would find and follow. And yet, with her experiences concerning surface elves, Donnia knew that it was a clumsy passage, at best. The more she looked, the more Ad'non's subtle suggestion that the trail had been left on purpose for Drizzt rang true to her. The elves thought their enemies to be orcs, goblins, and giants, and thought that a dark elf was numbered among their allies. The orcs who had witnessed the massacre had indeed noted that the surface elves and the dark elf had parted ways immediately following the fighting; perhaps the surface elves wanted to make sure that Drizzt Do'Urden knew how to find them should he need them.

Shall we go and find our pleasure? Ad'non's fingers waggled.

Donnia brought her hands up before her, a movement of accentuation and exclamation, and tapped the outsides of her thumbs together.

Indeed!

Tension hung thick in the air by the time Kaer'lic and Tos'un entered Obould's great tent. One glance at Gerti, the giantess sitting cross-legged (which still put her head near to the arched deerskin ceiling) between a pair of grim-faced guards, told the two drow that the meeting had not gone well to that point.

"Nesmé has been overrun in the south," Gerti resumed as soon as the two newcomers took their places across from her and to Obould's right. "Proffit and his wretched trolls have made more progress than we and in a shorter time."

"Their enemies were not nearly as formidable as ours," Obould countered. "They battled humans in open villages, while we try to dislodge dwarves from their deep holes."

"Deep holes?" Gerti roared. "We have gotten nowhere near to Mithral Hall yet. All you and your worthless son have encountered are minor settlements and a small force of dwarves on open ground! And Urlgen has not even been able to push a minor force over the cliff face and back to Mithral Hall. This is not victory. It is standstill, and all the while, Proffit the wretch marches from the Trollmoors!"

Proffit? Tos'un signed to Kaer'lic, spelling the unknown name phonetically.

Leader of the trolls, Kaer'lic replied, an assumption, of course, for she really had little knowledge of what was happening in the southland.

Kaer'lic turned her full attention back to the giantess and orc leader as she signed, though, and the expression on Obould's face rang out bells of alarm.

"King Obould's son claims the head of Bruenor Battlehammer as a trophy," the drow female interjected, trying to diffuse the situation.

Kaer'lic was only beginning to understand the depth of the change in the orc king, and it occurred to her that with his newfound confidence and prowess, Obould might not be above challenging Gerti or siccing his legions upon her and her minions.

"*I* have not seen any Battlehammer head," Gerti sharply replied.

"His fall was witnessed by many," Kaer'lic pressed. "As the tower fell."

"My giants claim no small part in that kill."

"True enough," Kaer'lic replied before Obould could explode—as he surely seemed about to do. "And so our victories to date at least equal those of this troll . . . Proffit?"

"Proffit," Obould confirmed. "Who has bound the trolls and bog blokes under his command. Who has led them from the Trollmoors in greater numbers than ever before."

"He will squeeze Mithral Hall from the south?" Kaer'lic asked.

Obould leaned forward and dropped his chin in his hand, mulling it over.

"Better from the tunnels," Tos'un reasoned, and the eyes of the three leaders turned over him.

"Let Proffit keep the pressure on the dwarves," the drow went on. "Let him and his minions keep them fighting in their tunnels after we seal them in Mithral Hall. We will raze the land and claim our boundaries and turn our attention to the beleaguered dwarves."

Kaer'lic's face remained impassive, but she did flash a signal of gratitude to Tos'un for his clever thinking.

"The fall of Nesmé and the presence of the trolls will more likely incite Silverymoon to action," Kaer'lic added. "That, we do not want. Let them go underground and do battle with Mithral Hall, as the son of Barrison Del'Armgo suggests. Perhaps then our greater enemies will think that Proffit and his wretched creatures have retreated back to the Trollmoors, where even Lady Alustriel would not go in pursuit."

Obould was nodding, slightly, but what caught Kaer'lic's attention most was the scowl stamped upon Gerti's face and the set of her blue eyes that never once left the specter of King Obould. There was more going on than the lack of recent progress in the march to Mithral Hall, Kaer'lic understood. First and foremost, Gerti was seething about the apparent transformation of Obould. Was it jealousy? Fear?

For a moment, the notion terrified Kaer'lic. A rift between the giants and the orcs at such a critical juncture could allow the dwarves to regroup and wipe out their gains.

It was but a fleeting thought, though, for it occurred to Kaer'lic that watching the giants and orcs turn against each other might be as fine a show as watching their combined forces rolling over the dwarves.

"The suggestion intrigues me," Obould said to Tos'un. "We will speak more on this. I have sent word to Proffit to turn east to the Surbrin and north to Mithral Hall's eastern gate, where we will meet with him as we chase the dwarves into their hole."

"We must go straight to the south and push the resistance from in front of your worthless son," Gerti demanded. "Urlgen's forces are being slaughtered, and while it pains me not at all to see orcs and goblins shredded, I fear that the losses are too great."

A look of utter contempt came over Obould at those remarks, and Kaer'lic immediately began preparing a spell that would provide cover so that she and Tos'un could flee should the orc king launch himself at Gerti.

But to his credit, Obould settled back, staring hard at the giantess.

"My ranks have swelled threefold since the fall of Shallows," the orc king reminded her.

"The dwarves are slaughtering your son's forces," Gerti replied.

"And the dwarves are taking heavy losses in the process," said the orc king. "And they are growing weary, with few to replace them on the battle line, while fresh warriors join Urlgen's ranks every day. If more giants joined in the fray, the dwarf losses would increase even more."

"I do not sacrifice my warriors."

Obould began to chuckle and said, "Giants will die in this campaign, Dame Orelsdottr."

The sheer power of his tone had Kaer'lic tilting her head to study his every movement. Clearly the ceremony had done something to Obould, had instilled in him the confidence to deal with Gerti in a manner even beyond that which the drow cleric had anticipated.

"The choice remains yours to make," Obould went on. "If you fear losses, then retreat to the Spine of the World and the safety of Shining White. If you wish the rewards, then press on. The Battlehammers will be beaten back into their hole, and the Spine is ours. Once secured, we will flush the dwarves from that hole, and Mithral Hall will be renamed the Citadel of Many-Arrows."

That bit of news brought surprise to everyone in the room who was not an orc. Since the day she had met Obould, Kaer'lic had seen in him a singular desire: to retrieve lost Citadel Felbarr. Had he abandoned that course in favor of the closer dwarven settlement of Mithral Hall?

"And how will King Emerus Warcrown react to this?" Gerti said slyly, picking up on the same discrepancy and not-so-subtly reminding Obould of that other goal.

"We cannot cross the Surbrin," Obould countered without the slightest hesitation. "I'll not allow the greater powers of the North to ally against us—not now. Citadel Felbarr will send aid and warriors to Clan Battlehammer, of course, but when Mithral Hall is lost to them, with King Bruenor dead, the dwarves in the east will more likely welcome the refugees of Mithral Hall to their own deep holes. Then, once the adjoining tunnels are secured, our victory is complete and all the land from the mountains to the Surbrin, south to the Trollmoors, will be ours."

A smaller bite, Tos'un signaled to Kaer'lic.

A wiser course, Kaer'lic flashed back. *Obould seeks more than vengeance and battle now. He seeks victory.*

The notion astonished Kaer'lic even as her delicate fingers communicated it to Tos'un. While quite worthy among his inferior kin, Obould had always seemed to Kaer'lic so much less refined than that. From the day she'd met him, the orc king had spoken almost exclusively of retaking Citadel Felbarr, which, with the reclamation of Mithral Hall and the solidification of the alliances between the dwarven triumvirate—Mithral Hall, Citadel Felbarr, and Citadel Adbar—seemed completely unattainable. Even in fostering this alliance and campaign, the four plotting dark elves had always assumed that Obould would reach for that goal, to abject disaster. Kaer'lic and her associates had never considered any real and lasting victory, but rather a simple state of resulting chaos from which they could find enjoyment and profit.

Had the shaman Arganth's ceremony granted some sort of greater insight to the orc king? Had the dwarves' blasphemy with the idol of Gruumsh brought the possibility of true and lasting victory to Obould and his swelling ranks of minions?

Kaer'lic took care not to let those thought spiral out of control, reminding herself that they were but orcs, after all, whatever their numbers. All she had to do was look at the simmering hatred in Gerti's eyes to recognize that Obould's designs could splinter and shatter at any moment.

"We seal the region under our domain at the onset of winter," Obould explained. "Put the dwarves in their hole and secure all the land above to the corner of the mountain range. We will fight through Mithral Hall's tunnels throughout the winter."

"The dwarves will prove more formidable in their underground halls," Kaer'lic said.

"But how long will they deign to remain there in battle?" Obould asked. "King Bruenor is dead, and they will have no trade unless they try to break out."

It made a lot of sense, Kaer'lic had to admit to herself, and the thought was both optimistic and fear-inspiring. Perhaps Obould was making too much sense. Ever skeptical of the entire endeavor, the drow priestess could see both a higher potential climb and a higher potential fall.

The worst part of it was her confirmation that King Obould had suddenly become much less malleable to the designs and deceptions of the dark elves.

That could make him dangerous.

Kaer'lic looked at Gerti and recognized that the giantess was thinking along pretty much the same lines.

11

UNSHACKLING

In a rare moment of respite, the exhausted Wulfgar leaned back against a boulder and stared out over Keeper's Dale, his gaze drawn to the western gates of Mithral Hall.

"Thinking of Bruenor," Catti-brie remarked when she joined him.

"Aye," the big man whispered. He glanced over at the woman and nearly laughed at the sight, though it would have been a chuckle of sheer resignation and nothing out of true amusement. For Catti-brie was covered in blood, her blond hair matted to her head, her clothing stained, her boots soaked with the stuff. "Your sword cuts too deep, I fear," he said.

Catti-brie ran a hand through her sticky hair and gave a helpless sigh.

"Never thought I'd admit to being sick of killing orcs and goblins," she said. "And no matter how many we kill, seems there're a dozen more to take the place of each."

Wulfgar just nodded and gazed back across the valley.

"Regis has given the order to all the clerics now that Bruenor is not to be tended," Catti-brie reminded.

"Should we be there when he dies?" Wulfgar asked, and it was all he could do to keep his voice from breaking apart.

He heard the woman's approach but did not turn to her, afraid that if he looked into her eyes at that moment he would burst out in sobs. And that was something he could not do, something none of them could afford.

"No," Catti-brie said, and she dropped a comforting and familiar hand on Wulfgar's broad shoulder, then moved in closer to hug his head against her breast. "He's already lost to us," she whispered. "We witnessed his fall in Shallows. That was when our Bruenor died, and not when his body takes its last breath. The priests have been keeping him breathing for our own sake, and not for Bruenor's. Bruenor's long gone already, sitting around a table with Gandalug and Dagnabbit, likely, and grumbling about us and our crying."

Wulfgar put his own huge hand over Catti-brie's and turned to look at her, silently thanking her for her calming words. He still wasn't sure about all of it, feeling almost as if he was betraying Bruenor by not being by his side when he passed over to the other world. But how could Banak and the others spare him and Catti-brie at that point, for surely the efforts of the pair were doing much to bolster the cause?

And wouldn't Bruenor slap him across the head if he ever heard of such a thing?

"I can hardly say my farewells to him," Wulfgar admitted.

"When we thought you dead, taken by the yochlol, Bruenor fretted about for tendays and tendays," Catti-brie explained. "His heart was ripped out from his chest like never before." She moved around, placing one hand on either side of Wulfgar's face and staring at him intently. "But he did go on. And in those first days, with the murdering dark elves still thick about us, he let his anger lead the way. No time for mourning, he kept muttering, when he thought none were about to hear him."

"And we must be equally strong," Wulfgar agreed.

They had been over it all before, of course, saying many of the same words and with the same determination. Wulfgar understood that the need he and Catti-brie had to repeat the conversation came from deep-seeded doubts and fears, from a situation that had so quickly spun out of their control.

"Bruenor Battlehammer's rest with his ancestors," he continued, "will be easier indeed if he knows that Mithral Hall is safe and that his friends and family fought on in his name and for his cause."

Catti-brie kissed him on the forehead and hugged him close, and with a deep breath, Wulfgar let go of his pain—temporarily, he knew. All the world had changed for him, and all the world would change again, and not for the better, when they buried King Bruenor beside his ancestors. Catti-brie's words made sense, and Wulfgar understood that Bruenor had died gloriously, as a dwarf ought to die, as Bruenor would have chosen to die, in the fight at Shallows.

That realization did make it a little easier.

Just a little.

"And what of you?" Wulfgar asked the woman. "You are so concerned with how everyone else might be feeling, and yet I see a great pain in your blue eyes, my friend."

"What creature would I be if losing the dwarf who raised me as his own child didn't wound me heart?" Catti-brie replied.

Wulfgar reached up and grabbed her firmly by the forearms.

"I mean about Drizzt," he said quietly.

"I do not think he's dead," came the emphatic reply.

Wulfgar shook his head with every word, agreeing wholeheartedly.

"Orcs and giants?" he said. "No, Drizzt is alive and well and likely killing as many of our enemies as this whole army of us are killing here."

Catti-brie's responding expression was more grit than smile as she nodded.

"But that is not what I meant," Wulfgar went on. "I know the confusion that you now endure, for it is clear to all who know you and love you."

"You're talking silliness," Catti-brie answered, and in a telling gesture, she tried to pull away.

Wulfgar held her firm and steady.

"Do you love him?" he asked.

"I could ask the same of Wulfgar, and get the same answer, I'm sure."

"You know what I mean," Wulfgar pressed. "Of course you love Drizzt as a friend, as I do, as Regis does, as Bruenor does. I knew that I would find my way from the drink and from my torment when I returned to you four, my friends. My true friends and family. And you understand that which I now ask. Do you love him?"

He let go of Catti-brie, and she did step back, though she didn't turn her eyes from his crystalline blue gaze and did not even blink.

"When you were gone . . ." she started to reply.

Wulfgar laughed at her obvious attempt to spare his feelings.

"This has nothing to do with me!" he insisted. "Except in the manner that I am to you a friend. Someone who cares very deeply for you. Please, for your own sake, do not avoid this. Do you love him?"

Catti-brie gave a deep sigh, and she did look down.

"Drizzt," she said, "is special to me in ways beyond that of the others of our group."

"And are you lovers?"

The blunt and personal question had the woman snapping her gaze back up at the barbarian. There was nothing but true compassion in his eyes, though, and so Catti-brie did not lash out.

"We spent years together," she said quietly. "When ye fell and were lost to us, me and Drizzt spent years together, riding and sailing with Deudermont."

Wulfgar smiled at her and held up his hand, gently telling her that he had heard enough, that he understood well her meaning.

"Was it love or friendship that guided your way through those years and those roads?" Wulfgar asked.

Catti-brie pondered that for a bit, glancing off into the distance.

"There was always friendship," she said. "We two never let go of that. Friendship and companionship above all else sustained me and Drizzt on the road."

"And now you're pained because it was more than that for you," Wulfgar reasoned. "And when you thought you were dead with those orcs, the sting was all the more because you've all the more to lose."

Catti-brie stood staring at him and making no move to answer.

"So tell me, my dear friend, are you ready to surrender that road?" Wulfgar asked. "Are you ready to forsake the adventures?"

"No more than Bruenor ever was!" Catti-brie snapped at him without the slightest bit of hesitation.

Wulfgar smiled widely, for it was all sorting out for him then, and he believed that he might be able to actually help his friend when she needed him.

"Do you wish to have children?" he asked.

Catti-brie stared at him incredulously.

"What kind of question is that for you to be asking me?"

"The kind a friend would ask," said Wulfgar, and he asked it again.

Catti-brie's stern gaze dissipated, and it was obvious to Wulfgar that she was really looking inward then, honestly asking herself that very same question for perhaps the first time.

"I don't know," she admitted. "I always thought it'd be an easy choice, and of course, I'd want to have some of me own. But I'm not so sure of meself, though I'm guessing that I'm running out of time to decide."

"And do you wish to have Drizzt's children?"

A look of panic came over the woman, her eyes going wide with apparent horror, but then softening quickly. She was torn, Wulfgar could clearly see, and had certainly expected. For this was the crux of it all, the rough rub in their relationship. Drizzt was a drow, and could Catti-brie honestly go down that path? Could she honestly have children who were half-drow in heritage?

Certainly the answer here was twofold, a heartfelt yes and a logical no, and both were emphatic.

Wulfgar began to chuckle.

"You're mocking me," Catti-brie said to him, and Wulfgar noted that as she became agitated, she seemed to sound more like a dwarf!

"No, no," Wulfgar assured her, and he held up his hands defensively. "I was considering the irony of it all, and it amuses me that you are even listening to my words of advice. I, who have taken a wife from the most unlikeliest of places and who am raising a child that is neither mine nor that of my unlikely wife."

As that message sank in, a smile widened over Catti-brie's face as well.

"And we of a family with a dwarf father who raises two human children as his own," she replied.

"And should I begin to list the ironies of Drizzt Do'Urden?" Wulfgar asked.

Catti-brie's laughter had her holding her sides then.

"Can we be saying," she said, "that Regis is the most normal among us?"

"Then be afraid!" Wulfgar replied dramatically, and Catti-brie laughed all the harder. "Perhaps it is just those ironies about us that drive us on along this road we so often choose."

Catti-brie sobered a bit at that remark, then stopped her giggling, her expression going suddenly more grim—and Wulfgar understood that the conversation had led her right back to where they had started, right back to the state of Bruenor Battlehammer.

"Perhaps," the woman agreed. "Until now, with Bruenor gone and Drizzt out there alone."

"No!" Wulfgar insisted, and he came up from the rock, standing tall before her. "Still!"

Catti-brie sighed and started to reply, but Wulfgar cut her short.

"I think of my wife and child back in Mithral Hall," the warrior said. "Every time I walk out of there, I know that I might not see Delly and Colson again. And yet I go, because the road beckons me—as you yourself just admitted it so beckons you. Bruenor is gone, so we must accept, and Drizzt . . . well, who can know where the drow now runs? Who can know if an orc spear has found his heart and quieted him forever? Not I, and not you, though we both hold fast to our prayers that he is all right and will return to us soon.

"But even should he not, and even if Regis accepts a permanent position of steward, or counselor, perhaps, if Banak Brawnanvil becomes King of Mithral Hall, I will not forsake the road. This is my life, with the wind upon my face and the stars as my ceiling. This is my lot, to wage battle against the orcs and the giants and all others who threaten the good folk of the land. I embrace that lot and revel in it, and I shall until I am too old to run about the mountain trails or until an enemy blade lays me low.

"Delly knows this. My wife accepts that I will spend little time in Mithral Hall beside her." The barbarian gave a self-deprecating chortle and asked, "Can I really call her my wife? And Colson my child?"

"You're a good husband to her and a fine father to the little one."

Wulfgar gave a nod of thanks to the woman for those words.

"But still I will not forsake the road," he said, "and Delly Curtie would not have me forsake the road. That is what I have come to love most about her. That is why I trust that she will raise Colson in my absence, should I be killed, to be true to whomever it is that Colson is meant to be."

"True to her nature?"

"Independence is what matters," Wulfgar explained. "And it is more difficult by far to be independent of our own inner shackles than it is of the shackles that others might place upon us."

The simple words nearly knocked Catti-brie over. "I said the same thing to a friend of ours, once," she said.

"Drizzt?"

The woman nodded.

"Then heed your own words," Wulfgar advised her. "You love him and you love the road. Why does there need to be more than that?"

"If I'm wanting to have children of me own. . . ."

"Then you will come to know that, and so you will redirect the road of your life appropriately," Wulfgar told her. "Or it might be that fate intervenes, against all care, and you get that which you're not sure you want."

Catti-brie sucked in her breath.

"And would it truly be such a bad thing?" Wulfgar asked her. "To mother the child of Drizzt Do'Urden? If the babe was possessed of half his skills and but a tenth of his heart, it would be among the greatest of all the folk of the northland."

Catti-brie sighed again and brought a hand up to wipe her eyes.

"If Bruenor can raise a couple of human brats as troublesome as us. . . ." Wulfgar remarked with a smirk, and he let the thought hang in the air.

Catti-brie laughed and smiled at him, with warmth and gratitude.

"Take your love and your pleasure as you find it," Wulfgar advised. "Do not worry so much of the future that you let today pass you by. You are happy beside Drizzt. Need you know more than that?"

"You sound just like him," Catti-brie answered. "Only not when he was advising me, but when he was advising himself. You're asking me to go to the same place that Drizzt found, the same enjoyment in the moment and all the rest be damned."

"And as soon as Drizzt found that place, you began to doubt," Wulfgar said with a coy smile. "When he found the place of comfort and acceptance, all obstacles were removed, and so you put one up—your fears—to hold it all in stasis."

Catti-brie was shaking her head, but Wulfgar could tell that she wasn't disagreeing with him in the least.

"Follow your heart," the big man said quietly. "Minute by minute and day by day. Let the course of the river run as it will, instead of tying yourself up in fears that you may never realize."

Catti-brie looked up at him, her head beginning to nod. Glad that he had brought her some comfort and some good advice, Wulfgar bent over and kissed his friend on the forehead.

That elicited a wide and warm smile from Catti-brie, and she seemed to him, for the first time in a long time, to be at peace with herself. He had forced her emotions back into the present, he knew, and had released her from the fears that had taken hold. Why would she sacrifice her present joys—the wild road, the companionship of her friends, and the love of Drizzt—for fear of some uncertain future wishes?

He watched her continue to visibly relax, watched her smile become more and more genuine and enduring. He could see her emotional shackles falling away.

"When'd you get so smart?" she asked him.

"In Hell and out of it," Wulfgar replied. "In a hell of Errtu's making, and in a hell of Wulfgar's making."

Catti-brie tilted her head and stared at him hard.

"And are you free?" she asked. "Are you really free?"

Wulfgar's smile matched her own, even exceeded it, his boyish grin so wide and so sincere, so warm and, yes, so free.

"Let's go kill some orcs," he remarked, words that were truly comforting music to the ears of Catti-brie.

12

SUBTERFUGE

They swept across the vale between Shallows and the mountains north of Keeper's Dale like a massive earthbound storm, a great darkness and swirling tempest. Led by Obould-who-was-Gruumsh and anchored by a horde of frost giants greater than any that had been assembled in centuries, the orc swarm trampled the brush and sent the animals small and large fleeing before it.

For the first time in tendays, King Obould Many-Arrows met up with his son, Urlgen, in a sheltered ravine north of the sloping battleground where the dwarves had entrenched.

Urlgen entered the meeting full of fury, ready to demand more troops so that he could push the dwarves over the cliff and back into their holes. Fearing that Obould and Gerti would blame him for his lack of a definitive victory, Urlgen was ready to go on the offensive, to chastise his father for not giving him enough force to unseat the dwarves from the high ground.

As soon as he entered his father's tent, though, the younger orc's bluster melted away in confusion. For he knew, upon his very first glance, that the brutish leader sitting before him was not his father as he had known him, but was something more. Something greater.

A shaman that Urlgen did not know sat in place before, below, and to the side of Obould, dressed in a feathered headdress and a bright red robe. To the side, against the left-hand edge of the tent, sat Gerti Orelsdottr, and she seemed to the younger orc leader not so pleased.

Mostly though, Urlgen focused on Obould, for the brash young orc was barely able to take his eyes off his father, off the bulging muscles of the intense orc's powerful arms, or the fierce set of Obould's face, seeming on the verge of an explosion. That was not so uncommon a thing with Obould, but Urlgen understood that the danger of Obould was somehow greater than ever before.

"You have not pushed them back into Mithral Hall," Obould stated.

Urlgen could not tell if the statement was meant as a mere recitation of the obvious or an indictment of his leadership.

"They are a difficult foe," Urlgen admitted. "They reached the high ground before we caught up to them and immediately set about preparing their defenses."

"And those defenses are now entrenched?"

"No!" Urlgen said with some confidence. "We have struck at them too often. They continue to work, but with arms weary from battle."

"Then strike at them again, and again after that," Obould demanded, coming forward suddenly and powerfully. "Let them die of exhaustion if not at the end of an orc spear. Let them grow so weary of battle that they retreat to their dark hole!"

"I need more warriors."

"You need nothing more!" Obould screamed right back at Urlgen, and he came right out of his seat then and put his face just an inch from his son's. "Fight them and stab them! Crush them and grind them into the stone!"

Urlgen tried hard to match his father's stare, but to no avail, for more than anger was driving the younger orc then. Obould had marched in with a force ten times the size of his own, and with a horde of giants beside him. One concentrated attack would force the dwarves into complete retreat, would chase them all the way back into Mithral Hall.

"I go east," Obould announced. "To seal the dwarves' gate along the Surbrin and chase them underground. There I will meet with the troll Proffit, who has overrun Nesmé, and I will arrange for him to begin the underground press upon our dwarf enemies."

"Let us close this western gate first," Urlgen suggested, but his father was snarling and shouting "No!" before he ever finished.

"No," Obould repeated. "It will not be enough to let these smelly dwarves run back into Mithral Hall. Not anymore. They have chosen to stand against us, and so they will die! You must hold them and batter at them. Keep them in place, but keep them weary. I return soon, and we will see to the end of them."

"I have lost hundreds," Urlgen protested.

"And you have hundreds more to lose," Obould calmly replied.

"My warriors will break rank and flee," Urlgen insisted. "They splash through the blood of their kin. They climb over orc bodies to get to the dwarves."

Obould let out a long, extended growl. He reached up and grasped Urlgen by the front of his tunic. Urlgen grabbed Obould's hand with both of his own, and tried to twist free, but with a flick of his wrist, Obould sent his startled son flying across the room to crash down by the flap of the tent.

"They will not dare flee," Obould insisted. He turned to the red-robed shaman as he spoke. "They will see the glory of Obould."

"Obould is Gruumsh!' Arganth Snarrl insisted.

Urlgen stared incredulously at his father, stunned by the sheer strength of Obould and the sheer intensity in his simmering yellow eyes. A glance to Gerti showed Urlgen that she was horrified by the display and similarly frustrated. Most of all, Urlgen recognized that frustration, and only then did it occur to him that Gerti had not said a word.

Gerti Orelsdottr, the daughter of the great Jarl Greyhand, who had always held the upper hand in all dealings with the orcs, had not said a word.

Like a great yawning river, the swarm of King Obould's orcs began their pivot and deliberate flow out to the east.

Urlgen Threefist, stung and afraid, watched the turn and march from a high ridge at the back of his own forces. His father had reinforced him, but with nothing substantial. Enough to hold on, enough to keep the dwarves under pressure, but not enough to dislodge them.

For suddenly King Obould didn't want to dislodge them. His reasoning had seemed sound—keep the dwarves fighting and separated so that they could completely cut them off and kill as many as possible before Mithral Hall's western door banged closed—but Urlgen could not dismiss the feeling that part of the delaying tactic was for no better reason than to push the credit for success squarely off of Urlgen's shoulders and squarely onto Obould's.

A noise from behind and below turned Urlgen from his contemplations.

"I feared you would not come," the orc said to Gerti as the giantess climbed up to stand just below him, which put her face level with his own.

"Was it not I who asked you to come out here at this time?" the giantess replied.

Urlgen bit back a sharp retort, for he still had not reconciled within himself the value of any dialogue with Gerti, whom he hated.

"You have come to fear my father," the orc did say.

"Can you state any differently?" Gerti asked.

"He has grown," Urlgen admitted.

"Obould seeks to dominate."

"King Obould," Urlgen corrected. "You would ask me to help the giants prevent the rise of the orcs?"

"Not of the orcs," Gerti clarified. "I would ask you, for the sake of Urlgen and not of Gerti, to check the rise of King Obould. Where will Urlgen fit in under the god-figure that Obould is fast becoming?"

In light of the weight of that question, Urlgen didn't question Gerti's omission of his father's title.

"Will Urlgen find any credit and glory?" Gerti asked. "Or will he serve as convenient scapegoat at the first sign of disaster?"

Urlgen's lip curled in a snarl, and as much as he wanted to lash out at the giantess (though of course he would never dare do anything of the sort!), his anger came more from the fact that Gerti's reasoning was sound than from the obvious insult to him. Obould was holding him from gaining a great victory there and, but should he fail, Urlgen held no doubts of the severity of his powerful father's judgment.

"What do you need from me?" Gerti surprised him by asking.

Urlgen glanced back at the marching thousands, then turned to Gerti once more, staring at her curiously, trying to read the message behind her words.

"When the time comes to destroy the dwarves before you, you wish to make certain that the orcs praise Urlgen," Gerti reasoned. "I will help you to do that."

Urlgen narrowed his eyes but was nodding despite his cynicism.

"And that the orcs praise Gerti," he remarked.

"If we share in Obould's glory, we will help ensure that we do not suffer all the blame."

It made sense, of course, but to Urlgen, it all seemed so surreal. He had never been close to Gerti in any form. He had often argued with his father against even enlisting the giants as allies. And for her part, Urlgen understood that Gerti despised him even more than she hated Obould and the other orcs. To Gerti, Urlgen had never been anything more than a wretch.

And yet, there they were, sharing plans behind the back of Obould.

Urlgen led Gerti's gaze to the south, to the steeply rising ground and the distant dwarven encampment.

"I need giants," he said. "To secure my lines and throw huge stones!"

"The high ground gives the dwarves the advantage of range," Gerti replied. "I will not see the orc bodies covered by those of my kin."

"Then what do you offer?" Urlgen asked, growing more and more frustrated.

Gerti and Urlgen both scanned the area.

"There," the giantess said, pointing to the high ridge far to the west. "From there, my kin will be out of the dwarves' range and on ground as high as that of our enemies. My kin will serve as your flank and your artillery."

"A long throw for a giant."

"But not for a giant-sized catapult," said Gerti.

"There are tunnels beneath the ridge," Urlgen explained. "The dwarves have taken them and secured them. It will be difficult to—"

"As difficult as arguing your cause when your father declares that you have failed?"

That straightened Urlgen, and straightened his thinking as well.

"Take the ridge, and I will give you the warriors to secure it and to strike out against the dwarves, for the glory of us both," Gerti promised.

"No easy task."

Gerti led Urlgen's gaze back up the slope, to the piles and piles of orc bodies rotting in the morning sun, letting the implication speak for itself.

*   *   *

"Bash! They're fightin' again, and we're stuck here watching!" the old dwarf Shingles McRuff grumbled to Torgar Hammerstriker.

Torgar moved to the opening in the ridge's eastern wall, overlooking the mountain slope that had served as battlefield for so many days. Sure enough, the charge was on again in full, with orcs and goblins running up the steep ascent, howling and hooting with every stride. A look back to the south told the dwarf that his kin were ready to meet that charge, their formations already composing, Catti-brie's devastating bow already sending lines of sizzling arrows streaming out at the oncoming horde. Every now and then, there came a small explosion among the front ranks of the charging orcs, and Torgar smiled, knowing that Ivan Bouldershoulder had put that clever hand crossbow of his to work.

Even though he held all confidence that Banak and the others would stave off the assault, Torgar was soon chewing his lower lip with frustration that he and half the dwarves of Mirabar could not stand beside them.

"They were needing us here," Shingles reminded Torgar, and he dropped his hand hard onto Torgar's strong shoulder. "We're serving King Bruenor well."

"In holding tunnels that ain't getting attacked," Torgar muttered.

The words had hardly left his mouth when shouts echoed back at him and Shingles from the deeper tunnels to the north.

"Orcs!" came the cry. "Orcs in the tunnels!"

Shingles and Torgar turned wide-eyed expressions at each other, both fast shifting into snarling battle rage.

"Orcs," they muttered together.

"Orcs!" Shingles echoed loudly, for the benefit of all those dwarves nearby, particularly those back toward the southern entrance. "Get yer axes up, boys. We got orcs to kill!"

With energy, enthusiasm, and even glee, the dwarves of Mirabar set off to predetermined positions to support those farther to the north, where, they learned almost immediately from ringing steel and cries of rage and pain, the battle had already been joined.

Torgar barked out orders with every stride, reminders that he knew he really didn't have to offer to his disciplined warriors. The Mirabarran dwarves understood their places, for in the days they had been in the tunnels, they had come to know every turn in every corridor and every chamber where defenses could be, and had been, set. Still, Torgar barked reminders, and he told them to fight for the glory of Bruenor Battlehammer and Mithral Hall, their new king, their new home.

Torgar had set the defenses purposefully, designing them with every intent that he and Shingles would not be left out of the fighting. The pair rushed down one descending corridor and came out onto a ledge overlooking an oval-shaped chamber, and below they found their first orcs, engaged with a force of more than a dozen Mirabarran dwarves.

Hardly slowing, Torgar leaped from the ledge, crashing in hard among the orc ranks, bringing a pair down beside him. He was up on his feet in an instant, his axe sweeping back and forth—but in control. Shingles was airborne by that time, along with several others who had followed the pair to that room.

Those dwarves up front pressed on more forcefully with the arrival of the reinforcements, hacking their way through orcs as they tried to link up with Torgar and the others. Almost immediately, the battle turned in favor of the dwarves. Orcs fell and orcs tried to flee, but they were held up by their stubborn kin trying to filter out of the tunnel and join in the fray.

"Kill enough and they'll run off!" Torgar roared, and of course, that was indeed the expectation when fighting orcs.

Many minutes later and with the floor covered in orc blood, the dwarves had reached the tunnel entrance, driving back the invaders. With Torgar centering them, the dwarves formed an arc around the narrow opening, so that many weapons could be brought to bear against any orc that stepped through. Surprisingly, though, the orcs still came through, one after another, taking hits and climbing over the fast-piling bodies of their fallen kin. On and on they came, and five orcs fell for every dwarf that was forced back with wounds.

"Damn stubborn lot!" Shingles cried at Torgar's side.

He accentuated his shout with a smash of his hammer that laid yet another brute low.

"Too stubborn," Torgar replied—quietly, though, and under his breath.

He didn't want the others to take note of his alarm. Torgar could hardly believe that orcs were still squeezing out of that tunnel. Every other one never even got a single step back into the room before being chopped down, but still they came.

Cries echoing from the tunnels near to them told Torgar that it was not a unique occurrence in that particular battle, that his boys were being hard-pressed at every turn.

More minutes passed, and more orcs crowded into the room, and more orcs died on the floor.

Torgar glanced back at the ledge, where an appointed dwarf was waiting.

"Position two!" he cried to the young scout and the dwarf ran off, shouting the call.

"Ye heard him!" Shingles cried to the others in the room. "Tighten it up!"

As he finished, Shingles spun around a large rock that had been set in place at the side of the tunnel entrance, bracing his back against the unsteady stone.

"On yer call!" Shingles cried.

Torgar pressed his attack on the nearest orc, shifting as he swung so that he could directly confront the next creature as it tried to come out of the tunnel. Behind him, his boys went into a frenzy, finishing those in the room.

As soon as he thought the door temporarily secured, Torgar shouted, *"Now!"*

A great heave by Shingles sent the rock falling across the door, and Torgar had to scamper back to avoid getting clipped.

"Go! Go! *Go!*" Shingles cried.

The dwarves gathered up their wounded and dead and retreated fast to the opposite end of the room and out to the south.

Before they could get through that other door, though, the orcs had already breached the makeshift barricade and a pair of spears arced out, one scoring a hit on poor Shingles.

"Ah, me bum!" he cried, grabbing at the shaft that was protruding from his right buttock.

Though he already had one unconscious dwarf over his other shoulder, Torgar hooked his dearest friend under the arm and pulled him along, out of the room and down the southern tunnel, where a series of stone drops had been set in place to slow any pursuit in just such a situation. All across the tunnel complex beneath the western ridge, the dwarves were forced into organized retreats, but they had been in the tunnels for several days and that was more than any dwarves ever needed to prepare a proper defense.

Torgar was back in battle soon enough, and even a limping Shingles returned to his side, hammer swinging with abandon. They and a handful of other dwarves had made a stand in a stalagmite-filled room that sloped up to the south behind them. Figuring to make the orcs pay for every foot of ground across the wide chamber, the dwarves battled furiously, and again, the orc blood began to flow and the orc bodies began to pile.

But still the stubborn creatures came on.

"Damn stupid lot!" Shingles cried out yet again.

Torgar didn't bother replying to the obvious or to the hidden message of his friend. They were beginning to catch on that the orcs meant to take the tunnels, whatever the cost. That troublesome thought only gained even more credence a few moments later when another group of dwarves unexpectedly crashed into the room from a western corridor.

"Giants!" they cried before Torgar could even ask them why they had abandoned the organized retreat that would have had them bypassing that chamber altogether. "Giants in the tunnels!"

"Giants?" Shingles echoed. "Too low for giants!"

The dwarves charged across and launched themselves into the fray, slaughtering the orcs that stood between them and Torgar's group.

"Giants!" one insisted when he came up before the leader.

Torgar didn't question him, for in looking over his shoulder, the dwarf leader saw the truth of the words in the form of a giant, a giantess actually, crouching, even crawling in places, to arrive at the entrance of the western corridor.

"Get that one!" Torgar demanded, eager to claim that greater prize.

His boys rushed past him, and past those who had just entered, lifting warhammers to throw and ignoring the warning cries of their newly arrived companions to stay back.

A dozen hammers went spinning across the expanse, and every throw seemed true—until the missile neared the pale, bluish-skinned creature and simply veered away.

"Magic?" Torgar whispered.

Almost as if she had heard him, almost as if she was mocking him, the giantess smiled wickedly and waggled her fingers.

Torgar's boys began their charge.

Then they were stumbling, slipping, and blinded, as a sudden burst of sleet filled the room, slicking up the floor.

"Close ranks!" Torgar shouted above the din of the magical storm.

A bright burst of fire appeared, reaching down from the chamber's ceiling and immolating a trio of dwarves who were trying to do just that.

"Run away!" yelled Shingles.

"No," Torgar muttered, and with rage burning in his eyes almost as brightly as the magical fire of the giantess, the refugee from Mirabar stalked through the sleet at the kneeling behemoth.

She looked at him, her eyes blazing with hatred, and she began to mutter yet another spell.

Torgar increased his stride into a run and lifted his axe. He roared above the din, denying the storm, denying his fear, denying all the magic.

Two strides away, he threw himself forward.

And he was hit by wracking pains, by a sudden, inexplicable magical grasp that closed upon his heart and stiffened him in midflight. He tried to bring his arms forward to strike with his axe, but they wouldn't move to his call. He could not get past that burst of agony, that grasp of ultimate pain.

Torgar smashed into the giantess, who didn't move an inch, and he bounced away. He tried to hold his balance for just a moment, but his legs were as useless as his arms. Torgar fell back several stumbling steps. He stared at the giantess curiously, incredulously.

Then he fell over.

Behind him, dwarves swarmed into the room, crying for their leader, bending their backs against the continuing sleet, and Gerti (for it was indeed Gerti herself who had entered the fray), her most powerful enchantments spent, wisely retreated, covering her departure by launching a host of orcs into the fray behind her.

Ignoring the pain in his rump, ignoring the fresh flow of blood down the back of his leg and the new wounds, Shingles scrambled to Torgar's side. He slapped Torgar hard across the face and shouted for him to wake up.

Gasping, Torgar did manage to look at his friend.

"Hurts," he whispered. "By Moradin, she's crushed me heart!"

"Bah, but yer heart's stone," Shingles growled at him. "So quit yer whinin'!"

And with that, Shingles hoisted Torgar over his shoulder and started back the other way, determinedly and carefully putting one foot in front of the other as he struggled up the icy slope with his dear friend.

They did get out of the room and out of many more, and while the fighting raged outside, the dwarves from Mirabar battled and battled for every inch of ground.

But stubborn indeed were the orcs, and willing to lose ten-to-one against their enemies. By the sheer weight of numbers, they gained ground, corridor to corridor and room to room.

Back near the southern end of the tunnel complex, Shingles reluctantly ordered the last and most definitive ceiling drops.

He told all his boys, even the wounded, "Ye dig in and be ready to die for the honor o' Mithral Hall. They took us in as brothers, and we'll not fail them Battlehammers now."

A cheer went up around him, but he could hear the shallowness of it. For nearly a third of their four hundred were down, including Torgar, their heart and soul.

But the dwarves did as Shingles ordered, without a word of complaint. The last ground in the tunnels, the first ground they had claimed in entering the complex, was the best prepared of all, and if the orcs meant to push them back out the exits near to the cliff overlooking Keeper's Dale, they were going to lose hundreds in the process.

The dwarves dug in and waited.

They propped those with torn legs against secure backing and gave them lighter weapons to swing, and waited.

They wrapped their more garish wounds without complaint, some even tying weapons to broken hands, and waited.

They kissed their dead good-bye and waited.

But the orcs, with three quarters of the ridge complex conquered, did not come on.

"The most stubborn they been yet," Banak observed when the orcs and goblins finally turned and retreated down the slope. For more than an hour they had come on, throwing themselves into the fray with abandon, and the last battle piled more orc and goblin bodies on the blood-slicked slope than all the previous fights combined. And through it all, the dwarves had held tight to their formations and tight to their defensible positions, and never once had the orcs seemed on the verge of victory.

But still they had come on

"Stubborn? Or stupid?" Tred McKnuckles replied.

"Stupid," Ivan Bouldershoulder decided.

His brother added, "Hee hee h—"

Pikel's laugh was cut short, and Banak's response did not get past his lips, for only then did they see the very telling movement in the west of Torgar's retreat, only then did they see the lines of wounded dwarves streaming out of the tunnels, those able enough carrying dead kin.

"By Moradin," Banak breathed, realizing then that the huge battle on the open slopes had been nothing more than a ruse designed to prevent reinforcements from flocking to Torgar's ranks.

Banak squinted, a prolonged wince, as the lines of limping wounded and borne dead continued to stream out from the southern entrance of the complex. Those dwarves had just joined Mithral Hall—most of them had never even seen the place that had drawn them from the safety of their Mirabar homes.

"The retreat's organized," Ivan Bouldershoulder observed. "They didn't get routed, just pushed back, I'm guessin'."

"Go find Torgar," Banak instructed. "Or whoever it is that's in charge. See if he's needing our help!"

With an "Oo oi!" from Pikel, the Bouldershoulders rushed off.

Tred offered a nod to Banak and ran right behind.

Two others came up to the dwarf leader at just that moment, grim-faced and covered in orc blood.

"What's the point of it?" Catti-brie asked, observing the lines. "They gave so many dead to take the tunnels, but what good are those tunnels to them anyway? None connect to Mithral Hall proper—not even close."

"But they don't know that," said Banak.

Catti-brie didn't buy it. Something else was going on, she believed, and when she looked at Wulfgar, she could see that he was thinking the same way.

"Let's go," Wulfgar offered.

"I got them Bouldershoulders and Tred going to Torgar now," Banak told him.

Wulfgar shook his head. "Not going to Torgar," he corrected. "There is nothing in those tunnels worth this to our enemies," he added, sweeping his arm out to highlight the sheer carnage about the mountain slopes.

Banak nodded his agreement but kept his real fear unspoken. It was coming clearer to him and to the others, he knew, why the orcs had so desperately played for those tunnels.

Giants.

Wulfgar and Catti-brie sprinted away, actually catching and passing by the three dwarves heading to find Torgar.

"We're going up top," Catti-brie explained to them.

"Then take me brother!" Ivan called. "He's more help out of doors than in."

"Me brudder!" shouted Pikel, and he veered from his dwarf companions toward the duo.

Without complaint, having long before learned to not underestimate and to appreciate the dwarf "doo-dad," Catti-brie and Wulfgar continued along. They got to the southern end of the ridge and began to scale, beside the tunnel entrance from which came the line of wounded.

"We're holding!" one badly injured but still-walking dwarf proudly called to them.

"We never doubted that ye would!" Catti-brie yelled back, allowing her Dwarvish accent to strike hard into her inflection. In response, the dwarf punched a fist into the air. The movement had him grimacing with pain, though he tried hard not to let it show.

Wulfgar led the way up the rocky incline, his great strength and long legs allowing him to scale the broken wall easily. At every difficult juncture, he stopped and turned, reaching down and easily hoisting Catti-brie up beside him. A couple of points presented a more difficult challenge concerning short Pikel, though, for even lying flat on the stone, Wulfgar couldn't reach back that low.

Pikel merely smiled and waved him back, then went into a series of gyrations and chanting, then stopped and stared at the flat stone incline, giggling all the while. The green-bearded dwarf reached forward, his hand going right into the suddenly malleable stone. He reshaped it into one small step after another. Then, giggling still, the dwarf simply walked up beside the two humans and motioned them to move along.

The top of the ridgeline was broken and uneven but certainly navigable, even with the wind howling across the trio, left to right. Downwind as they were of the western slopes, they actually caught scent of the enemy before ever seeing them.

They fell back behind a high jut and watched as the first frost giant climbed to the ridge top.

Catti-brie put up Taulmaril and took deadly aim, but Pikel grabbed the arrow, shook his hairy head, and waggled the finger of his free hand before her, then pointed out to the north.

Where more giants were coming up.

"One shot," Wulfgar whispered. He grasped Aegis-fang tightly. "Be running as you let fly."

"Ready," Catti-brie assured him, and she motioned for Pikel to let go of her arrow, then for him to be off.

With a porcine squeal, Pikel sprinted out from behind the jut, running full out to the south. The nearest giant howled and pointed and started to give chase.

But then a streaking arrow hit the behemoth in the chest, staggering him backward, and a spinning warhammer followed the shot, striking in almost exactly the same place. The giant staggered more and tumbled off the western side of the ridge.

Wulfgar and Catti-brie heard the roar but didn't see it, for they were already in a dead run. They caught up to Pikel near to the southern descent, and without a word, Wulfgar merely scooped the dwarf up in his powerful grasp and ran on, hopping from ledge to ledge all the way back to the ground. Soon after they came down, boulders began to skip all around them, and the trio worked hard to help those dwarves still in the area back into the shelter of the tunnel.

Not so far in, they rejoined Ivan and Tred, along with Shingles McRuff and a very shaken Torgar Hammerstriker.

"Casters," Shingles explained to them. "Giant witch reached out and nearly crushed me friend's heart!"

As he finished, he patted Torgar on the shoulder, but gently.

"Hurts," Torgar remarked, his voice barely audible. "Hurts a lot."

"Bah, ye're too tough to fall to a simple witch trick," Shingles assured his friend, and he started to slap Torgar again, but Torgar held up a hand to deny the blow.

"Giants up above," Wulfgar explained to the dwarves. "We should move in deeper in case they come down."

"They won't move south," Catti-brie reasoned. "They wanted the high ground, and so they got it."

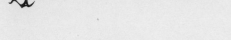

"And them orcs ain't coming on anymore, neither," said Shingles. "We dropped the roof on them, but they could've gotten to us by now if they'd wanted to."

"They have what they came for," Catti-brie replied.

She glanced back to the southern exit, and all seemed calm again, the rock shower having ended. Still, Wulfgar and the others gave it some time before daring to exit the tunnel again. The long shadows of twilight greeted them, along with an unsettling quiet that had descended over the region.

Catti-brie looked back to the main dwarven force, far to the east.

"Too far for a giant's throw," she said, and she glanced back up at the ridge.

Wulfgar started up immediately, and the woman went right behind. Back on the ridge top, even in the deepening gloom of night, they quickly came to understand what the assault had been all about. Far to the north on the ridge, giants were hauling huge logs up the western slope, while others were assembling those logs into gigantic war engines. Catti-brie looked back to the dwarves' position, with alarm. The distance was too far for a giant's throw, indeed, but was it too far for the throw of a giant-sized catapult?

At that moment, it truly hit the woman just how much trouble they were in. For the orcs to sacrifice so many, for them to allow hundreds of their kin to be slaughtered simply to earn a tactical advantage in the preparation of the battlefield, revealed a level of commitment and cunning far beyond anything the woman had ever seen from the wretched, pig-faced creatures.

"Bruenor's often said that the only reason the orcs and goblins didn't take over the North was that the orcs and goblins were too stupid to fight together," the woman whispered to Wulfgar.

"And now Bruenor is dead, or soon will be," Wulfgar replied.

His grim tone confirmed to Catti-brie that he had come to fathom the situation along similar lines.

They were in trouble.

13

DEFINING THE BORDER

"By the gods, old William, ye could sleep the day away gettin' ready for yer nighttime rest," said Brusco Brawnanvil, first cousin to Banak, the war leader who was making his amazing reputation across the mountains to the west, on the other side of Mithral Hall.

"Yep," old William—Bill to his friends—HuskenNugget answered, and he let his head slide back to rest against the stone wall of the small tower marking the eastern entrance to the dwarven stronghold. Below their position, the Surbrin flowed mightily past, sparkling in the afternoon light.

Soon after the first reports had filtered back to Mithral Hall of monsters stirring in the North, a substantial encampment had been constructed just north of their current position, along the high ground of a mountain arm. But with the desperate retreat from Shallows and the advent of the war in the west, that camp had been all but abandoned, with only a few forward scouts left behind. The dwarves simply didn't have any to spare, and the orcs were pressing them hard in the mountains north of Keeper's Dale. Rumors from Nesmé had forced Clan Battlehammer to tighten the defenses of their tunnels as well, fearing an underground assault.

In the east, there was nothing but the dance of the Surbrin and the long hours of boredom, made worse for the veteran dwarves because of their knowledge that their kin were fighting and dying in the west.

Thus, with Banak, Pwent, and their charges—along with the dwarves of Mirabar—making their names in a heroic stand against the pursuing hordes, Brusco, Bill, and the others still in the east just closed their eyes and rested their heads and hoped there'd be orcs enough for them to kill before the war ended.

"Ain't seen Filbedo in a few days," Brusco remarked.

Bill cracked open one sleepy eye and said, "He went through to the west, and out across Keeper's Dale, from what I'm hearing."

"Aye, that he did," said Kingred Doughbeard, who was up above them in the tower, sitting beside the open trapdoor, his back resting along the waist-high wall that ringed the structure's top. "We're not to be relieved fifteen for fifteen no more. Only twenty-five of us left on this side o' the halls, so some'll be pulling shifts two times in a row."

"Bah!" Brusco snorted. "Wished they'd asked. I'd've gone off to the west!"

"So would us all," Kingred answered, and he gave a snort. "Exceptin' Bill there. Bill's just looking to sleep."

"Yep," Bill agreed. "And I'll take the two-times watch. Three times, if ye're wanting. Nine Hells, I'll stay out here all day and all the night."

"Snoring all the while," said Kingred.

"Yep," said Bill.

"Found himself a comfortable spot," Brusco remarked and Kingred laughed again.

"Yep," said Bill.

"Well, if ye're gonna sleep, then switch with Kingred," Brusco demanded. "Give me someone to roll bones with, at least."

"Yep," said Bill.

He yawned and somehow rolled to his side and up on his feet, then wearily began to climb.

The noise below, of Kingred, Brusco, and a couple of others they had coaxed from the tunnels to join in their gambling, did little to inhibit the ever-tired dwarf, and soon he was snoring contentedly.

Halfway up the outside wall of the tower, nestled in the dark crevice where the shaped tower edge met the natural stone of the mountain wall, Tos'un Armgo heard the entire conversation. The drow paused at one comfortable juncture and waited, cursing silently—and not for the first time!—the absence of Donnia and Ad'non. They were the stealthy ones of the group, after all, whereas Tos'un was

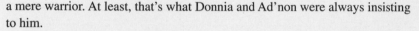

a mere warrior. At least, that's what Donnia and Ad'non were always insisting to him.

Kaer'lic had given Tos'un a few enchantments to help him as he ran forward scout for Obould, but still, he wasn't overly thrilled with being so exposed, out alone in a nest of tough dwarves.

Obould wasn't far behind, he told himself. Likely the orc and his minions would overrun the feeble defenses of the encampment to the north within a short time.

That notion made the drow take a deep breath and turn around, picking his handholds. The cursed, burning ball of fire in the sky had moved behind the mountains by this time, thankfully, extended long shadows over all the area on this eastern slope. Still, it was uncomfortably light by Tos'un's estimations.

But it was growing darker.

The time of the drow.

Brusco blew into his cupped hands, then shook them vigorously, rolling the bones around in the cup of his gnarly fingers and callused palms. Then he blew into them again and whispered a quick prayer to Dumathoin, the god of secrets under the mountain.

He repeated the process, and again, until the other dwarves around the cleared, rolling area began complaining, and one even cuffed him off the back of the head.

"Throw the damned things, will ye?"

Of course, the dwarf's annoyance had an awful lot to do with the fact that most of the silver pieces were set before Brusco by that point, as the dwarf had gotten onto a winning streak since sunset, some hours before.

"Gotta wait for good ol' Dum to tell me what's what," Brusco replied.

"Throw the damned things!" several shouted at once.

"Bah!" Brusco snorted and brought his hands back to roll.

And a horn blew, loud and clear and insistent, and all the dwarves froze in place.

"South?" one asked.

The horn blew again. Expecting it, they were able to discern that it had indeed come from the south.

"What d'ye see, Bill?" Kingred called up.

The others scrambled out of the tower, moving to higher points so that they could look for the signal fires from their watch-outposts in the southland.

"Bill?" Kingred called again. "Wake up, ye dolt! Bill!"

No answer.

And no snoring, Kingred realized, and there had been none for some time.

"Bill?" he asked again, more quietly and more concerned.

"What do ye know?" asked Brusco, running back in.

Kingred stared up, his expression speaking volumes to the other dwarf.

"Bill?" Brusco shouted.

He rushed to the ladder and began a fast climb.

"Trolls to the south!" came a cry from outside, from the distance. "Trolls to the south!"

Brusco paused on the ladder and thought, Trolls? What in the Nine Hells are trolls doing up here?

Another horn blew, from the north.

"Get to the crawls!" Brusco shouted down to Kingred. "Get 'em all to the crawls and get ready to shut 'em tight!"

Kingred scrambled out, and Brusco looked back up the ladder. He could see one of Bill's feet, hanging out over the open trapdoor.

"Bill?" he called again.

The foot didn't move at all.

A nauseous feeling came over Brusco then, and he forced himself up, slowly, hand over hand. Just below the lip, he slowly reached up and grabbed Bill's foot, giving it a tug.

"Bill?"

No movement, no response, no snoring.

And suddenly, Brusco was blind, completely in darkness. Instinctively, he simply let go and tucked, dropping to the stone floor and landing in a bumpy roll. By the time he came out of it, the veteran warrior had his sword in hand, and he was glad at least to find that he was not blind, that the spell that had dropped over him was an area of darkness and nothing that had actually affected his vision.

"Get in here!" he cried to his companions. "Magic! And something's got Bill!"

Other dwarves, led by Kingred, charged back into the tower.

"Set a catch blanket!" Brusco ordered.

He rushed back to the base of the ladder and started up again, moving much more quickly. The other dwarves grabbed a pair of blankets, doubling them up. Each taking a corner, they stretched it wide under the trapdoor.

They heard a commotion above, shouts from Brusco for Bill, and a grunt.

A dwarf came tumbling down, hitting the side of the blanket and rolling off to thud hard against the floor.

"Bill!" the four dwarves cried together, abandoning the blanket and rushing to their fallen comrade, a bright line of blood showing across his throat.

"Get him in to a priest!" one cried, and began to drag Bill away.

The dwarves rolled toward the door, then stopped and shouted for Brusco when they heard another commotion up above.

Brusco fell from the darkness, landing hard on the floor. He tried to stand and staggered to the side and would have fallen had not Kingred rushed over and caught him.

"Damned thing sticked me!" Brusco gasped.

He reached back and brought a blood-covered hand back in front. All strength left him then, and Kingred had to set himself firmly to hold the heavy dwarf up.

"A hand!" he called, and another dwarf rushed to the opposite side of the wounded Brusco.

"To the crawls," Brusco managed to remind them, coughing blood between each word.

By the time they got out of the small tower, two carrying Bill and two supporting Brusco, they caught sight of other companions charging up from the south and heard the calls of those rushing back from the north as well.

In the south, they shouted, *"Trolls!"*

From the north came the cries of, *"Orcs!"*

Kingred handed Brusco over fully to the other dwarf and sprinted ahead, drawing a hammer from his belt as he approached the huge iron doors of Mithral Hall. He went in hard, hammering away, once, twice . . . a pause, and a third time. He waited a few moments and banged out the coded signal again and again, and more emphatically when he thought he heard the locking bar being lifted behind the door.

The last thing he wanted at that moment was for those impregnable doors to open!

A grinding noise began off to the side of the main entrance and a small rock slid aside, revealing a dark crawl tunnel. In went the dwarves, one after another, with Kingred standing beside the tunnel, urging them on. Dwarves came from the north and from the south, each group barely outdistancing the advancing force—trolls in the south, orcs in the north. Kingred saw the truth of it; even though a second crawl tunnel had been opened, all the dwarves couldn't possibly get in ahead of the monsters. He almost called for his fellows to open the main doors then, but he held off the urge and bit back his fear. He and some others would have to stay out, would have to hold back the invaders to the bitter end.

Kingred took up his sword and strapped on a shield, and he continued to order those rushing up into the crawls.

"Go! Go! Go!" he called to them. "Keep yer butt down and keep yer butt moving!"

The trolls were the first monsters to arrive, their horrid stench filling Kingred's nostrils as he rushed out to meet them. His strong arms worked tirelessly, slashing away at the beasts, driving them back. A claw raked his shoulder, drawing a deep line, but he shrugged it off and turned, swinging, at that attacker. One after another, Kingred drove them back. Fighting like a dwarf possessed, a dwarf who knew that all, for him, was lost, Kingred growled and pressed on.

A great two-headed troll, as ugly as any creature Kingred had ever seen, as ugly a nightmare as Kingred had ever believed possible, shoved some of the other trolls out of the way and stepped up before him. Swallowing his fear, Kingred roared and charged headlong into the beast, but a huge spiked club whipped across to intercept and the dwarf was lifted from the ground and launched far, far away.

At that moment, the orcs arrived on the scene, sweeping down from the north, howling and hooting and throwing stones as they charged in with abandon.

"We got a dozen left out there!" cried Bayle Rockhunter, one of the inner gate guards. "Open them durned doors!"

The dwarf slapped a heavy pick across his hands and charged for the portal, and many others fell in behind him.

"It ain't to be done!" the wounded Brusco cried. "Ye know yer place!"

That reminder slowed the charge to the great doors—portals that were not to be opened in any event without express permission from the clan leaders back in the western reaches of the complex. The dwarves at the eastern gate were not an army by any means, but merely lookouts and sentries, holding the hall at all costs. Opening those doors would be engaging an apparently powerful force, one that could then flow into the hall.

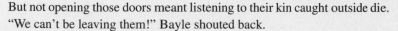

But not opening those doors meant listening to their kin caught outside die.

"We can't be leaving them!" Bayle shouted back.

"Then ye're stealing all meaning from their deaths," Brusco responded, much more quietly.

That tone as much as the words themselves seemed to steal all the fire from the angry young dwarf.

"Hold the crawl tunnels open as long as ye can," another dwarf remarked.

Two score dwarves got into the safety of Mithral Hall that fateful evening, while some dozen stood with Kingred outside the crawl tunnels and the great, barred doors. Eventually, those inside reluctantly pulled the levers that dropped the counterweights that slid the stones back over the crawl entrances, sealing their kin outside, sealing their fate. Brusco and the others shut the crawl tunnels with heavy hearts and with promises that Kingred and the others wouldn't be forgotten, that songs would be written and sung, tavern to tavern.

King Obould, Gerti Orelsdottr, and Proffit the troll stood back from the tower and the doors, watching the work as giants, orcs, and trolls piled heavy stones before Mithral Hall's eastern entrance. All sound from inside the hall indicated that the dwarves were doing likewise, but Obould didn't want to take any chances. His goal had been to seal the eastern gates, and so he was doing just that.

"The land is ours to the Surbrin," the orc announced to his fellow leaders. From the shadows, Kaer'lic and Tos'un listened carefully.

He forgets that his son has not quite sealed in the dwarves, as yet, Kaer'lic flashed to her companion.

Tos'un appreciated the sarcasm, though he was more impressed with Obould's progress. Given the pressure that Urlgen was placing on Clan Battlehammer in the west, the victory had been all too easy. A few dead orcs, a few dead dwarves, and Obould controlled the western bank of the Surbrin, all the way from the Spine of the World to the end of the mountains south of Mithral Hall. With defensive positions already being constructed along the river north of their current position, that was no small thing.

"The dwarves will find another way out," Gerti remarked, and Tos'un could tell that she, like Kaer'lic, simply wanted to deflate the glorious orc king a bit.

Obould offered a quick scowl at the giantess but turned his attention to the two-headed troll, Proffit.

"You have done well," he congratulated. "Your march was impressive."

"Troll no . . ." said the left-side head.

". . . get tired," added the right.

"And so you will go right back to the south when we are finished here," Obould said, and both heads nodded.

"We stretch our line the length of the Surbrin," Obould explained to Gerti. "Hold our gains against any who would deny them. And our main force goes back to the west and north."

"And Proffit goes back to the Trollmoors?" Gerti asked.

Her disgust for the smelly troll was easy to see.

"To the tunnels in the south," Obould corrected. "Tunnels that connect to Mithral Hall. Proffit and his people will begin the battle for the dwarven stronghold within. We will defeat the dwarves without and claim our new kingdom."

He has a vision, Kaer'lic flashed.

Tos'un hid his smile, for he could tell that his companion was growing very uneasy with Obould. The four clever drow had incited all of it, but never had they actually believed that Obould would orchestrate something definitive and winnable! What would happen, Tos'un wondered (and he knew that his drow companions were also wondering), if the orc king managed to secure all the North between the Trollmoors and the Spine of the World, from the Surbrin to the Fell Pass? What would happen if, with such a base to serve as a kingdom, Obould did finally rout the dwarves from Mithral Hall? What would Silverymoon do? Or Mirabar? Or Citadel Adbar or Citadel Felbarr?

What could they do? More orcs were pouring forth from the mountains, by all reports. Had Tos'un and his companions inadvertently elevated Obould beyond their control?

An orc kingdom nestled within the various strongholds—human, dwarf, and elf. Would other tribes flock in to join in Obould's glory? Would Obould seek treaties, perhaps, and trade with the other cities?

It all seemed so preposterous to Tos'un, and also amusing. When he looked at Gerti, though, her expression grim even as she outwardly agreed with the orc king, the dark elf was reminded that there remained many potential pitfalls.

Only then did Tos'un realize that Kaer'lic was walking out to join the three leaders and that Obould was calling to him as well. He moved out beside the priestess of Lolth.

"You go with Proffit," Obould instructed the warrior of Barrison Del'Armgo.

"I?" Tos'un asked incredulously, and with more than a little revulsion at the less than appetizing thought.

"Proffit will travel the upper Underdark to do battle with the dwarves," Obould explained. "Much as your city did."

Tos'un looked at Kaer'lic with surprise, wondering how the orc king might have garnered that information.

It is for the best, Kaer'lic secretly flashed to him, alleviating all his doubts concerning the source.

"You know the tunnels leading to Mithral Hall," Obould reasoned to Tos'un. "You have been there."

"I know little," the drow argued.

"And that is more than anyone else," said Obould. "We must soon begin our attack within the hall, if the surface is to be secured. You will guide Proffit in this hunt."

There was no debate in Obould's tone, and when Tos'un started to argue anyway, Kaer'lic flashed an emphatic, *It is better!*

"I will go with him," Kaer'lic then announced. "I know some tunnels, and better for Proffit to have two dark elves directing his forces."

Obould nodded and turned to other matters, mostly the continuing sealing of the great doors.

Why have you done this? Tos'un's fingers asked Kaer'lic as the pair drifted back from the main conversation.

We should be away, came the reply.

What of Ad'non and Donnia?

Kaer'lic shrugged and replied, *They will fend for themselves. They always do. For now, it is best that we go to the south.*

Why?

Because Drizzt Do'Urden is in the north.

Tos'un stared curiously at his surprising companion. Kaer'lic had expressed great concern about Drizzt, but to go far away simply because the renegade drow was operating in the region? It made no sense.

He couldn't know Kaer'lic's suspicions, though. Ever since Tos'un had joined the band of renegades with his tales of Menzoberranzan's Mithral Hall disaster, Kaer'lic Suun Wett had feared that Drizzt Do'Urden might be something more than any of the Menzoberranyr drow had ever appreciated.

Beyond his fighting skills, there was something special about that particular renegade drow, something god-blessed. Kaer'lic had always been a clever one, but she almost hated her cunning, for in the grip of her suspicions, the drow priestess understood that she might be, in effect, condemning herself. Might that not be the price of enlightenment?

Unknown to her companions, the priestess of Lolth was convinced of something both unnerving and perfectly wicked: Drizzt Do'Urden had the favor of Lolth.

ELVEN GNATS

Weapons flying, feet flapping, the two orcs had no desire to continue any battle with the deadly elf warrior on his flying horse—seeing three of their kin already down and dead was more than enough for their cowardly sensibilities, so they threw their weapons and ran away, sprinting along the rocky trail and shouting for help.

Behind and above them came the elf, astride his beautiful white charger, great wings driving them on. The orcs couldn't outrun him, certainly, nor could they hide unless they found a way underground.

And they would not, the elf knew.

He brought Sunrise out to the left, herding the pair back on the main, narrow trail.

Oblivious to anything but the pegasus and the elf, the orcs willingly veered and ran on at full speed. They came around a bend, one behind the other, and charged up a slight incline around another boulder.

At least, they tried to get around the boulder.

The second elf appeared, as beautiful as she was deadly. She came out in a spin from the left, from behind the boulder. The lead orc gave a shriek and stopped cold, throwing its hands out before it, but the elf didn't even strike at it. She rolled right around it, using the orc as an optical barrier to its running partner. The second orc pulled up fast, seeing its companion unexpectedly stopped, and didn't even notice the lithe form coming around on its companion's right until it was too late.

A sword skewered the orc through the chest.

The first orc opened its eyes again, and thought it had survived the attack, that the female elf had somehow gone right past it. Apparently, not one to pause and consider such a fortunate turn, the orc started to run again.

It got almost one full step before a sword bit it in the kidney. It got almost a second full step before the blade struck again. It got almost a third full step before the deadly sword came in yet again, across the back of its neck.

"I'm beginning to understand why Drizzt Do'Urden enjoys this existence," Tarathiel remarked, walking his mount up beside Innovindil.

"I do not think he enjoys it," Innovindil replied. She looked out across the rocks and gave a whistle. Sunset appeared, trotting her way. "He is driven by rage and is beyond all joy. We saw that when we came to his aid. He could not even accept our generosity."

Tarathiel wiped his bloody sword on the ratty tunic of one felled orc. His partner was right, he knew. He had hoped to begin a relationship with the dark elf when he and Innovindil had come upon Drizzt at the river. Tarathiel had hoped to speak with him about Ellifain, to learn what he might about her or to warn Drizzt that she was beyond reason and hunting for him.

But their discussion that day had never gotten even close to that point, and for exactly the reasons Innovindil had just espoused.

"Somewhere deep inside him, he must take some pleasure at killing these foul creatures," Tarathiel did respond. "He must recognize that his actions are for the betterment of the world."

"Let us hope," said Innovindil, in a less-than-convincing tone.

She looked up and around as she spoke, as if scanning for some sign of Drizzt.

The two moved along soon after, knowing that other orcs were converging on the area, rushing to investigate the screams of the five orcs the elves had killed. They kept the pegasi on the ground for the most part, trotting along, but used the flying mounts to cross ravines and small cliff faces to discourage any pursuit. They held high confidence that the grounded orcs could not possibly catch up.

The elves didn't return directly to their cave that night, though, preferring to scout out even wider in search of more prey.

Drizzt might be acting out of rage, but for Tarathiel and Innovindil, there was indeed a sense of accomplishment and even pleasure at the sport. And there was no shortage of orcs to hunt.

Donnia didn't even have to signal her pleasure to Ad'non when the glow of warmth led them to the pile of manure, for her evil smile summed it up perfectly.

Ad'non's expression showed that he was no less pleased.

The drow could see that most of the heat was gone from the pile, and they had a point of reference so that they could use that to determine the time the manure had been there. Dark elves were taught to judge heat dissipation from droppings from an early age, and the pile was similar in texture and size to that typical of the rothé cattle the dark elves farmed in their underground cities.

The pair flashed coordinating messages, and they set off on a roundabout path up the mountainside. Moving from bluff to bluff, from stone to stone, and from tree to tree, the pair made leap-frogging progress. Another pile of manure brought grins.

Then some more, down below them as they looked out from a flat stone.

Cave, Ad'non signaled, falling to his belly off to Donnia's right.

The two dark elves didn't know it, but they were atop the very same stone from which Drizzt had first glimpsed the cave of Tarathiel and Innovindil.

Donnia flicked a series of signals back to Ad'non, then slid forward on her belly to the very lip of the flat stone. A glance around and at Ad'non to ensure that he had his hand crossbow at the ready, and Donnia rolled right over the stone, holding securely to its lip, then skipping down the ten feet to hit the ground running across from the cave. At the side of the dark entrance, she drew out sword and hand crossbow.

Up above, Ad'non went over in a similar manner and quick-stepped his way to the wall opposite the entrance from Donnia.

Warm ashes within, Donnia flashed, a sure sign that the place was being used as a campsite.

Ad'non fell low and peered around, taking his time with the scan.

Empty, he silently told his companion. *But not deserted.*

Neither had to signal the other that they should set an ambush.

The drow elves moved around outside the cave, looking for some promising vantage points for an ambush. They didn't remain too close to the entrance, though, nor did they go in, showing proper respect for their dangerous adversaries. Soon after, Donnia stumbled upon something even more promising: a second cave.

This one is deeper, she signaled.

Ad'non came up to the lip of the small tunnel. He studied the descent within and the general angle of the corridor, then measured both against the location of the cave the surface elves were obviously using as a base. He motioned Donnia back, then fell to his belly and turned his head away as he gingerly slid his hand into the cave, delicate and practiced fingers working around the rim in search of any cunning traps. Gradually, Ad'non's arm went in deeper, feeling every inch.

With a glance at Donnia, the drow male slithered into the small hole, disappearing from view.

Donnia moved to the lip and glanced in just in time to see Ad'non's feet slip around the first bend in the corridor. With a look all around, she gently put one ear to the stone. The tapping of a predetermined code sent her into motion, falling flat and slipping in. The going was tight and tighter still when she worked around that first bend, and she came to a hole in the floor that could be negotiated only by going in head first, and blindly. Few rational creatures would have continued through such an uncomfortable obstacle, but to the dark elves, who had spent so many decades working through countless similar corridors in the honeycombed Underdark, it was not so daunting.

The corridor below the hole was a bit wider, though the ceiling was too low for Donnia to lift her head as she crawled along. It widened even more and opened into a higher chamber, and there she found her companion, sitting on a stone.

We should go down lower, Ad'non reasoned, and he motioned to the several choices offered to them: a pair of corridors winding out of the chamber, a wider area up a steep incline that seemed to extend over a wall of piled stones, and a broken-walled, rocky hole winding down deeper.

Donnia knew better than to argue with Ad'non concerning underground direction sense, for the scout had always shown a remarkable ability to navigate such tunnels. He was possessed of a keen instinct for that type of searching, as if he could innately sense the structure of any cave complex, as if he could somehow step back from the smaller areas visible to them at any given time and view the whole of the region. Perhaps it was the flow of the air or gradations of heat or light, but however he did it, Ad'non always seemed to follow the best course along a maze of tunnels.

And sure enough, after squeezing down the rocky shaft, crawling under a low overhang of rock and following yet another winding tunnel, the dark elves came into a small chamber. A slight breeze blew through the far wall. Not much of a wind, but one that sounded clearly to the keen ears of the drow.

Dead end? Donnia asked.

Ad'non signed her to be patient, then he moved to that far wall and began feeling along the stone. He looked back and grinned wickedly, and when Donnia rushed up to join him, she soon understood.

For they had come into a chamber adjacent to the cave the surface elves were using as their camp, and while there was no access between the chambers, the dark elves were able to work enough of the stone to give them a view of the other room.

They carefully replaced the stones and went back out into the night.

Drizzt went down to one knee and stared out across the early-morning landscape. Mist rose from the many mountain streams, dulling the sharp lines of ridges and outcroppings and adding a surreal quality to the morning light, dispersing it in a haze of orange and yellow. That mist dulled the sounds, too. The cry of birds, the rumble of loose stones, the babble of running water.

The scream of orcs.

Drizzt followed those screams out across a valley to another ridge across the way, and he made out the winged form of one pegasus, lifting into the air, then diving suddenly, and again, while its rider let fly a line of arrows from a longbow.

That would be Tarathiel, Drizzt supposed, for he was usually the one chasing the orcs into Innovindil's ambush.

Drizzt shook his head and gave a grin at their efficiency, for the pair had been out hunting before the last sunset and were out again at the first signs of dawn. He doubted that they had even returned to their cave during the night. He watched the chase a bit longer, then padded off softly for a secluded glade that he knew of nearby. Once there, he found a quiet place off to the side where he could watch the grassy area unnoticed, and he waited.

Sure enough, barely half an hour later, a pair of pegasi trotted onto the meadow, the two elves walking beside them and talking easily. The mounts needed to rest and to eat and needed to be wiped down as well, for their white coats glistened with sweat.

Drizzt had figured as much, and thus, he had expected the elf pair. Once again, the thought of going to them nagged at him. Was it not his responsibility to tell them of Ellifain and the tragedy in the west?

And yet, as the minutes passed, with Tarathiel and Innovindil untacking the pegasi, the drow did not move.

He watched their movements as they gently watered down the marvelous steeds with water from a nearby brook. He watched Tarathiel bring a bucket up before each pegasus in turn, gently stroking the sides of their heads as they bent low to drink. He watched Innovindil bring forth some type of root. She put it in her mouth and stood before her mount teasingly, and the pegasus reached out and took the root from her in what could only be described as a kiss. The stallion reared then, but not threateningly, and Innovindil merely laughed and did not move as the great equine creature waved its front hooves in the air before her.

Drizzt's hand went to his belt pouch and the onyx figurine at the sight of the intimate interaction, for the way Tarathiel and Innovindil acted with their pegasi seemed a deeper level than master and creature, seemed a friendship more than anything else. Drizzt above all others understood such a relationship.

Again the drow felt the urge to go to them, to talk to them and to tell them the truth. He paused and looked down, then closed his eyes and relived that fateful battle with the disturbed Ellifain. For many minutes, he sat there quietly, remembering the encounter and the one previous with Ellifain, in the Moonwood and with Tarathiel nearby. He understood the pain Tarathiel would feel upon hearing of Ellifain's fate, for he had seen the compassion Tarathiel had shown to the disturbed elf female.

He didn't want to bring that pain to those two.

But they had a right to know, and he a responsibility to tell them.

Yes, he had to tell them.

But when he looked up, the elves were already gone. Drizzt moved from his hiding place, a low crook on a tree nestled among several others. He went to the edge of the meadow, scanning, and he saw the pegasi lift into the air from over the other end.

Drizzt knew that they weren't going hunting. The mounts were too weary and so were the elves, likely. He watched their progress and figured their direction.

They were going back to their cave.

Drizzt wondered if he really had the strength to go to them and tell them his tale.

"We should return to the Moonwood and gather the clan," Tarathiel said to his companion as the two elves settled their pegasi outside the antechamber of their cave shelter.

"Are you ready to abandon Drizzt Do'Urden when you have not yet learned of Ellifain?" Innovindil replied.

"Soon," Tarathiel replied.

He began stripping off his bloodstained clothing and carefully hung his sword belt on a natural wall hook above his bedroll, then pulled off his tunic. Noticing a wound on his shoulder, he went back to the sword belt and reached into his pouch to produce a jar of salve.

Across from him, Innovindil was similarly stripping down and carefully laying out her dirty clothes.

"One scored a hit on you," she remarked, seeing the long scratch along Tarathiel's shoulder and upper arm.

"A branch, I believe," Tarathiel corrected, and he winced as he rubbed the cleansing salve over the wound. "During Sunrise's dive."

He replaced the top on the jar of salve and dropped it down to his bedroll, then pulled off his breeches and knelt down, straightening the blankets.

"Not too deep?" Innovindil asked.

"Not at all," came the assurance from Tarathiel, but the reply ended abruptly, and when Innovindil turned to regard him, she saw him crumple down on the bedroll.

"Are you that weary?" she asked lightheartedly, at first thinking nothing of it.

A few seconds slipped past.

"Tarathiel?" she asked, for he hadn't responded at all and lay very still. Innovindil moved over to him and bent low. "Tarathiel?"

A slight noise turned her head up to look at the back wall, and she spotted the hole in the stones and the small contraption—a hand crossbow—set in it.

The click of its release halted her questioning gasp, and she watched the small dart zoom across the short expanse. She tried to dodge but was too close. She threw her hand up instinctively to block, but the dart was already past that point—already past the waving hand and sticking deep into the base of her neck, just above her collarbone.

Innovindil staggered backward, her hand still held out before her. The hand was trembling, and violently, she realized only by looking at it. Even then the drow poison was coursing through her veins, numbing her extremities, dulling her thoughts. She realized she was sitting, though she hadn't intended to.

Then she was on her back, staring up at the ceiling of the cave. She tried to call out, but her lips wouldn't move to her command. She tried to turn her head to regard her companion, but she could not.

Behind the wall, Ad'non and Donnia exchanged grins and quickly moved away. They moved out of the back tunnel in a few moments' time and rushed around the hill to the front entrance of the cave. They each reached into their innate magic and summoned a globe of darkness, one over each of the pegasi milling around the entrance. The pegasi whinnied and stomped the ground in protest, and the dark elves rushed past them quickly.

Ad'non led the way up to the two paralyzed surface elves, Innovindil lying on her back before him and Tarathiel beyond her, crumpled in the fetal position.

"Beautiful, naked, and helpless," Ad'non remarked as he lewdly regarded the elf female.

With a wide grin and a quick glance back to Donnia, the drow crouched over and began stroking the elf's bare shoulder. Innovindil shuddered and jerked spasmodically, obviously trying to curl up and cower away from the touch.

That brought a chuckle from Ad'non, and from Donnia, who was enjoying the show.

"Beautiful, naked and helpless," Ad'non said again, and he glanced back at his drow companion. "Just the way I like my fairies."

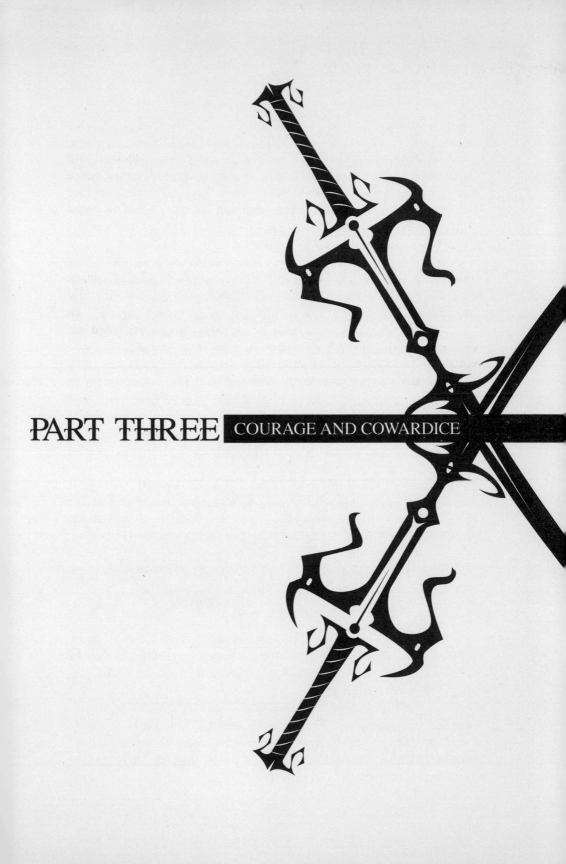

PART THREE COURAGE AND COWARDICE

How strange it was for me to watch the two elves come to my aid that day at the river. How out of sorts I felt, and how off-balance. I knew the hunting pair were in the area, of course, but to actually confront them on such terms took me to places where I did not dare to venture.

Took me back to the cave in the west, where Ellifain, their friend, lay dead at the end of my bloody blade.

How convenient the situation was to me in that moment of recognition, for there was truth in my advisement that we should flee along separate trails to discourage pursuit. There was justification in my reasoning.

But that cannot hide the truth I know in my own heart. I ran off down a different path because I was afraid, because courage in battle and courage in personal and emotional matters are often two separate attributes, and an abundance of one does not necessarily translate into an ample amount of the other.

I fear little from enemies. I fear more from friends. That is the paradox of my life. I can face a giant, a demon, a dragon, with scimitars drawn and enthusiasm high, and yet it took me years to admit my feelings for Catti-brie, to let go of the fears and just accept our relationship as the most positive aspect of my entire life.

And now I can throw myself into a gang of orcs without regard, blades slashing, a song of battle on my lips, but when Tarathiel and Innovindil presented themselves to me, I felt naked and helpless. I felt like a child again in Menzoberranzan, hiding from my mother and my vicious sisters. I do not think those two meant me any harm; they did not aid me in my battle just so they could find the satisfaction of killing me themselves. They came to me openly, knowing my identity.

But not knowing of my encounter with poor Ellifain, I am fairly certain.

I should have told them. I should have confessed all. I should have explained my pain and my regret, should have bowed before them with sorrow and humility, should have prayed with them for the safekeeping of poor Ellifain's spirit.

I should have trusted them. Tarathiel knows me and once trusted me with one of the precious horses of the Moonwood. Tarathiel saw the truth and believed that I had acted nobly on that long-ago night when the drow raiding party had crept out of the Underdark to slaughter Ellifain's clan.

He would have understood my encounter with Ellifain. He would have seen the futility of my position and the honest pain within my heart and soul.

And he should know the fate of his old friend. By all rights, he and Innovindil deserve to know of the death of Ellifain, of how she fell, and perhaps together we could then determine why she fell.

But I couldn't tell them. Not there. Not then. The wave of panic that rolled through me was as great as any I have ever known. All that I could think of was how I might get out of there, of how I might get away from these two allies, these two friends of dead Ellifain.

And so I ran.

With my scimitars, I am Drizzt the Brave, who shies from no battle. I am Drizzt who walked into a verbeeg lair beside Wulfgar and Guenhwyvar, knowing we were outmatched and outnumbered but hardly afraid! I am Drizzt, who survived alone in the Underdark for a decade, who accepted his fate and his inevitable death (or so I thought) rather than compromise those principles that I knew to be the true guiding lights of my existence.

But I am also Drizzt the Coward, fearing no physical challenge but unable to take an emotional leap into the arms of Catti-brie. I am Drizzt the Coward, who flees from Tarathiel because he cannot confess.

I am Drizzt, who has not returned to Mithral Hall after the fall of Shallows because without that confirmation of what I know to be true, that my friends are all dead, I can hold a sliver of hope that somehow some of them managed to escape the carnage. Regis, perhaps, using his ruby pendant to have the orcs carry him to waiting Battlehammer arms. Wulfgar, perhaps, raging beyond sensibility, reverting to his time in the Abyss and a pain and anger beyond control, scattering orcs before him until all those others ran from him and did not pursue.

And Catti-brie with him, perhaps.

It is all folly, I know.

I heard the orcs. I know the truth.

I am amazed at how much I hide behind these blades of mine. I am amazed at how little I fear death at an enemy's hands, and yet, at how greatly I fear having to tell Tarathiel the truth of Ellifain.

Still, I know that to be my responsibility. I know that to be the proper and just course.

I know that.

In matters of the heart, courage cannot overcome cowardice until I am honest with myself, until I admit the truth.

My reasoning in running away from the two elves that day in the river was sound and served to deflect their curiosity. But that reasoning was also a lie, because I cannot yet dare to care again.

I know that.

—Drizzt Do'Urden

15

TACTICAL DISADVANTAGE

Catti-brie threw her back against a flat stone, avoiding the rock that whistled across beside her, clipped the ground, and rebounded out over the drop to Keeper's Dale. The woman couldn't afford to watch that missile, though, for she was already being hard pressed by the pair of orcs that remained of the trio charging her position.

She had taken one of them down with Taulmaril, but then came the barrage from those distant giants on the western ridge. They couldn't reach the dwarves' position with any large stones, so they were throwing slabs of shale instead, the thin, sharp missiles catching drafts of air in wild and arcing spins. Most of the throws went far wild, spinning crazily, turning up on end and soaring far to one side or the other, but some cut in too close to be ignored.

Another arrow went up on the bowstring, and Catti-brie drew back just as the lead orc came around, the side of the stone, club raised, teeth bared.

She blew the creature away, her arrow blasting it right in the chest, lifting it from the ground and throwing it a dozen feet backward to the stone.

Instinctively, the woman dropped the bow straight down, caught it at its end and stabbed out with it behind her to intercept the attack of a second orc. The curve of the bow brought the free tip up under the orc's chin, and Catti-brie kept the pressure on as she turned around, reversing her grip and pressing forward. She had the orc straining to its tiptoes then, and it reached up to grab the bow and push it aside.

But Catti-brie moved more quickly, turning slightly and putting her back in tight against the stone, angling the bow out. She twisted and shoved, and the orc had to retreat and twist away.

Unfortunately for the orc, it happened to be standing on the edge of Keeper's Dale. It managed to grab the bow as it started to fall, forcing Catti-brie to let go. She grimaced as she saw Taulmaril go over the edge. She didn't dwell on the loss, but rather quickly drew out Khazid'hea and spun back to face the threat.

An ugly orc face greeted her, leering at her from across the flat stone. The creature did a feint to the right, and the woman sent her sword out that way. It went back to the left quickly, and Catti-brie reacted accordingly. The orc shifted fast back to center and moved as if to scramble over the stone.

But Catti-brie tired of the game and thrust straight ahead, her fabulous sword slicing through the stone and right through the chest of the orc up against it.

The creature's bloodshot eyes stared at her incredulously over the sheared rock.

"Ye almost fooled me," Catti-brie said with a wink.

Another orc leaped at her then, suddenly and without warning, coming in from far and wide.

No, not leaped, she realized as the flailing creature soared right past, soared right out over the drop to the dale.

Catti-brie understood as Wulfgar appeared, hammer in hand.

"Ready your bow," he bade her. "We are turning them yet again!"

Catti-brie held up her free hand helplessly and started to motion toward the cliff. But she just shrugged when she realized that Wulfgar wasn't watching, having already turned back to the main fight. She leaped ahead, scrambling to the top of the stone and away in fast pursuit of her barbarian friend.

Side by side, they waded into the closest group of orcs, Aegis-fang swiping back and forth, scattering the closest enemies.

Catti-brie darted out to the side, where an orc presented a shield against her. It was a feeble defense against Khazid'hea. The blade bit right through the wooden shield, right through the arm strapped against its other side, and right through the orc's chest.

Catti-brie slashed across to intercept the charge of a second creature, and the fine blade, so aptly nicknamed Cutter, sliced through bone and flesh and wood to tear free of its first victim. Turning it down, Catti-brie caught the second orc's thrusting spear and dropped its tip harmlessly. She snapped the blade back up with two quick stabs—two clean holes in the orc's chest. The creature staggered backward and tried to regroup, but the swiping Aegis-fang caught it in the back and sent it flying past Catti-brie.

She put Cutter into its side for good measure as it went by.

How fine I eat this night! came a thought in her mind.

Though the words hardly registered, the sensation of bloodthirst surely did. Before she could even consider the implications, before she even realized that the sentient sword had awakened and found its way into her conscious once more, the woman charged ahead, past Wulfgar, rushing with abandon into a throng of orcs.

Ferocity replaced finesse, with Cutter lashing out wickedly at anything that moved near. Out to the left she thrust, across her chest and through one shield and arm. A quick retraction and the blade slashed across in front of her, forcing the two orcs before her to stumble backward and taking the tip from the spear of another that was coming in from her right. Catti-brie turned her trailing foot and swung her hips, then charged out suddenly to the right, stabbing repeatedly, poking hole after hole into the curling and screaming orc.

Recognizing her vulnerability, the woman turned back to face the remaining two, and she dived aside as something flew past.

Aegis-fang, she realized when one of the two orcs seemed to simply disappear.

He shares our plate! Khazid'hea protested, and the sword compelled the woman to charge forward at the remaining orc.

Terrified, the creature threw its sword at her and turned and fled, and though the weapon smacked against her, it hardly slowed her. She caught the orc as it joined up with a pair of its fellows and still didn't slow, coming in with fury, stabbing and slashing. She took a hit and ignored the pain, willing to trade strike for strike, orc weapon against marvelous Khazid'hea.

The three were down, and Catti-brie ran on.

"Wait!" came a cry behind her.

It was Wulfgar's cry, but it seemed distant and not insistent. Not as insistent as the hunger in her thoughts. Not as insistent as the fire coursing through her veins.

Another orc fell before her. She hit another, thinking to rush past with a following stab on the creature behind it. But her strike was too strong, and the fine blade slashed through the orc's upper arm, severing the limb, then bit deeply into the creature's side, cutting halfway through its torso. There the blade halted and got stuck, for the momentum of the slash was stolen by too-eager Catti-brie, her weight coming past before she had finished the move. The dying orc flopped about and the woman nearly lost her grip on the blade. She turned and tugged fiercely, knowing she had to get it free, seeing the next creature barely feet away.

"Bah! Ye're taking all the fun!" that creature called at her.

Only then did Catti-brie stop struggling with the stuck sword. Only then did she realize that she had already reached the end of the dwarven line.

She offered a sheepish smile at the dwarf, keeping the thought private that if she hadn't accidentally caught her blade on the orc, that dwarf would likely have fallen to the hunger of Khazid'hea.

Spurred by that thought, the woman silently swore at the sword, which of course heard her clearly. She planted a foot on the dead orc and tried again to pull Khazid'hea free but was stopped by a large hand gripping her shoulder.

"Easy," Wulfgar bade her. "We fight together, side by side."

Catti-brie let go of the blade and stepped back, then took a long and steadying deep breath.

"Sword's hungry," she explained.

Wulfgar smiled, nodded, and said, "Temper that hunger with common sense."

Catti-brie looked back at the path of carnage she had wrought, at the sliced and slashed orcs, and at herself, covered head to toe in orc blood.

No, not all of it was orc, she only then realized and only then felt the burning pain. The thrown sword had opened a gash along her left arm, and she had another wound on her right hip and another where a spear tip had cut into her right foot.

"You need a priest," Wulfgar said to her.

Catti-brie, jaw clenched against the pain, stubbornly stepped forward and grabbed Khazid'hea's hilt. She roughly tore it free—and yet another fountain of orc blood painted her.

"And a bath," Wulfgar remarked, half in humor and half in sadness.

Banak Brawnanvil shoved two thick fingers into his mouth and blew a shrill whistle. The orcs were in retreat yet again, and the dwarves were giving chase, holding perfectly to their formations as they went. But those orcs were veering, Banak realized from his high vantage point back near the cliff face. They were sidling west in their run down the slope.

Banak whistled again and again and called for his nearby commanders to turn the dwarves around.

Before that order ever reached the pursuing force, though, all the dwarves, commander and pursuer alike, came to understand its intent and urgency. For in their bloodlust, the dwarves had moved too far to the north and west, too close to the high ridge and the waiting giants. As one, the formation skidded to a stop and swung around as giant boulders began to rain down upon them.

Their focused turn became an all-out retreat, and the orcs who had baited them turned as well, making the pursuers the pursued.

"Damned clever pigs," Banak grumbled.

"They've got the tactical advantage with them giants on the ridge," agreed Torgar, who stood at Banak's side.

That advantage was likely leading to complete disaster. Those orcs in pursuit, with the artillery support of the giants, would likely cut deep into the dwarven lines.

The two dwarf commanders held their breaths, praying that the errant band would get out of the giants' effective range and would then be able to offer some defense against the orcs. Banak and Torgar measured the ground, both calling out commands to support groups, moving all the remaining dwarves into position to catch and bolster their running kin.

Their plans took a sudden turn, though, as one group from the fleeing dwarves broke away from the main force, turning back upon the orcs with sudden ferocity.

"That'd be Pwent," Banak muttered.

Torgar tipped his helmet in admiration of the brave Gutbusters.

Pwent and his boys hit the orc line with abandon, and that line broke almost immediately.

The giants turned their attention to that particular area. Boulders rained down, but there were many more orcs than dwarves, a ratio of more than five to one—and that ratio held up concerning the numbers dropped by giant-thrown stones.

The pursuit was over and the main dwarven force was able to return to their defensive positions. All eyes turned back to the area of carnage, to see a group of Gutbusters, less than half of those who had bravely turned and charged, come scrambling out, running zigzags up the inclining stone.

Banak's charges cheered for them, urging them on, shouting for them to, "Run!" and, "Duck!" and, "Keep going!"

But rocks smashed among the zigzagging group, and whenever one of Pwent's boys went down, the cheering dwarves gave a collective groan.

One figure in particular caught the attention of the onlookers. It was Pwent himself, running up the slope with not one, but a pair of wounded dwarves slung over his shoulders.

The cheers went up for him, for "Pwent, Pwent, Pwent!"

He lagged behind, so he became the focus of the giants as well. Rocks smashed down all around him. Still he charged on, roaring with every step, determined to get his wounded boys out of there.

A rock hit the ground behind him and skipped forward, slamming him in the back and sending him flying forward. The wounded dwarves rolled off to either side, all three hitting the ground hard.

Up above, cheers turned to stunned silence.

Pwent struggled to get up.

Another stone clipped him and laid him face down.

Two figures broke out from the dwarf ranks then, running fast on longer legs, sprinting down the slope toward the fallen trio.

Amazingly, Pwent forced himself back up and turned to face the giants. He swung one arm up, slapping his other hand across his elbow so that his fist punched high in the air—as rude a gesture as he could offer.

Another boulder smashed the stone right in front of him, then bounced up over him and clunked down behind.

And there stood Pwent, signaling curses at the giants.

Catti-brie wished that she had her bow with her! Then, perhaps, she could at least offer some cover against that suicidal charge.

Wulfgar outdistanced her, his hands free, for he had left Aegis-fang back up with the dwarves.

"Get to Pwent!" the barbarian cried, and he veered for one of the two more seriously wounded warriors.

Catti-brie reached the stubborn battlerager and grabbed him by the still-cursing arm.

"Come on, ye dolt!" she cried. "They'll crush you down!"

"Bah! They're as stupid as they are tall!" Pwent shouted.

He pulled his arm from Catti-brie, hooked a finger of each hand into either side of his mouth, and pulled it wide, sticking out his tongue at the distant behemoths.

He sobered almost at once, though, and not from Catti-brie's continuing pleas, but from the specter of Wulfgar crossing before him, an unconscious dwarf over one shoulder. Pwent watched as Wulfgar moved to the second fallen Gutbuster, a huge hand clasping over the scruff of the dwarf's neck and hoisting him easily.

When Catti-brie tugged again, Pwent didn't argue, and the woman pulled him along, back up the slope. The rain of boulders commenced with full force, but luck was with the trio and their unconscious cargo, and Wulfgar was hardly slowed by the burden of the two injured dwarves. Soon enough, they were out of range of the boulders. The frustrated giants went back to their shale then, filling the air with spinning and slashing sharp-edged stones.

Dwarves cheered wildly as the group of five approached. As one, the hundreds lifted their arms in rude gestures and stood defiantly against the whizzing missiles of slate.

"Get yer bandages ready," Banak shouted to Pikel Bouldershoulder, who was off to the side, jumping around excitedly.

"Oo oi!" the dwarf yelled back, and he turned and lifted an arm in salute to Banak.

The slate flew past, taking Pikel's raised arm at the elbow. The green-bearded dwarf put on a puzzled look and stumbled forward, then shrugged as if he didn't understand.

And his eyes went wide as he saw the severed limb—*his* severed limb!—lying off to the side.

His brother Ivan slammed into him from the side, slapping a cloak tightly around Pikel's blood-spurting stump, and other dwarves nearby howled and rushed to help.

Pikel was sitting then, ushered down by his brother.

"Oooo," he said.

16

EMBRACING THE HUNTER

Ad'non Kareese's long, slender fingers traced a line down over Innovindil's delicate chin, down the moon elf's birdlike neck and to the base of her throat.

"Can you feel me?" the drow teased, though he believed, of course, that the paralyzed surface elf couldn't understand his language.

"Have your way with the creature and be done with her," Donnia said from behind him.

Ad'non smiled, keeping his head turned away from his companion so that she could not see the amusement he was taking at her obvious consternation. She understood his intended action as debasement more than any real emotional connection, of course—and as she was drow herself so she was certainly going to find her own pleasures with their paralyzed playthings—but still, there sounded a bit of unmistakable agitation around the edges of her voice.

Amusing.

"If I find you soft and warm, perhaps I will keep you alive for a while," Ad'non said to Innovindil.

He watched the surface elf's eyes as he spoke and could see that they were indeed reacting to the sound of his voice and the feel of his touch. Yes, she couldn't outwardly make any movements—the drow poison had done its job well—but she understood what was happening, understood what he was about to do to her, and understood that she had no chance to get out of it.

That made it all the sweeter.

Ad'non ran his hand lower, across the female's small breasts and down over her belly. Then he stood up and stepped back. He glanced back at Donnia, who stood with her arms crossed over her chest.

"We should drag them to a different cave," he said to his companion. "Let us keep them prisoner."

"Her, perhaps," Donnia replied, indicating Innovindil. "For that one, there will be only death."

It seemed fine enough to Ad'non, and he glanced back at the female elf and grinned.

And he couldn't see her—a ball of blackness covered her and her companion.

Never to be taken completely by surprise, the two dark elves swung around, Ad'non unsheathing his swords, Donnia drawing a blade and her hand crossbow. The form behind them, by the entrance, was easily enough distinguishable. It was a drow standing calmly, standing ready, scimitars drawn.

"Traitor!" Donnia growled, and she lifted her crossbow and fired.

Drizzt trembled with rage when he first entered the cave, seeing the two elves lying flat, and the two drow standing over them. He had known of the trouble before he'd ever come in, for the calls and stomping hooves of the pegasi outside had alerted him from some distance away. Without thinking twice, the drow ranger had broken into a run, leaping down the flat rock from which he'd often observed the area, and charging between the winged horses even as the darkness globes dissipated.

So alarmed was Drizzt that he hadn't even paused long enough to bring forth Guenhwyvar.

And he faced the drow pair.

He didn't even see the movement, but he heard the distinctive *click,* and remembered well enough that telltale sound. The ranger spun, pulling his cloak in a wide sweep around him.

His quick defense caught the dart in the swinging cloak, but even as the dart stuck in place, the second *click* sounded. Drizzt spun again, but the second dart got past the flying cloak and struck him in the hip.

Almost immediately, Drizzt felt the numbing chill of the drow poison.

He staggered back toward the exit and thought to call in Guenhwyvar. He couldn't reach for his belt pouch, though, for it was all he could do to hold fast to his weapons.

"How wonderful of you to join us, Drizzt Do'Urden," said the female drow who'd shot him.

Her words, spoken in the language of his homeland, brought him drifting back across the years, brought him back to images of Menzoberranzan and his family, of House Do'Urden and Zaknafein, of Narbondel glowing with heat and the great structures of the drow palaces, stalagmite and stalactite palaces, shaped and set with sweeping balconies and decorated with multicolored accents of faerie fire.

He saw it all so clearly—the early days beside his sisters and training with the weapons masters at Melee Magthere, the school for drow warriors.

The sound of metal clinking against stone woke him up, and only then did he realize that he was leaning heavily on the wall and that he had dropped one of his blades.

"Ah, Drizzt Do'Urden, I had hoped you would put up a better fight than this," said the male drow. The sound of his voice alone told Drizzt that his enemy was steadily approaching. "I have heard so much of your prowess."

Drizzt couldn't keep his eyes open. He felt the numbness flowing through his lower extremities so that he couldn't even feel the ground beneath his feet. The only reason he was still standing, he understood through the haze that was filtering his thoughts, was because of his angle against the wall.

The poison crept in, and so did the sword-wielding drow.

Drizzt tried to fight back against the numbness, tried hard to find his center, tried hard to shake his mind clear of the cloudy disorientation.

He could not.

"Now perhaps we have found a true plaything, Ad'non," he heard the drow female remark from somewhere so very, very distant.

"Too dangerous is this one, my dear Donnia," the male argued. "He dies quickly."

"As you will . . ."

Her voice trailed away, and it seemed to Drizzt as if he was falling far away, into a pit of blackness from which there could be no escape.

Wulfgar lay on the stone, peering down, trying to discern the best angle of approach toward the ledge where Taulmaril balanced precariously.

Behind him, Catti-brie tied a rope around her waist and checked the length of the cord.

"The devilish sword almost had me enthralled," the woman admitted as Wulfgar turned around and sat up facing her. "I've not felt its call so insistently in many months."

"Because you are tired," Wulfgar replied. "We're all tired. How many times have our enemies come at us? A dozen? They give us no rest."

"Just hit the damned thing with a rock, send it tumbling to the floor, and go get it," said Torgar, coming over with Shingles McRuff beside him.

Both of them were limping, and Shingles was holding one arm protectively close against his side.

"We've tried," Wulfgar replied.

"How is Pikel?" Catti-brie asked. "And Pwent?"

"Pwent's hopping mad," Shingles replied.

"Nothing new there," the woman remarked.

"And Pikel's said nothing but 'oooo' since he lost the arm," Shingles added. "I'm thinking it'll take him a bit afore he's used to it. Banak sent him down to Mithral Hall for better tending."

"He'll live, though, and that's more than many can say," added Torgar.

"Well, be quick about getting yer bow," Shingles said. "Might that we'll all be going inside the hall soon enough." He glanced back over his shoulder toward the distant ridge and the giants. "We can hold firm so far, as long as we're not stupid enough to chase the damned orcs back in range of the brutes. But they're bringin' up big logs and building giant-sized catapults. Once them things are throwing, we'll be fast out o' here."

Wulfgar and Catti-brie exchanged concerned looks, for neither had any answer to that logic.

"Banak would've called for the retreat to begin already," said Torgar, "except now we've got a force set west of Keeper's Dale, and he knows that if he surrenders this ground, they'll have the dickens getting back to the gate, since they'd be crossing the dale right under giant fire."

Again the two humans exchanged a concerned look. Their enemies had gained a huge tactical advantage, one that would drive the dwarves from the area, and yes, back into Mithral Hall. That much seemed certain.

What did that mean for all the other towns nearby?

What did that mean for Mithral Hall, with no surface trade and no way to get out in numbers sufficient to take back the land?

And for Wulfgar and Catti-brie, there remained one more nagging problem.

If they were forced back underground, what did it mean for Drizzt Do'Urden? Would he ever be able to find his way back to them?

He saw Zaknafein falling into the acid pit.

He saw Ellifain falling against the wall.

He saw Bruenor falling atop a tower.

He felt the keen sting of each loss, the pain and the anger, and he did not push them away. No, Drizzt embraced them, called those emotions to him, basked in them and heightened them.

He imagined Regis being torn apart by orcs.

He imagined Wulfgar falling amidst a bloody sea of enemy spears.

He imagined Catti-brie, down and helpless, surrounded by enemies, bleeding from a hundred wounds.

He imagined, and those conjured images blended with the very real and painful images he had known in his life, the visions of sorrow and despair, the scenes of his life that had brought him to a place of emotional darkness.

He felt the Hunter rising within him. All the images ran together then, one long line of pain and loss and sorrow and regret, and most of all, of pure rage.

A sword stabbed in at Drizzt's left side, but the ring of metal on metal sounded clearly, a warning bell to his two attackers that their poison could not defeat the Hunter. For across came the backhand slash of a scimitar, in the blink of an astonished drow eye, whipping up and around in an instant to catch the thrusting sword and turn it up and out.

The second sword followed, predictably low, but even in anticipation of the coming blade and given the attack angle, the defender seemingly had no practical chance of either snapping down his first scimitar or of getting to his second, which lay on the floor.

But he was the Hunter, and not only did that first scimitar blade come back down, rapping the sword and driving it out to the right out in front of him as he turned, but the Hunter fell into a crouch with the parry, scooping up the fallen Twinkle. As he came up fast, blades working in perfect harmony, the retrieved scimitar came in and over the sword and rode it out even more.

That first scimitar reversed and snapped back up, hard, ringing the first sword again.

And so the attacker, Ad'non, stood helpless, swords out wide to either side, two deadly scimitars *inside* them.

A sudden and brutal ending, or so it would have been for the surprised Ad'non, had not his companion come in then hard at the Hunter's back. A sudden jerk shoved Ad'non's blades out even more, and he had to step back to hold any sort of defensive position. But he needed no defense at that moment, for the Hunter spun away from him, blades cutting the air in a protective weave before him as he turned left to right.

Donnia squealed at the surprising deflection of her sword, but the skilled female warrior followed the flow of the scimitars and quick-stepped in behind for a dagger thrust.

The Hunter's hip was already moving, keeping him out of reach.

And Drizzt spun again, defeating Ad'non's double-thrust, scimitars rolling up and across, hitting the swords a dozen times in rapid succession before he continued around, the whirling blades forcing that dirk back, then driving hard against Donnia's sword once more.

The Hunter continued to spin, rolling blades striking one side and the other, always coming around at the exact angle to intercept, as if the lone drow was anticipating each attack, as if he was seeing it before it ever began.

His attackers were not novices, though, and they had fought together many, many times. They kept opposite each other and kept their attacks coordinated—and they were expending far less energy than the spinning drow defender. Still, as they struck and leaped back, every thrust, high or low, left or right, was met by the ringing impact of a perfectly aimed scimitar.

Then, suddenly, the twirl stopped, and the pair attacked, but the Hunter went back around the other way. Again came the ring of metal on metal, two scimitars striking hard against three swords.

That spin ended almost immediately, though, leaving the Hunter sidelong to both attackers.

In came Ad'non, double-thrust high.

The Hunter ducked below it and stabbed for the male's knees, then leaped straight up over Donnia's slashing sword as Ad'non retracted. Drizzt landed in a fast step toward Ad'non, snapping his scimitars up in a cross between Ad'non's leveled blades, stabbing them high until his arms crossed and the hilts caught at the blade, then snapping them out across again, out wide, nearly tearing the swords from Ad'non's grasp.

Ad'non threw himself backward, but so did the Hunter, leaping into a backward somersault right above and over the stabbing sword of Donnia. He landed lightly, still backstepping.

As he crossed over, defeating her attack, the dexterous Donnia flipped her dirk in her hand and whipped it at his chest.

But the defending drow's right scimitar snapped up to cleanly block, and before the deflected dirk could bounce away, the left-hand scimitar locked up under it, pinning it against the first blade for just a moment before slashing back to the left, redirecting the dirk into a swift flight at his retreating adversary. Ad'non desperately dived back and around but got clipped across the cheek as he tumbled away.

Donnia pressed the attack, drawing a whip from her belt as she thrust ahead with her sword.

That sword thrust never got close, as the Hunter's right reversed down and around, turning it, then lifting it as the left hand came back in, striking it again, lifting it higher. The right scimitar climbed that parrying ladder in turn, knocking it still higher.

Donnia accepted the blocks with only a minimal attempt to break free, for her second hand worked perfectly then, sending the whip in a teasing forward slide, then snapping it suddenly for the Hunter's face.

A scimitar picked it off, but it did not cut the enchanted whip, and the same magic that prevented the tear also reacted to Donnia's willful call, the living tentacle wrapping fast around the blade.

Her eyes blazing with apparent victory, the female yanked the scimitar free. She was surprised at how easily she got it from the strong drow—only until she realized that he had let it go, turning as he did and pulling his cloak from around his neck.

Ad'non came in hard from the side, but the Hunter quick-stepped ahead and to the opposite side, moving around Donnia to use her as a screen. As he went, he brought his cloak up above his head in a spin, and as Donnia snapped the whip, so he launched the cloak.

She felt her whip crack hard against his shoulder and got wrapped about the head by the flying cloak in return—which she accepted as more than an even trade.

Until she felt the sudden sting at the side of her neck, and she realized that her dart was hanging in that cloak and that the vicious and sneaky warrior had angled the throw perfectly to get its poisoned tip near to her.

With a shriek, the female fell back and threw aside the garment.

One scimitar against two swords, the Hunter still slapped and parried perfectly, never letting Ad'non get close to hitting. He backstepped as he parried, swiftly working his way in perfect balance to his lost scimitar.

Following that maneuver, Ad'non increased his attack, even went into a sudden and furious charge.

The Hunter leaped aside, to Ad'non's left, and the skilled killer redirected his left-hand blade out immediately, and when it got slapped aside, he followed with a thrust of the right.

That, too, was parried, and the Hunter turned inside both, putting his back to Ad'non. A quick double-pump of his arm brought his scimitar forward and back twice, brought its pommel hard into Ad'non's face—twice.

Staggered, the drow stumbled backward, his blades working furiously in desperate defense. They hit only air, though, and a look of abject terror flashed across the drow's face.

Except that the Hunter hadn't pursued. Instead, he'd turned and sprinted for his lost scimitar.

A globe of darkness covered him as he reached the blade, and he responded with one of his own, right where he remembered the female to be.

Grabbing up the scimitar, he went out furiously, diving into a roll, then charged right through the second globe, his own globe, sliding in low, blades working all around.

He came out to find the female sprinting across toward the male, who had warm blood trickling down his face.

Unafraid, the Hunter stalked in.

"Together and to the sides," the Hunter heard the male say, and Ad'non started to the left.

And the female felt at the side of her neck, a look of panic on her face.

The Hunter covered her in blue-glowing flames, harmless faerie fire that marked her as a clearer target.

As Ad'non charged, she turned and ran.

They worked their blades so quickly that the ring sounded as one long call. Ad'non stabbed with one sword then the other and got hit with a double-block left and a double-block right, each of his attacks being picked off by not one, but both of the Hunter's scimitars.

A slash across hit nothing but air as the Hunter ducked. A thrust flew freely as the Hunter deftly turned, and that blade got smacked hard on the retraction, nearly tearing it free of Ad'non's grasp.

"Donnia!" he screamed.

He growled and worked his own blades magnificently as a sudden series of diagonal slashes, tap-tapping each scimitar just enough to make it slide past him harmlessly. So fast did those scimitars come, though, that Ad'non was forced to steadily retreat and couldn't begin to think of any possible counters.

But those blades did gradually slow, leaving a slip of an opening.

One that Ad'non leaped through, offering a devastating double-thrust low.

Amazingly, the scimitars somehow fell into the only possible defense, double-cross-down, which left the two at a draw for that particular routine, so Ad'non thought. For Ad'non Kareese was not of Menzoberranzan and did not know that his foe, Drizzt' Do'Urden, had long-ago found the solution for the routine-end.

With amazing dexterity and balance, the Hunter's foot came up right between the crossed scimitars and smashed Ad'non squarely in the face, sending him staggering backward yet again.

He tried to mount a defense, but the scimitars led the way, batting his swords aside, and as he slammed hard against the wall, he could not block the diving, curved blade.

It hit him squarely in the chest, and he screamed.

And the Hunter growled, thinking the fight at its end.

But the scimitar did not penetrate! Nor did its sister blade score a mortal wound as it came in hard against Ad'non's side. Oh yes, the two blades had hurt the drow warrior, but neither had found its way in for the kill.

And suddenly, the Hunter was off-balance, was caught by surprise.

Across came a sword, knocking both scimitars aside, and the Hunter went into a spin, right-to-left. But Ad'non went to his right behind him, pressing the attack, forcing him to run past or get skewered.

But there was a wall there, Ad'non knew, and he smiled, for the devilish drow renegade had nowhere to go. In Ad'non charged, both blades going for the kill.

But the Hunter was not there.

Ad'non's blades clipped the bare stone, and he stopped suddenly, eyes wide.

"O cunning Drizzt," he said as he figured out that Drizzt had gone right over him, running up the wall and flipping a back somersault to stand behind him.

The scimitar came slashing across just above Ad'non's shoulder, cleanly lopping off his head.

Drizzt glanced across the way to the two paralyzed elves and even started toward them, just a step. But then, his anger far from sated, the Hunter ran out of the cave and off into the night. He paused and glanced around and saw the blue glow of his faerie fire along a slope to the west. His eyes cast determinedly as if set in stone, the Hunter drew forth his onyx figurine and called to Guenhwyvar.

The blue glow still showed when the great panther materialized beside him, and Drizzt pointed it out.

"Catch her, Guen," the drow instructed. "Catch her and hold her for me."

With a growl, the panther charged off into the night, gaining great expanses with every mighty leap.

17

STEWARDSHIP AND ESPIONAGE

Regis squeezed Bruenor's hand and stared down at his friend, wondering if it would be last time he would see the dwarf king alive. Bruenor's breaths seemed more shallow to him, and the dwarf's color was even more grayish, as if he was made of stone. Stumpet and Cordio had told Regis that it likely wouldn't be much longer, and he could see that plainly.

"I owe you this," the halfling whispered, barely able to get his voice out through the lump in his throat. "We all do, and know as you rest that Mithral Hall will stand strong in your absence. I will not let this place fall."

The halfling gave another gentle squeeze, then laid the dwarf's hand down across his chest. For a moment, he saw no movement in Bruenor's chest, and he wondered if the dwarf had heard him and had at last let go.

But then Bruenor took a breath.

Not yet.

Regis patted the dwarf's hands and briskly walked out of the room, overcome and trying hard to bring himself emotionally back to center. He moved quickly along the tunnels, knowing that he was late for a meeting with Galen Firth of Nesmé. He still didn't know how he would handle the fierce warrior. What aid might he offer with Mithral Hall under such duress? The eastern door was sealed—the dwarves had even dropped the tunnels behind it to make sure that any enemies trying to come in that way would have to claw through more than twenty feet of stone.

Reports from the north were no more promising, for Banak Brawnanvil had sent word that he was not certain how long he could hold his position. The giants were setting catapults on the western ridge, and soon enough, Banak feared, his forces would be under terrible duress.

He had asked for Regis to swing the force that had settled in the western end of Keeper's Dale around to the north to overrun the ridge from the west, but the request had come with a caveat: *if* it was feasible. Even Banak, settled in an increasingly desperate situation, recognized the danger of following such a course. Not only would that be exposing one of his two remaining surface armies to a potentially devastating situation, but in moving them out of their defensive position in Keeper's Dale, Regis would be risking leaving a wide-open path to Mithral Hall's western gate.

And Nesmé was sorely pressed—likely even overrun—so the halfling had to keep the western approach protected from potential enemies moving up from the south.

Too many problems flitted through the halfling steward's mind. Too many issues confronted him. He hardly knew where he was half the time, and in truth, all he wanted was to go eat a big meal or two and settle down in a warm bed, with nothing troubling him more than the all-important decision of what he would choose to eat for breakfast.

With all of that weighing down his little shoulders, Regis started away. But he stopped and glanced back at the candlelit room where King Bruenor lay, and he remembered his words to his dying friend.

Regis straightened his shoulders immediately, bolstered by his sense of duty. His promise had not been idly given, and he did indeed owe Bruenor at least that much, and surely even more.

First things first, Regis decided, and he moved off more quickly and determinedly for his meeting with Galen Firth. He found the man in the appointed audience room, a smaller and more personable sitting area than the grand chamber. It was appointed with comfortable chairs—three padded ones with arm rests and wide-flaring backs—set on a thick-woven rug patterned in the foaming mug emblem of Clan Battlehammer. Completing the square of the sitting area was a stone hearth, wherein burned a small and cozy fire.

Despite the obvious comforts, Galen Firth was pacing, his hands behind his back, his fingers running all around, his eyes cast down at the floor. Regis had to wonder if this man was ever anything but agitated.

"Well met again, Galen Firth of Nesmé," the halfling steward greeted as he entered the room. "Forgive my tardiness, I beg, for there are many pressing prob-lems all needing my attention."

"Your tardiness this day is more forgivable than the tardiness of Mithral Hall's answer to Nesmé's desperate call," the disagreeable man replied rather harshly.

Regis gave a sigh, walked past Galen and plopped himself down in one of the chairs. When the warrior made no move to join him in the sitting area, the halfling pointedly gestured to the seat directly across from him, to the right of the fire as his was to the left.

Never blinking and never taking his eyes from the halfling, the Rider of Nesmé moved to the chair.

"What would you have me do?" Regis asked as Galen at last sat down.

"Launch an army of dwarves to the aid of Nesmé, that we can drive the trolls back into their brackish waters and restore my town."

"And when this army marches south and a greater army of orcs and giants offers pursuit, then what would you have any of us do?" Regis reasoned, and Galen's eyes narrowed. "For that is what will happen, you do understand. The orcs press us on the north and have sealed the door to Mithral Hall on the east—you have heard of this latest battle, yes? I have one force up on the cliff north of Keeper's Dale waging battle daily against the orcs, but if the reports of the size of the attacking force in the east were anywhere near to accurate, my warriors will soon be even harder pressed and likely forced to forfeit the ground.

"You do not fully comprehend what is transpiring all around us, do you?" the halfling asked.

Galen Firth sat there staring, grim faced.

"It is no accident that Nesmé was attacked just now," Regis explained. "These enemy forces, north and south, have coordinated their movements."

"That cannot be!"

"Did you hear no details of the fall of Mithral Hall's eastern gate?"

"Few, nor do I care to—"

"The forces out there were besieged by giants and orcs from the north and by a host of trolls from the south," Regis interrupted, and Galen's bluster fell away as clearly as his suddenly drooping jaw.

"It would seem that our common enemies are sweeping all the land from the Surbrin to Nesmé, from the Trollmoors to the Spine of the World," Regis went on. "That leaves only a handful of settlements, Mithral Hall, and Nesmé to stop them, unless we can elicit help from the neighboring lands."

"Then you admit that we must join our forces," Galen reasoned. "Then you see the wisdom of sending a force fast for Nesmé."

"I do," said Regis, "and I do not. We must stand together, and so we shall, but I believe your desire to hold our ground at Nesmé is ill considered. Mithral Hall will hold, but outside of our gates, all is lost—or soon shall be."

"What foolishness is this?" Galen Firth demanded, leaping from his chair, his eyes ablaze with anger.

"We fight for every inch of ground," Regis countered, and his voice didn't waver in the least, nor did he tense up or shy away from the imposing man. "And when we cannot hold, we retreat into the defensible tunnels of Mithral Hall. From here, we keep the lines of tunnels open to Citadel Felbarr; they will be our eyes, ears, and mouth to the outside world. From here, we continue to implore Silverymoon and Sundabar to mobilize their forces. I already have emissaries hurrying along their way through tunnels to find Lady Alustriel of Silverymoon and the leaders of Sundabar. From here, we hold the one remaining fortress against the onslaught of monstrous enemies."

"While my people die?" Galen Firth spat.

"No," said Regis. "Not if we can help them. From the moment you arrived, I had dwarf scouts striking out to the southwest, underground, seeking a course to Nesmé. Their progress has been strong, and I expect that they will find an exit to the surface near enough to your town to join up with your people."

"Then send an army, and let us drive the trolls back!"

"I will send what I can spare, but I expect that will be far fewer than needed for the task you espouse," said Regis.

"Then what?" the warrior's voice suddenly mellowed, and he even slumped back in the chair.

He turned his head and rested his chin in his hand, staring into the flames.

"Let us find your people and help them as we may," Regis explained. "We will fight beside them, if that remains a viable option. And if not, or when it becomes not, we will retreat, with your people in tow, back into the Underdark and back to Mithral Hall. Though my dwarves will not be able to defeat our enemies aboveground, I have little doubt that they can hold their own tunnels against pursuing monsters."

Galen Firth said nothing, just kept staring into the fire.

"I wish I could offer more," Regis went on. "I wish I could empty Mithral Hall and charge south to overrun the trolls. But I cannot, and you must understand."

Galen sat there quietly for a long while, then turned to Regis, his features softened.

"You truly believe that the orcs and giants work in concert with the Trollmoors trolls?"

"The fall of the eastern gate would indicate as much," the halfling replied.

"And it tells, too, that my people are in dire trouble," Galen said. "If the trolls had enough strength to send a force as far east and north as your gates on the Surbrin. . . ."

"Then tarry no more," Regis said. He reached into his vest and produced a rolled parchment, tossing it across to the man. "Take that to the Undercity and Taskman Bellows. The expedition is outfitting even now and will be ready to march this very day."

Again Galen Firth paused, staring at the parchment, then back at Regis as he slowly climbed out of the chair once more. He said nothing more, but his nod held enough appreciation for Regis to see that the man understood the reasoning, even if he did not necessarily agree.

He gave a slight bow and left the room and the halfling steward breathed a sigh of relief, thinking he had one less issue pressing.

Regis slid back in his chair and turned to the fire, but before he could even begin to relax, a knock on the door turned him back.

"Enter, please," he said, expecting it to be a returned Galen Firth.

The door pushed open and in walked a soot-covered dwarf, Miccarl Ironforge by name, one of Mithral Hall's best blacksmiths. So dirty was this one that the color of his wide, short beard (rumored to be red) was impossible to tell. He wore a thick leather apron and a black shirt with only one sleeve, covering his left arm completely and sewn as one with a heavy heat-resistant glove. His bare right arm, streaked with soot, was nearly twice the girth of his left, muscled from years and years of lifting heavy hammers.

"The gnome again?" Regis asked.

Miccarl had sought him out twice before in the last tenday, offering reports that their little visitor from Mirabar had been acting overly curious in snooping around the Undercity.

"The little one's been in the maps again," Miccarl explained.

"Same maps?"

"Western tunnels—mostly unused."

"Where is he now?"

"Last I saw was him moving down those same tunnels," Miccarl explained. "I'm thinking that he's thinking he's found something there."

"And what might be there?"

"Nothing that I'm knowing, nor that anyone else's knowing. Them tunnels

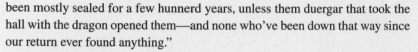

been mostly sealed for a few hunnerd years, unless them duergar that took the hall with the dragon opened them—and none who've been down that way since our return ever found anything."

"Then what? A way out—a way to bring an army from Mirabar in?" Regis asked. "Ore that could be stolen for Mirabar's forges?"

"Nothing there—not even good ore," Miccarl answered. "Never was nothing there but shale and coal for the forges. If the little one's come all the way to find a source for that, then he's a bigger fool than ye know, for there's not much worth in the stuff and Mirabar's already got more than she'd ever need."

"Tunnels to Mirabar?"

Miccarl snorted and said, "We got enough already known. We could get far west of here in a day's time and be aboveground beyond the reach of our enemies and well on our way to Mirabar. The little one's got to know that."

"Then what?" Regis asked again, but quietly, and more to himself than to the dwarf.

What might Nanfoodle be doing? As he pondered the possibilities, the halfling's hand instinctively went up to the chain around his neck.

"Find Nanfoodle and bid him join me," Regis instructed the dwarf.

"Aye," Miccarl readily agreed. "Ye wanting me to drag him or knock him black and carry him?"

"I'm wanting you to coerce him," Regis replied. "Tell him that I have some news for Mirabar and need his advice forthwith."

"Not as much fun," Miccarl muttered, and he left.

A procession of informants followed the departure of the blacksmith, with news from the east and news from the west, with reports about the fighting outside and from the progress in securing and scouting the tunnels. Regis took it all in, paying strict attention, weighing all the possibilities, and mostly, formulating a line of questions for his dwarf advisors. He recognized that he was more the synthesizer of information than the decision maker, though he found that his advice was carrying more and more weight as the dwarves came to trust his judgment.

That pleased him and frightened him all at the same time.

His dinner was delivered to him in the same room, coming in alongside yet another messenger, one reporting that the expedition of fifty dwarves had set off for the south with Galen Firth.

Regis invited the dwarf to join him, or started to, but then Miccarl Ironforge appeared at the door.

"More work," Regis explained to the first messenger.

The halfling gave an apologetic shrug and motioned to the plates of food set on the small table between the chairs.

"Yup," replied the dwarf, and he stepped over, piled a few pounds of meat on a plate and filled the largest flagon to its tip with mead.

He gave a nod to Regis, which sent some mead spilling over the front of the flagon, then took his leave.

In walked Miccarl and Nanfoodle.

"Got work to do," the sooty blacksmith explained, and after moving over to similarly outfit himself with meat and mead for the trek back to the Under-city, he too took his leave.

"Sit and eat and drink," Regis offered to the gnome.

"They left little," Nanfoodle remarked with a grin, but even as he spoke the words, a pair of dwarves entered with refills of both food and drink.

Both the halfling and the gnome, not to be outdone by any dwarf, began their long, hearty meal.

"I am told you have news of Mirabar, or for Mirabar," Nanfoodle said between gulps of the golden liquid. "Master Ironforge was not explicit."

"I have a request for Mirabar," Regis explained between bites. "You understand the weight of our present dilemma, I hope."

"Many monsters, yes," Nanfoodle replied, and he took another bite of lamb and another gulp of mead.

"More than you know," Regis replied. "Pressing all the region. No doubt word has already reached your marchion from besieged, and perhaps already overrun, Nesmé. I know not how long we might hold any presence on the surface, and so Mirabar must mobilize her forces."

"For the good of Mithral Hall?" asked the gnome.

So surprised was he that a bit of mead fell out of his mouth as he blurted the words. He quickly dabbed it up with his napkin and took another big swallow.

"For the good of Mirabar," Regis corrected. "Are we to assume that these monsters will end their march here?"

It seemed to him that the gnome was growing a bit more concerned, and in his nervousness, Nanfoodle seemed to be taking more and more drink and less and less food. That was good, Regis thought, and so he kept the conversation going for some time, detailing the fall of the eastern gate and the fears that the trolls of the south had joined with the orcs and giants from the north, or perhaps that the groups had been working in concert all along. He spared no detail at all, drawing out the conversation for as long as possible, and letting Nanfoodle drink more and more mead.

At one point, when the servers arrived with even more food and drink, Regis called one over and whispered into his ear, "Cut the next bit of drink with Gutbuster." The halfling glanced at the gnome, trying to get a measure of his present sensibilities. "Twenty-to-one mead," he explained to the server, not wanting to knock the poor gnome unconscious.

An hour later, Regis was still talking, and Nanfoodle was still drinking.

"But you and your sceptrana claim that you came here to check on Torgar and to strengthen the bond between our towns," Regis said suddenly, and with increased volume. He had been steering the conversation that way for a bit, moving away from the particulars of the monsters and the fighting and toward the issue of relations between Mirabar and Mithral Hall. "That is true, is it not?"

Nanfoodle's eyes opened wide—or at least, as wide as the somewhat inebriated gnome could open them.

"W-well . . . yes," Nanfoodle sputtered. "That is why we came here, after all."

"Indeed," said Regis.

He shifted forward in his chair, leaning near to Nanfoodle. He fished his necklace out of the front of his vest and fiddled with the ruby pendant, sending it into a little spin.

"Well, we all want that, of course," the halfling said, and he noted that Nanfoodle had glanced at the ruby and up, and again at the ruby. "Better relations, I mean."

"Yes, yes, of course," said the gnome, his eyes more and more focused on the tantalizing spin of the enchanted ruby pendant.

Regis would never have tried it on the gnome normally. Nanfoodle was a brilliant alchemist, so Torgar and Shingles McRuff had told him, and also was known to dabble in illusionary magic. Add to that obvious intelligence the natural resistance of a gnome to such enchantments as the ruby might cast, and the pendant would never have been effective.

But Nanfoodle was drunk.

He didn't even turn his eyes from the pendant anymore, obviously mesmerized by its continuing sparkling and spinning.

"And do you seek those relations in the westernmost tunnels of Mithral Hall?" Regis asked casually.

"Eh?" Nanfoodle remarked.

"You were there, were you not?" Regis pressed, but quietly so, not wanting his suspicions to break the charm. "In the western tunnels, I mean. You have been going there quite a bit, from what I hear. The dwarves find that curious, even amusing, for there is nothing down there . . . or is there?"

"Sealed tunnels, pitch-washed," Nanfoodle answered absently.

"Then what importance might they offer to your mission in coming all this way?" the halfling asked. "Since you came to check on Torgar, did you not? And to better the relationship between Mirabar and Mithral Hall?"

Nanfoodle gave a snort and a shake of his head.

"If only that were so," said the gnome.

Regis froze in place, resisting the urge to fall back in his chair. He gave the pendant another spin.

"Indeed, if only!" he enthusiastically agreed. "So tell me, good gnome, why have you really come?"

The hair on the back of Shoudra Stargleam's neck rose inexplicably when a dwarf informed her that her friend was sitting with Steward Regis, and had been for more than two hours. The sceptrana moved along the corridors, half-running and often slowing as she tried to sort things out. Why was she so bothered and nervous, after all, for wasn't Nanfoodle a reliable companion?

She came into an anteroom where a trio of dwarves stood calmly, each holding a nasty-looking polearm.

"Well met yerself," one of them said to Shoudra, and he motioned for the door to the audience room.

A second dwarf, standing beside the door, pushed it open, and Shoudra heard laughter from within and saw the glow of a comfortable fire. Still, she didn't calm down; something wasn't sitting well with her. She moved to the opening and peered in to see Nanfoodle laughing stupidly on one cushy chair, while a more sober Regis, his wounded arm back in its supporting sling, sat across from him.

"So nice of you to join us, Sceptrana Shoudra," the halfling said, and he motioned to the empty chair.

Shoudra took one step into the room, then jerked suddenly as the door slammed behind her.

"Nanfoodle and I were just discussing the disposition of the relationship between our respective communities," Regis explained, and again he indicated the empty chair to the unmoving sceptrana.

Shoudra hardly heard him, for her attention followed her scan around the room. The walls were all hung with tapestries, save the one that held the hearth, and the heavy hangings were not flat against the wall. Shoudra's gaze went lower, and she noted the toes of more than one pair of boots below the bottom fringe.

Slowly, the sceptrana turned her gaze to Regis.

"It is an interesting relationship, don't you agree," the halfling said, and there was no missing the sudden change in his tone.

"One we hope to strengthen," Shoudra replied, her gaze going to the obviously drunk Nanfoodle.

"Truly?" Regis asked.

Shoudra turned back to him.

"To strengthen our relationship by weakening Mithral Hall's ore?" the halfling asked, and he pulled a large pouch out from behind him on the chair and tossed it on the floor at Shoudra's feet.

Shoudra slowly bent and retrieved the pouch but didn't even have to open it to know what was inside: Nanfoodle's weakening solution.

The sceptrana turned her stunned expression over the gnome, who burst out in great laughter and nearly fell off the chair.

"My new friend Nanfoodle told me everything," Regis stated.

He snapped his fingers in the air, and the tapestries were pulled aside, revealing a trio of grim-faced dwarves. The door behind Shoudra opened as well, and the sceptrana knew that polearms were aimed at her back.

"He has told me," Regis went on, "of how you came here on orders of the marchion to sabotage our ore. Of how Mirabar intended to wage a trade war upon Mithral Hall through such means, to ruin our reputation and steal our customers."

Shoudra began to shake her head.

"You must understand . . ." she started.

"Understand?" Regis interrupted. "Weakened metal in our hands as we battle the orc hordes? Weakened metal on the barricades we construct to keep the monsters out of our halls? What is there to understand, Sceptrana?"

"We didn't know you were at war!" Shoudra blurted.

"Oh, then of course your spying and espionage are not so important!" came the halfling's sarcastic reply.

"No, you must understand the temperament of Marchion Elastul," Shoudra tried to explain. She moved beside Nanfoodle as he spoke and casually draped an arm across his shoulders. "This is his . . . his way. Marchion Elastul fears Mithral Hall, and so he instructed Nanfoodle and I to come here and learn if Torgar was divulging the secrets of Mirabar. You must admit that Mithral Hall has gained a sudden advantage in the trade war, with four hundred of Mirabar's dwarves deserting our city to come to yours."

"Yes, a tremendous advantage with hordes of orcs knocking on our doors."

"We did not know." Shoudra took a deep breath and went on, "And I doubt that Nanfoodle or I would have had the heart to cause any mischief even if there was no war. Neither of us approve of the marchion's tactics here, nor of his disposition concerning King Bruenor and Mithral Hall. We two seek a better way."

"You would say that now, of course," Regis interrupted.

Shoudra closed her eyes and blew a long sigh, then began muttering under her breath.

"Take them and lock them away—and separately," Regis instructed.

The six dwarves advanced on the pair, but then they were gone, winking out of sight.

"The door!" Regis cried, and the dwarf closest the exit rushed back and slammed the portal shut.

Shoudra and a very surprised-looking Nanfoodle appeared suddenly on the far side of the room, and the dwarves hooted and charged.

They disappeared again, reappearing a few moments later in front of the hearth.

"She's casting again! Stop her!" Regis cried, noting Shoudra's renewed chant.

"Watch for fireballs!" cried the dwarf by the door.

He pulled it open, and Shoudra and Nanfoodle appeared right there, as fortune would have it. The dwarf fell away with a shriek.

Nanfoodle giggled stupidly, and Shoudra yanked him out of the room and into a run through the anteroom and out into the corridor, chased every step by the shouting dwarves.

"You silly gnome!" Shoudra scolded, and Nanfoodle giggled even more.

With the dwarves gaining and Nanfoodle lagging, Shoudra gave an exasperated growl and scooped Nanfoodle up.

They went through a door, which Shoudra shut and promptly barred, and out the other side of the room into another corridor. On they ran for the western gate, cries of alarm sounding all around them.

Soon the dwarves had them located once more, a dozen shouts echoing down every side passage they crossed. Finally, the pair turned into the long main corridor, which ended on a wide landing lined by statues of the kings of Mithral Hall. A descending staircase beyond that landing led to a smaller room and across that the last rays of daylight were streaming through the great hall's open western doors.

Doors that weren't to remain open for long, Shoudra realized, for dwarves down there were already pushing aside the doorstops, while others were forming a defensive line across the opening.

"Well, they got us," Nanfoodle said with a chuckle. "Time for torture!"

"Shut up, you fool," Shoudra scolded.

She looked all around, then at the last moment, tugged Nanfoodle into the shadows behind the nearest statue. And not a moment too soon, for a group of dwarves came charging through the moment they were out of sight, all of them shouting to, "Hold the door!" or, "Bar the way!"

Nanfoodle started to cry out in response, but Shoudra clamped a hand over his mouth and held him tight. She took a deep breath and gathered her courage, then she peeked out at the outside door and the area beyond. After finally calming the drunken gnome, the sceptrana began to cast another spell.

She whispered out a chant and the tips of her two index fingers began to glow bright blue. With them, the sceptrana then drew out the lines of a door in the air.

"There!" came a shout—Regis's shout, and Shoudra glanced back to see the halfling and a group of dwarves charging her way.

Without hesitation, the sceptrana hoisted Nanfoodle once more, and as the great western doors of Mithral Hall banged closed, she carried Nanfoodle through her portal.

The dimensional door closed right behind her, and Shoudra breathed a sudden sigh of relief to realize that she and her companion were outside the closed doors, standing alone in Keeper's Dale.

"You got so many tricks," Nanfoodle squeaked, and he laughed again.

Shoudra's eyes shot darts at the foolish alchemist.

"More than you know," she promised.

She hoisted him higher and moved off to the side of the gates, to a hollow area already dark with shadows.

There, the glum Shoudra sat, but not until she had forced Nanfoodle down to the ground. He tried to rise, but Shoudra dropped both of her legs over him, pinning the unsteady gnome.

He started to protest, but Shoudra flicked her finger against the underside of his long and pointy nose.

"Hey!" Nanfoodle cried.

"Shhh," Shoudra insisted, putting her finger over her pursed lips. In a voice low and threatening, she added, "You be quiet, or I'll make you quiet. I've a few magic tricks left."

Those words seemed to take a bit of the drunk off Nanfoodle. He swallowed loudly and said no more.

They sat there as afternoon turned to twilight and twilight to night.

And Shoudra had no idea what they were going to do.

18

THE FRIENDSHIP DARE

Drizzt pulled himself up over the dark stone and dexterously moved his foot atop the abutment. He started to leap over, quickly sorting out his landing area, but he relaxed and paused, noting that Guenhwyvar had the situation completely under control.

There stood the female drow, weapons in hand, but talking to the cat, bidding Guenhwyvar to back off and not kill her.

"Perhaps if you threw your weapons to the ground, Guenhwyvar would not seem so hungry," Drizzt called down, and he was surprised at how easily the little-used drow language came back to him.

"And when I do, you will instruct your panther to slay me," came the reply.

"I could instruct her so right now," Drizzt argued, "and could be down beside her quickly enough, I assure you. Your choices are few. Surrender, or fight and die."

The female glanced up at him—even from a distance, he could see her sneer—but then she looked back at Guenhwyvar and angrily threw her sword and dagger to the ground.

Guenhwyvar continued to circle her but did not advance.

"What is your name?" Drizzt asked, scrambling over the stone and picking a rocky path down to the small stone hollow where the cat had cornered the female.

"I am of family Soldou," the female replied tentatively. "Is that a name known to you?"

"It is not," Drizzt announced, suddenly right behind her, having fast-stepped around the bowl, out of sight. The suddenness of his arrival startled the female. "And in truth, your surname is not important to me. Not nearly as important as your purpose in being here."

Slowly, the female turned to face him. She was quite pretty, Drizzt noted, with her hair parted so that long strands covered half her face, including one of her reddish eyes—not the spidery bloodshot lines he often saw in orcs, but a general reddish hue.

"I escaped the Underdark much as you did, Drizzt Do'Urden," she answered, and though he did well to hide it, the references to him, the apparent knowledge of his course, did indeed surprise Drizzt. "If you knew of family Soldou, you would understand that we lost favor with the Spider Queen, by choice. As one, we forsook that wicked demon queen, and so we were destroyed almost to a one."

"But you got out?"

"Here I stand."

"Indeed, and in company quite fitting a follower of Lolth," Drizzt remarked, and he brought Twinkle up in a flash, the edge of the blade resting against the side of the female's neck.

She didn't flinch.

"Only so that I could survive," the female tried to explain. "I came out and still have not adapted to this fiery orb that burns its way across the high ceiling."

"It takes time."

"I found the other drow—his name is Ad'non—"

"Was," Drizzt corrected, and he shrugged.

The female didn't flinch.

"I would have killed him soon enough anyway," she went on. "I could not tolerate his vileness any longer. As soon as he stripped down to take advantage of the paralyzed elf, I meant to run him through."

Drizzt nodded, though of course he did not believe a word of it. For a supposed convert against the drow nature, she seemed quite willing to put a dart or two into him, after all.

"You still have not told me your name."

"Donnia," she answered, and Drizzt was somewhat relieved that she had not lied to him on that, at least. He had heard the male call her by name, after all. "I am Donnia Soldou, who seeks the blessing of Eilistraee."

That reference put Drizzt somewhat off his center, obviously so.

"You have heard of the Lady of the Dance?"

"Rumors," said Drizzt.

He believed that the female was lying, of course, but still, he couldn't help but be intrigued, for he had indeed heard whispers of the goddess Eilistraee and her followers—supposedly drow of like heart to his own.

"I am sorry that I turned on you in the cave of the elves," Donnia went on. She lowered her gaze. "You must understand that my companion was a powerful warrior and that I was alive only by his good graces. If he suspected that I was a traitor, he would have long-ago killed me."

"And you found no opportunities in all this time to be rid of him?"

Donnia stared up at him.

"Or is he not the only companion you have found?"

"Only Ad'non," Donnia said. "Well, Ad'non and his friends, the giants and the orcs. He has been here for many years, a rogue not unlike yourself—though his intent is far different. He haunts the tunnels among the upper Underdark and about the Spine of the World, finding his pleasures where he can."

"Then why did you not rid yourself of him and be on your way?" Drizzt asked.

Donnia nodded and rubbed a hand across her face.

"Then I would have been alone," she whispered. "Alone and up here, in this place I do not know. I was weak, Drizzt Do'Urden. Can you not understand?"

"I can indeed," Drizzt admitted.

He sheathed Icingdeath and moved Twinkle from Donnia's neck. With his free hand he began patting the female down. He found a dagger at her belt and took it away, along with her hand crossbow and a belt pouch filled with darts. One of those darts came out quickly and quietly, the ranger sliding it into his belt. Drizzt patted lower, along her leg, and noted the slightest lump at the top of one of her soft boots. He purposely ignored that bulge as he slid his hand down across her ankles. It was a knife, of course, and he made it look like he had just missed it in his inspection.

"Your weapons are drow-made," he remarked, tossing the discovered dagger and hand crossbow to the ground beside the sword and the other dagger. "They will do you little good up here if you plan to remain under the light of the sun." He slid Twinkle into its sheath. "Come along then," he instructed, and he started away, pointedly walking right past the discarded weapons.

He looked back at Donnia as he did, and noting that she wasn't paying him any heed at the moment, he hooked the hand crossbow with his foot and brought it up fast to catch it with his free hand and hook it on his belt.

"Come along," he instructed her once more, and he started away.

He heard Donnia suck in her breath slightly as she moved past the pile of weapons, and he knew what she was thinking. She believed that he was testing her, that he was ready to pull forth his blades and defend should she grab at one of those discarded weapons.

When they crossed by, the weapons still in their pile, Drizzt knew that Donnia believed she had passed that test. Little did she understand that first opportunity to be no more than a ruse.

"Guenhwyvar," the ranger called, baiting the trap all the more sweetly. "Too long have you tarried here. Go home now, I bid!"

Drizzt glanced sidelong at Donnia, watching her as she observed the great panther begin stalking in a circle, round and round until Guenhwyvar's lines blurred and she became a drifting gray mist, initially in the shape of a cat, but then drifting apart to nothingness.

"Guenhwyvar's time here is limited," Drizzt explained. "She tires easily and must return to her Astral home to rejuvenate."

"A marvelous companion," Donnia remarked.

"One of three," Drizzt replied. "Or five, if you count the pegasi, and I assure you that they should be counted."

"You are allied with the surface elves then?" Donnia asked, and before Drizzt could answer, she added, "That is good—they are fine companions for one of our kind who has forsaken the Spider Queen."

"Mighty companions," Drizzt agreed. "The female is a high priestess of an elf god, Corellon Larethian. She will wish to speak with you, no doubt, to determine your veracity."

He noted the slight hesitation in Donnia's step as she moved along right behind him.

"She has spells she will cast upon you," Drizzt pressed. "But fear not, for they are merely to detect if you are lying. Once she has seen the truth of Donnia Soldou . . ."

He ended his words with a sudden spin left to right, drawing Icingdeath from the sheath on his right hip as he turned. As he expected, the panicked Donnia was coming at him, dagger drawn from her boot and arm extended.

Drizzt's leading right hand slapped down over Donnia's wrist and turned her stabbing blade up high and wide, and in rushed the scimitar to poke hard against the female's ribs, drawing a long gash. Donnia spun and scrambled away, but not before she got hit again across the extended arm, hard enough so that she

let go of her blade. Clutching her right arm and holding it in tight against the wound to her right side, Donnia stumbled.

Drizzt ran past her.

"All of it a lie—as if I should have ever expected anything else from a drow!" he cried, and he rushed to the side as Donnia veered.

"I will have the truth now, or I will have your head!" Drizzt demanded. "Why are you here? And how many of our kin are in your band?"

"Hundreds!" Donnia yelled at him, and still she scrambled, looking for some escape. "Thousands, Drizzt Do'Urden! And all of them with the edict to bring your head to the Spider Queen!"

Drizzt rushed to block the way before her, and Donnia summoned a globe of darkness around him.

She charged right into it, guessing correctly that he would go out one side or the other. She got past and rushed out of the darkness, coming to the lip of a long drop. Without hesitation, the drow leaped out, again bringing forth the innate magic of her station and race. Before she had plummeted twenty feet, she was drifting down slowly.

"You so disappoint me," she heard Drizzt say behind and above her, and she sensed sincerity in his voice, as if perhaps he truly wanted to believe her tale.

And indeed, he had wanted to believe her. How badly Drizzt wanted to find a drow companion! Another of like mind to him to share his adventures, to truly understand the solitude that was ever in his heart.

Donnia had barely gotten the smile onto her face when she heard the click of a hand crossbow from behind and above, and she felt the sudden sting atop her shoulder. She held her place in midair, counteracting the pull of the ground completely with the levitation. Then she stared at the dart and felt the poison beginning to seep into her shoulder.

She was motionless, helpless, hanging there.

Drizzt looked down at her and sighed deeply. He dropped the hand crossbow—Donnia's own hand crossbow that he had scooped up from the pile as they had set out—and watched it drop past her, down, down, the two hundred feet to shatter on the stones below.

Drizzt fell into a crouch and put his head in his hand. He didn't look away, though, determined to bear witness.

The levitation soon expired and the paralyzed Donnia dropped. She couldn't even scream out as she fell, for her vocal chords could not function against the potent poison.

Drizzt looked away at the last second, not wanting to watch her hit. But then he looked back, to see the drow female splayed across the stones, warm blood pooling around her.

The ranger sighed again, though he wasn't really surprised it had ended like that. Still, the one emotion that dominated Drizzt Do'Urden at that moment was anger, just anger, at the futility of it all.

He gathered himself up a few moments later, reminding himself that Tarathiel and Innovindil were likely still fairly helpless in their cave, and he started back at a fast run. He found them safe and sound, and even beginning to move a bit once more.

Innovindil was reaching for her clothing as Drizzt entered, so he promptly retrieved the items and gave them over, then moved back near the entrance and began cleaning up the mess that was Ad'non.

"Well met again, Drizzt Do'Urden," Tarathiel said to him. "And a most fortunate meeting it is, for us at least."

"You have dealt with the remaining drow?" Innovindil asked.

"She is dead," Drizzt confirmed, his tone somber. "She fell from a cliff face."

"Did it pain you to kill them?" Innovindil asked.

Drizzt's head snapped around at her, his eyes narrow.

"Did it?" Innovindil asked again, not backing away at all.

Drizzt's visage softened.

"It always does," he admitted.

"Then your soul is intact," Tarathiel remarked. "Be afraid when the killing no longer affects you."

How profound that simple remark seemed to Drizzt at that moment, to the creature who seemed to be caught somewhere between his true self and the Hunter. Certainly he felt more soulless at those times when he was the Hunter. The deaths didn't bother him in that mode. He had felt nothing but the satisfaction of victory when he had beheaded Ad'non, but the death of Donnia had stung more than a little. There had to be some middle ground, Drizzt knew, a place where he could fight as the Hunter and yet hold on to his soul. He thought back across the years and believed that he had found that place before. He could only hope that he would find it again.

Drizzt rummaged through Ad'non's pockets, searching for some clue as to who the dark elf might be and why he was there. He found little, other than a few coins that he did not recognize. One other thing did catch his eye though: the fine light gray silk shirt that Ad'non wore under his cloak. That shirt had

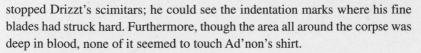
stopped Drizzt's scimitars; he could see the indentation marks where his fine blades had struck hard. Furthermore, though the area all around the corpse was deep in blood, none of it seemed to touch Ad'non's shirt.

"Strong magic," Innovindil remarked, and when Drizzt looked to her, she motioned for him to take the shirt as his own. "To the victor. . . ." she recited.

Drizzt began removing the shirt. His own chain mail, forged by Bruenor, was in sore need of repair, with many broken links, and some of them rubbing him uncomfortably.

"We are most grateful," Tarathiel remarked. "You understand that, of course?"

"I could not let them harm you, as I believe you would have come to my aid—indeed, as you have come to my aid," Drizzt replied.

"We are not your enemies," Tarathiel said, and the tone of his voice made Drizzt pause and consider him.

"I have never desired the enmity of any surface elf I have ever known," Drizzt replied, both his tone and his words leading.

He didn't miss the movement as Innovindil and Tarathiel exchanged concerned glances.

"We must tell you that you have made an enemy of one," Innovindil admitted. "Through no fault of your own."

"You remember Ellifain," Tarathiel added.

"Keenly," Drizzt assured him, and he sighed and lowered his gaze. "Though when I last met her, she was called Le'lorinel and was masquerading as a male."

Again the two elves looked to each other, Tarathiel nodding.

"That was how she evaded us in Silverymoon," he said to his partner.

"She came after you," Innovindil reasoned. "We knew that such was her course, though we knew not where you might be. We tried to stop her—you must believe us when we tell you that Ellifain was beyond reason and was acting on her own and against the wishes of our people."

"She was beyond reason," Drizzt agreed.

"And you met her in battle?" Tarathiel quietly asked, his voice full of concern.

Drizzt glanced up at him but lowered his eyes almost immediately and sighed yet again.

"I had no desire to . . . had I known, I would have . . ." he stammered. He took a deep breath and looked directly at the pair. "I caught up to her in the company of some thieves that I and my companions were pursuing. I had no idea of who she was—or even that she was a 'she'—when we joined in combat. It was not until . . ."

"Until you struck the killing blow," Tarathiel reasoned, and Innovindil looked away.

Drizzt's responding silence spoke volumes.

"I feared that it would end this way," Tarathiel said to Drizzt. "We tried to save Ellifain from herself—no doubt you did as well, or that you would have, had you known."

"But she was full of a rage that transcended all rationality," Innovindil added. "With every tale we heard about your exploits in the service of the goodly races, she grew even more outraged, convinced that it was all a lie. Convinced that Drizzt Do'Urden was all a lie."

Drizzt didn't blink as he responded, "Perhaps I am."

"Is that what you believe?" Innovindil asked, and Drizzt merely shrugged.

"We do not judge you harshly for defending yourself against Ellifain," Tarathiel remarked.

"It would change nothing if you did," said Drizzt, and that seemed to take the pair off their balance a bit.

"And so we can fight together in our common cause," Tarathiel went on. "Side-by-side."

Drizzt stared at him for a short while, then looked back at Innovindil. It was a tempting offer, but it entailed a commitment that Drizzt was not yet ready to take. He looked back to Tarathiel and shook his head.

"I hunt alone," he explained. "But I will be there to support you if I may, in times when you are in need."

He gathered up the marvelous silken shirt then and started to go.

"We will always be in need of your help," Tarathiel said from behind him. "And would you not be stronger if . . ."

"Let him go," Drizzt heard Innovindil remark to her companion. "He is not yet ready."

The next morning, Drizzt Do'Urden sat on a bluff looking back at the area of the elves' cave, mulling over the generous offer Tarathiel had given him. He had just admitted to killing their friend and kin, and yet, neither had judged him at all harshly.

It put a whole new light on the unfortunate Ellifain incident for Drizzt Do'Urden, but he just wasn't certain of how that light might yet shine.

And he was confronted with the prospect of new friendship, of new allies, and while the thought tempted him on a very basic level, it also frightened him profoundly.

He had known great friends once and the greatest allies anyone could ever hope to command.

Once.

So he sat and he stared, torn apart inside, wondering what might be and what should be.

Always, always, he found the image of the blasted tower tumbling, taking Bruenor down with it.

Drizzt felt an urgent need to go back to his own cave then, to feel the one-horned helmet, to smell the scent of Bruenor, and to remember his lost friends. He started off.

Before the end of the day, though, he was drawn back to that bluff, looking across the stones to the lair of Innovindil and Tarathiel.

He watched with great interest as one of the pegasi swooped past, bearing Tarathiel down to the cave entrance. To his surprise, the elf dismounted and did not go right in, but rather, ran out his way and called to him.

"Drizzt Do'Urden!" Tarathiel cried. "Come! I have news that concerns us all!"

Despite his reservations, despite the deep pain that pervaded his every fiber, Drizzt found himself trotting along to join the pair.

※

"Yet another tribe crawls from its dark hole," Innovindil said to Drizzt when he entered the cave. "Tarathiel has seen them marching along the foothills of the Spine of the World."

"You called me in to tell me of orcs in the area?" Drizzt asked incredulously. "There is no shortage of—"

"Not just any orcs, but a new tribe," Tarathiel interrupted. "We have seen them flocking to this cause, one tribe after another. Now we have found a group that has not yet linked up."

"If we strike at them hard, they might go back to their holes," Innovindil explained. "That would be a great victory to our cause." When Drizzt didn't overtly react, she added, "It would be a great victory for those dwarves defending Mithral Hall."

"How many?" Drizzt heard himself asking.

"A small tribe—perhaps fifty," Tarathiel replied.

"The three of us are to kill fifty orcs?" Drizzt asked.

"Better to kill ten and turn the other forty around," Tarathiel replied.

"Let them whisper in their tunnels about certain death awaiting any who go to the call of the orc leader," Innovindil added.

"The orcs and giants have amassed a great army," Tarathiel explained. "Thousands of orcs and hundreds of giants, we fear, and truthfully, our efforts against such a great army will prove a minor factor in the end result. But the more ominous cloud for those in the region, the dwarves of Mithral Hall, the elves of the Moonwood, the people of Silverymoon, are the seemingly limitless reinforcements pouring out of the Spine of the World."

"Tens of thousands more orcs and goblins may flock to the call of whoever it is who leads this army," Innovindil put in.

"But perhaps we can stem that flow of vermin," said Tarathiel. "Let us turn back the orcs, that they warn their fellows about leaving the mountains. Our kills could be multiplied many times over concerning monsters who choose not to join in." He paused and stared hard at Drizzt.

"This is, perhaps, our chance to make a real difference in this war. Just we three."

Drizzt couldn't deny the potential of Tarathiel's plan.

"Quickly, then," Tarathiel remarked when it became obvious that Drizzt wasn't going to argue. "We must hit them before they travel far from the caves, before the fall of night."

Drizzt marveled at how precisely the two elves angled their descending mounts, putting themselves in line with the setting sun as they approached the orc force.

Beside the drow, Guenhwyvar gave an anxious growl, but Drizzt held her back.

In came the two elves and their winged mounts, and their bows began to hum. And the orcs began to shriek and to point up to the sky.

"Now, Guen," Drizzt whispered, and he turned the panther loose.

Guenhwyvar bounded away along a line north of the orcs, while Drizzt sprinted off the other way, hemming the tribe on the south. He found his first battle soon after, even as orcs across the way screamed out in terror at the sight of Guenhwyvar. Drizzt leaped atop a boulder and stood staring down at a pair of orcs who had taken cover from the elves' arrow barrage. He waited for them to finally look up before dropping between them.

Out went Twinkle, a killing blow to his left, while he turned Icingdeath to the flat side as he slapped hard at the orc on his right, sending the creature scrambling away.

Behind him and to his left, the pegasi set down, and the two elves let fly another round of arrows, then leaped free and drew their weapons.

"For the Moonwood!" Drizzt heard Tarathiel cry.

Despite the urgent moment, Drizzt Do'Urden was wearing a grin when he came out hard from behind that boulder, leaping into a devastating spin at the closest ranks of orcs.

At his side, Tarathiel and Innovindil linked arms and went into their deadly dance.

The orcs fell back. One tried to call out commands for them to regroup, but Drizzt immediately engulfed the creature in a globe of darkness.

Another shouted out a command—right before a flying Guenhwyvar buried it.

Within moments, the orcs were running back the way they had come, and when the last rays of daylight winked out, they were still running, and still with Guenhwyvar flanking them on the left and Drizzt on the right and Tarathiel and Innovindil and their powerful mounts pressing them from behind.

Soon after, Drizzt watched the last pair run into a dark, wide cave. He charged up behind them, calling out threats. When one slowed and started to glance back, he rushed ahead and cut the creature down.

Its companion did not look back.

Nor did any others of the tribe.

Drizzt stood in the cave entrance, hands resting against his hips, staring down the deep tunnel beyond.

Guenhwyvar padded up beside him, and soon he heard the clopping of pegasi hooves.

"Exactly as I had hoped," Tarathiel remarked, dismounting and moving to stand beside Drizzt.

He lifted a hand and patted the drow on the shoulder, and though he did flinch a bit initially, Drizzt did not pull away.

"Our technique will only strengthen with practice," Innovindil said as she walked up on Drizzt's other side.

The drow looked deeply into her eyes and saw that she had just challenged him yet again, had just invited him yet again.

He did not openly deny her, nor did he pull away when she moved very close to his side.

19

SETTLING INTO
THE ORC KING'S SHADOW

The work along the western bank of the Surbrin moved at a frenetic pace, with orcs and giants constructing defensive fortifications at all of the possible fords near the southern edge of the mountains around the closed gate of Mithral Hall. King Obould deemed one crossing particularly dangerous, where the river was wide and shallow and an entire army could cross in short order. And so Obould set most of his orcs into action, bringing tons of stones down to the water and packing them tightly together, then filling in with tons of sand, forming a levy that tightened up the river and deepened and strengthened the flow.

Not to be outdone, and taking no chances, Gerti Orelsdottr ordered her giants to ensure that the dwarven gate would not soon be opened, at one point even bringing a landslide down from the mountains. She would not have Clan Battlehammer sneaking out at her backside!

The work went on day and night, with high walls quickly constructed at every crossing point. Giants piled boulders suitable for bombardment at every outpost, ready to meet any crossing with heavy resistance, and orcs similarly filled rooms with hastily made spears. If reinforcements meant to come across the Surbrin, Gerti and Obould meant to make them pay dearly for the ground.

The two leaders met every night, along with Arganth, who was fast becoming Obould's principal advisor. The discussions were usually civil, a discourse about how to best and quickly secure their gains, but it did not escape Gerti's notice that Obould was leading the way at every turn, that his plans made great sense, that his vision had suddenly clarified to a keen and attainable edge. Thus, when the giantess was leaving the nightly meetings, she was usually in a foul mood, and increasingly, she went into the meetings gnashing her teeth.

So it was that night a tenday after the fall of Mithral Hall's eastern gate.

"We must move back to the west," Gerti began, the litany she spoke to open every meeting of late. "Your son remains locked in a stalemate with the dwarves, and he has not the giant allies he needs to dislodge them."

"You are in a hurry to chase them into Mithral Hall?" Obould casually asked.

"One less problem for us when we do."

"Better to let attrition take a heavy toll on them while we have them out here in the open," the orc king reasoned. "Deplete the resources they would employ against Proffit and his smelly trolls."

The notion of the orc king referring to any other race as "smelly" struck Gerti as laughable, but she was in no mood for mirth.

"Do you believe that a few trolls will chase Clan Battlehammer from its ancestral home?" she scoffed.

"Of course Proffit will not succeed," Obould admitted. "But we do not need him to succeed. He will soften them and tighten the noose around them. The tighter we squeeze them in their tunnels, the better the resolution."

"That we wipe them from the North?" Gerti asked, a bit confused, for it did not seem to her that Obould was moving along that line, though it had always before been his stated intent.

"That would be wonderful," the orc king remarked. "If we can. If not, perhaps with their outer doors sealed and pressed in the tunnels, Clan Battlehammer will seek to negotiate a settlement."

"A treaty between conquering orcs and dwarves?" Gerti asked incredulously.

"What is their option?" asked Obould. "Will they carry on their trade through tunnels to Silverymoon and Felbarr?"

"They might."

"And when we at last locate and drop those tunnels?" Obould asked, seeming perfectly confident in that. "Will the dwarves follow the way of that wretched Do'Urden creature and begin doing trade with the drow of the Underdark?"

"Or perhaps they will do nothing of the sort," Gerti argued. "Surely Mithral Hall is self-contained and self-sustaining. Clan Battlehammer may be content to remain in their hole for a century, if necessary." She leaned forward over her crossed legs. "Your kind has never been known for its long-term resolve, Obould.

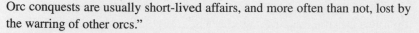

Orc conquests are usually short-lived affairs, and more often than not, lost by the warring of other orcs."

That particular reference was purposely worded and aimed to sting Obould, for not long in the past the orc king had made a great conquest indeed, sweeping the dwarves from Citadel Felbarr and renaming it the Citadel of Many-Arrows. But then had come the inevitable squabbling, orc against orc, and the dwarves under King Emerus Warcrown had wasted little time in chasing Obould's distracted and chaotic invaders back out. Gerti had launched her not-too-subtle reminder of that disaster just to drop her counterpart's mounting ego a few pegs. The giantess was surprised, though, and more than a little disappointed, at how composed Obould remained.

"True enough," the orc king even admitted. "Perhaps we have learned from our mistakes."

Gerti honestly wanted to ask that strange creature who he truly was and what he had done with that sniveling fool, Obould.

"When the region is secured and our numbers great enough, we will build orc cities," Obould explained, and he seemed to be looking far away then, as if he was visualizing that of which he spoke. "We will find our own commerce and trade and seek out surrounding towns to join in."

"You will send an emissary to Lady Alustriel and Emerus Warcrown seeking trade agreements?" Gerti blurted.

"Alustriel first," Obould calmly replied. "Ever has Silverymoon been known for tolerance. I expect that King Warcrown will need more persuading."

He looked directly at Gerti and grinned wickedly, his tusks curling over his upper lip.

"But we will have barter," Obould asked, "will we not?"

"What goods might you produce that they cannot get elsewhere?"

"We will hold the key to Clan Battlehammer's freedom," Obould explained. "Perhaps we allow for the reopening of the eastern door of Mithral Hall. Perhaps we even construct a great bridge at that point over the Surbrin. We allow Mithral Hall to trade openly and aboveground once again, and all for a tithe, of course."

"You have gone mad," Gerti snapped at him. "Dwarves fall before orc blades! King Bruenor himself was killed by your son's charges. Do you believe they will so quickly forget?"

"Who can know?" the orc king said with a shrug, and he seemed to hardly care. "They are just the options, all the more possible because of our successes. If all this land becomes an orc stronghold, will the peoples of the region band together and fight us? How many thousands will they sacrifice? How long will they hold their resolve when their kin die by the score? By the hundred, or thousand? And all of that with the option of peace honestly offered to them."

"Honestly?"

"Honestly," Obould replied. "We cannot take Silverymoon, or Sundabar, if all my kin and all your kin and all the trolls of the Trollmoors banded together. You know this as I know this."

The admission nearly had Gerti choking with disbelief, for she had known that truth from the beginning, of course, but had never believed that Obould would ever truly understand his real limitations.

"Wh-what about Citadel Felbarr?" she did manage to stammer, hoping once more to throw the orc king off his guard.

"We will see how far our victories take us," Obould replied. "Perhaps Mithral Hall will be conquered—that is no less a prize than Felbarr. Perhaps even the Moonwood will fall to us in the months it will take to secure any peace. We will be in need of lumber, of course, and not so that we might dance about the living trees as do the foolish elves."

He looked to the side again, as if staring far away, and gave a little guttural chuckle.

"We get too far ahead of ourselves," the orc king remarked. "Let us secure what we now have. Close the Surbrin to those who would support Mithral Hall. Let Proffit work his disaster in the southern tunnels, and let Urlgen then drive the dwarves fully into their hole and close the western door. Then we might decide our next march."

Gerti settled back against the wall of the stone room and stared at her counterpart and at the smug shaman sitting next to him. She resisted the urge to reach out and crush the life out of Arganth, though she dearly wanted to do just that, if only because he was such an ugly little wretch.

And she wondered, honestly, if she should spring forward and crush the life out of Obould first. The creature who was sitting before her was constantly amazing her, was constantly putting her off her balance. He was not the sniveling orc who had once brought her dwarf heads as a present. He was not the overreaching and doomed-to-disaster warrior leader whom she had played as an ally out of amusement. Obould was biding his time over in the west against the dwarves, sacrificing short-term gain and swift victory for a long-term benefit. What orc ever thought like that?

It seemed to Gerti as if Obould honestly had it all planned out, and even more amazing, it seemed as if he had a real chance of succeeding. What she had to wonder, however, was what plans the orc king might have in store for her.

"They smell like rothé dung in fetid water," Tos'un complained.

Despite her generally foul mood, Kaer'lic Suun Wett didn't argue the point—her nose wouldn't let her.

"And Proffit is the smelliest of the bunch," Tos'un rambled on.

Kaer'lic shot him a look reminding him that they were two drow amidst an army of trolls and that it might not do well to so openly insult the leader of the brutes.

"Perhaps that is how he got so elevated," Tos'un added, amusing himself, Kaer'lic figured, for she found nothing at all amusing about their current state of affairs. Particularly concerning her own state of indecision.

Tos'un continued to grumble and began to stalk around. He stopped suddenly and took a closer look at the small cave Kaer'lic had taken for her temporary shelter. Glyphs and runes had been etched here and there, and the priestess's ceremonial robes were set out.

When Tos'un turned to more closely scrutinize her, she did not hide the fact that she had been beginning to change into those garments when he had burst in.

"This is not a ceremonial day, is it?" the male asked.

"No," the priestess answered simply.

"Then you are communing . . . perhaps to locate our lost companions?"

"No."

"To gain spells that will help us with the trolls?"

"No."

"Am I to guess every possible purpose, then? Or is it that you would not tell me in any case?"

"No."

Tos'un paused and studied her, obviously not quite sure of where that last answer fit in exactly.

"Your pardon, high priestess," he said with clear sarcasm, and he dipped a bow that was full of his frustration. "I forget my place as a mere male."

"Oh, shut up," Kaer'lic replied, and she moved toward her vestments and began further disrobing. "I am as confused as you are," she admitted.

She gave a little laugh as she considered that—why shouldn't she tell Tos'un the truth, after all, since he was the only drow companion she was going to know for some time?

"It does not surprise me that Ad'non and Donnia sneaked away," Tos'un said.

"Nor does it surprise me," Kaer'lic replied. "My confusion has nothing to do with them."

"Then what? Obould?"

"He would be part of it, yes," said the priestess. "As would be whatever intervention his brutish god offered."

"It was an impressive ceremony."

Kaer'lic turned on him suddenly, caring not at all that she was stripped to the waist.

"I fear that I have angered Lolth," she admitted.

It didn't seem to sink into Tos'un at first, and he started to respond. But then, with her continuing stare, the weight of her words nearly bowled the male over. He glanced around, as if expecting some creature of the Abyss to leap out of the shadows and devour him then and there.

"What does that mean?" he asked, his voice shaky.

"I do not know," Kaer'lic replied. "I do not even know if I am correct in my assessment."

"Do you think the intervention of Gruumsh One-Eye to be—"

"No, it was before that ceremony," Kaer'lic admitted.

"Then what?"

"I fear it is because of your advice," Kaer'lic honestly replied.

"Mine?" the male protested. "What have I done that holds any sway to the Spider Queen? I have offered nothing—"

"You suggested that we would be better served in avoiding Drizzt Do'Urden, did you not?"

Tos'un rocked back on his heels, his eyes darting around, seeming like a trapped animal.

"I fear that I am trapped within a web of my own suspicions," said Kaer'lic. "Perhaps my unwillingness to engage the traitor, as you advised, has cost me Lolth's favor, but in truth, I fear that going against Drizzt Do'Urden and slaying him would anger the Spider Queen even more!"

Tos'un looked as if a slight breeze would have knocked him over.

"She denies you communion?"

"I am afraid to even try," the priestess admitted. "It is possible that my own fears work against me here."

"Your fears of Drizzt?" he asked, shaking his head, so obviously at a complete loss.

"Long ago, I came to some conclusions concerning the renegade of House Do'Urden," Kaer'lic explained. "Even before I knew of Matron Baenre's march against Mithral Hall. The name of Drizzt was not unknown to us even before you joined our little band. So many of our priestesses have come to errant presumptions concerning that one, I fear . . . and I believe. They see him as an enemy of the Spider Queen."

"Of course," said Tos'un. "How could he be anything but?"

"He is a facilitator of chaos!" Kaer'lic interrupted. "In his own beautiful way, Drizzt Do'Urden has brought more chaos to your home city than perhaps any before him. Would that not be the will of Lolth?"

Tos'un's eyes widened so much that it seemed as if they might simply roll out of their sockets.

"You believe the road of Drizzt Do'Urden to be Lolth-inspired?" he asked.

"I do," said Kaer'lic, and she turned away. "Clever Kaer'lic! To see the irony of the rebel. To imagine the beauty of Lolth's design."

"It does make sense," the other drow admitted.

"And either way, whether my guess is correct or not, I am trapped by my own cleverness," said Kaer'lic.

Tos'un moved around to stare at her curiously.

"If I am wrong," the priestess explained, "then we should have engaged the renegade with all our powers, as I believe Ad'non and Donnia now seek to do. If I am right, then I have exposed a design that is far beyond . . ."

Her voice trailed away.

"If you are right, the mere fact that you have solved the riddle of Drizzt brings weakness to Lady Lolth's designs," the male reasoned.

"And we cannot know."

Tos'un began shaking his head and trembling.

He said, "And you told me."

"You asked."

"But . . ." the male stammered. "But . . ."

"We do not know anything," Kaer'lic reminded him, holding up her hand before the quivering fool to calm him. "It is all speculation."

"Then let us break free of these wretched trolls and seek Drizzt out, that we might learn the truth," Tos'un offered.

"To reveal my discovery fully?"

Tos'un seemed to quickly come to see her point, his sudden, apparent eagerness fast wilting.

"Then what?" he asked.

"Then I will seek my answers as we travel with Proffit," Kaer'lic explained. "I must find my heart for the call to the handmaidens, though I fear the machinations of Lady Lolth and the fate that awaits those who seek to look through her plans."

"The Time of Troubles marked the greatest chaos in Menzoberranzan," he told her. "When House Oblodra, fortified by their psionic powers when the magic of all others seemed to fail about them, aspired to the mantle of First House and nearly won it. Of course, Lady Lolth then returned to the pleas of Matron Baenre . . . never have I seen such a catastrophe as that which befell the Oblodrans!"

Kaer'lic nodded, for the male had told her and her fellows that story before, in great and gory detail.

"It is a confusing time," she said again. "If my fears of Lolth's purpose concerning Drizzt Do'Urden weren't enough, we witness a rare display of true orc shaman might."

"You fear Obould," Tos'un stated more than he asked.

"We would be wise to stay wary of that one," Kaer'lic replied, not denying a thing. "And not because he is suddenly so much physically stronger and so much quicker. No, we must watch Obould carefully because, so suddenly, he is right!"

"Perhaps we were wrong in our estimation of the gifts Gruumsh has placed on that one. Perhaps the shamans imbued him with more than muscle and agility," Tos'un reasoned. "Is it possible that the ceremony gave to him the gift of insight as well?"

"At the least, he learned well his priorities," said Kaer'lic. "Forgoing his anger and hunger for a level of reason beyond anything I ever expected of the pig-faced creature. Consider this mission we find ourselves along—consider how easily and completely Obould is using Proffit and his trolls. If Obould can secure the area and keep the flow of orcs and goblins coming strong from the mountains, all the while holding firm his alliance with Proffit, then there is every reason to believe that he might just succeed in creating an orc nation in the North. Is it possible that Obould will bring his people to parity with Silverymoon and Sundabar, that he will force treaties, perhaps even trade agreements?"

"They are orcs!" Tos'un protested.

"Too smart for orcs, suddenly," lamented Kaer'lic. "We would do well to carefully watch these developments and to take no course contrary to Obould for the time being."

Once again, both Kaer'lic and Tos'un found themselves back on their heels at the observation; the two had been over it all before, but every time, they came to the same inescapable conclusion, and both were amazed.

"I wish that Ad'non and Donnia had not gone running off," Tos'un lamented. "It would be best if we were all together now."

"To retreat?"

"If it comes to that," the warrior from House Barrison Del'Armgo admitted. "For where and how shall we fit into Obould's kingdom?"

"From afar, in any case," Kaer'lic answered. "But fear not, for we shall find our fun. Even if Obould's vision comes to pass and he secures the realm he will claim as his own, how long will the orc kingdom hold? How long did it hold when Obould had Citadel Felbarr in his grasp? They will fall apart soon enough, do not doubt, and we will find enjoyment throughout the process, so long as we are cunning and careful."

Her own lack of confidence as she spoke that thought struck the blustering priestess profoundly. Was she uncomfortable because of her fears concerning the ultimate power behind the renegade Do'Urden? Or had the orc ceremony so unsettled her? Kaer'lic had to wonder if her lack of confidence was well founded, and directly proportional to her growing confidence in Obould's capabilities.

"And our enjoyment now?" Tos'un asked sarcastically.

"Yes, the trolls smell terribly," Kaer'lic replied. "But let us lead them as we were asked, through the tunnels toward Mithral Hall. You and I stay out of the way and out of the fighting—let the trolls and the dwarves slaughter each other with abandon. What do we care which side emerges victorious?"

Tos'un considered the words for a few moments, then nodded his agreement. He looked around at the hastily decorated chamber.

"Do you think you will find your confidence in Lolth's graces once more?" he asked.

"Who can know Lolth's will?" Kaer'lic said, with more than a little defeat obvious in her tone. "The enigma of the renegade Do'Urden troubles me greatly. In this time of chaos, I am the main representative of Lady Lolth and in the face of great presence of Gruumsh One-Eye. If through my cleverness or folly, I have compromised my own position in this, I have removed Lady Lolth from a deserved position in this delicious conquest."

"Or is there a personal remedy?" Tos'un remarked with a sly grin.

"I am not yet ready to embrace that notion and go chasing after Drizzt Do'Urden," Kaer'lic replied. "If Lolth is angry with me for my suspicions of her intentions concerning the rogue, then I will need guidance, and I will need to be well equipped with her blessing."

Tos'un nodded and glanced around once more.

"I wish you well in your search," he said. He turned to leave, adding, "for both our sakes."

Kaer'lic appreciated that last remark and felt better about her decision to reveal her weakness to the warrior. Normally, a dark elf would never offer advantage to another dark elf, fearing a dagger in the back. Might Tos'un figure to gain favor with Lolth by killing Kaer'lic? The priestess pushed that unsettling notion aside, reminding herself that their little band wasn't typical for the drow. The four of them were more reliant on each other than normal, for defense, for profit, and yes, even for companionship. How horrible the journey would be for her if Tos'un was not beside her. And he felt the same way, she knew, and that had guided her instincts that it would be acceptable to reveal the truth to him.

Because if it was personal, if Lolth was angry at her for purposefully turning away from Drizzt Do'Urden, then she would need Tos'un's assistance—and Ad'non's and Donnia's as well, if the renegade's reputation was to be believed.

Yes, Kaer'lic was thinking very much along the same lines as Tos'un. She wished those other two had not run off.

"What is it?" Gerti asked as she entered the wide cave beside the river that Obould had taken as his temporary quarters. The orc king sat on a stone to one side, his head resting in one hand and a look of concern on his brutish face— more concern than Gerti had seen since that troublesome ceremony.

"News from the north," Obould replied. "The Red Slash emerged from the Spine of the World to join in our cause."

His word choice alone reminded Gerti that he was not the same orc king who had often before come sniveling into her cave.

Obould looked up at her and said, "They were turned back."

"Turned back?" Gerti asked, and her voice turned snide. "Have your people already reverted to their self-destructive ways? Are they preparing the way for a counterattack before victory has even been achieved?"

"They were turned back by elves," Obould sourly replied, and he glared at the giantess, as open a threat as Gerti had ever seen from any orc.

"The elves have crossed the Surbrin?" the giantess asked, but not with too much concern.

"They were turned back by a *pair* of elves . . . and a drow," Obould clarified. "Does that ring familiar?"

"These Red Slash orcs—a small tribe?"

"Does it matter?" Obould replied. "They will run back into the tunnels now, and alert any others who were considering coming out to join with us."

"But Arganth spreads the word of the glory of Obould," said Gerti, "and Obould is Gruumsh, yes?"

As Obould narrowed his eyes, Gerti knew that he had caught on to the underpinnings of sarcasm in her voice, and she was glad of that. She might not overtly go against him just then, but she was more than willing to let him know that she remained less than impressed.

"Do not underestimate the advantages that Arganth and his shamans have brought to us," Obould warned.

"To us, or to Obould?"

"To both," the orc said definitively. "Their call sounds deep in the tunnels. I have brought forth perhaps fifteen thousand orcs, and thousands of goblins as well, but there are ten times those numbers still available to us if we can coax them forth. We cannot have these puny enemies turning the retreat of a few into a tactical advantage for our enemies."

Gerti wanted to argue of course—mostly because she just wanted to argue with everything Obould said—but she found that she really could not find flaws in the logical reasoning. "What will you do?" she heard herself asking.

"The preparations here are well underway, so we will take the bulk of our force and march off at once, back to the west and the north," Obould announced. "We will send some to reinforce Urlgen so that he can continue the fight on the north ridge for as long as the dwarves are foolish enough to stay and battle. Whatever his losses, we can afford them much more easily than the dwarves can afford theirs.

"I had planned to swing immediately around to the west," Obould went on, "and close the vice on the place the dwarves call Keeper's Dale, driving them into Mithral Hall. But first I will go north with Arganth and some others to see to this problem."

Gerti eyed him suspiciously, trying not at all to hide her trepidation.

"I expect that you will afford me a few of your kin for my journey," Obould answered that look. "You can come along or not, at your pleasure. Either way, I will have a pair of elf heads and a drow's to hang on the sides of my carriage."

"You do not have a carriage," the giantess remarked.

"Then I will build one," Obould replied without missing a beat.

Gerti didn't answer but merely turned and exited, and that act alone signified to her the change that had come over her relationship with Obould. Always before, it had been the orc king coming to Shining White, her icy mountain home, to speak with her, but lately, she more often than not seemed the visitor in Obould's growing kingdom.

With that unsettling thought reverberating within her as she walked out into the daylight, the giantess also heard the orc king's dismissive, "you can come along or not, at your pleasure," echoing in her mind.

Gerti pointedly reminded herself that she could not afford to let Obould move her too far to the margins. Her thoughts began to crystallize around the realization that if the orc king's confidence continued to grow into such impertinence, she might have to kill him. The timing would be everything, the giantess realized. She had to let Obould play his hand out, let him chase the dwarves into the tunnels and begin the full-fledged flushing of Clan Battlehammer, and let him stand as the center point of war with the larger communities in the North, if it came to that.

If there was to be a fall, Gerti wanted Obould to take it. If there was to be only glory and gain, then she would have to give Obould his fall and step into the vacated position.

The giantess would enjoy crushing the life out of the impertinent and ugly orc. She had to keep telling herself that.

DELAYING THE INEVITABLE

"That's it then? We just leave?" Nanfoodle asked Shoudra.

The little gnome assumed a defiant posture, folding his little arms over his chest and tapping his foot impatiently, his toes, which could not be seen, flapping the front of his red robes.

"You would have us go back in there after your revelations to Steward Regis?" the sceptrana returned, pointing back over Nanfoodle's shoulder at the closed door of Mithral Hall. "I prefer to report in person to Marchion Elastul, if you please, and not simply by having my disembodied head delivered to him on a Clan Battlehammer platter!"

Nanfoodle's bluster did diminish a bit at the reminder that he had been the one to betray them, and his foot stopped tapping quite so insistently.

"It . . . it was the truth," he stammered. "And when they hear the whole truth, they will understand—I never meant to follow through with Marchion Elastul's stupid mission anyway."

"So just march in and tell that to Regis," Shoudra offered. "I am certain he will believe you."

Nanfoodle muttered under his breath and went back into his defiant mode.

"Of course we cannot go back in there!" said the gnome. "Not yet. We have to prove ourselves to the dwarves—and why should we not? We did come here under false pretenses and with nefarious designs. So let us show them the truth of Nanfoodle and Shoudra and of how the truth is different from that of Marchion Elastul."

"Well said," Shoudra remarked, her sarcasm still dripping. "Shall we go and destroy the orc hordes? Perhaps we can return to the halls before the afternoon beer and cookies . . ."

She stopped, seeing Nanfoodle's eyes go wide and for a moment, she thought he was staring incredulously at her. But then Shoudra heard the wailing behind her and she spun around to see a trio of dwarves approaching from the north. Two flanked the green-bearded one in the center, the dwarf on Pikel Bouldershoulder's right holding him under the shoulder, while the dwarf on his left, his brother Ivan, held a blood-soaked cloth up to the stump that remained of his left arm.

"Oooo," Pikel whined.

Nanfoodle and Shoudra rushed across the expanse to meet up with the trio.

"Oooo," said Pikel.

"They got me brother good," Ivan bellowed. "Took his arm off clean with that slate them giants're chucking. Damned unlucky shot!"

"They've got the high ground now, and once they get their war engines built, there will be many more coming down," said the other dwarf supporting Pikel. "This wound'll be a little one compared to what we're soon to see."

The trio hustled by, heading straight for the door, and Shoudra and Nanfoodle wisely moved farther out of the way.

"We cannot abandon them in this dark hour," Nanfoodle insisted.

Shoudra peeked around a boulder as the great doors opened and the trio were hustled inside. The sceptrana fell back quickly, though, for a couple of dwarf guards came out and began glancing all around.

"What would you have us do, Nanfoodle the alchemist," she replied, putting her back to the stone and seeming, in that dark moment, as if she truly needed it for support. "Perhaps we can join with the orcs, and you can poison their weapons with your concoction."

It was meant as a joke, of course, but Nanfoodle seemed to brighten suddenly as he stared at Shoudra. He snapped his stubby fingers in the air.

"We just might do that!" he declared.

He started away toward the north, staying close to the cover of the uneven, broken wall.

"What are you talking about?" Shoudra demanded, pacing him easily.

"They need us up there, so let us go and see where we might fit in," the gnome replied.

Shoudra grabbed him by the shoulder and halted him.

"Up there?" she echoed, pointing up to the top of the northern cliff. "Up there, where the battle rages?"

Nanfoodle fell back into his cross-armed, toe-tapping stance.

"Up there," he answered.

Shoudra scoffed.

"You know that I am right in this," the gnome argued. "You know that we owe it to Clan Battleham—"

"We *owe* it to Clan Battlehammer?" the sceptrana asked.

"Yes, of course," said Nanfoodle, and it was his turn to bathe his words in sarcasm. "We owe them nothing. Not even in common cause against monstrous armies. Not even though they might be the only thing standing between these orc and giant hordes and Mirabar herself! Not even because they have offered Torgar Hammerstriker and his followers the friendship of brothers. Not even because they welcomed us into their homes, trusting us even though they had no sound reason to. Not even because—"

"Enough, Nanfoodle," said Shoudra, and she waved her hands in surrender. "Enough."

The tall, beautiful woman gave a long sigh as she looked back up at the high cliff and at the lines of rope ladders hanging down, crossing from ledge to ledge.

"Up there," she stated more than asked.

"Perhaps you have a spell that will carry us up to them?" the gnome asked hopefully.

Shoudra looked back at him and shook her head.

His look was crestfallen, but that was quickly pushed aside by renewed determination as little Nanfoodle the alchemist led the way to the base of the cliff and the nearest rope ladder. He gave one look over at Shoudra, and he began to climb.

It took the pair more than an hour to get up the side of the cliff, pausing to rest at every available ledge. When they finally did near the top, the first faces that greeted them were not dwarves', to their surprise.

"Regis sent you?" Catti-brie asked, peering over at the two.

She reached her hand down toward Nanfoodle, while Wulfgar fell flat beside her and extended his strong arm to Shoudra.

"We came on our own," Shoudra answered as she climbed up and brushed herself off. "We were preparing to leave—back home to Mirabar—but thought to check in and see if we might be of some use up here."

"We can use all the help we can find," Wulfgar answered. He turned and stepped aside, giving the pair a wide view of the lands below them to the north, where the vast orc and goblin army was regrouping. "They have come at us regularly, several times each day."

Lowering her gaze to encompass the descending ground between the dwarves and the orcs, Shoudra could see the truth of the barbarian's words, as evidenced by the scores of hacked orc and goblin bodies. Blood was so thick about the battleground by that point that it seemed as if the gray stone itself had taken on a deeper, reddish hue.

"We're killing them twenty to one," Catti-brie remarked. "And still they're coming."

Shoudra glanced over at Nanfoodle, who nodded grimly.

"We will help where we may," the sceptrana assured the two human children of King Bruenor.

"Ye'd be helping more if ye might be finding a way to take out them giants," came the call of a dwarf, Banak Brawnanvil, as he stalked over to greet the pair of new recruits.

He turned as he approached, motioning back to the ridge in the distant west, a mountain arm running north-south.

"They cannot reach us with their stones," Catti-brie explained. "But they've improvised well, hurling flat pieces of—"

"Slate," Shoudra finished, nodding. "We met up with the unfortunate Bouldershoulder down in Keeper's Dale."

"Poor Pikel," said Catti-brie.

"The giants will become more of a problem than that soon enough," Banak put in.

He didn't elaborate, but he didn't have to, for as she scanned the giants' position far to the northwest, Shoudra could see the great logs that had been brought up to the ridge, some of them already assembled into wide bases. No stranger to battle, Shoudra Stargleam could guess easily enough what the behemoths might be constructing.

"The slate is troublesome and unnerving," Wulfgar explained. "But in truth, they cannot often get the soaring pieces anywhere near to us, despite Pikel's misfortune. But once they assemble and sight in those catapults, we will have little cover from the barrage."

"And I'm thinking that they'll have a couple up and launching tomorrow," Banak added.

"Their advantage will drive you from the cliffs," Nanfoodle reasoned, and no one disagreed.

"Well, we're glad to have ye, for as long as we can have ye," Banak said suddenly and enthusiastically, brightening the dampened mood. He turned to Wulfgar and Catti-brie. "The two of ye show them about so they might figure how they'll best fit in."

Despite the many forays by their enemies, the dwarves had done a fine job of creating defensive positions, Shoudra and Nanfoodle quickly realized. Their walls were neither high nor thick, but they were well angled to protect from flying slate and well designed to allow for the bearded warriors to move from position to position along the trenches created behind them. Most of all, the dwarves had forced a series of choke points up near the cliff, areas where the orc advantage in numbers would be diminished by lack of room. Shoudra could well imagine that the last orc charge, if designed to drive the dwarves over the cliff, would prove very costly to the aggressors.

And the dwarves were preparing for the eventuality of that retreat as well. With several hundred to evacuate, it seemed clear to Shoudra that many would be killed on the journey down the rope ladders—taken down by missiles from above and perhaps tumbling away when ropes were slashed. Shoudra recognized many of the dwarves, Mirabar engineers, hard at work on the answer to that dilemma. They were digging a tunnel, a slide actually, with a wide hopper area leading to a narrower channel that wound down within the stone, paralleling the descent of the cliff itself.

"Would you even fit down there?" Shoudra asked the huge Wulfgar.

"They've set drop-ropes as well," the barbarian explained. "The slide is for those last dwarves leaving."

"Ye think ye got a spell or two to grease the run?" came a familiar voice from out of the hole.

Nanfoodle fell flat and peered in to see Shingles McRuff climbing up from the darkness.

"It is good to see you well," Shoudra said when the dwarf emerged from the hole.

"Well enough, I suppose," Shingles replied. "But we lost many kin when them ugly orcs took the tunnels in the west."

"Tunnels?"

"Under the ridge," Catti-brie explained. "Torgar, Shingles, and the others from Mirabar tried to hold them, but the onslaught was too great." The woman glanced over at the dirty dwarf. "But more orcs died than dwarves, to be sure," she added, and Shingles managed a smile.

"Tunnels under the ridge?" Nanfoodle inquired.

"A fair network," Shingles explained. "Not too wide and not too many, but running one end to the other."

Nanfoodle's expression suddenly became very intrigued, and he looked up at Shoudra.

"And no easy access up to the ridge," Catti-brie remarked, "if you're thinking we should fight our way back in there and rush up at the giants."

Nanfoodle merely nodded and began tapping his finger against his chin. He moved off for a moment and glanced back over the cliff at Keeper's Dale.

"What's he thinking?" Shingles asked.

"With him, who can tell?" came Shoudra's answer, given with a shrug. "Pray tell me, my old friend, how fares Torgar?"

"He's well," Shingles reported.

He looked down to the northeast, to a group of dwarves holding a tight formation behind a low wall, ready to spring up and counter any orc charge. Studying the group, Shoudra thought she could make out the familiar figure of Master Hammerstriker, whose actions in Mirabar carried effects for them all that seemed to go on and on.

"Well as can be," Shingles added. "He's not much happy about losing the tunnels."

"Too many orcs," Catti- brie said. "And too many giants, and some with dark magic. The Mirabarran dwarves did well to hold as long as you did."

"Yeah, yeah," came Shingles's dismissive answer.

"Perhaps you'll get the chance to take it back," Nanfoodle offered, rejoining the group.

"Might that we will, but I'm not for seeing any reason," Shingles replied. "Won't do us much good in getting rid o' them giants, and them giants're the big trouble now. Can't see how we're to stop 'em."

Nanfoodle looked at Shoudra, who gave a great sigh and walked off a couple of steps to the northwest, cupping her hand over her eyes and looking off at the high ridge.

"Solutions are often complicated," Nanfoodle said, and the gnome was grinning widely. "Unless you follow them logically, one little step at a time."

"What're you thinking?" Catti-brie asked.

"I am thinking that I have been presented a problem. One in need of a solution in short order." Still smiling, the gnome turned back to Shoudra—to her back, actually, for she continued her scan of the ridge. "And what are you thinking, Shoudra?" he asked.

"I am thinking that I know what you can do to metal, my friend," the sceptrana answered. "Would you have a similar solution for wood?"

Nanfoodle looked back to the puzzled expressions of Catti-brie, Wulfgar, and Shingles.

He offered them another wide smile.

The feeling of flying was strange indeed to Wulfgar—almost as much so as the spell Shoudra had cast upon him so that he could see in the night as well as any elf. He was the only one enchanted with the power of flight—the others were simply levitating—so he was the guiding force, pulling them all across the broken terrain of the mountain ridge.

He kept glancing back at them, though since they were invisible, he couldn't see them or the tow ropes. He knew they were there, for he could feel the resistance on the separate ropes from all four: Catti-brie, Torgar, Shoudra, and Nanfoodle.

Remembering Shoudra's warning that magical flight was unpredictable, Wulfgar set down as soon as it seemed to him that the remaining run to the giants and their war engines was smooth enough to easily traverse. He set himself firmly and ducked low, understanding that the levitating foursome would continue to fly past him. One by one, he caught them and broke their momentum as their different lengths of rope played out to the end, and though all of them did their best to remain quiet against the tug, there came a slight grunt from Nanfoodle that had them all holding their breath.

The giants didn't seem to notice.

It took the five a short while to untangle and untie themselves and get together, for only Shoudra and Nanfoodle, enchanted with spells of magical vision, could see the others. Finally, they were all settled behind a small jut.

"We were wise in coming out," Shoudra whispered. "The giants' catapults are nearing completion."

"I will need five minutes," Nanfoodle whispered in reply.

"Not so long a time," said Shoudra.

"Longer than you think, with a score of giants about," Catti-brie whispered.

Nanfoodle set off then, and Shoudra guided her three invisible companions around to the east of the giants, to a defensible position.

"Just say when to go," Catti-brie offered.

"As soon as you attack, the invisibility spell will dissipate," Shoudra reminded her.

In response, Catti-brie lifted Taulmaril over the lip of the jut, settling the bow into the general direction of the closest group of giants. Only then did she realize that she couldn't rightly aim the invisible weapon, for she had no reference points with which to sight it in.

"You two here, then," Shoudra agreed. "You will hear the first sounds soon enough." The sceptrana took Torgar's hand and led him away, circling even more to the east and north of the giant encampment.

"I'd be feeling a bit more comforted if I could see you ready beside me," Catti-brie whispered to Wulfgar.

"Right here," he assured her.

He went silent and so did she, for a giantess moved very near to their position.

Many minutes slipped past in tense silence, broken only by the hum of the wind whistling through the many broken stones. Even the wind was not loud that night, as if all the world was hushed in anticipation.

And it began. Catti-brie and Wulfgar jumped back in surprise at the abrupt commotion off to the north, a great din that sounded as if an entire dwarf army had gone on the attack. The giants reacted at once, leaping up and turning that way.

Catti-brie let the nearest of the behemoths get a few long strides farther away, then let fly a sizzling blue bolt, slamming the giantess right in the center of her back. She howled and had just started to turn when Aegis-fang smacked her across the shoulder, sending her sprawling to the stone.

"To the glory of Moradin!" came a great roar, a magically enhanced blast of Torgar's voice, Catti-brie realized.

Then came a lightning bolt, splitting the darkness and sending a handful of giants tumbling aside.

Catti-brie let fly another arrow into the giantess, and as soon as his magical warhammer reappeared in his waiting hand, Wulfgar launched it at the next nearest giant, who was turning to see to his fallen companion.

More cries to the dwarf god echoed from the north, another lightning bolt lit up the night, then came a sudden storm, a downpour of sleet pelting the stones near to Wulfgar and Catti-brie.

The woman hardly slowed her shooting, letting fly arrow after arrow, and many giants turned and charged at her position.

And many giants slipped on the slick stones. One nearly navigated his way all the way to the jut, but Aegis-fang smashed him in the chest. Though the giant seemed to handle the heavy blow well, he staggered backward under its weight, his feet sliding out from under him.

Catti-brie hit him in the face with an arrow as he sat there on the wet and shiny stones.

A great hand appeared right in front of her, the scrambling giantess finally crawling to the other side of the jut. She pulled herself up with a roar, and Catti-brie was suddenly falling away.

It wasn't from anything the giantess had done, though, the woman soon realized. Wulfgar had tossed her aside, taking her place, and as the giantess's head came up over the jut, the barbarian gave a roar to his god of war and brought Aegis-fang sweeping down from on high.

Catti-brie winced at the sharp retort, a sound like stone clacking against stone, and the giantess disappeared from view.

But more were coming, as fast as they could manage across the slippery surface. Others took a different tack, finding stones and sending them sailing at the pair. It was Catti-brie's turn to pull Wulfgar aside, as she dived behind the cover of the jut, catching him by his thick shock of blond hair and forcing him down beside her. And not a moment too soon, for barely had the barbarian hit the ground when a boulder smashed the tip of the jut and went rebounding past.

The two quickly untangled, trying to regroup, and both cried out in surprise as a blue line appeared in the darkness, running straight up to a height of about six feet. That line widened and stretched, forming a doorway of light, and through it stepped Shoudra and Torgar.

"Just run!" Shoudra cried, pulling at Catti-brie as she began her sprint to the south.

"Nanfoodle?" Catti-brie cried.

"Just run!" Shoudra insisted.

And there seemed no other choice, for the giants were closing and were soon to be out of the icy area, and more rocks began to skip all around them.

They scrambled and they tumbled, and whenever one fell, the others hoisted him up and pulled him along. At one point, a rather wide and seemingly bottomless chasm, Wulfgar grabbed Catti-brie and tossed her across. A protesting Torgar got the treatment next, then Shoudra. With giant-thrown rocks cracking the stone all around him, Wulfgar made the leap himself.

On they ran, too afraid to even look back. Gradually, the bombardment thinned and the yells of outrage behind them diminished to nothingness.

Huffing and puffing, the foursome pulled up behind a wall of stone.

"Nanfoodle?" Catti-brie asked again.

"If we're lucky, the giants never even knew he was there," Shoudra explained. "He has potions that should allow him easy escape."

"And if we're not lucky?" Wulfgar asked.

Shoudra's grim expression was all the answer he needed. Wulfgar had seen enough of giants in his day, and enough of frost giants in particular, to understand the odds Nanfoodle would face if they noticed him.

"I don't know . . . that we killed any . . . but there's one . . . giantess who is sure to be . . . wishing we hadn't come," Catti-brie remarked between gasps.

"I am sure that my lightning stung a few," Shoudra added. "But I doubt I did any serious harm to any."

"But that wasn't the point, now was it?" Torgar reminded them. "Come on, let's get off these rocks before the next orc charge. I didn't get no swings at the damned giants, but I mean to have me a few orcs' heads!"

He stomped off, and the others followed, all of them nursing more than a few cuts and bruises from their nighttime run, and all of them glancing back repeatedly in hopes of seeing their gnome companion.

They should have been looking ahead instead, for when they arrived back at the main encampment, they found Nanfoodle resting against a stone, an oversized pipe stuffed into his mouth, his smile stretching wide to either side.

"Should be an interesting morning," the gnome remarked, grinning from ear to ear.

Soon after dawn the next day, the first giant barrage began—almost.

All the dwarves watched as in the distance, a pair of great catapults, baskets piled with stones, bent back, giants straining to set them.

From below, the orcs howled and began their charge, thinking to catch the dwarves vulnerable under the giant-sized volley.

Beams creaked . . . and cracked.

The giants tried to release the missiles, but the catapults simply fell to pieces.

All eyes in the area turned to Nanfoodle, who whistled and pulled a vial out of his belt pouch, holding it up before him and swishing greenish liquid around inside it.

"A simple acid, really," he explained.

"Well, ye bought us some time," Banak Brawnanvil congratulated the fivesome, and he looked down the slope at the stubbornly charging orcs. "From them giants, at least."

The dwarf ran off then, barking orders, calling his formations into position.

"They'll need many new logs if they hope to reconstitute their war engines," Nanfoodle assured the others.

Of course, none of them were surprised later that same day, when scouts reported that new logs were already being brought in to that northwestern ridge.

"Stubborn bunch," the little gnome observed.

21

TWO HELMETS

The diamond edge held his gaze, its glaring image crystallizing his thoughts.

Drizzt sat in his small cave, Icingdeath laid out before him, Bruenor's lost helmet propped on a stick to the side. Outside, the morning shone bright and clear, with a brisk breeze blowing and small clusters of white clouds rushing across the blue sky.

There was a vibrancy in that wind, a sense of being alive.

To Drizzt Do'Urden, it shamed him and angered him all at the same time. For he had gone there to hide, to slide back into the comfort of secluded darkness—to put his feelings behind a wall that effectively denied them.

Tarathiel and Innovindil had assaulted that wall. Their forgiveness and apology, the beauty of their fighting dance, the effectiveness of their actions beside him, all showed Drizzt that he must accept their invitation, both for the sake of the cause against the invading orcs and for his own sake. Only through them, he knew, could he begin to sort out the darkness of Ellifain. Only through them might he come to find some closure on that horrible moment in the pirate hideout.

But seeking those answers and that closure meant moving out from behind the invulnerable wall that was the Hunter.

Drizzt's gaze slipped away from the diamond edge of Icingdeath to the one-horned helmet.

He tried to look away almost immediately, but it didn't matter, for he wasn't really looking at the helmet. He was watching the tower fall. He was watching Ellifain fall. He was watching Clacker fall. He was watching Zaknafein fall.

All that pain, buried within him for all those years, came flooding over Drizzt Do'Urden there, alone in the small cave. Only when the first line of moisture slid down his cheek did he even realize how few tears he had shed over the years. Only when the wetness crystallized his vision did Drizzt truly realize the depth of the pain within him.

He had hidden it away, time and again, beneath the veil of anger in those times when he became the Hunter, when the pain overwhelmed him. And more than that—more subtly but no less destructive, he only then realized—he had hidden it all away beneath the veil of hope, in the logical and determined understanding that sacrifices were acceptable if the principles were upheld.

Dying well.

Drizzt had always hoped that he would die well, battling evil enemies or saving a friend. There was honor in that, and the truest legacy he could ever know. Had anyone died more nobly than Zaknafein?

But that didn't alleviate the pain for those left behind. Only then, sitting there, purposefully tearing down the wall he had built of anger and of hope, could Drizzt Do'Urden begin to realize that he had never really cried for Zaknafein or for any of the others.

And under the weight of that revelation, he felt a coward.

It started as the slightest of movements, a jerk of the drow's slender shoulders. It sounded as a small gasp at first, a mere chortle.

For the first time, Drizzt Do'Urden didn't let it end at that point. For the first time, he did not let the Hunter build a wall of stone around his heart, nor let the justifications of principle and purpose dull the keen edge of pain. For the first time, he did not shy from the emptiness and the helplessness; he did not embrace them, but neither did he run.

He cried for Zaknafein and for Clacker. He cried for Ellifain, the most tragic loss of all. He considered the course of his life—but not with lament, stubbornly throwing aside all the typical regrets that he should have turned his friends from the course into the mountains, that he should have ushered them straight to Mithral Hall. They had walked with eyes wide. All of them, knowing the dangers, expecting the inevitable. Circumstance and bad luck had guided Drizzt's journey to that fallen tower and to the helmet of his lost friend. His journey had taken him to the saddest day of his life, to a moment of the greatest loss he could

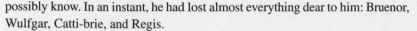
possibly know. In an instant, he had lost almost everything dear to him: Bruenor, Wulfgar, Catti-brie, and Regis.

But he had not cried.

He had run away from the pain. He had built the wall of the Hunter, the justification being that he would continue the fight—heighten it—and pay back his enemies.

There was truth in that course. There was purpose and there was, undeniably, effectiveness.

But there was a price as well, Drizzt understood on a very basic level, as the wall fell down and the tears flowed. The price of his heart.

For to hide away behind the stone of anger was to deny, as well, the pleasures of being alive. All of that separated him from the orcs he killed. All of that gave true purpose to waging the war, the difference between good and evil, between right and wrong.

All of that had blurred with the fall of Ellifain.

All of that blended within the veil of the Hunter.

Drizzt thought of Artemis Entreri then. His arch-nemesis, his . . . alter ego? Was that Hunter within Drizzt in truth who Entreri was, a man so full of pain and anguish that he denied his own heart? Was Drizzt destined to follow that uncaring road?

Drizzt let the tears flow. He cried for them all, and he cried for himself, for the profound loss that had so emptied the joy from his heart. Every time the anger welled, he threw it back down. Every time he visualized his blades taking the head from an orc, he instead forced forth the image of Catti-brie smiling, or of Bruenor tossing him a knowing wink, or of Wulfgar singing to Tempus as they trotted along the mountain trails, or of Regis lying back, fishing line tied to his toe, on the banks of Maer Dualdon. Drizzt forced the memories to come forth, despite the pain.

He was hardly conscious of the deepening shadows of nightfall, and he lay there, somewhere between sleep and memory throughout the night.

By the time morning dawned once more, Drizzt had at last found the strength to take the first steps along a necessary road to follow the elves, who had moved their encampment. To accept their invitation to join with them in common cause.

He put away his scimitars and took up his cloak, then paused and looked back.

With a bittersweet smile on his face, Drizzt reached in and lifted Bruenor's helmet from the supporting stick. He rolled it over in his hands and brought it close so that he could again catch Bruenor's scent. Then he put it in his pack and started away.

He paused only a couple of steps out from the entrance, though, and nearly laughed aloud when he looked down at his callused feet.

A moment later, the drow held his boots in his hand. He considered putting them on, but then just tied them together by the laces and slung them over one shoulder.

Perhaps there was a happy medium to be found.

At the same time Drizzt was rolling Bruenor's helmet over in his hands, another, not so far away, was likewise studying a different armored headpiece. That helm was white as bone and resembled a skull, though with grotesquely elongated eyes. The "chin" of the helmet would hang down well over Obould's own chin, offering protection for his throat. The elongated eye holes were the most unique part of the design, though, for they were not open. A glassy substance filled them, perfectly translucent.

"Glassteel," Arganth explained to the great orc. "No spear will pierce it. Not even a great dwarven crossbow could drive a bolt through it."

Obould growled softly in admiration as he rolled the helmet over in his hands. He slowly brought it up and fitted it over his head. It settled low, right to his collarbones.

Arganth held up a scarf, laced with metal.

"Wrap this around your neck and the helmet will settle upon it," the shaman explained. "There will be no opening."

Behind the glassteel, Obould narrowed his eyes. "You doubt my ability?" he demanded.

"There can be no opening," Arganth bravely replied. "Obould is the hope of Gruumsh! Obould is chosen."

"And Gruumsh will punish Arganth if Obould fails?" the orc king asked.

"Obould will not fail," the shaman replied, dodging the question.

Obould let it go at that and considered instead the seemingly endless line of precious gifts. Every time he clenched his fist, he could feel the added strength in his arms; every easy step he took across the broken ground reminded him of the additional balance and speed. Beneath his plate mail he wore a light shirt and breeches, enchanted, so said the shamans, to protect him from fire and ice.

The shamans were making him impregnable. The shamans were building around him a failsafe armor.

But he could not let that notion permeate his thoughts, Obould understood, or he would inevitably relax his guard.

"Does it please you?" Arganth asked, his excited voice nearly a squeal.

Still growling, Obould removed the helm and took the metal-laced scarf from the shaman.

"Obould is pleased," he said.

"Then Gruumsh is pleased!" Arganth declared.

He danced away, back to the waiting cluster of shamans, who all began talking excitedly. No doubt pooling their thoughts toward a new improvement for their god-king, Obould realized. The orc king gave a grating chuckle. Always before, he had demanded devotion and exacted it with fear and with muscle. But the growing fanaticism was something completely different.

Could any king hope for more?

But such fanaticism came with expectations, Obould understood, and he looked around at the dark mountains. They had forced marched north in short order, through the day and through the night, because a threat loomed before his grand design.

Obould meant to eliminate that threat.

A quick glance to the west told Tarathiel that he was pushing his luck, for the sun's lower rim was almost to the horizon and his and Innovindil's camp was some distance away. When the sun went down, he'd have to bring Sunrise to the ground, for flying around in the dark of night was no easy task, even with the elf and his keen eyesight guiding the pegasus.

Still, the elf's adrenaline was pumping with the thrill of the hunt—he had a dozen orcs running scared along the mountain trail below him—and even more so that day because he knew that Drizzt Do'Urden was about. After their joint efforts in turning the orc tribe back to the Spine of the World, the drow had gone off again, and Tarathiel and Innovindil hadn't seen him for a few days. Then Tarathiel, out hunting alone, had spotted Drizzt moving along a trail toward the cave he and Innovindil were using as their new base. Drizzt had offered a wave; not much of an assurance, of course, but Tarathiel had noticed a couple of hopeful signs. Drizzt was carrying the helmet of his lost friend— Tarathiel had spotted its one remaining horn poking out of the drow's shoulder pack—and perhaps even more notably, Drizzt was carrying his boots.

Had his resistance to the advances of the two elves begun to break down?

Tarathiel meant to return to Innovindil, and hopefully Drizzt, with news of another victory, albeit a minor one. He meant to have at least four kills under his belt that day before going home. He already had two, and with a dozen targets still scrambling below him, it did not seem unlikely that he would get his wish.

The elf settled more comfortably in his saddle and leveled his bow for a shot, but the orcs cut down into a narrow stone channel, dropping from sight. Tarathiel brought Sunrise around, sweeping over that crevice, and saw that the creatures were still running. He circled his pegasus and came in over the channel, following the line, looking for a shot.

His bow twanged, but off the mark as both the channel and the targeted orc cut to the right. Again the elf had to circle, so that he didn't overfly the group.

He was back in sight shortly, and his arrow struck home, marking his third kill. Again, he then had to fly his mount in a wide circle. Tarathiel glanced west at the lowering sun as he did and realized that he didn't have too much time remaining.

Again he bore down on the fleeing orcs. The channel descended along the mountainside and cut sharply between two high juts of stone, where the ground opened up beyond. Tarathiel told himself that he'd catch them as they exited the crevice and seek out whichever one scattered in the general direction of his cave.

Smiling widely, eager for that last kill, Tarathiel brought Sunrise soaring through the gap.

And as he did, two long poles rose up before him, crossing diagonally and going upright to either side. It wasn't until Sunrise plowed right in that the elf even realized that a net had been strung to the poles.

The pegasus let out a shocked whinny and it and Tarathiel balled up, wings folding under the press. They continued forward for just a bit as the poles crossed again behind them, netting them fully, and the whole trap slid down to the ground.

Tarathiel twisted and slipped underneath Sunrise as soon as they touched down, using the free area beneath the pegasus to draw out his sword and begin cutting at the net. With a few links severed, the elf scrambled out. He looked around, expecting enemies to be fast closing.

He sucked in his breath, seeing that the netting poles had been held not by orcs, but by a pair of frost giants.

They weren't approaching, though, and so Tarathiel spun around and went to fast work on the net, trying desperately to free Sunrise.

He stopped when torches flared to life around him. He stopped and real-ized the completeness of this trap.

Slowly the elf moved away from the struggling pegasus, walking a defen-sive circle around Sunrise, sword out before him as he eyed the torchbearers, a complete circle of ugly orcs. They had set him up, and he had fallen for it. He had no idea how he could possibly get himself and Sunrise out of there. He glanced back at the pegasus to see that Sunrise was making some progress in extracting himself—but certainly not quickly enough. The elf had to get back and cut more of the netting, he knew, and he turned.

Or started to.

There before him, emerging from the line of orcs, came a creature of such stature and obvious power that Tarathiel found he could not turn away. Suited in beautifully crafted, ridged and spiked plate mail and a skull-shaped white helmet with elongated eyes and shining teeth, the large orc stepped out from the line. Tarathiel noted the carved hilt of a huge sword protruding up diagonally from behind the brute's right shoulder.

"Obould!" the other orcs began to chant. "Obould! Obould! Obould!"

It was a name that Tarathiel, like every other worldly creature across the Silver Marches surely knew, the name of an orc king who had brought a pow-erful dwarven citadel to its knees.

Tarathiel wanted to turn back for Sunrise and the net. He knew he had to, but he could not. He could not tear his eyes away from the spectacle of King Obould Many-Arrows.

The burly orc strode toward Tarathiel, reaching up his thick right arm to grasp the carved hilt. Slowly, the orc extended his arm, drawing up the great-sword. He lifted the weapon clear of its half-sheath, to a horizontal position above his head. Still stalking in, hardly slowing, not changing his expression one bit (as far as Tarathiel could see through the huge eye holes), the determined crea-ture swept the weapon down to his side.

The blade flamed to life.

Tarathiel moved his free left hand to the small of his back, to the hilt of a throwing dagger. He had to finish the orc quickly, he understood, to stun the onlookers and buy himself time to get back to Sunrise. He forced aside his fears and studied the incoming orc, looking for an opening, any opening.

Only its bloodshot eyes appeared vulnerable—not an easy throw, but to Tarathiel, a necessary one.

He slid the dagger free of his belt and casually lowered his arm to his side, concealing the weapon behind his hand, with its blade running up behind his arm.

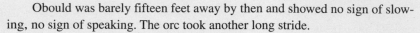

Obould was barely fifteen feet away by then and showed no sign of slowing, no sign of speaking. The orc took another long stride.

Tarathiel's arm snapped forward, the small dagger spinning out.

Obould didn't move fast to dodge or block, but he did stiffen suddenly, staring without a blink.

Tarathiel started to break to the side at once, back toward Sunrise, thinking that his missile would surely drop the brute. But even as he took the first step away, the elf noted the impact. The dagger's tip clipped against the translucent shield of glassteel and ricocheted harmlessly aside.

Beneath the skull teeth of that awful helmet, King Obould widened his grin and gave an eager growl.

Tarathiel stopped in his tracks and spun back to face the orc's sudden charge. He ducked the orc's surprisingly swift one-armed cut of the greatsword, feeling the heat of its flames as it passed above him. Ahead stepped the elf, his own sword stabbing hard for Obould's belly.

But the orc didn't jump back, again trusting in his armor, and instead caught up his own sword in both hands and came over and down diagonally back the other way.

Tarathiel's sword did connect, but before he could slip it around in search of an opening or drive it in harder to test the plate, he found himself leaping aside, spinning as he went, every muscle working to keep him away from the orc's mighty sword.

As he turned his back to Obould, before completing the spin, the elf quickstepped straight away. He felt the pursuit, felt the hunger of his adversary, and suddenly completed the spin, reversing direction and ducking into a squat as he flashed past the lumbering Obould. The elf turned again and drove his sword hard into Obould's lower back. The orc howled as he spun to catch up, his greatsword splitting the air with a *swoosh* of flame and ferocity.

Tarathiel didn't leave his feet, didn't even move his feet, as he threw himself backward, arms flying out wide to either side. Down he tumbled, the deadly fiery sword passing above his chest and face as he fell nearly horizontal. And, with an amazing display of agility and leg strength, the elf popped right back up to the vertical, his sword stabbing ahead once and again.

Sparks flew from the orc king's black armor as the fine elven blade struck hard, but if either of the strikes had hurt Obould, the orc didn't show it.

Again, that greatsword came across, and again, Tarathiel fell back, coming out of the stiff movement with a wise backstep. Obould didn't overswing again and had his sword in stubborn pursuit.

But Tarathiel had one advantage, his quickness, and he knew that if he did not err, he could stay away from that terrible sword. He had to bide his time, to take his opportunities where he found them, and hope to wear down the great orc. He had to fight defensively, always one step ahead of his opponent, until the weight of that massive sword began to take a toll on Obould's strong arms, forcing them down so that Tarathiel could find some weakness in that suit of armor, find some place to score a mortal wound on the orc.

Tarathiel understood all of that immediately, but a glance to the side, where Sunrise was still struggling under the net, reminded him that time was a luxury he could not afford.

On came Obould, driving the elf. Then the elf went suddenly out to the side, spinning and turning around that stabbing greatsword. As he sensed that mighty weapon coming back in pursuit, the elf fell flat to the ground and scrambled suddenly at the orc's thick legs, driving in hard, thinking to trip him up.

He might as well have tried to knock over a pair of healthy oaks, for Obould didn't budge an inch, and the impact against the orc's legs left the elf's shoulders numb.

Tarathiel did well to emotionally dismiss the surprise, to continue moving around the orc king's legs, angling to ensure that he gave no opening for that pursuing sword. He came back to his feet, falling into a defensive stance as Obould came around to face him.

With a sudden roar, the orc came on, and again, Tarathiel was dancing and dodging, searching for some opening, searching for some sign that Obould was tiring.

Surprisingly, though, the orc only seemed to be gaining momentum.

Innovindil looked with some distress at the dipping sun, knowing that Tarathiel should have arrived by then. She had moved out to join him, guessing the general area where he would herd any potential enemies and figuring that she would find some way to assist in his hunt.

But there had been no sign.

And the sun was going down, which would likely ground the pegasus.

"Where are you, my love?" the female whispered to the night breeze.

She caught the movements of a dark figure off to the north of her position and smiled, somewhat comforted by the knowledge that Drizzt Do'Urden was flanking her hunt.

She told herself that Tarathiel had to be close and quickly reminded herself of all those times when her bold companion had run off into the night in pursuit of fleeing orcs. How Tarathiel loved to kill orcs! Innovindil gave a helpless and exasperated sigh, silently promising herself that she would scold him for worrying her so. She moved on, heading up the side of one ridge so that she could get a better view of the ground to the northwest.

She heard the chanting, like the low rumbling of a building thunderstorm. "Obould! Obould! Obould!" they said in the communal croaking voice, and even though she did not at first recognize the reference and the name, Innovindil understood that there were orcs around—too many orcs.

Normally, that notion would not have phased the elf. Normally, she would have then simply figured that Tarathiel was in hiding nearby, probably gaining a fair estimate of the nearby force, probably even finding some weaknesses among the orc ranks that they two could exploit. But for some reason, Innovindil had the distinct feeling that something was amiss, that Tarathiel was not safe and secure behind a wall of mountain stone.

Perhaps it was the insistent tone of the chanting, "Obould! Obould!" with an undercurrent that seemed hungry and elated all at the same time. Perhaps it was just the lengthening shadows of a dark night. Whatever the reason, Innovindil found herself moving once more, running as fast as she could manage across the broken and rocky slope, veering inevitably toward that distant chanting.

When she at last crested the ridge in the north, coming over and continuing down the other side across the craggy rocks, the elf's heart dropped. For there in the rocky vale before her flickered the torches of scores of orcs, all in a wide ring, all chanting.

Innovindil did recognize the name, and before she could even fully register the implications. Her eyes scanned across the lines, toward the center of the circle, and her heart fell away. For there was Tarathiel, dodging and diving, always a fraction of a step ahead of a fiery greatsword. And there behind him in the shadows was Sunrise, struggling, pinned by a net.

Gasping for breath, Innovindil fell back against the stone, mesmerized by the dance of the combatants and by the spectacle of the onlookers. Her love, her friend, dived and rolled, spun a beautiful turn, and rushed in hard, his sword flashing, sparks flying.

Then he was diving again, the greatsword slashing across just above him.

Innovindil looked around the orc ring, trying to find some way she could penetrate it, some way she could get down there beside Tarathiel. She silently

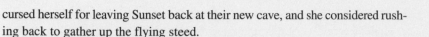

cursed herself for leaving Sunset back at their new cave, and she considered rushing back to gather up the flying steed.

But could Tarathiel possibly hold out for that long?

Innovindil started back up to the south, then she paused and turned back to the north. She realized that she had no other option, and so she spun again to the south and her cave, looking back and praying to the elf gods to protect Tarathiel.

She stopped suddenly, mesmerized once more by the intensity of the fight, the dance. Tarathiel went by Obould and stabbed hard, and the greatsword flashed down across in front of the backing elf. Innovindil blinked—and she understood that Tarathiel had, too—when that sword-fire suddenly blinked out.

Innovindil's eyes bulged as her mouth widened in a silent scream, recognizing that the blackout had frozen Tarathiel's eye for just an instant, the last flash of fire holding his attention and making him think that the blade was still down low.

But it was not.

It was up high again and back the other way.

"Obould! Obould! Obould!" the orcs chanted for their mighty and cunning leader.

The burly orc leaped forward and brought his sword down and across in a great diagonal swipe.

Tarathiel leaped back as well, and when he didn't fly away, Innovindil believed for a moment that he must have somehow backed out of range. She knew that to be impossible, but he was still standing there before the orc king.

How had the strike missed?

It hadn't. It couldn't have.

Not breathing, not moving, Innovindil stared down at Tarathiel, who stood perfectly still, and even from a distance, she could tell that he wore a perplexed look.

The sword had not missed; the mighty cut had slashed through Tarathiel's collarbone and down and across, left to right, to come out just under his ribs on the other side. Still staring, he just fell apart, his torso sliding out to the left, his legs buckling under him.

"Obould! Obould! Obould!" the orcs screamed.

Innovindil screamed as well. She leaped away, charging down the rocky slope, drawing forth her slender sword.

Or trying to, for then she got tackled from the side, and before she hit the ground, before she could cry out in surprise, a slender but strong hand clamped hard across her mouth. She struggled futilely for a moment before finally recognizing the voice whispering into her ear.

Drizzt Do'Urden stayed tight against her on the ground, holding her, telling her that it would be all right, until at last her muscles relaxed.

"There's nothing to do," the drow said over and over again. "Nothing we can do."

He pulled Innovindil up into a sitting position against him and together they looked down on the rocky vale, where the orc king, his sword aflame once more, stalked around the halved body of Tarathiel, where more netting was being thrown over poor Sunrise, holding the pegasus down, where scores of orcs and more than a few giants cheered and danced in the torchlight.

The couple sat there for a long, long time, staring in disbelief, and despite Drizzt holding her as tightly as he could, Innovindil's shoulder bobbed with great sobs of despair and grief.

She couldn't see it, for her eyes were transfixed on the horrible scene before her, but behind her, Drizzt, too, was crying.

PART FOUR WHEN DARKNESS FALLS

I watched the descent of Obould's sword.

With my heart undefended, risking friends once more, I watched, and again my heart was severed.

All is a swirl of confusion again, punctuated by pinpricks of pain that find my most vulnerable and sensitive areas, stinging and burning, flashing images of falling friends. I can build the stone wall to block them, I know, in the form of anger. To hide my eyes and hide my heart—yet I am not sure if the relief is worth the price.

That is my dilemma.

The death of Tarathiel was about Tarathiel. That is obvious, I know, but I must often remind myself of that truth. The world is not my playground, not a performance for my pleasure and my pain, not an abstract thought in the mind of Drizzt Do'Urden.

Bruenor's fall was more poignant to Bruenor than it was to me. So was Zaknafein's to Zaknafein, and that of all the others. Aside from that truth, though, there is my own sensibility, my own perception of events, my own pain and confusion. We can only view the world through our own eyes, I think. There are empathy and sympathy; there is often a conscious effort to see as a friend or even an enemy might—this is an important element in the concept of truth and justice, of greater community than our own wants and needs. But in the end, it all, for each of us, comes back to each of us individually, and everything we witness rings more important to each of us than to others, even if what we witness is a critical moment for another.

There is an undeniable selfishness in that realization, but I do not run away from that truth because there is nothing I, or anyone, can do about that truth. When we lose a loved one, the agony is ours as well. A parent watching his or her child suffer is in as much pain, or even more, I am sure, than the suffering child.

And so, embracing that selfishness at this moment, I ask myself if Tarathiel's fall was a warning or a test. I dared to open my heart, and it was torn asunder. Do I fall back into that other being once more, encase my spirit in stone to make it impervious to such pain? Or is this sudden and unexpected loss a test of my spirit, to show that I can accept the cruelty of fate and press on, that I can hold fast to my beliefs and my principles and my hopes against the pain of those images?

I think that we all make this choice all the time, in varying degrees. Every day, every tenday, when we face some adversity, we find options that usually run along two roads. Either we hold our course—the one we determinedly set in better and more hopeful times, based on principle and faith—or we fall to the seemingly easier and more expedient road of defensive posture, both emotional and physical. People and often societies sometimes react to pain and fear by closing up, by sacrificing freedoms and placing practicality above principle.

Is that what I have been doing since the fall of Bruenor? Is this hunting creature I have become merely a tactic to forego the pain?

While in Silverymoon some years ago, I chanced to study the history of the region, to glance at perspectives on the many wars faced by the people of that wondrous community throughout the ages. At those times when the threatened Silverymoon closed up and put aside her enlightened principles—particularly the recognition that the actions of the individual are more important than the reputation of the individual's race—the historians were not kind and the legacy did not shine.

The same will be said of Drizzt Do'Urden, I think, by any who care to take notice.

There is a small pool in the cave where Tarathiel and Innovindil took up residence, where I am now staying with the grieving Innovindil. When I look at my reflection in that pool, I am reminded, strangely, of Artemis Entreri.

When I am the hunting creature, the reactionary, defensive and closed-hearted warrior, I am more akin to him. When I strike at enemies, not out of community or personal defense, not out of the guiding recognition of right and wrong or good and evil, but out of anger, I am more akin to that closed and unfeeling creature I first met in the tunnels of duergar-controlled Mithral Hall. On those occasions, my blades are not guided by conscience or powered by justice.

Nay, they are guided by pain and powered by anger.

I lose myself.

I see Innovindil across the way, crying still for the loss of her dear Tarathiel. She is not running away from the grief and the loss. She is embracing it and incorporating it into her being, to make it a part of herself, to own it so that it cannot own her.

Have I the strength to do the same?

I pray that I do, for I understand now that only in going through the pain can I be saved.

—Drizzt Do'Urden

THE CALL OF DESPERATE TIMES

"Uh oh," Nanfoodle whispered to Shoudra.

When the sceptrana looked his way, the little gnome motioned his chin toward a group of dwarves holding a conversation near the lip of the cliff. Torgar and Shingles were there, as well as Catti-brie, Wulfgar, Banak, and Tred of Citadel Felbarr. Tred had just returned from Mithral Hall with word of Pikel, no doubt, and also of the duo from Mirabar.

At around the same time Banak and the others all turned to regard the gnome and Shoudra, and their expressions spoke volumes.

"Time for us to go," Shoudra whispered back, and she grabbed Nanfoodle's shoulder.

"No," the gnome insisted, pulling away. "No, we will not flee."

"You underestimate—"

"We helped them in their dilemma here. Dwarves appreciate that," Nanfoodle said, and he started off toward the group.

"I thought it from the first," Torgar Hammerstriker said when Nanfoodle arrived, Shoudra moving cautiously behind. "Ye still can't see the truth o' that damned marchion."

"We didn't flee, did we?" Nanfoodle replied.

"Ye'd probably be smart in keeping yer mouth shut, little one," offered Shingles, and his tone wasn't threatening as much as honest, even sympathetic.

"Ye've got yerself in enough trouble by-the-by. These folk'll treat ye fair and put ye on yer way back home soon enough."

"We could be well on our way home already, if that was the course we chose," Nanfoodle stubbornly replied. "But we did not."

"Because ye're a dolt?" Torgar remarked.

"Because we believed we could be useful," Nanfoodle countered.

"To us or to them orcs?" Banak Brawnanvil put in. "Ye came here to ruin our metal, so ye told Steward Regis yerself."

"That was before we knew of the orc army," Nanfoodle explained.

He tried to focus and find his center, tried to calm his breathing, telling himself to trust in the truth.

"And that's making it any better?" Banak demanded.

"We came here under orders to do exactly what you have stated," Shoudra Stargleam admitted. She came forward to stand beside Nanfoodle and managed to release herself from Banak's imposing stare long enough to shoot her little friend a comforting look. "Your departure brought great fear and distress to Mirabar," she went on, addressing Torgar directly. "And weakened our city greatly."

"That's not me problem," the stubborn dwarf answered.

"No, it is not," Shoudra admitted. "It is the duty of the marchion to protect his people."

"He'd do better protecting them if he could tell the difference between friends and enemies," Torgar shot back, poking a stubby finger Shoudra's way.

The sceptrana held her hands up to calm him, patting them in the air.

"This is not the time to rehash the debate," she said.

"Good a time as any, as far as I'm seein' it," said Torgar.

"We came here not to sabotage . . ." the sceptrana began.

"The little one admitted it," said Tred, who had brought the news up to the cliff.

". . . but to investigate," Shoudra went on. "We had to know if there was any danger to Mirabar—surely you can understand that. Perhaps the emigrating dwarves harbored resentment that would bring them back upon our city, with a host of Battlehammers behind them."

"Ye're talking stupid," said Torgar.

Shoudra started to respond, then sighed and nodded.

"I am telling you things from the perspective of Marchion Elastul, who is charged with the security of Mirabar," she explained.

"Like I said," came Torgar's dry reply.

"Barring any imminent threat to Mirabar—which Nanfoodle and I did not expect to find—we would never have used the formula. In fact, it was that same formula that Nanfoodle used to destroy the giant catapults. Have you so quickly forgotten our help?"

"Course we ain't," said Banak. "Which makes this news all the more painful. We're in a war here, so ye come here as friends or ye come here as enemies. Ain't no middling ground when the blood is flowing."

"We are here as friends," Nanfoodle said without hesitation. "We could have run home, but we did not. We were free in Keeper's Dale and would have been long off to the west before any word came out of Mithral Hall had we chosen to flee. But how could we, when we knew that you were fighting our common enemy up here? How could we when we knew that we could bring valuable assistance to your cause? Judge not my drunken words to Regis—never did I desire to poison Mithral Hall's metal. It is a mission I resisted every step out of Mirabar, and one that I only embarked upon with the intention of turning aside its course. And no less can be said of Shoudra Stargleam, who has ever been a friend of Torgar Hammerstriker and Shingles McRuff."

Banak, Tred, Catti-brie, and Wulfgar all turned to the Mirabarran dwarves, and the pair nodded their agreement with Nanfoodle's assessment.

"Then what would ye have me do, little one?" Banak asked. "Let ye run free down the road to Mirabar?"

Nanfoodle looked to Shoudra, then, smiling, back at the dwarf.

"No," he insisted. "Take me to Regis that I might make my case. In chains, if you must."

He held out his hands to the dwarf, who pushed them aside.

"Ye helped us here. Ye bought us needed time," Banak said. "If ye're wanting to run, now's the time for it. We'll look away long enough for ye to be long gone."

Again Nanfoodle glanced at Shoudra before eyeing the dwarf directly.

"If we thought we could be of no more assistance, we would accept your generous offer, good dwarf." Nanfoodle glanced back to the ridge, where new logs were already piling up, and said, "You must deal with those giants, and I think I can help. So no, I will not leave at this time and will accept the judgment of Steward Regis."

"Sounds like the little one's got a plan," said Catti-brie.

Nanfoodle's smile widened even more.

Regis sat back in his comfortable chair, dropped his chin into one hand and stared down at the many maps and diagrams Nanfoodle had spread out on the floor.

"I don't understand," he admitted, and he looked to Shoudra.

The sceptrana seemed equally perplexed and could only shrug in response.

"Is he always this abstract?" the halfling asked.

"Always," Shoudra admitted.

In the chair beside Regis, Ivan Bouldershoulder pored over a group of other diagrams Nanfoodle had given him, and it took him some time to realize that the other three were staring his way.

"Easy enough," the dwarf told them, particularly Regis. "The box at least. Simple enough contraption."

"The open-ended metal cylinders will prove no more complicated," Nanfoodle said.

"Agreed, except for the number ye're wanting," said Ivan, and he looked to Regis. "Ye'd have to set every furnace in Mithral Hall working day and night to get it done in time."

Regis shook his head, seeming more perplexed than negative.

"If I am right . . ." Nanfoodle started to say.

"You don't even know if those tunnels are open," Regis replied. "Nor do you know what you'll find if they are."

"Then let me go and look, at least," said the gnome.

"I can't commit my smiths to the task until we're sure," the steward replied.

Despite the denial, or more so because of the wording of the denial, Nanfoodle's grin nearly took in his abundant ears.

"Yes, go," Regis relented. He looked down at the mass of maps and diagrams and shook his head in disbelief and open skepticism. "It seems a fool's errand, but we have nothing better."

Nanfoodle bowed, again and again, as if he was bobbing with happiness— as indeed he usually was when someone in power offered him the opportunity to chase down another of his often wild proposals. Eventually, he managed to turn back to Ivan, whose reputation as a craftsman had long preceded him to Mithral Hall.

"You will construct the box?" he asked.

"Got all I need," said the dwarf. "Except this flame water potion."

"Leave that to me, when the time is near," Nanfoodle assured him. The brightness on the gnome's face dimmed then, as he added, "Where might I find your brother?"

"Sitting in the dark," Ivan replied. "And I'm wishing ye luck on getting him to go tunneling with ye. He's not much in the mood for anything right now."

"We shall see," said Nanfoodle.

"With your permission, I will return to Master Brawnanvil," Shoudra put in then.

"I feel the fool for trusting you after what he admitted to me," Regis said to her. "I should throw you both in chains and have Marchion Elastul pay a high ransom for your safe return."

Shoudra smiled at him and said, "But you will not."

"Go to Banak," Regis said with a wave of his little hand.

Shoudra started out of the room but paused and looked back as the gracious steward added, "And thank you."

As she left the room, the sceptrana told herself pointedly that when she returned to Mirabar, she would oppose Marchion Elastul's every move against this neighbor and ally.

As he moved up to the door, Nanfoodle heard the soft, "Oooo" and winced in sympathy for the poor dwarf. The gnome lifted his fist to knock but held back and slowly dropped that hand to the dragon-shaped doorknob and quietly turned the latch. The perfectly balanced and well-oiled portal made not a sound as it swung open.

There sat Pikel in the middle of the floor, head down, his remaining hand absently drawing designs on the stone floor of the room. So distracted and dis-traught was the green-bearded dwarf that he didn't even look up as Nanfoodle approached, moving right beside him. Every now and then, the dwarf gave another plaintive, "Oooo."

"Does it still hurt?" Nanfoodle quietly asked.

Pikel looked up at him.

"Uh uh," he said, and he waved his stumped forearm in Nanfoodle's direction.

"Then you are sad," Nanfoodle said, and Pikel looked at him as if that should be obvious enough. "Do you believe that you have nothing to offer to Clan Battlehammer now?"

"Eh?" the green-bearded dwarf replied.

He held up his hand and waggled his fingers.

"You are still able to cast your spells then?"

"Yup yup," said Pikel.

"What are you doing there on the floor?" the gnome asked.

He came forward and leaned over the still-sitting Pikel—to see that the dwarf wasn't just sliding his hand over the stone in swirling designs, he was actually swirling the stone itself around. A grin widened on Nanfoodle's face, for that was exactly one of the purposes he had in mind for Pikel Bouldershoulder.

Nanfoodle moved around in front of Pikel and squatted down to look the dwarf directly in the eye.

"Your brother is working for me," he said.

"Eh?"

"I needed a craftsman, an engineer," Nanfoodle explained. "I was told that Ivan was among the best."

"Yup. Hee hee, me brudder."

"And Regis was very interested in telling Ivan to help me because he understands that my plan could well change the battle raging up on top of the cliff." He paused and studied the dwarf to make sure that he had Pikel's attention. "You want to help them, yes?"

Pikel's expression was perfectly perplexed.

"Yup yup."

"You see, I have many different needs right now," Nanfoodle tried to explain. "Important things must be done, but many of the tasks are a bit different than the dwarves could normally offer. Oh, there are a few that Steward Regis knew who might be able to assist me with one task or another, but there was only one name that came through repeatedly, for every task."

"Pikel?" the dwarf asked, pointing to himself—with a finger that was covered in fast-hardening stone.

"Pikel," Nanfoodle confirmed. He pointed down to the designs on the floor. "For that, and because I need help from animals—they won't be injured, I assure you. Not if we are smart and quick."

"Hee hee hee."

It did Nanfoodle's heart good to see that he had brought a smile to the despondent dwarf's face. Pikel seemed such a gentle soul to him; the mere thought of such a person suffering so grievous an injury pained Nanfoodle greatly. But Nanfoodle also understood that Pikel's pain was more emotional than physical, and that, in such cases as his, a person's self-worth was often the greatest casualty.

"Come on," he cheerfully offered to the dwarf, extending his hand to help Pikel to his feet. "We have much to do."

———◦———

"Ye're pulling me beard," said Wocco Brawnanvil, brother of Brusco and proud cousin of Mithral Hall's heroic war commander.

"I ain't, and if I was, ye'd be kneeling, don't ye doubt," Ivan Bouldershoulder replied.

"This little gnome's a troublesome one, then," said Wocco. "He's not for building them damn arky-busses, is he? Heared them things blow up in yer face more'n they boom yer enemies."

"Nah, none o' them," Ivan confirmed.

Wocco and all the other blacksmiths standing around him breathed a sigh of relief. Ivan thought discretion necessary. If those dwarves, miners all, understood what Nanfoodle had in mind, they wouldn't be pleased.

"So ye're just wanting a tube of metal?" another dwarf asked.

"But all gotta be the same diameter," Ivan replied.

"And length?"

"Long as ye can make 'em."

The blacksmiths all looked around at each other.

"And Regis wants us doing this?" one asked.

"Got his mark, don't it?" Ivan asked, pointing to the parchment he had handed over, complete with diagrams and instructions and the signature of the Steward of Mithral Hall.

"*All* the forges?" one of them asked.

"We got lots of weapons to fix, with the fighting up above," Wocco explained. "We're behind already, after outfitting the band Regis sent running down the southern tunnels."

"This comes first," said Ivan. "Bah, if ye're quick about it and make a proper mold, ye'll put them out a dozen at a time!"

Again the blacksmiths looked around at each other, but a couple, at least, were nodding.

"How many ye need?" asked Wocco.

"Just ye keep making them," said Ivan.

He grinned and pulled out another rolled parchment, opening it wide for the other dwarves to see. It contained a diagram, one far more complicated than the instructions for the simple rolled metal tubes.

"And I'm working with impact oil," Ivan said with a snicker.

"Boom?" asked Wocco.

"I'm hopin' I don't slip with me hammer," Ivan said with a laugh, and the others joined in.

"Boom!" several said together.

Wocco lifted the parchments in salute, then motioned for his companions to follow him back to the lines of forges.

Ivan, whose work would be much more delicate, turned and moved off the other way, back to the smaller work area Regis had afforded him near the audience chambers.

He did pause long enough to look across the Undercity to the northwest, to the doors blocking the little-used tunnels, and his smile fast faded. Pikel was down there, with Nanfoodle.

Ivan could only hope that his brother would be all right, and that he would find his heart again, and his laugh.

Pikel held his shortened arm up and the small bird sitting on it shifted nervously. The dwarf druid brought the delicate creature in close and whispered reassuring words, then lowered the arm and started off down the side passage, which was lit with a soft, reddish glow.

"You are sure of this?" Nanfoodle asked the dwarf. "I have little in the way of weaponry about me and am not even certain that my more potent spells would affect such creatures."

In response, Pikel looked back at Nanfoodle and scrunched up his face, closing his eyes tight, a reminder that the gnome had insisted that they use no fire in the potentially disastrous tunnels.

"Yes, but . . ." Nanfoodle started to protest.

Pikel just gave a, "Hee hee hee," and started away.

Nanfoodle turned back to the five dwarf warriors assigned as escort and merely shrugged, and so did they, seeming more amused than worried.

"Just bugs, little one," one of the group explained. "Big bugs, but bugs all the same."

To reassure the gnome, the group presented their weapons, including the two enchanted, glowing long swords that had been providing all of their light.

They didn't need those weapons, though, for Pikel had little trouble in persuading the potential enemies that there was no battle to be found, and soon after,

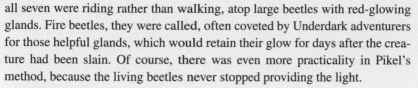

all seven were riding rather than walking, atop large beetles with red-glowing glands. Fire beetles, they were called, often coveted by Underdark adventurers for those helpful glands, which would retain their glow for days after the creature had been slain. Of course, there was even more practicality in Pikel's method, because the living beetles never stopped providing the light.

All along the tunnels, the green-bearded dwarf communicated to his new "friends" with a series of clicks and pops, and he even (so he said) managed to glean a bit of useful information out of the giant insects.

Whether or not that claim was true, the dwarf did lead the party to a most curious tunnel, sloping down to the north and reeking of a particularly nasty odor. Streaks of color lined the dark walls, though it was hard to distinguish its true hue in the red light.

"Yellow," Nanfoodle told them, for the gnome knew the smell of sulfur. "Keep a careful watch on your bird, Pikel. You don't want him to fall over dead."

Pikel gave a squeak of protest and brought the brave little bird up close to his face. Almost immediately, the bird began to panic, and Pikel whispered into its ear and sent it flying back up to clearer air.

Beside him, Nanfoodle understood the positive sign, and he pressed on through the reek.

The tunnel ended in a wide, high chamber full of stalagmites that narrowed as they rose, then widened again as they joined with the great stalactites hanging down from above. A haze filled the room, and even the sturdy dwarves had to pull the cloths Pikel had prepared up before their faces.

"Gonna lose me breakfast," one announced, and the others all nodded in agreement.

Nanfoodle, though, was simply too excited to consider such possibilities. He urged his beetle mount up ahead, then quickly dismounted and moved between the pillars of stone to the edge of an underground pool.

His smile erupted when he at last managed to peer through the haze, to see the source of that sulfuric fog, for the water roiled and bubbled, a sure sign of gasses escaping.

"If you lit a torch in here, we would all be incinerated," the gnome somberly announced.

"Hope that breakfast wasn't too spicy, then," chortled one dwarf, motioning over to another who was on his hands and knees gagging.

Those who were able moved up beside Nanfoodle to view the spectacle.

"The gas we need is invisible and has no odor," the gnome explained.

"Could o' fooled me," said one dwarf.

"No no," the gnome explained. "It mixes with other gasses in the pressure below. But you see how it escapes?" he asked, pointing to the bubbles. "Yes, yes, it is all in place."

"Got no idea what ye're talking about, gnome," said a dwarf. "But ye found it, yep? So now we can be leaving?"

"In a few moments," Nanfoodle replied. "We have to know the texture of the stone. We must be prepared when we return, for this will be no easy task."

He looked to Pikel, who was already falling within himself, eyes closed, arms waving.

The dwarf finished, giggled, and lay down, then simply melted into the stone, disappearing from view.

"That one's just not right," muttered a thoroughly shaken dwarf.

"Shut yer trap and get on yer beetle," another sarcastically remarked.

"Doo-dad. . . ." said a third, shaking his head.

Nanfoodle just smiled through it all.

A short while later, Pikel's form reappeared in the stone, like a bas relief carved into the floor. He came forth fully and hopped up, brushing himself off.

"Whew!" he said.

"How thick?" the excited Nanfoodle asked.

Pikel tapped himself on the head three times.

"Fifteen feet," Nanfoodle muttered.

"How'd he know that?" one dwarf asked another.

"Three Pikel's deep," reasoned another.

"Ye're scarin' me, gnome," a third remarked.

"Can we get through that much?" Nanfoodle asked Pikel, ignoring the others.

"Hee hee hee," said the green-bearded dwarf.

23

ELF MUSING,
GIANT FEARS

Drizzt sat on a high stone on the eastern slope, watching as the sky brightened before him, as pinks and violets grew from the deep blue of predawn. He was glad when he heard the soft footfalls of Innovindil behind him, for it was her first journey out of the cave since Tarathiel's fall, two days before.

She walked up beside him and leaned on the stone.

"It will be a beautiful dawn," she said.

"They all are," Drizzt replied. "Even when the clouds lay thick about the horizon, the glow of the sun is a most welcomed sight to my Underdark weary eyes."

"Even after all these years?"

Drizzt looked over at Innovindil, at the warmth of her elf features—seeming less angular in the soft, predawn light—and at the depth of her blue eyes. Dawn was a time befitting her beauty, he thought. The softness and the quiet. The opposite of the hardened warrior he had witnessed in battle. Only then, in that flavor, did Drizzt truly begin to appreciate her depth.

"How old are you?" he asked before he could even consider the propriety of the question.

"This time marks the end of my third century," she answered. "Tarathiel was older than I, by many decades."

"That seems inconsequential to us of elf heritage."

Drizzt closed his eyes as he spoke, considering his own statement. What was waiting for him in his second century of life? he wondered. Was each existence among the shorter lived races a replay of the previous? A simple continuation?

He glanced at the sunrise and wondered, hoped, that perhaps it was not, that perhaps each "existence" as measured by the life span of a human or even a dwarf, would instead place layers upon knowledge already gained. He looked down at Innovindil, hoping that perhaps there might be some clue to be found in the depths of her eyes, but he found her smiling widely at him, a look that seemed almost condescending.

"You do not understand what it is to be an elf, do you?" she asked him.

Drizzt just stared at her. He understood what she was hinting at and even believed that there was more than a little truth in her words.

"You left the Underdark when you were but a child," Innovindil went on.

"Not so young."

"But never trained in the perspectives of elven culture," Innovindil said.

Drizzt shrugged and had to agree, for in his time in Menzoberranzan, he had spent his hours training to fight and to kill.

"And up here," she went on, "you have mostly been in the company of shorter-lived races."

"Bruenor counts his age in centuries, as do you," Drizzt reminded.

"Dwarves do not have an elf's perspective."

"You speak as if it is a tangible thing."

Drizzt paused then, as did Innovindil, for the eastern sky brightened with brilliant pinks and purples. The dawn came on gloriously, for there were just enough clouds, all drifting in distinct clusters and lines, to catch the morning rays and reflect them in myriad hues and textures.

"Was the beauty of that sunrise a tangible thing?" Innovindil asked.

Drizzt smiled and surrendered with a sigh.

"You must come to understand what it is or what it will be to live for several centuries, Drizzt Do'Urden," she said. "For your own sake, should you be fortunate enough to dodge your enemies and see those long years. You have picked your friends among the lesser races, and you must understand the implications of those choices."

"Lesser . . ." Drizzt started to ask, but Innovindil cut him short by explaining, "Lesser-*lived* races."

Drizzt started to respond again, but he fell silent and let his gaze drift back to the east. He concentrated on the beauty of the continuing sunrise, trying to hide behind it and not show the pain that had come into his heart.

"What is it?" Innovindil pressed him.

He held silent. He felt Innovindil's hand softly touch his shoulder, and he couldn't deny that her warm touch was drawing him away from the wall of anger that was building again around his heart.

"Drizzt?" she asked quietly.

"Good friends," he said, his voice quavering.

Innovindil's hand continued to hold him until he at last turned to regard her.

"More than friends?" she asked.

Drizzt's lips went very tight.

"The daughter of Bruenor," Innovindil reasoned. "You love the human daughter of Bruenor Battlehammer, the one named Catti-brie."

Drizzt swallowed hard.

"Loved," he corrected.

It was Innovindil's turn to put on a curious look.

"She fell at Shallows, with Bruenor, Wulfgar, and Regis," Drizzt mustered the strength to say. "I picked my friends and could not have found better companionship, but . . ."

His voice cracked apart, and he turned fast back to the dawn, locking himself into the spectacle of colors, even held his stare against the sting of the rising sun itself, as if its burn on his sensitive eyes could somehow block out the other, more profound pain.

Innovindil squeezed his shoulder hard and asked, "Do you question your choice?"

"No," Drizzt insisted without the slightest hesitation.

"And your choice to love a human?"

"Was I wrong for that?" Drizzt asked. His defiance melted suddenly, and he asked again, more quietly, as if searching for an honest answer, "Was I wrong for that?"

Drizzt had to pause then and take a deep breath, and another, and he turned back to the rising sun, his eyes moist from more than the bright light's sting.

"Do you think it unwise for an elf, who might live for seven or more centuries, to fall in love with a human who will not know the end of one?" Innovindil asked him. "Do you think it a terrible notion that if you had children with a human, they would age and die before you?"

Drizzt winced at both questions.

"I do not know," he admitted, his voice barely a whisper.

"Because you do not know what it is to be an elf," Innovindil said with certainty.

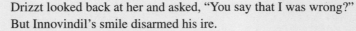

Drizzt looked back at her and asked, "You say that I was wrong?"

But Innovindil's smile disarmed his ire.

"Our curse is to outlive so many of those we will know and love," she said. "I have known two human lovers."

Drizzt eyed her, not knowing what to make of the admission.

"The first man I fell in love with was a human, and he was not a young man, by human counting," Innovindil went on, and it was her turn to look to the rising sun. "He was a good man, a wizard of great talent, if little ambition." She gave a wistful chuckle. "But how I loved him—as greatly as I have ever loved anyone. I buried him when I was still a child by an elf's counting—younger even than you are now. How that pained me. . . .

"Nearly a century passed before I was able to dare to love another human," the elf went on, still staring to the east, not blinking at all.

"And he died as well," Drizzt reasoned.

"But not before we had three wonderful decades together," Innovindil replied, her smile widening. She paused for a long while, then turned and looked directly at Drizzt once more. "You really do not understand what it is to be an elf, Drizzt Do'Urden, because no one has shown you."

Her tone told Drizzt clearly that her words were an offer.

But could he dare to take her up on that offer? Could he dare to leave his heart open wide once more, where it would possibly get seared yet again?

"We have business to attend," the drow announced, his voice strong and determined. "Tarathiel's death will not go unavenged."

"You will kill the orc who slew him?"

"On my word," Drizzt declared through clenched teeth.

It took him a while to realize that Innovindil was staring at him hard. He turned to her, his determination ebbing as he looked into her wide-eyed, angry glare.

"That is our purpose then?" Innovindil asked. "To avenge Tarathiel?"

"Is it not?"

"It is not!" the elf growled at him, and she seemed to grow tall and terrible, seemed to rise up and tower over Drizzt. "Our purpose—my purpose—is not a journey of hatred and vengeance."

Drizzt shrank back from her.

"Not while Sunrise is held captive by such unmerciful and brutal masters," Innovindil explained. She settled back then and seemed herself once more. "I will not let my anger get in the way of my purpose, Drizzt Do'Urden. I will not let anger cloud my vision or turn me one step to the side of the path I must take. Sunrise is my charge—I will not fail him to satiate my anger."

She looked at Drizzt for a moment longer, then turned and walked back to the cave.

Leaving Drizzt alone on the rock in the slanting rays of early morning.

"He cut the elf in half," the giant, one of two who had come in to see their dame, told Gerti. "He wields that sword with the strength of *Tierlaan Gau,*" he added, using the giants' name for members of their race.

Gerti Orelsdottr tightened her jaw. Obould had won again, an impressive show in front of creatures who already thought him a god.

"What of the drow and the other elf?"

"Of Drizzt Do'Urden, we have heard nothing . . . perhaps," the giant replied, and he turned and looked to his partner, also recently returned from the incidents up north.

"Perhaps?"

"A body was found," the giant explained.

"That of a drow," said the other.

"Drizzt?"

"Donnia Soldou," the first giant replied, and Gerti's eyes widened.

"Dead among the rocks," the other giant added. "Murdered by fine blades."

Gerti mulled over the words for a bit. Had Donnia met up with Drizzt? Or perhaps with the surface elves? Gerti couldn't help but chuckle as she considered that perhaps Donnia had angered her own three companions. That was the thing about drow, was it not? They were so often busy killing each other that they could never manage any real conquests.

"I will miss her," Gerti admitted. "She was . . . amusing."

The other two relaxed, obviously relieved that Gerti wasn't taking the death of Donnia very hard.

"Obould slew one of the elves that has been terrorizing the region," the giantess stated.

"And captured his winged horse," the scout reported.

Again Gerti's eyes went wide.

"A pegasus? Obould is in possession of a pegasus?"

"We would have preferred to kill it," the scout explained. "That elf and his beast made up half the pair who assaulted us in the fight at Shallows."

"A bit of horseflesh would taste good," said the other.

Gerti thought it over for a moment, then said, "You should have slaughtered the creature. While Obould was battling the elf, you should have walked over and crushed its head!"

The two looked startled, but Gerti pressed on, "They are creatures of beauty, yes, and I would favor one for myself. But I do not wish to see King Obould Many-Arrows flying about above the battlefields, calling out orders to his charges. I do not wish to see him up on high, riding about, godlike."

"W-we did not know," the scout stammered.

"We could not have killed the winged beast, in any case," said the other. "We would have been battling scores of orcs had we tried."

Gerti dismissed them both with a wave and turned away, her mind whirling from the surprising news. Obould was the hero once more, which would be beneficial in bringing forth more of the orc and goblin tribes. His glory had bound them together.

But where did that glory leave her? Beneath him on the field while he soared around on his winged steed?

A horn brought the giantess from her contemplations, and she turned north to see the returning host of orcs, King Obould walking at their head.

"Walking," she whispered, thinking that a good thing.

She caught sight of the pegasus, moving along to the side, bound and hobbled by short ropes tied leg to leg. Indeed it was a beautiful creature, majestic and with a brilliant white coat and mane. Too wondrous for the likes of an orc, to Gerti's thinking. She decided right then that she would demand the pegasus in time—true, she could never ride it, but what a wonderful addition to Shining White such a magnificent beast would prove!

As the column neared, Obould motioned for his charges to continue, then he veered toward Gerti, the miserable Arganth trotting along at his heels.

"We found just one," he told her. "But that one will be enough to bring the orcs from the tunnels."

"How can you know?" Gerti asked, and she wasn't looking at the orc king but rather at the pegasus as it was pulled past on her distant right.

"Yes, a mount for a king," Obould remarked. "We have begun the breaking. I will fly the beast when that bitch Alustriel of Silverymoon comes pleading that we do not continue our march."

Gerti glanced back as the pegasus moved past, and she could clearly see the signs of the brutal orc breaking. Whip marks marred the pegasus's white coat. Every time the steed tried to lift its head proudly, the orc tugging it along yanked down on the lead, and the horse bowed. Gerti could only imagine the bite of the nasty bit the orc must be using to so bend the powerful pegasus.

"I have been informed of Donnia's demise," Gerti said, turning back to the orc king.

"Dead and rotting on the mountainside," said Obould.

"Then Drizzt Do'Urden is still around, and other elves, no doubt."

Obould nodded and shrugged as if it didn't really matter.

"We will stay in the region for a while," he explained, "to better coax out any tribes who choose to join us. Arganth will lead some back into the northern tunnels to better spread the word of my victory and to give hope to the orcs. Perhaps we will find Drizzt Do'Urden and the other elf or elves, and they too will fall to my blade. If they are wise, they will flee across the Surbrin and back into the Moonwood, though perhaps they will not be safe there, either."

Behind Obould, Arganth snickered.

Gerti studied the orc king carefully. Was his dimwit resurfacing? Would he begin to believe the accolades others were putting on his shoulders and change his mind about securing the borders of his planned kingdom? Gerti knew that crossing the Surbrin would prove a huge, and likely fatal, error.

Despite herself, she hoped Obould would do it.

"My king," Arganth Snarrl said from behind. "Methinks you should go south to your son and be done with the dwarves."

"You question me?"

"No, my king, no!" Arganth said, bowing repeatedly. "I fear . . . Drizzt Do'Urden and the elf's companion are still about . . . there is . . ."

Obould glanced back at Gerti, then turned back to Arganth, looking somewhat confused. He gave a sudden, great belly laugh.

"You fear for my safety?"

"Obould is Gruumsh!" Arganth said, and he fell flat to the ground. "Obould is Gruumsh!"

"Get up!"

Arganth jumped to his feet but continued to genuflect.

"Were you afraid when I battled the elf?" Obould asked.

"No, my king! He was nothing against you!"

"But Drizzt Do'Urden. . . ."

"Is nothing to you, my king!" Arganth screeched. "Not in fair battle. But he is drow. He will cheat. He will come in when you are asleep, methinks. I fear—"

"Silence!" growled Obould.

Arganth gave a whine and seemed as if he would faint away.

Obould turned back to Gerti, his face a mask of anger.

Gerti couldn't hide her amusement, and didn't even try to.

"Forgive me, my king," Arganth whispered, moving up behind Obould.

A backhand slap sent the fool flying away.

"I do not fear this rogue drow, nor a host of the elf's companions," the orc told Gerti. "If all the Moonwood came forth to avenge their dead, I would rush to that battle eagerly."

And die horribly, Gerti thought and hoped.

"We already have enough resources to put the dwarves in their hole and to defend the Surbrin," the giantess remarked.

"Not yet," Obould replied. "I want them to pay in deep pools of blood for trying to hold ground against Urlgen. Let him continue the battle outside of Mithral Hall a while longer. Proffit will need time to being the press from the south."

"You will find little hunting in this region beyond Drizzt and any other elves who might be around. The humans are all dead or have wisely fled."

Obould stared at her for a short while, then just muttered under his breath, "I will consider our movements," and walked away.

Gerti nearly slugged him as he passed, for merely presuming to count her and her giants into his considerations. How dare he act as if his decisions would so affect her? How dare he . . .

Gerti let her bluster die away, a private admission that, just then at least, she would be wise to perhaps play along with Obould. The sheer number of followers he had amassed could press her giants greatly should she make an enemy of him.

The giantess glanced around at the hundreds of orcs and the handful of giants. It struck her then that she had unwisely spread out her forces, with so many working along the Surbrin and the score she had given to Urlgen.

Hopefully that fool of an orc had used those giants as intended and had already driven the dwarves back into Mithral Hall.

Gerti wanted the glory to begin to spread out, instead of simply falling onto Obould's broad shoulders at every point.

She'd find out soon enough, she learned a short while later, when word reached her of Obould's decision to return to the south and Urlgen's battlefield.

24

PREYING ON FLEETING HOPES

Regis ruffled the pile of papers—scouting reports—then pushed them all aside. Up on the cliff, Banak was holding strong. But how? Or the better question, why? The force of orcs and giants—to say nothing of the trolls!—that had closed the eastern gate of Mithral Hall had by all accounts been huge. Fortifications were being constructed all around the fords of the Surbrin and yet the bulk of the monstrous forces had departed, with the trolls marching south and the main force of orcs turning back to the north. If that main force linked up with the orcs opposing Banak, then the valiant dwarf and his charges would be pushed over the cliff to Keeper's Dale and all the way back into Mithral Hall. There could be no doubt.

The question nagged at Regis's thoughts: Why hadn't the orcs already done that?

The halfling looked up to Catti-brie, who sat across the way. He started to say something, but her expression caught him and held him in place. She seemed relaxed, physically at least, leaning back in the soft chair, her legs crossed at the knee, her head turned to the side and looking off into nowhere, one hand up, one finger absently playing about her chin and lips. Exhaustion was written across her face, a mask of weariness but also of resolve.

Regis looked closer, noticed the bruises on her hand, the small cuts on her extended finger, rubbed raw from the draw of her powerful bow. He noted the dried blood in her auburn hair, the streaks and clumps. And most of all, he noted the look in her blue eyes, the quiet determination, but undercut by something darker, some sense that, for all their efforts, they could not prevail.

"They are fortifying the western bank of the Surbrin," the halfling informed her, and Catti-brie slowly turned her head to regard him. "Every ford and shallow."

"To keep the elves in the Moonwood and Alustriel in Silverymoon," Catti-brie replied. "To keep Felbarr from joining."

"Felbarr's soldiers will come through the tunnels," Regis corrected.

"Aye, but then if they're to go up and fight, they'll be filtering in beside Clan Battlehammer's own. We'll put no vice on the orcs if we're all coming out the same hole."

"It will fall to the humans, then," said Regis. "To Alustriel and Silverymoon, and to the folk of Sundabar, if they can be raised. We need them."

He heard the pain in his own voice, the realization that crossing the Surbrin would likely take a terrible toll on those hoped-for allies.

"The orcs're counting on the pain of the Surbrin defenses to keep them at bay," Catti-brie said, as if she had read the halfling's mind.

"Some advisors have hinted that I should reopen an eastern exit and strike at the Surbrin fortifications from behind. We could sneak a few hundred dwarves out, and that few hundred could cause more damage than an army of ten thousand across the river."

Catti-brie's expression immediately turned doubtful.

"We would need to coordinate it precisely with the arrival of any allies, of course," the halfling clarified. "Else the beasts would chase us back in and just rebuild their defenses."

Catti-brie began to shake her head.

"You do not agree?"

"You've more than a thousand up with Banak and thousands more digging in on the west end of Keeper's Dale," she explained. "We're hearing the sounds of trolls in the southern tunnels, and you've got dwarves running south to find if any're surviving Nesmé."

"We cannot spare five hundred at this time," Regis replied.

"Even if we could . . ." Catti-brie said, her voice halting, and still shaking her head.

"What do you know?"

"It seems amiss . . ." the woman started and stopped with a sigh. "They could put us in our hole, but they're not."

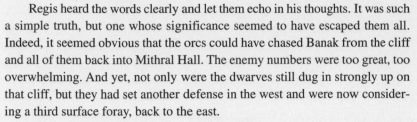

Regis heard the words clearly and let them echo in his thoughts. It was such a simple truth, but one whose significance seemed to have escaped them all. Indeed, it seemed obvious that the orcs could have chased Banak from the cliff and all of them back into Mithral Hall. The enemy numbers were too great, too overwhelming. And yet, not only were the dwarves still dug in strongly up on that cliff, but they had set another defense in the west and were now considering a third surface foray, back to the east.

"We're being baited," Regis heard himself saying, and he could hardly believe the words as they left his mouth. He came forward in his chair, eyes wide with the terrible recognition. "They're forcing us to fight on terms more favorable to them."

"The hundreds of orc and goblin dead on the slopes in the north wouldn't be agreeing with you," Catti-brie replied. "Banak's slaughtering them."

Then Regis was the one shaking his head.

"They're accepting the losses for the sake of the bigger gain," he explained. "We kill a thousand, two thousand, ten thousand, but they can replace them. Our replacements come harder, and keeping us fighting aboveground continues the clarion call to the neighboring communities to come forth and join in the battle."

It made sense to Regis. The orcs were driving the issue to the bitter end. That great force that had marched back to the north after sealing Mithral Hall's eastern gate would indeed turn their sights upon Banak and drive the dwarves into their hole. But by that time, Silverymoon and perhaps Sundabar would have played their hands, would have come forth or not. And all on terms favorable to the orcs and giants. Regis fell back in his seat, running his chubby fingers through his curly brown hair.

"The orcs want us to stay out there," he said.

"So you're thinking we should come in?"

Regis pondered Cattie-brie's words for a moment, then stared at the woman in confusion.

"We cannot ignore the damage Banak is inflicting," he said. "And there are reports of refugees making their way to the west, north of the battle." He paused and riffled through a pile of parchments, looking for the report that indicated such an emigration. "If we break off the fighting, any left in the area will be without hope, for the orcs could turn their full attention against them."

"That would include Drizzt," Catti-brie remarked, and the thought had Regis stammering as he tried to continue.

"Don't fret," Catti-brie offered. "The choice won't be your own for long. Banak's thinking he's got less than a tenday before the giants bring their catapults to bear—and we won't be stopping them this time. Once those great engines of war begin throwing, he'll have to retreat or be wiped out."

"And if they get the high ground above Keeper's Dale, we'll have no choice but to come inside. All of us," Regis said.

"And if they're thinking of coming in behind us, we'll cut them down," Catti-brie grimly offered.

It seemed a hollow potential to Regis, though, understanding that all of it—the fighting and the timing—was being controlled by their enemies.

Catti-brie pulled herself out of her chair.

"I'm to be heading back to Banak," she stated.

She pulled up Taulmaril from the side of her chair and slung the bow over her shoulder in a determined and even angry motion. But Regis could see the weariness creeping behind that determination.

Before the woman even turned to leave, there came a knock on the door, and in walked the two emissaries from Mirabar, the gnome's arms filled with dozens of rolled parchments.

"We can do it," Nanfoodle declared before anyone even had the chance for proper greetings. "We can do it!"

"Do it?" Catti-brie asked, turning to Regis.

Regis held up his hand to stop the questions from the woman.

"As you suspected?" the halfling asked the gnome.

"Of course," said Nanfoodle. "And fortune is with us, for the deposit is under the northern edges of Keeper's Dale and close enough to open tunnels so that we will not need to dig through much stone at all."

"What's the little one talking about?" Catti-brie quietly demanded.

Nanfoodle bobbed over, a more somber Shoudra in tow.

"With the help of Pikel Bouldershoulder, we can string the metal tubes in short order," Nanfoodle explained. "Within a single day, if you offer enough dwarves to aid us."

"Tubes?" Catti-brie asked, and she looked from Nanfoodle to Shoudra, who merely shrugged, then back to Regis.

"What do you know of it?" Regis asked the sceptrana.

"I know that Nanfoodle is excited by the prospects," Shoudra replied, stating the obvious, for the little gnome was bobbing about, hopping from foot to foot.

"We can do it, Steward Regis," Nanfoodle insisted. "Only give the word and I will commence the organization of the workers. Twenty should accomplish the task, along with Pikel, Ivan, and myself. More than that would likely get in each others' way! Ha ha!"

"Regis?" Catti-brie demanded more insistently.

The halfling put his palms over his eyes and blew a deep sigh. He was surprised by the gnome's success in finding the gasses, and not necessarily pleasantly surprised. For despite Nanfoodle's obvious exuberance, that new development only upped the stakes for troubled Regis. True, he had diverted his forges to satisfy the gnome's requirements for "tubes," but that action had involved little real risk, after all. To move forward with the gnome's planning, the halfling steward would have to order dwarves into dangerous battle, with the risks much greater to all of them, particularly to Banak and his forces on the northern cliff.

And what would happen if Nanfoodle proved correct and brought his plan to fruition?

A shudder coursed through Regis's spine, and he turned to Catti-brie. "Can we take the tunnels underneath the ridge again?"

"Below the giants?"

"That ridge, yes."

The woman looked again at the gnome, curiously, then sat back and considered the problem. She had no idea of how determinedly the orcs were holding those tunnels, with the giants in place above. Likely the resistance would be greatly diminished, since the strategic importance of the labyrinth seemed negligible.

"I would expect that we could," she answered.

Nanfoodle gave a little squeal and punched his fist into the air.

"Won't be an easy fight, though," the woman added, just to dampen the little one's spirits a bit.

Regis looked from Nanfoodle to Shoudra and back again, then back at Shoudra, his eyes asking her quite clearly to help him, to tell him if he could really trust the gnome's wild planning. The woman, apparently catching the cue, gave the slightest of nods.

"How long before those giant catapults come to bear?" the halfling asked Catti-brie again.

"Within the tenday," she replied. "Might be as few as three days."

"Then go to Banak and prepare a force. Get me the tunnels back the morning after next," the steward instructed. "Nanfoodle will send up specifics this very afternoon."

"Ivan Bouldershoulder will meet you up there with instructions," the gnome put in.

"You think ye might be telling me what this is all about?" Catti-brie asked.

Regis looked to the other two again, then he snorted and shrugged.

"I'm afraid to do that," he admitted. "You would not believe me, and if you did, you might just cut me down where I sit."

All eyes went to Nanfoodle then, the obvious architect of all of it all.

"We can do it," the little gnome assured them.

Tred McKnuckles came upon Torgar Hammerstriker and Ivan Bouldershoulder shortly after hearing that Banak had put out a call for volunteers to go and retake the tunnels beneath the western ridge. The pair were distracted as Tred approached, and so they did not seem to notice him. Their attention was fixed upon a small box held by Torgar, one side of it as shiny as any mirror, the other three, and top and bottom, smooth wood.

"Well met," the dwarf of Citadel Felbarr greeted the pair.

"And to yerself," said Ivan.

Torgar nodded and smiled, then went back to inspecting the box.

"Is yerself to lead the fight for the tunnels?" Tred asked Torgar. "Might that I could be joinin' ye?"

"Aye, and aye," Torgar replied. "We'll be going in the morning to drive them smelly orcs out. Me and me boys'll welcome yer company."

"Any word on why?" Tred asked. "I'm not thinkin' we can get to them stinking giants from the holes beneath 'em."

Torgar and Ivan exchanged a grin, and Torgar held up the box.

"Here's why," he explained.

Tred reached for it, but Torgar pulled it back.

"Handle it carefully," the dwarf warned.

"Full o' the oil from me darts," Ivan explained, and he slipped his hand under his bandoleer of explosive crossbow darts and held it forward. "And a concoction the little gnome made—bottle of firewater that blows up when it touches the air."

Tred scrunched up his face and retracted his hand.

"We're going in with bombs, then?" Tred asked.

"Nah, we'll use our axes and hammers to be rid of the durned orcs," said Torgar. "The bombs're for later."

Tred looked curiously from dwarf to dwarf, but both of them merely shrugged and returned his expression.

"It's all beyond us," Torgar admitted. "But Banak's wanting them tunnels taken, and so we're for taking them. We'll see what magic the gnome's got later on."

"Could be worse," Ivan put in. "Least we're getting to smash some orcs."

"Always a good thing," Torgar agreed, and Tred nodded.

"Eleven-hunnerd more feet!" Wocco Brawnanvil cried when Nanfoodle laid out the diagrams before him.

"Eleven hundred and thirty," Nanfoodle corrected.

"Ye'll tie up all the forges for another tenday, ye stupid gnome!"

"Another tenday?" asked the gnome. "Oh no, I need this tomorrow—all of it. My assistants will be pulling it right out of the cooling troughs, piece by piece."

Wocco sputtered for several moments, his flapping lips forming curse after curse, but his incredulity beating every word back before it could get out.

"Seven foot lengths," he finally managed to say. "It's a hunnerd and fifty pieces!"

"A hundred and sixty-two," Nanfoodle corrected. "With half of one left over."

"We can't be doing that!"

"You have to," the gnome countered. "If this was a merchant's order needing to be filled, you would pump those furnaces hot and get the job done."

"Merchants're paying," Wocco dryly answered.

"And so am I," Nanfoodle insisted.

"And what's yer pay, little one?"

"A score of giants," Nanfoodle answered with a great flourish, for he saw that he had many of the other blacksmiths watching him. "A score, I say, and victory for Banak Brawnanvil and Mithral Hall. I offer you nothing less than that, good Master Brawnanvil."

"We build weapons for that," came the smithy's protest.

"This is a weapon," Nanfoodle assured him. "As great a weapon as you've ever built. A hundred and sixty-two. You can do this."

Wocco glanced over at the other blacksmiths.

"It's a lot o' metal," one of the smiths remarked.

"It'll take more than half our stores," said another.

"Much more," a third put in.

"You can do this," Nanfoodle said again to Wocco. "You must do this. Time is running out for Banak and his forces. Would you fail them and have them pushed over the cliff?"

That hit a nerve, the gnome saw immediately, for Wocco puffed out his chest and tightened his jaw, his wide mouth puckering up into an angry pout.

For a moment, Nanfoodle thought the dwarf would surely punch him, but the gnome did not back away an inch, and even added, "This is Banak's only chance to hold out against the hordes. Without your superior efforts here, he will be forced into a disastrous retreat."

Wocco held the pose but did not come forward to throttle the gnome, and gradually, the dwarf's anger seemed to melt into resolve. He looked to the other blacksmiths.

"Well, ye heared him. We got work to do." Wocco turned back to Nanfoodle and said, "Ye'll get yer hunnerd and sixty-two and a few extra for good measure, in case yer own measure weren't so good."

As the chief blacksmith stormed back to his forge, Nanfoodle settled back against the table. He moved to begin collecting his many diagrams but stopped and brought his hand to cover his eyes, overwhelmed suddenly. He could hardly believe that he was really doing it, that the dwarves were trusting him enough to take such a risk.

He hoped that trust wasn't misplaced, for he understood that he was reaching to the ends of common sense, and though he had so vigorously defended his plans to Regis, Shoudra, Wocco Brawnanvil, and all the others, he had to privately admit that his words were stronger than his thoughts.

Nanfoodle sincerely hoped he didn't destroy all of Mithral Hall.

25

SILENCING THE CHEERS

"Obould is Gruumsh!" Arganth Snarrl shouted at the tribe of orcs exiting the tunnel along the eastern side of one mountain. "He killed the elf demon— all of us witnessed this great victory! He is the chosen! He will lead us to glory!"

The dozen of his comrades behind the shaman took up the chant, and those orcs coming out from their mountain homes glanced around but gradually came to similar chanting.

"He is a dangerous one," Innovindil remarked to Drizzt, the two of them crouched behind a low wall of stone off to the side. They had been listening to Arganth for some time and were both somewhat overwhelmed by the sheer intensity of the orc shaman in his praise for Obould.

"He truly believes that Obould is the avatar of his vile god," Drizzt replied.

"Then he will watch his vile god die."

Innovindil hadn't turned to face Drizzt as she spoke the angry vow, but he could feel the intensity in her eyes and heart as she spat every word. He thought to point out to her that she had scolded him for just the same angry attitude not so long before, bidding him to look past his thirst for vengeance. But crouching behind and to the side of the elf, looking down at her fair profile, Drizzt could recognize the pain there. Of course she was hurting. And despite her wise words to him, that pain could slip past her guard and bring her uncharacteristic moments of weakness. Drizzt, who had recently witnessed the fall of a dear friend, could surely understand.

"The orc king has gone south with his force, but this one remains," Drizzt remarked.

"To rouse the rabble who crawl out of their mountain holes," said Innovindil.

"We cannot underestimate the importance of that," said Drizzt. "And this one is close to Obould—he may have information."

Innovindil turned around and looked up at the drow, and her expression told him that she understood his reasoning completely.

"They will likely camp within the tunnels," she said.

Drizzt looked to the east and agreed, for already the lighter blue of dawn was blossoming beyond the horizon. Also, while the new orc additions had come forth from the tunnel, they hadn't come out very far.

"They will not move off until late afternoon, likely," said Innovindil.

Drizzt scanned the area, then patted Innovindil's shoulder and motioned for her to follow him off to the side.

"Let us go underground before them and learn our way around," he explained. "We will take the shaman while he sleeps. There is much I wish to hear from that one."

The two drow moved swiftly along the tunnels, their keen eyes scanning every crevice, every jut, every uneven grade, in the darkness. Well in advance of Proffit's lumbering trolls, Kaer'lic and Tos'un paused many times and listened—and more often than not, found their scouting inhibited by the ruckus of the trolls.

They do roll along, Kaer'lic's fingers flashed to her partner, and she gave a disgusted shake of her face.

Eager for dwarf blood, came Tos'un's response. *Will Proffit be so eager to meet with dwarven fire? For the bearded folk know how to battle trolls!*

Before Kaer'lic could begin to signal her agreement, she caught a whisper of noise reverberating through the stone. Her fingers stopped abruptly, and she left one extended to signal her companion to silence, then she eased her head against the stone. Yes, there it was, unmistakably so, the march of heavy dwarven boots.

Tos'un came up beside her.

Our friends again? his fingers asked.

Kaer'lic nodded.

"A sizable force," she whispered. "Two score or more, I would guess."

How far? asked Tos'un's fingers.

Kaer'lic paused and listened for a moment, then shook her head.

Not far . . . she started to sign.

But parallel, Tos'un's movements interrupted. *And who knows where these tunnels might intersect?*

One thing is certain, Kaer'lic replied, *our enemies are heading past us to the south. Back toward the Trollmoors.*

Reinforcements for Nesmé? asked Tos'un.

Kaer'lic looked back at the stone wall, her expression doubtful.

"Ornamental, if so," she whispered. "A gesture by Mithral Hall, perhaps, to show support for their neighbors."

Sounds echoed down the corridor behind them as the trolls closed ground. The two drow looked at each other, each silently asking the same question.

"Proffit will wish to chase the dwarves down, but the diversion will cost Obould the desired pressure on the dwarves underground, perhaps for several days," reasoned Tos'un.

That possibility didn't bother Kaer'lic greatly, as she let her expression show.

"We might perhaps find some enjoyment if the dwarf band is not so large," Tos'un went on, a smile widening on his face.

"Run along with all speed and find a place where we might cross over to the tunnels used by our enemies," Kaer'lic instructed. "Better to pursue them out to the south than to backtrack and hope to find their tunnel's exit on the cursed surface."

Tos'un gave a deferential nod, then turned to leave.

"With all care!" Kaer'lic called after him.

The drow priestess found that her own words surprised her. Were those not the words of a friend? And since when did Kaer'lic Suun Wett consider anyone a friend? Donnia and Ad'non had been her companions for years, and never once in all the trials of their journeys did she ever so dramatically warn them to take care. On several occasions she had believed one or the other dead, and never once had she wept, or even really cared, beyond her own inevitable needs. Why, then, had she just been so insistent with Tos'un?

Because she was afraid, she realized, and because she feared that she was vulnerable. And with Donnia and Ad'non off who-knew-where, Tos'un was her only real companion.

The stench of troll began to grow around her as Proffit and his band closed in, and that only reinforced for the priestess the value of her lone drow companion. She'd hardly find life tolerable without Tos'un.

For a long, long while, Kaer'lic stared at the dark tunnel down which Tos'un had disappeared, pondering that realization.

Though he had tried to become a creature of the surface, as soon as he moved deep into the gloom of the tunnels, Drizzt Do'Urden realized just how much he remained a denizen of the Underdark. Beside him, Innovindil moved with an elf's grace, but in the tunnels, it was not nearly as fluid and easy a stride as the dark elf's. In the Underdark, Drizzt was as much superior to her as she was to him in the open daylight.

They made their way across some broken ground and up into a natural chimney, branching off the main corridor of the complex. In looking at Innovindil as they set themselves, Drizzt could see her reservations. And why not? He had placed them in the center of the main corridor, and if the orcs did come in, they would surely pass that way in force and would even possibly camp in that very spot, perhaps right below the pair.

But Drizzt merely looked back to the tunnel below and hid his smile. Innovindil did not understand the level of stealth a drow in such places could achieve. She didn't understand that even if the orcs set their main encampment right below the natural chimney, the drow could slip down among them with ease.

He did look back at Innovindil then, offering her an assuring nod, and the two sat still and quiet, letting the minutes slip past.

Drizzt's sensitive eyes showed him that the gloom lessened just a bit; the heightening of morning outside, he knew. Soon after, there came the shuffling of orc feet and the procession began below them. Drizzt estimated that perhaps two dozen orcs had come in, and as they moved past, he motioned for Innovindil to hold her place, then crept down the chute, head first, spiderlike. Pausing for a moment to listen, he poked his head out into the corridor and scanned both ways. The orcs had moved deeper in, but not far. They were milling around, he could hear, likely setting their camp.

Back up he went.

"Two hours," Drizzt whispered into Innovindil's ear.

The patient elf nodded. The two settled in more comfortably, and to Drizzt's surprise, Innovindil pulled him close to her so that his head was resting comfortably against her bosom. As he relaxed, she gently stroked his long and thick white hair, and even kissed him once atop the head.

It was a comfortable place and a tender sharing, and Drizzt allowed himself to relax more than he had in a long, long while.

The two hours passed all too swiftly for him then, but he was able to pull himself from his zone of comfort and rouse the hunting instincts within. Again, he motioned to his companion to hold her place, and again, he went down the chute, head first.

The corridor was clear. Drizzt hooked strong fingers on the lip of the chimney chute, then rolled himself over, dropping silently to a standing position in the tunnel. He drew out his blades, crept along deeper into the complex, and found the orc camp soon after, set in the corridor and in a pair of small chambers to the side.

The twisting and uneven corridor offered him a plethora of vantage points as he studied his enemies. A few were awake, milling around a small cookfire, and a couple were off to the side, against the far wall, eating and talking. Beyond them was an opening, leading into a slightly higher chamber wherein several orcs snored. Across the way sat the other chamber, with more sleeping brutes. Drizzt did spot one orc dressed in a garb that seemed to mark him as a shaman, but it was not *the* shaman, not that Arganth creature who seemed so valuable to King Obould.

The drow slid his scimitars away and crept closer, looking for an opportunity. Many minutes passed, but finally the camp settled down a bit more, with all but a couple of the orcs lying back and closing their eyes. Drizzt didn't hesitate. He pulled his cloak tight around him and crept in closer, moving in the shadows on the wall opposite the small cookfire—which was really no more than a few glowing embers by then. He paused just past that main area until those orcs still talking seemed more distracted, then he slipped right by them and into the small room across the way.

He saw Arganth, sleeping soundly.

Back out again, the drow reversed his movements and went back to the chimney, where he found Innovindil waiting. He considered the setup once again, then offered her his plan using short whispers, stopping often to listen and ensure that he had not alerted any nearby enemies. He considered then that perhaps he should try to teach Innovindil the drow sign language, and the thought nearly had him laughing aloud.

He had tried to teach the language to Regis once, but the halfling's stubby fingers, despite his exceptional dexterity, simply could not form the proper

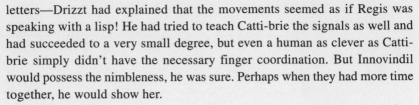

letters—Drizzt had explained that the movements seemed as if Regis was speaking with a lisp! He had tried to teach Catti-brie the signals as well and had succeeded to a very small degree, but even a human as clever as Catti-brie simply didn't have the necessary finger coordination. But Innovindil would possess the nimbleness, he was sure. Perhaps when they had more time together, he would show her.

"You may have trouble getting out afterward," the elf replied when Drizzt finished explaining his plan.

Drizzt was touched that her only concern seemed to be with his safety—particularly considering that if things went accordingly, she was the one who would be pursued by most of the orcs.

They went back out into the night then, to ensure that the orc tribe that had come out of the mountains hadn't camped too close.

Then they were back into the tunnels, just around the bend from the nearest point of the orc encampment. They exchanged pats on the shoulder and nods, then Drizzt slipped ahead, mimicking his earlier movements. It took some time, for the group seated by the opposite room were stirring and arguing, but the stealthy drow finally managed to get into the chamber with Arganth and several others.

One by one, he slit their throats, leaving only the lead shaman alive.

Arganth was rudely awakened, a hand over his mouth and a scimitar tip up tight against his back.

"If you squirm in the least, I will cut out your heart," Drizzt promised, his voice merely a buzzing in the terrified shaman's ear.

He pulled Arganth back against the wall and down to the floor, shielding himself with the shaman in case any should look in. He even managed to hook a filthy blanket and pull it up over them somewhat as a further precaution.

Drizzt waited. He had told Innovindil to give him plenty of time to get the shaman nabbed.

A shriek told him that the elf had gone to work.

Outside the small chamber, orcs began to scramble all around, some running past to Drizzt's right, deeper into the tunnels but most heading the other way, or scrambling around. One came to the entryway and called out for help, but of course, none in the room moved or responded. Drizzt grabbed Arganth all the tighter and slumped lower beneath the blankets.

Another shriek outside told him that Innovindil had scored a second hit with her bow.

A few moments later, the drow wriggled his legs under him and yanked

Arganth to his feet, then dragged the shaman to the door. Drizzt saw his moment and slipped out, moving to the left, deeper into the tunnels. He slipped into a side passage as soon as one presented itself, and he pulled Arganth into a sheltered cubby.

He waited once more, as the sounds in the main corridor lessened. He waited a few moments longer, then moved his prisoner back out, and managed to get past the orc encampment without seeing a living enemy. Drizzt noted that three orcs were dead in the corridor, shot down by Innovindil.

The drow and his prisoner got all the way out into the night, and only then did Drizzt release the shaman.

"If you cry out, I will cut out your throat," he promised, and he knew from the responding expression that the clever Arganth had understood every word.

"Obould will ki—" the shaman started to say, but he went silent when a scimitar's fine edge flashed up against his throat.

"Yes . . . Obould," Drizzt replied. "We will speak about Obould at length, I promise you."

"I will tell you nothing!"

"I beg to differ." The scimitar went in even tighter. "I don't think that you want to die."

At that, Arganth put on a weird smile and, surprisingly, pressed even tighter against the blade.

"Gruumsh is with me!" he proclaimed, and he suddenly threw himself forward.

But Drizzt was quicker, retracting the scimitar and bringing his other one from its sheath and across, pommel leading. It smacked against Arganth's skull, and he crumbled to the ground. He tried to move and tried to cry out, but Drizzt hit him again, and again, until he went very still.

Cursing under his breath, Drizzt slipped his blades away and scooped the shaman up over his shoulder, then ran off into the night.

He was relieved to find Innovindil back at their cave, as they had arranged. Her expression didn't change a bit as the drow dumped the unconscious shaman at her feet.

"You killed three in the cave," he told her.

"And several more outside," she answered, and she looked up at him grimly. "I would have killed them all had their pursuit been more dogged."

Drizzt let it go; he didn't want to raise Innovindil's ire at that time. He methodically went about tying up Arganth, then dragged the shaman to the wall and propped him into a sitting position.

"He will give us the information we need to avenge Tarathiel," Drizzt said.

His mention of the dead elf brought a pained grimace to fair Innovindil.

"And to help defeat this scourge of orcs," she did manage to reply, her voice soft, almost breaking.

"Of course," Drizzt said, offering a smile.

Arganth stirred a bit, and Drizzt kicked him hard in the shin. It was time to talk.

"The Nesmé dogs are scattered," said one of Proffit's heads.

"And running," added the other.

"And hiding," they both said together.

Kaer'lic looked from one to the other and back again, trying not to let on how unsettling it truly was in dealing with that ugly, two-headed beast.

"Perhaps the dwarves seek them," the drow replied.

"Then we follow dwarves," said Proffit's first head.

"And kill them," the second added.

"And squish them," the first put in.

"And eat them," they both decided.

"Just a small group of trolls should stay for eating dwarves and Nesmé dogs," the first head explained. "The rest go on to start the fight inside Mithral Hall."

Kaer'lic hid her grimace.

"But there were scores and scores of dwarves, perhaps," she replied. "A formidable force. We would be foolish to underestimate them."

"Hmm," the troll's heads pondered.

"Better that we all follow the dwarves out to the south," Kaer'lic reasoned. "Let us eat well, then turn back for Mithral Hall."

"But Obould. . . ."

"Is not here," Kaer'lic interrupted. "Nor has he begun to pressure Mithral Hall in any real way. We have time to finish this band of dwarves and the Nesmé dogs, then turn back and begin the war inside Mithral Hall."

For a moment, the drow considered explaining to Proffit that Obould was using him, was throwing his trolls into the fray inside the Clan Battlehammer tunnels knowing full well that their losses would be horrendous and without any real plan to come in support from the upper gates. The drow resisted the temptation, though, realizing that an angry two-headed troll would be likely to strike out at anything convenient—including a lone drow priestess. Besides, as much as Kaer'lic was becoming wary of Obould, she didn't think the pressure on Clan Battlehammer would be a bad thing. And if a few score trolls got slaughtered in the process, where would be the loss?

Proffit started to respond—to agree, Kaer'lic knew—but he stopped short as another figure came into sight, trotting easily down the passageway.

"We can rotate over to the tunnel the dwarves used not too far from here," Tos'un explained to them. "The joining corridor will be tight for our friends, but they will get through."

He looked at the gigantic Proffit as he said that, and his expression was less than complimentary.

Of course, the dim-witted troll didn't catch the subtle look.

"Off we go then," Kaer'lic remarked. "We'll follow them right out and, hopefully, to the Nesmé refugees, and . . ." she paused and looked over at Tos'un, "we'll eat well."

Her drow companion screwed up his face with disgust, but both of Proffit's heads were laughing, and both of his toothy mouths were drooling.

Such a thoroughly disgusting creature, Kaer'lic signaled to Tos'un. *But useful indeed in angering Obould.*

Tos'un's answer came in the sudden flash of nimble fingers. *A worthy cause, then.*

26

ĐURNEĐ GNØME

Regis gave a resigned sigh and dropped the parchment that the scout had just delivered. He watched it float down, gliding left then right before landing on the edge of his desk and hanging there precariously. How fitting, the halfling thought, for it was just one more troubling document in a pile of worry. The scout had come from the south to report that some trolls had turned around in apparent pursuit of Galen Firth and the band Regis had sent to the aid of Nesmé.

The halfling's instincts told him to muster an army and go retrieve the fifty dwarves.

But how could he? He had nearly a thousand still up on the cliff fighting with Banak and another even larger group settled into the western reaches of Keeper's Dale, holding Banak's flank and the course to Mithral Hall's western door. Those limited numbers of dwarves still within Mithral Hall proper had more than enough to keep them busy, between patrolling the tunnels, ferrying supplies up to and bringing wounded down from Banak—and replacing his losses—and running the forges nonstop, crafting the items for Nanfoodle.

A sour look crossed Regis's face when he thought of those forges, and for a moment he considered shutting Nanfoodle's crazy scheme down then and there. He could free up some dwarves at least and send them off to the south.

Another sigh escaped the halfling's lips, and he dropped his face into his palms. Hearing a rap on his door, he rubbed his face briskly, looked up, and bid the knocker to enter.

In came a dwarf arrayed in battle gear, except that his head was wrapped with a bandage instead of encased in a helmet.

"Fighting's begun in the tunnels under the giant ridge," the dwarf reported. "Banak told me to tell yerself."

"When you came down to get your wounds tended," Regis reasoned.

"Bah, just a scratch," said the dwarf. "Came down to get some long spears so we can build a few new defenses."

He nodded and started back out.

"How goes the fighting in the tunnels?" Regis asked after he recovered from the dwarf's statement.

The warrior looked much worse than he was letting on. One side of the head-wrap was dark with blood and his armor showed dozens of tears and dents. The dwarf turned back.

"Ye ever try to push an enemy outta a tunnel?" he asked. "An enemy that's dug in and ready for ye?"

Regis tried not to grimace as he shook his head. The dwarf just nodded grimly and walked away.

That brought yet another sigh from Regis, but not until the dwarf had closed the door—he didn't want to show any outward display of despair or weakness after all. But it was getting to him, truly wearing at his emotional edges. Dwarves were fighting and dying, and ultimately, it was his decision to keep them there. As steward, the halfling could recall Banak and his forces, could bring all of Clan Battlehammer and all of the newcomers to the halls back within the defenses of Mithral Hall itself. Let the orcs try to move them out then! And given his own revelation that this continuing battle might be exactly what the orcs were hoping for, perhaps recalling the forces would be the most prudent move.

But such a move would, in effect, be handing all the region over to the invading orcs, would be abandoning Mithral Hall's standing as the primary kingdom in their common cause of the defense of the goodly folk in the wild lands beneath the shadows of the eastern stretches of the Spine of the World.

It was all too confusing and all too overwhelming.

"I am no leader," Regis whispered. "Curse that I was put in this role."

The moment of despair passed quickly, replaced by a wistful grin as Regis imagined the answer Bruenor would have had for him had he heard him utter those words.

The dwarf would have called him Rumblebelly, of course, and would have backhanded him across the back of his head.

"Ah, Bruenor," Regis whispered. "Will you just wake up then and see to these troubles?"

He closed his eyes and pictured Bruenor, lying so still and so pale. He went to Bruenor each night, and slept in a chair right beside the dwarf king's bed. Drizzt was nowhere around, and Catti-brie and Wulfgar were both tied up with Banak in the fighting, but Regis was determined that Bruenor would not die without one of his closest companions beside him.

The halfling both feared and hoped for that moment. He couldn't understand why Bruenor was even still alive, actually, since all the clerics had told him that the dwarf would not survive more than a day or so without their tending—and that had been several days before.

Stubborn old dwarf, Regis figured, and he pulled himself out of his chair, thinking to go and sit with his friend. He usually didn't visit Bruenor that early in the evening, certainly not before he had taken his supper, but for some reason, Regis felt that he had to go there just then. Perhaps he needed the comfort of Bruenor's company, the reminder that he was the dwarf king's closest friend, and therefore was correct in accepting the call as Steward of Clan Battlehammer.

Or maybe he could simply find strength in sitting next to Bruenor, recalling as he often did his old times beside the toughened dwarf. What an example Bruenor had been for him all those years, standing strong when others turned to flee, laughing when others crouched in fear.

As he was moving through the door, another thought struck Regis and took from him every ounce of comfort that the notion of going to Bruenor had seeded within his heart and mind.

Perhaps, he suddenly realized, he had felt the need to go to Bruenor because somehow Bruenor's spirit was calling out to him, telling him to get to the king's bedside if he truly wanted to be there when his friend breathed his last.

"Oh no," the halfling gasped, and he ran off down the corridor as fast as his legs would carry him.

The speed of his approach and the unusually early arrival time in Bruenor's chamber brought to Regis an unexpected enlightenment, for as he moved through the door, he found not only Bruenor Battlehammer, lying still as death on the bed, but another dwarf crouching over him, whispering prayers to Moradin.

For a moment Regis thought that the priest was helping to usher Bruenor over to the other side and that perhaps he had arrived too late to witness his friend's passage.

But then the halfling realized the truth of it, that the priest, Cordio Muffinhead, was not saying good-bye but was casting spells of healing upon Bruenor.

Wide-eyed, wondering if Bruenor had done something to elicit such hope as healing spells, Regis bounded forward. His sudden movement alerted Cordio to his presence, and the dwarf looked up and fell back, sucking in his breath. That nervous movement clued Regis in that his hopes were for naught, that something else was going on there.

"What are you about?" the halfling asked.

"I come to pray for Bruenor's passing every day," the dwarf gruffly replied, a half-truth if Regis had ever heard one.

"To ease it, I mean," Cordio tried to clarify. "Praying to Moradin to take him gently."

"You told me that Bruenor was already at Moradin's side."

"Aye, and so his spirit might be—aye, it . . . it must be," Cordio stammered. "But we're not for wanting the body's passing to be a painful thing, are we?"

Regis hardly heard the response, as he stood there considering Bruenor, considering his friend who should have died days before, soon after he gave the order to the priests to let him be.

"What are you about, Cordio?" the halfling started to ask, but he stopped short when another rushed into the room.

"Steward's comi—" Stumpet Rakingclaw started to say, until she noted that Regis was already in the room.

Her eyes went wide, and she seemed to mutter some curse under her breath as she stepped back.

"Aye, Cordio Muffinhead," Regis remarked. "Steward's coming, so end your spells of healing on King Bruenor and be gone quick."

He turned on Cordio as he spoke the accusation, and the dwarf did not shrink back.

"Aye," Cordio replied, "that would've been close to Stumpet's own words, had ye not been in here."

"You're healing him," Regis accused, engulfing them both in his unyielding glare. "Every day you come in here and cast your magic into his body, preserving his life's breath. You won't let him die."

"His body's here, but his spirit's long gone," Cordio replied.

"Then let him die!" Regis ordered.

"I cannot," said Cordio.

"There is no dignity!" the halfling yelled.

"No," Cordio agreed. "But Bruenor's got his duty now, and I'm seeing that he holds it. I cannot let King Bruenor's body pass over."

"Not yet," said Stumpet.

"But you are the ones who told me that you cannot bring him back, that soul and body are far separated and will not hear the call of healing powers," the halfling argued. "Your own words brought forth my decision to let Bruenor go in peace, and now you defy my order?"

"King Bruenor cannot fully join his ancestors until the fighting's done," Cordio explained. "And not for Bruenor's sake—this's got nothing to do with Bruenor."

"It's got to do with the king, but not the dwarf," Stumpet added. "It's got to do with them who're out there fighting for Mithral Hall, fighting under the name o' King Bruenor Battlehammer. Ye go and tell Banak Brawnanvil that Bruenor's dead and see how long his line'll hold against the orc press."

"This ain't for Bruenor," said Cordio. "It's for them fighting in Bruenor's name. Ye should be understanding that. Mithral Hall's needing a *king*."

Regis tried to find an argument. His lips moved, but no sound came forth. His eyes were drawn low, to the specter of Bruenor, his friend, the king, lying so pale and so still on the bed, his strong hands drawn up one over the other on his once-strong chest.

"No dignity. . . ." the halfling did whisper, but the complaint sounded hollow even to him.

Bruenor's life had been about honor, duty, and above all else, loyalty. Loyalty to clan and to friend. If staying alive meant helping clan and friend, even if it meant great pain for Bruenor, the dwarf would put an angry fist in the eye of anyone who tried to stop him from performing that duty.

It pained Regis to stand there staring at his helpless friend. It pained Regis to think that those clerics were going against the wishes of Catti-brie and Wulfgar, the two who held the largest claim over the fate of their adoptive father.

But the halfling could find no argument against the logic of Cordio and Stumpet's reasoning. He glanced at the two dwarves and without either affirming or denying their work, he put his head down and walked out of the room, yet another weight on his burdened shoulders.

The two heavy iron tubes clanged down to the stone floor and bounced around for a moment until Nanfoodle finally managed to corral them and hold

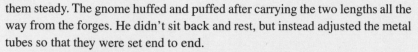

them steady. The gnome huffed and puffed after carrying the two lengths all the way from the forges. He didn't sit back and rest, but instead adjusted the metal tubes so that they were set end to end.

Pikel Bouldershoulder looked at the items curiously, then down at the pile of mud set before his crossed legs. The enchantment would soon fade on the mud, he knew, reverting it to its former solidity. The green-bearded dwarf scooped a handful and slid over to the two pipes, then lifted the end of one and examined it.

"Heh," he said appreciatively, noting that the dwarves had put a lip on either end of each piece.

He waved Nanfoodle over to his side, and the gnome took up the other tube and carefully held it up to the end Pikel had elevated.

Pikel helped press them together, and Nanfoodle quickly wrapped the area of the joint round and round with a strip of cloth. Pikel brought his hand in, slopping the mud all around the joint, all over the cloth wrap. He worked the mud around, then he and Nanfoodle carefully laid the two pieces back on the floor. Nanfoodle quickly gathered some small stones and buffered them against the curving sides of the two pieces, securing them in place while Pikel's stone hardened.

And harden it did, sealing the two pieces together into a single length.

"Ssssss," Pikel explained, pointing down at the joint, and he pinched his nose.

"Yes, it will leak if we leave it as is," Nanfoodle agreed. "But we shall not."

He rushed out and returned a few moments later bearing a heavy bucket, the handle of a wide brush protruding over its lip. Setting the bucket down, Nanfoodle lifted the brush, which was dripping with heavy black tar. Again, the gnome bent low to the joint, washing over it with the tar.

"No ssssss," he said to Pikel, waggling his finger in the air.

"Hee hee hee," the green-bearded dwarf agreed.

It did Nanfoodle's heart good to see Pikel in such fine spirits. Since the loss of his arm, the dwarf had been sullen, and even less talkative than usual. Nanfoodle had watched him carefully, though, and had come to the conclusion that Pikel's despair was wrought more from being helpless in the face of the current adversity than in his own sudden disadvantage.

Engaging the green-bearded dwarf so completely in his plan—and indeed, Pikel was the best suited of all for such a task—had brought energy back to the dwarf and had rekindled the dwarf's wide smile. Sitting there with his stone-turned-to-mud, Pikel even offered the more-than-occasional "Hee hee hee."

"They're fighting up above," Nanfoodle remarked.

"Oooo," Pikel replied.

He started to rise and turn, as if he meant to run right off to the battlefield.

"The tunnels under the giants," Nanfoodle explained, grabbing Pikel's arm and holding him in place. "If we are fortunate, the battle will be over before we could even get up to join it. But we cannot ask our friends to hold those tunnels for long—doing so will deplete Banak's resources greatly."

"Oooo."

"Only we can help alleviate that, Pikel," Nanfoodle said. "Only you and I, by working hard and working fast."

He glanced down at the lengths of metal tubing.

"Uh huh," Pikel agreed, and he fell back to work, gathering up his large bucket of mud, which was fast turning back to its previous solid state.

Nanfoodle nodded and took a deep breath. It was indeed time to begin in earnest. He considered the course he had to lay out and quickly estimated the maximum number of dwarves he could press into service before creating a situation with simply too many workers. Regis would be easy to convince, the gnome understood, for up above, the truly brutal work, the clearing of the tunnels, was already underway.

Nanfoodle imagined some of the scenes of battle that were no doubt occurring even then.

A shudder coursed his short spine.

"Damned archers!" Tred McKnuckles cried.

He fell to the side of the tunnel, throwing himself behind a rock. The dwarves had easily enough gained the outer areas of the tunnels, the southern stretches nearest to Keeper's Dale, but as they had moved in deeper, the resistance had grown more and more stubborn. Tred's group, which included Ivan Bouldershoulder and Tred's Felbarr friend Nikwillig, had hit fortified resistance along one long and narrow tunnel.

A short distance from them, the orcs had dug in behind a wall of piled stones and held several vantage points from which they could fire their bows and throw their light spears.

"Torgar's pressing on to our left," Ivan, who had similarly dived for cover on the opposite side of the corridor, called back to Tred. "He'll move past us to the wider halls. He's to be needing our support!"

"Bah!" Tred snorted, and he determinedly leaped out from behind the rock—and promptly got hit by a trio of arrows that had him slumping back from where he'd started.

"Ah, ye fool!" Ivan cried.

"That one's hurtin'," Tred admitted, clutching at one of the quivering arrow shafts.

"We'll get ye outta here!" Ivan promised.

Tred held up his hand and shook his head, assuring the other dwarf that he was all right.

"We gotta get 'em pushed back," the Felbarr dwarf called back.

"Nine Hells!" spouted a frustrated Ivan.

He pulled a crossbow quarrel from his bandoleer and eyed it carefully. His friend Cadderly had designed those bolts, with Ivan's help. Solid on both ends, they were partially cut out in the middle, designed to hold a small vial in their cubby. That vial was full of enchanted oil, designed to explode under the impact of the dart's collapse.

Ivan fitted the bolt to his small hand crossbow—another design that he and Cadderly had worked to perfection—then fell flat to his belly, eased himself out, and launched the missile down the corridor.

Without much force behind it, for it was merely a hand crossbow after all, the bolt looped down toward the orcs. It hit one of the rocks that formed their barricade and collapsed on itself. The oil flashed and exploded, blowing away a piece of the rocks.

"Let me chip away at their walls," Ivan called to Tred. "We'll send them pigs running!"

He fitted another bolt and let it fly, and another small explosion sounded down the tunnel.

And the tunnel began to tremble.

"What'd ye do?" a wide-eyed Tred asked.

Ivan's eyes were no less open.

"Damned if I'm knowing!" he admitted as the thunder began to grow around them. Ivan looked down at his bandoleer, and even pulled forth another dart. "Just a little thing!" he cried, shaking his head, and he looked back down toward the orcs.

He realized only then that the reverberations were behind his position, not in front.

"Tweren't me, then!" Ivan howled, and he looked back in alarm.

"Bah! Cave-in!" cried Tred, catching on. "Get 'em out! Get 'em all out!"

But it wasn't a cave-in, as the two dwarves and their companions learned a moment later, when the leading edge of the thunder-makers came around the corner behind them, charging up the tunnel with wild abandon.

"Not a collapse!" one dwarf further down the corridor called.

"Gutbusters!" cried another.

"Pwent?" Ivan mouthed at Tred, and both wisely rolled back tighter against their respective wall.

His answer came in one long, droning roar: the cry of sheer outrage, the scraping of metal armor, and the stamp of heavy boots. The column rushed past him, Thibbledorf Pwent in its lead, and bearing before him a great, heavy tower shield. Arrows thunked into that shield, and one skipped past, catching Pwent squarely in the shoulder. That only made him yell louder and run faster, leaning forward eagerly.

Orc bows fired repeatedly, and orc spears arced through the narrow passage, but the Gutbusters, be it from courage or stupidity, did not waver a single step. Several took brutal hits, shots that would have felled an ordinary dwarf, but in their heightened state of emotion, the Gutbuster warriors didn't even seem to feel the sting.

Pwent hit the rock barricade at a dead run, slamming against it, and the dwarves behind him hit him at a dead run too, driving on, forming a dwarven ramp over which their buddies could scramble.

And the wall toppled.

A few orcs remained, some firing their bows, some just swatting with flimsy weapons, others drawing swords.

The Gutbusters responded heart and soul, leaping onto their enemies, thrashing them with wickedly ridged armor, skewering them with head spikes, or slugging them with spiked gauntlets.

By the time Ivan helped the stung Tred hobble down to the toppled barricade, no orcs remained intact, let alone alive.

"Gotta take 'em fast and not let 'em shoot ye more'n a few times," the smelly Thibbledorf Pwent explained.

He seemed oblivious to the fact that a pair of arrows protruded from one of his strong shoulders.

"Get that tend—" Ivan started to say to him, but he was interrupted by a cry from farther along, calling out another barricade.

"Get 'em boys!" howled Pwent. *"Yaaaaaaaaaa!"*

He kicked the broken stones off of his shield and yanked it up. With a chorus of cheering all around him, Pwent set off again at a dead run.

"Hope we don't get to the wider areas too much afore Torgar," Ivan remarked.

Tred just snorted and shook his head, and Ivan helped him along.

Far down from the fighting, in the sulfuric chamber beneath the northern floor of Keeper's Dale, Nanfoodle, Pikel, and a host of dwarves had gathered, heavy cloths over their faces, protecting them from the nasty stench.

Pikel crouched in a pit that had been carved on the edge of the yellowish water. He was mumbling the words of a spell, waving his hand and his stump of an arm over the stone. Beside him, one burly dwarf held a long metal tube vertically, its bottom end capped with a spearlike tip. Pikel finished the spell and fell back, nodding, and the dwarf plunged the long tube into the suddenly malleable stone. Burly arms pressed on, sliding the metal down through the mud, until more than half its length had disappeared.

"Hit rock," he explained.

Pikel nodded and smiled as he looked at Nanfoodle, who breathed a sigh of relief. It would be the trickiest part of all, the gnome believed. First, with Pikel's help, they had excavated ten feet of stone, leaving a thin wall of about five feet to the trapped gasses. There was little room for error.

They waited until the enchanted mud turned back to stone, and on a nod from the gnome, a pair of mallet-wielding dwarves stepped forward and began tapping at the top of the tube.

Nanfoodle held his breath—he knew that one spark could prove utterly disastrous, though he hadn't shared that little tidbit with any of the others.

He didn't breathe again properly until one of the hammering dwarves remarked, "We're through."

The other dwarf, again on a nod from the gnome, pulled out a knife and cut the tie that was holding the spear tip tight against the bottom lip, allowing it to fall away, and almost immediately both the dwarves spat and waved their hands before them as a deeper stench came flowing through the tube.

Pikel gave a little squeal of delight and ran forward, capping the end with a gummy substance Nanfoodle had prepared, then falling down and further sealing the tube in place with more stone-turned-to-mud.

"Craziest damned thing I ever seen," one dwarf off to the side remarked.

"Durned gnome," another answered.

Beneath his cloth veil, Nanfoodle merely smiled. He couldn't really even disagree with their assessment. On his word alone, the dwarves had strung a line of metal out of the chamber, along several tunnels, and through another ten feet of stone to the floor of Keeper's Dale. On his word alone, other dwarves had taken that line all the way to the base of the cliff, more than fifty feet farther to the north and twice that to the east. On his word alone, still more dwarves were even then continuing the line up the side of the cliff—two or three hundred feet up—securing the tubes end to end with a series of metal pins so that Pikel could later seal them together with his stone-turned-to-mud.

Pikel went back to work, with all the dwarves in tow, some carrying buckets of mud, others carrying buckets of sealing pitch. While the pit had been carved, the green-bearded dwarf had connected nearly all of the underground tubes, and so within the matter of an hour, the crew was back above ground, crawling their way across Keeper's Dale to the base of the cliff. Pikel had become quite proficient at his work by that time, even perfecting the technique for "elbowing" the stone joint when the tubes had to turn a corner.

Nanfoodle led a second crew all along the joined metal line, painting more pitch on any possible weak areas and propping stones against the metal to further secure it. There was no room for error, the gnome understood, particularly in those stretches underground.

Every so often, the gnome went back to the sulfuric chamber, just to make sure that the critical first tube was still solidly in place.

Just to reassure himself that he wasn't completely out of his mind.

After Pwent's dramatic victory at the barricade, the battling dwarves had the majority of the tunnels beneath the giant-held ridge secured within another hour, forcing the remaining orcs to the very northern end of the complex. Not wanting to delay much further than that, Torgar ordered the area sealed off (which greatly disappointed Pwent, of course), his engineers dropping a wall of stone before their enemies. Inspecting the cave-in, Torgar declared the complex won.

The work was only beginning, though. The dwarves rushed back out of the tunnel's southern end, back near Keeper's Dale, and replaced weapons on their belts as they took up buckets of dark and sticky pitch. As part of Torgar's troupe went back underground, buckets and brushes in hand, another part began stringing the come-alongs and ropes down to the floor of Keeper's Dale. Within a short expanse of time, a bucket brigade had begun, with tar-filled pails coming up the ropes and empty buckets moving back down for refilling.

Inside, the dwarves worked to seal every crack and crevice they could find, plastering the walls and ceiling with the sticky substance.

Using the designs offered by Nanfoodle, other dwarves secured themselves to the long ropes with harnesses and eased down the cliff face, taking up equidistant positions from the canyon floor all the way to the top. They began hammering in eyelet supports, building a straight line of supporting superstructure from floor to ledge.

Torgar, Ivan, and Tred—who continued to stubbornly wave away any who thought to tend his wounds—began to inspect the region near the center of the tunnels within the ridgeline, seeking the thinnest area of stone blocking the way to the east and the continuing battlefield. Torgar moved along deliberately, tapping the stone with a small hammer and listening carefully for the consistency of the ring. Convinced he had found an optimal spot, Torgar sent his diggers to work, and the team quickly bored a hole out to the east, breaking through the line of the stony ridge so that they could feel the open air upon them.

"That wide enough?" Torgar asked.

Ivan held up the small box he had constructed to Nanfoodle's specifications, with its mirrored side.

"Looks like it'll fit," he answered.

He moved close and held the box up tight. The diggers went back to work at once, shaping the hole so that it would be a better and more secure fit, then they moved back and Ivan squeezed in as far as he could, pressing the box, mirror facing outward, as far to the edge as possible.

"Seal it tight in place," Torgar instructed his team, and he and the other two leaders moved back the other way.

"What's that durned gnome thinking?" Tred asked.

"Couldn't begin to tell ye," Torgar admitted. "But Banak told me to take the damned tunnels, so I taked the damned tunnels."

"That ye did," said Ivan. "That ye did."

"And good'll come of it," Tred offered with a nod.

"Aye," agreed Ivan. "These Battlehammers know how to win a fight."

Torgar patted his companions in turn, and it struck Ivan then how ironic it was that he, Torgar, and Tred had been given charge of so important a mission as retaking the cave complex, in light of the fact that not one of them was of Bruenor's clan.

The stomping of battlerager boots interrupted that thought, and their conversation. The three turned to see Thibbledorf Pwent leading his troops at a swift pace back to the south.

"Fighting's startin' again outside," Pwent explained to the three as he passed. He called back to his team, "Hurry up, ye dolts! We're missing all the fun!"

With a great cheer, the Gutbuster Brigade charged past.

"Glad he's on our side," Tred remarked, drawing a chortle from both of his companions.

Before the next dawn, with fighting continuing along the sloping ground to the east and with Tred sent along for some priestly tending, Torgar and Ivan stood at the edge of the southernmost of the complex tunnels, right near the lip of the cliff drop to Keeper's Dale.

"We spill good dwarf blood just to close it all off," Torgar remarked with a frustrated sigh.

"I'm thinking the gnome's meaning to stink them giants off the ridge," Ivan replied. He kicked at the length of tubing that had been laid down from the cliff face to inside the tunnel itself. "He's for bringing up the stink."

Before the pair, a group of dwarves worked fast, piling rocks all around the center reaches of the long metal tube, carefully placing the stones so that they supported each other without putting any pressure on the metal pipe.

"Have to be a pretty good stink," said Torgar, "to chase giants off the ridge."

"Me brother says it's a good one," Ivan explained.

As the workers scurried to the side, he nodded to the dwarf engineers standing to either side of the tunnel, warning them away. Torgar and Ivan took up heavy mallets and simultaneously knocked out wooden supports that had been set in place, and the end of the rocky tunnel collapsed, burying the entrance and the middle sections of the tubing.

"Seal it up good," Ivan explained to his workers. "Wash it all with pitch, pile it with dirt, then wash it all again. We're not wanting any of that stink backing up on us."

The dwarves nodded and went to work without complaint.

Ivan returned the nod, then glanced back over the cliff facing, at the line of harnessed dwarves hanging all the way down to the floor of the dale. Other ropes brought buckets of muddy stone and still others hauled length of the metal tubing.

So much metal tubing.

"Durned gnome," Ivan remarked.

CONSCIENCE DECISIONS

"How fortunate for you that those giants decided to join with you," Obould remarked to Urlgen when he caught up to his son at the rear of Urlgen's encampment. As he spoke, the orc king directed Urlgen's attention to the western ridgeline, where Gerti's frost giant warriors were busily reconstructing their catapults. "Good fortune that this group happened your way."

Neither Urlgen nor Gerti, who was standing beside Obould, missed the orc king's sarcasm, nor his clear inference that he knew Gerti and Urlgen had tried to circumvent his control of the situation.

"I did not refuse valuable help," Urlgen replied, glancing at Gerti for support more than once.

"Valuable in scoring a victory without Obould?" the orc king bluntly asked, and both Urlgen and Gerti bristled and shifted nervously. "And still, even with the assistance of, what—a score of frost giants?—the dwarves remain."

"I will drive them from the cliff!" Urlgen insisted.

"You will do as you are instructed!" Obould countered.

"You would deny me this victory?"

"I would deny you a minor victory when a greater one is within our grasp," Obould explained. "Have everything in place to drive the dwarves from the cliff. I will quietly double your forces, out of sight of the foolish dwarves. After that, Gerti and I will march southwest and attack the dale below from the west. Then you can drive the dwarves from the cliff. They will have nowhere to run."

He looked from Urlgen to Gerti, who was clearly angry and just as clearly perplexed as she surveyed the ridgeline to the west.

"This should have been ended long ago," the giantess admitted, addressing Urlgen more than Obould. "Explain this delay."

"Two days ago the catapults were ready to finish the task," Urlgen growled back at her. "But our enemies came against them, and your giants failed to defend the war engines. It will not happen again."

"But there are reports that the dwarves retook the tunnels beneath the catapults," Gerti reminded, for word of the recent battle had been filtering through the camp all the day long.

"True," Urlgen admitted. "They have lost dwarves in retaking tunnels that were not worth defending. By the time they can dig through the thick stone to attack the giants, the battle outside will be long over.

"But that doesn't even seem to be their intent," he went on. "They fill the tunnels with stink—too great a stink for us to counterattack, and so great that your giants complain of it. Look on them closely, and you will see that they wear veils over their faces to ward the stench."

"Will an odor drive them from the ridge?" Obould asked.

"It is an inconvenience and nothing more," Urlgen explained. "The dwarves have assured that we cannot attack them through those tunnels. They believe they have protected their flank, but it was not an attack we would make anyway. Their fight in the tunnels has brought them no relief, and no victory."

Obould squinted his bloodshot eyes and stared at the ridge. In any event, it seemed as if the catapults were nearly completed and that work was continuing on them at a steady pace.

"We have a ten-mile march to wage the fight west of the dale," Obould explained. "When battle sounds in the southwest, begin your drive against the dwarves. Engage them fully and to the end. Drive them from the cliff into my waiting army, and they will be destroyed, and Mithral Hall will never again realize its present glory."

Urlgen glanced again at Gerti and seemed more than a little shaken.

"All glory to Obould," the younger orc said, rather unconvincingly.

"Obould is Gruumsh," the orc king corrected. "All glory to Gruumsh!"

With that, and with a warning snarl at both his son and the giantess, King Obould walked away.

"His army has grown many times over," Gerti explained to Urlgen. "He will more than double your force. You'll not even need my warriors and the catapults."

"The smell of dwarven trickery will not force them from the ridge," Urlgen assured her. "Let the catapults throw their stones and crush the dwarves. Perhaps we can direct some throws over the cliff and near to Obould's march, eh?"

"Take care your words," Gerti warned.

But there was no hiding the smile that showed her to be somewhat entertained by the mere notion of "accidentally" squishing King Obould Many-Arrows beneath a giant boulder. She glanced over at the departing orc king, that arrogant little wretch who was so controlling the entirety of the campaign.

Her smile widened.

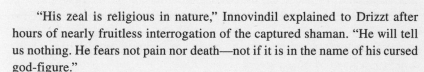

"His zeal is religious in nature," Innovindil explained to Drizzt after hours of nearly fruitless interrogation of the captured shaman. "He will tell us nothing. He fears not pain nor death—not if it is in the name of his cursed god-figure."

Drizzt leaned back against the cave wall and considered the truth of Innovindil's reasoning. He had learned that Obould had marched south—but he had all but figured that out previous to capturing the shaman, anyway. The only other tidbit that seemed even remotely useful was the admission by Arganth that it was Obould's own son, Urlgen, who had sacked Shallows and was pressing the dwarves in a fierce battle just north of Mithral Hall.

"Are you ready to go to the south?" Innovindil quietly asked the drow. "Are you ready to face the surviving dwarves of Mithral Hall and confirm your fears?"

Drizzt rubbed his hands over his face and pushed away the awful image of Withegroo's tumbling tower. He knew what he was going to hear when he went to Mithral Hall.

And he didn't want to hear it.

"Let us go south, then," the drow answered. "We have business with this King Obould and have a loyal pegasus depending upon our every move. I mean to get that mount back and mean to pay Obould back for his actions."

Innovindil was smiling then, and nodding. Drizzt glanced to the side, to the opening of the side chamber that held the shaman.

"What do we do with that one?" he asked. "He will surely slow us down."

Without saying a word, Innovindil stood, gathered up her bow, and walked to the entrance of the side chamber.

"Innovindil?" Drizzt asked.

She fitted an arrow to her bowstring.

"Innovindil?"

Drizzt jerked in shock as the elf drew back and let fly, and let fly again, and a third time.

"I show them more mercy than they would show to us, by making the kill swift and clean," the elf replied, her voice perfectly impassive.

She glanced at Drizzt, and they both heard a moan coming from the chamber. Without a word, Innovindil dropped her bow aside and drew out her slender sword, then stalked into the side chamber.

Her actions bothered Drizzt. He thought back briefly to a goblin he had once known, a misunderstood slave who had been wrongfully beaten and murdered by his human master.

But the drow shook that image away. The creature they had captured was not like that goblin. A fanatical follower of an evil god, the orc shaman had lived to destroy, to pillage, to burn, and to conquer. Drizzt knew that Innovindil's assessment of the situation, that she had shown more mercy than the orcs ever would, was perfectly correct.

He began gathering up their things, preparing to break camp. It was time to head south.

Past time, perhaps.

Regis sat in the dark, recalling old times with his friend Bruenor. How many days they had shared back in Icewind Dale. How many times Bruenor had found him on the banks of Maer Dualdon, casually fishing, or at least pretending to. Bruenor had berated him—Regis could hear the words in his ears even then.

"Bah, Rumblebelly! Ye do the laziest job ye can find, and ye don't even do that with any heart!"

A smile creased the halfling's face as he recalled that Bruenor would often then plop down beside him on the lakeside, to "show him how to do it."

A great way to enjoy those precious few warm days in Icewind Dale.

Bruenor was still alive. Regis suspected that Cordio and Stumpet were still going to him in the quiet night, casting their preserving healing spells upon him. They weren't going to follow his orders on that issue—they had made that fairly clear—and Regis's position as steward offered him little leverage against two of Mithral Hall's leading priests.

In a way, Regis was glad that they were making the choice for him. He didn't know if he could find the heart to once again demand that Bruenor be allowed to die.

But still, the halfling could not bring himself to fully agree with the assessment of the two stubborn clerics, that for the sake of Mithral Hall, Bruenor had to be kept alive. They argued the symbolism of Bruenor Battlehammer, but it seemed obvious to Regis that Bruenor wasn't a king to anyone then.

No king would lie there if he knew that all his minions were in dire battle, that so many were falling wounded or dead.

"There has to be an answer," Regis muttered softly in the dark room.

He rolled up to a sitting position and stared into the darkness. There had to be more options.

Regis straightened suddenly as his thoughts wound around and coalesced, drawing new patterns in his mind. He considered Cordio's words, and Stumpet's. He considered his old friend Bruenor and all the times they had once shared. He thought of the dwarf's stubbornness, of his pride, of his loyalty and generosity.

There in the darkness, Regis found the answer, found the joining of his heart and his mind.

With more determination and fire in his belly than the unsure halfling had known in a long, long time, Regis, Steward of Mithral Hall, stormed out of his room and across the dwarven complex to find Cordio Muffinhead.

NANFOODLE'S DRAGON

"Keep the squares tight!" Banak Brawnanvil yelled to his forces—his *depleted* forces.

Not only had attrition begun to take a real toll on the dwarf defenders, but Banak had several dozen of his dwarves off the lines and working with Nanfoodle. They were further securing the pieces of metal tubing that were running from the tunnels beneath Keeper's Dale all the way up the side of the cliff face. That left the dwarf warlord fighting defensively, warding the newest vicious attack, but withholding any counterstrikes.

Banak's dwarves were holding well and would continue to hold, as far as the orcs were concerned. But the dwarf warlord kept glancing to his left, to the northwestern ridge and the giants busily completing the assembly on their great catapults. Every so often, a flash of white from the far ridge caught Banak's attention. Reports from his scouts said that Nanfoodle's stink was thick around the behemoths, crawling up through the rocks and settling like a fetid yellow cloud upon the ridge. But to Banak's dismay, that discomfort hadn't driven the giants away. They had wrapped their large faces in treated cloth and had methodically continued, and were continuing, their work.

"We're running out o' time, Banak," came a voice from the side.

The warlord turned to regard Ivan Bouldershoulder.

"We'll hold them back," Banak replied.

"Bah, them orcs're nothing," said tough Ivan. "But the little trickster's trick ain't working. By yer own eyes, ye can seem them giants still at their work. Catapults'll be up and throwin' before the sun's next rising. From that angle, they'll flatten us to the stone."

Banak rubbed his bleary eyes.

"We might want to be dropping down to the dale," Ivan offered.

Banak shook his head.

"Little one's still working on it," he huffed. "I've got a hunnerd dwarves working with him."

"He's only securing the line, from what I'm hearing," Ivan countered.

He motioned for Banak to follow and started off to the west, toward the line of dwarves hanging along the cliff facing down to Keeper's Dale. They came in sight of Nanfoodle and Ivan's brother in short order, standing atop the cliff, looking over reams of parchments and diagrams. Every so often, Nanfoodle would lean out a bit and holler down the line, telling the dwarves to re-tar the joints—all the joints.

"This'll make the smell so bad them giants can't stay up?" Banak asked when he and Ivan neared the pair.

Nanfoodle looked up at him, and the blood drained from the clearly worried gnome's face.

"Easy, little one," Banak offered. "Yer stink's slowing them at least, and we're grateful to ye for that."

"They're not even supposed to smell it!" Nanfoodle shouted.

"Ptooey!" Pikel spat in agreement.

Ivan looked at his brother and shook his head.

"We're not supposed to be stinking up the ridge," Nanfoodle tried to explain. "That means that the hot air . . . the pitch was supposed to seal the tunnels . . . we need to build this level of concentration . . ."

He stammered and stuttered and held up a sheet parchment scribbled with numbers and formulae that Banak couldn't begin to decipher.

"Ye got what he's saying?" Banak asked Ivan.

"Giants shouldn't be stinking," Ivan clarified.

"But then they'd be building their war engines without any hindrance at all," the warlord reasoned.

"Yup," Ivan agreed.

"But then . . ." Banak started, but he stopped and shook his head.

He gave Nanfoodle a confused look out of the corner of his eye, then shook his head again as he looked down at the many dwarves working on securing the line of metal tubes tight to the cliff—dwarves who could have been strength-ening the defensive squares that were even then holding the line against the pressuring orcs.

With a snort, Banak moved back toward the area of battle.

"No, he doesn't understand," Nanfoodle pleaded to Ivan.

The yellow-bearded dwarf patted his gnarled hands in the air to calm the little one.

"And he never will," Ivan replied.

"The stink should not have escaped," Nanfoodle frantically tried to explain.

"I know, little one," Ivan assured him.

"Boom," Pikel quietly muttered.

"We needed to contain it, to thicken it . . ." Nanfoodle pressed.

"I know little one," Ivan interrupted, but Nanfoodle rambled along.

"The stench would never push them away—in the tunnels, maybe, where the concentration is greater . . ."

"Little one," Ivan said, and when Nanfoodle rambled on, he repeated his calm call again and again, until finally he caught the excited gnome's attention.

"Little one, I built yer box," Ivan reminded him.

He patted Nanfoodle on the shoulder, then hustled after Banak to help direct the battle.

Ivan glanced to the west as he departed, not to the ridgeline, but beyond it, where the sun had set and the twilight gloom was completing its hold on the land. Then he did lower his gaze to encompass the ridgeline and the dark silhouettes of the great working giants.

Ivan knew that their troubles would multiply before the next rising sun.

"The dwarves' plans did not work, boss," one of the orc undercommanders said to Urlgen.

The pair as standing in the center of the two armies at Urlgen's command: his own, which was continuing the battle up the slope against the dwarves; and those on loan from his father, who were still encamped and out of sight of their enemies.

Urlgen was looking to the west, to the ridge and the giants. The hourglass was flowing on the battle, as word had arrived from Obould that the assault in the west would begin in full at dawn. For Urlgen, that meant that he had to push those dwarves over the cliff, and doing that would be no easy task without the giant catapults.

"They will be ready," the orc undercommander remarked.

Urlgen turned to face him.

"The dwarves and their stink have not stopped the giants," the undercommander asserted.

Urlgen nodded and looked back to the west. He had assurances from the giants that the catapults would begin their barrage before the dawn.

Back in the north, the battle continued, not in full force, for that was not Urlgen's intent, but strongly enough to prevent the dwarves from retreating in full. He had to keep them there, engaged, until his father sealed off any possible escape.

The orc leader issued a low growl and curled his fists up at his side in eager anticipation. The dawn would bring his greatest victory.

He couldn't help but glance back nervously at the western ridge as he considered that without the giant catapults, his task would be much more difficult.

Nikwillig rolled the small mirror over and over in his hands. He glanced to the west and the ridge, then to the east and the taller peaks. He focused on one smaller peak at the edge of the cliff, a short but difficult climb. That was where he had to go to catch the morning rays. Returning from that place, should Banak lose, would prove nearly impossible.

"What am I hearing?" he heard Tred call to him, drawing him from the unsettling thought.

Nikwillig observed the swift approach of his Citadel Felbarr companion.

"What am I hearing?" Tred demanded again, storming up right before the seated Nikwillig.

"Someone's got to do it."

Tred put his hands on his hips and looked all around at the continuing bustle of the encampment. He had just come back from the fighting, dragging a pair of wounded dwarves with him, and he meant to get right back into the fray.

"I was wondering why ye weren't with us on the line," he said.

"I'm more trouble than help down there, and ye know it," said Nikwillig. "Never been a warrior."

"Bah, ye were doing fine!"

"It's not me place, Tred. Ye know it, too."

"Ye could've gone running back to King Emerus then, with news," Tred answered. "I bid ye to do just that—was yer own stubbornness that kept us both here!"

"And we belong here," Nikwillig was quick to reply. "We're owing that much to Bruenor and Mithral Hall. And to be sure, they're glad that Tred was up here fighting beside them."

"And Nikwillig!"

"Bah, I ain't killed an orc yet and would've been slain more than once if not for yerself and others pulling me out o' the fight."

"So ye're choosin' this road?" came the incredulous question.

"Someone's got to do it," Nikwillig said again. "The way I'm seeing it, I might be the most expendable one up here."

"What about Pikel?" Tred asked. "Or the durned gnome Nanfoodle—yeah, was his crazy idea in the first place."

"Pikel probably can't even make the climb with his one arm. And Nanfoodle might be needed here—ye know it. Pikel, too, since he's been so important to it all so far. Nah, Tred, shut up yer whining. This's a good job for meself and ye know it. I can do this as well as any, and I'll be the least missed here."

Tred started to argue, but Nikwillig rose up before him, his stern expression stealing the blustery dwarf's words.

"And I'm wanting to do it," Nikwillig declared. "With all me heart and soul. Now I'm paying back the Battlehammers for their help."

"Ye might find a tough time in getting back. In getting anywhere."

"And if that's true, then yerself and all them standing here will have hard a tough time of it, too," said Nikwillig. He gave a snort and a sudden burst of laughter. "Yerself's about to charge down headlong into a sea of smelly orcs, and ye're fearing for me?"

When he heard it put that way, Tred, too, gave a little laugh. He reached up and patted his longtime companion on the shoulder.

"I'm not liking that we might be meeting our ends so far apart," he said.

Nikwillig returned the pat, and the look, and said, "Nor am I. But I been looking to make meself as helpful as can be, and this job's perfect for Nikwillig." Again, Tred started to protest—reflexively, it seemed—but again, Nikwillig cut him short.

"And ye know it!" Nikwillig said flatly.

Tred went quiet and stared at his friend for a long moment, then gradually admitted as much with a hesitating nod.

"Ye be careful."

"Are ye forgetting?" Nikwillig replied with a wink. "I'm knowing how to run away!"

A shout from down the slope caught their attention then. The orcs had breached the dwarven line right between the two defensive squares—not seriously, but enough to put a few of the bearded folk in apparent and immediate danger.

"Moradin, put yer strength in me arms!" Tred howled, and he charged headlong down the slope.

Nikwillig smiled as he watched his friend go, then he turned back to the east and the dark silhouettes of the imposing mountains. He glanced back one more time to take his bearings and to better mark the critical area of the mountain spur, then, without another word, he tucked the mirror safely into his pack and trudged off on what he figured would be the last journey of his life.

Several hours later, the sky still dark but the eastern rim holding the lighter glow of the approaching dawn, word filtered up to Banak that an orc force had been spotted in the southwest, fast approaching the dwarf positions on the western edge of Keeper's Dale. The dwarf quickly assembled his leaders, along with Nanfoodle, Pikel, and Shoudra Stargleam, who had been the bearer of the information, having scouted the western reaches personally with her magical abilities.

"It is a sizable force," Shoudra warned them. "A great and powerful army. Our friends will be hard-pressed to hold out for very long."

The dispiriting news had all the dwarves glancing around to one another.

"Are ye saying that we should run down the cliff now and be done with it?" Banak asked.

Shoudra had no answer to that, and Banak turned to Nanfoodle.

"I'm hoping to steal a victory here," he explained. "But we're not to do that if them giants start throwing their boulders across our flank. It comes down to yer plan, gnome."

Nanfoodle tried to look confident—futilely.

"If we gotta leave, then we gotta leave," Banak said to them all. "But I'm thinkin' we need to hurt these pig orcs, and bad."

Thibbledorf Pwent growled.

"They're coming soon," Ivan Bouldershoulder put in. "They're stirring in the north, getting ready for another charge."

"Because they know the giants will soon begin their barrage," Wulfgar reasoned.

"But if them giants ain't throwing. . . ." Banak said slyly.

Again he turned to Nanfoodle, guiding the eyes of all the others to the gnome as well.

"Oo oi!" Pikel cheered in support of the hunched little alchemist.

"Is it gonna work?" Banak asked.

"Oo oi!" Pikel said again, punching his one fist into the air.

"The smell was not supposed to . . ." Nanfoodle started to reply, but then he stopped and took a deep breath. "I do not know," he admitted. "I think . . ."

"Ye *think?*" Banak berated. "Ye got more than a thousand dwarves up here, little one. Ye think? Do we hold the fight or get down now?"

Poor Nanfoodle had no idea how to answer and couldn't begin to take that heavy responsibility upon his tiny shoulders.

"Oo oi!" cried Pikel.

"It's gonna work," Ivan added.

"So we should stay?" Banak asked.

"That's yer own choice to make," Ivan replied. "But I'm thinking them giants're gonna be wishing we'd turned tail and run!"

He stepped over and patted Nanfoodle on the shoulder.

"Oo oi!" cried Pikel.

"Orcs're coming again," said another dwarf, Rockbottom the cleric. "Big charge this time."

"Good enough. I was gettin' bored!" said Thibbledorf Pwent, who was already covered in blood and gore from the evening's fighting—some of it his own, but most of it that of his unfortunate enemies.

"Dawn's another hour away," Ivan remarked.

"Less than that from Nikwillig's perch, if he got there," said Catti-brie.

"We got to hold then," Banak decided.

He turned to Nanfoodle and nodded, as much a show of support for the gnome's outrageous scheme as he could muster at that grim time. Banak was gambling a lot, and he knew it, and so did everyone else around him. With the giants throwing their boulders and the press of the orcs, the dwarves would have a difficult time getting over that cliff face and down to Keeper's Dale. If Shoudra's reports and assessment were correct, getting down to Keeper's Dale might prove to be the least of their problems and the worst of their decisions.

"Drive them back, Thibbledorf Pwent," Banak instructed. "Ye hold them pigs off us."

In response, Pwent held up a bulging wineskin, tapped it to his forehead in salute, and ran along to join his bloody and battered Gutbusters.

All eyes again went to Nanfoodle, who seemed to shrink under the press of those concerned gazes. His plan had to work, but the signs were not promising.

Soon enough, the sounds of battle again echoed up the slope as Pwent led the dwarves' counterassault.

Soon after that, the sounds of another battle echoed up from below, from the western reaches of Keeper's Dale.

And soon after that, the first of the giant catapults let fly. A huge boulder smashed and bounced across the back edge of the dwarven line, right along the cliff face.

"Ye got yer skins?" Thibbledorf Pwent asked his gathered Gutbusters as they circled back up and regrouped. To a dwarf, they produced the bulging bladders. "Some o' ye won't be needing them," he added solemnly. "And might be that some won't be able to get to them, but ye know yer place!"

As one, the Gutbusters cheered and roared.

"Get in and break their lines," the fierce dwarf instructed. "Drive them back and take yer dead place!"

Down went the force, another furious charge that slashed through the orc ranks. No defensive measure there, Pwent led his forces down the slope farther than any dwarves had previously gone, shattering the orc line and their supporting allies. Their goal was to cause more confusion than actual damage—no easy mind set for the carnage-hungry Gutbuster Brigade—and that's what they did.

The orc assault fell apart, with many forced to turn back and retreat before regrouping.

Thibbledorf Pwent kept his formation tight, not allowing the customary Gutbuster pursuit. He raised his waterskin in salute and reminder to the others. Then he found a broken weapon he could later use, offering a wink to those nearby so they would understand his intent.

Like an ocean tide, the orcs rolled back and gathered strength for the next wave. And during that brief lull, more of the giant catapults began heaving huge boulders through the predawn sky. Few had the range at first, and so the initial volleys were not so effective, but all the dwarves understood how quickly that might all change.

"We got to hold the east!" Tred cried at the others, mostly to Wulfgar, who had pretty much been anchoring that end of the line from the very beginning.

Wulfgar looked at him grimly, and that response alone quieted the Felbarr dwarf, reminding him of what he had known all along: that Nikwillig would have a hard time getting back to them.

Banak paced nervously around the cliff ledge, looking down to the south-west as often as he was looking at the raging battle down the slope to the north.

This is it, he thought.

It was the culmination of all his efforts and of all of his enemies' efforts. The orcs were closing their vice, north and west, as the giants were softening up the rear of Banak's position.

A boulder slammed down not so far away and bounced right past Banak, nearly clipping him off the cliff.

The tough dwarf didn't flinch, just continued his pacing, his eyes more and more going to the brightening eastern sky.

"Come on then, Nikwillig of Felbarr," he whispered, and even as he spoke the words, he saw the flash of a distant mirror, catching the first rays of dawn on the other side of the eastern ridge.

Others noted the same thing, some pointing excitedly to the east. Catti-brie came running Banak's way from the east, bow in hand, as did Nanfoodle, Shoudra, and Pikel, coming in fast from the west.

"Sight it, sight it," Shoudra coaxed quietly, watching the distant mirror.

Nanfoodle clenched his hands before him, hardly drawing breath.

"There!" Catti-brie said, pointing to the ridge, where the reflection of Nikwillig's roving sunbeam at last caught a second mirror, turning it to blazing brilliance. The woman lifted her bow.

Banak held his breath, as did the others.

Below them, the battle raged, orcs swarming up the slope in greater num-bers than before. An all-out assault, it seemed, and all around their position came the calls for retreat, even some terrified shouts for the dwarves to retreat all the way, to get down to Keeper's Dale.

"What're we doing, then?" Catti-brie asked, glancing, as were all the others, over at Nanfoodle.

Nanfoodle began to huff and puff, unable to catch his breath, and for a moment it seemed as if he would simply fall over. He glanced over to regard Pikel, who was sitting next to the tubing near one wide joint.

Nanfoodle found strength in that image, in the giddy confidence of the green-bearded dwarf.

The gnome took a deep breath and nodded to Pikel.

"Oo oi!" Pikel Bouldershoulder cried.

The druid waved his hand over the stone that joined the tubes, then pressed against the suddenly malleable stone, crushing it flat and sealing off the flow.

Another deep breath and another gulp, and Nanfoodle forced himself to steady.

"Shoot straight!" he yelled, and he whimpered and cast himself aside.

Catti-brie leveled Taulmaril, sighting in the shining mirror—the reflector Ivan had placed on the side of the box that had been set in the ridge.

More giant boulders crashed down—several dwarves cried out in terror as the great rocks smashed across the dwarven line.

Catti-brie pulled back, but the eastern mirror held by distant Nikwillig shifted a bit and the reflector in the ridge went suddenly dark.

The woman held her posture, held her breath, and held her bow ready.

"Breach!" came the cry of a dwarf from below and to the north.

"Shoot it, then!" Banak implored her.

She didn't breathe and didn't let fly, waiting, waiting, trusting in Nikwillig. She saw his reflected sunbeam crawling around the dark stones of the ridge, seeking its target.

"Come on then," Shoudra whispered. "Sight it."

Banak ran away from them.

"Fall back!" he yelled down to those engaged in battle. "Form a second line!" he cried to those reserves up nearer to the cliff—reserves who were scrambling around, trying to find cover from the increasing catapult barrage.

Catti-brie put it all out of her mind, holding herself perfectly still and ready, and focusing on that reflected sunbeam—only on that crawling line of light.

There came a flash in the darkness of the western ridge.

Taulmaril hummed, the silver-streaking arrow soaring out across the many yards. The woman fired a second and a third off at once, aiming for the general area.

She needn't have bothered, for that first shot had struck the mark, smashing through the glass of the mirror, then driving home into the piece of wood set in place behind it. The force of the blow drove the wood back, collapsing the large vial and the enchanted and explosive oil burst to life.

For a brief instant, nothing happened, then . . .

BOOM!

All the west lit up as if the sun itself had leaped out from behind that ridge. Flames shot out from every crack in the mountain spur, side, and ceiling, jumping up past the stunned giants and their great war engines, leaping higher than any flames any of the awestricken onlookers had ever seen. A thousand feet into the air went the orange fires of Nanfoodle, turning night to daylight and carrying dust and stone and huge boulders high into the sky with them.

The flames lasted only a brief instant, the gasses burning themselves out in one concussive blast, and the onlookers gaped and gasped. And a hot wave of shocking force rolled over them, over Catti-brie, Shoudra, and Nanfoodle, over squealing Pikel and wide-eyed Banak, over the battling warriors, dwarf and orc alike, throwing them all to the ground.

Within that hot wave of air came the debris, tons and tons of stones small and large sweeping across the battlefield slope. Since the main reaches of the slope were farther to the north, the orc hordes took the worst of it, with hundreds laid low in a single burst of power.

Back in the west, the ridge, once so evenly distributed, seemed a jagged and torn line. Catapults and giants alike—those few that were still somehow in place—were aflame, the war engines falling to pieces, the behemoths leaping wildly about.

Nanfoodle pulled himself off the ground and stood staring stupidly to the west.

"Remember that fireball you described to me from your visit to the mage faire those years ago?" he asked the equally stricken Shoudra.

"Elminster's blast, yes," the stunned woman replied. "The greatest fireball ever thrown."

Nanfoodle snapped his little fingers in the air and said, "Not any more."

"Oo oi!" Pikel Bouldershoulder squealed.

29

SHOCK WAVES

The gallant Sunset did not complain as he wound his way above the mountains with two riders sitting astride his strong back. Innovindil guided the pegasus from the front perch, with Drizzt sitting right behind her, his arms tight around her waist.

For Drizzt, flying was among the most amazing and wonderful experiences he had ever known. His traveling cloak and long white hair alike flew out behind him, waving in the wind, and he had to squint against the rush of air to keep his tears from flying. Though he was astride a mount and moving not of his own volition, the drow felt a profound sense of freedom, as if escaping the bounds of earth was somewhat akin to escaping the bounds of mortality itself.

Early on in the flight, he had tried to speak with Innovindil, but the wind was too loud around them, so that they had to shout to be heard at all.

And so Drizzt just rested back and enjoyed the ride, the rush of air and the predawn chill.

They were traveling south, far behind the mass of King Obould's army. Their destination weighed heavily upon Drizzt, though he had found some respite from his fears, at least, in the wondrous pleasures offered by the journey on the winged horse. They knew not what they might find as they approached Mithral Hall. Would Obould have the dwarves sealed away, with no chance for Drizzt and Innovindil to sneak through to communicate with Bruenor's kin? Would the dwarves be holding strong against the invaders, leaving Drizzt and Innovindil a field of torn orc corpses to cross? With so many possibilities spread wide before them, Drizzt had managed to settle back from them all, to simply enjoy the sensation of flight.

Ahead and to the right of the pair and their mount lay the soft darkness of predawn, but to the left, the east, the sky showed the pale blue of morning, above the pink rim created by the approach of the rising sun. Drizzt watched in awe as the red-glowing sun crested the horizon, the first streaks of dawn reaching out from the east.

"Beautiful," he muttered, though he knew that Innovindil could not hear him.

From that high vantage point, Drizzt followed the brightening line of morning as it spread east to west. He turned far ahead of it to catch one last glimpse of the departing night.

And there was daylight, so suddenly, everywhere at once! No, not daylight, Drizzt realized, but an orange glow, an orange flame leaping high into the sky, a fire so great that it brightened the landscape before him instantaneously. Into the air the fire leaped, so far up that the two pegasus-riding elves had to crane their necks and look up to see its apex.

Sunset pawed at the empty air and whinnied, and Innovindil, equally stunned and confused, eased the reigns and bade the mount to descend.

"What in all the world?" the female cried.

Drizzt started to similarly cry out, but then the hot shockwave of the explosion reached out to them, buffeting them with its winds, nearly dislodging both of them. The wind carried dust and small debris far from the fireball, and all three, elf, drow, and pegasus, squinted against the sting.

Down, down they went, Sunset frantic to get to the ground. Innovindil held tight and helped guide him, but Drizzt took the moment to survey the region lit up by the fast-dissipating fireball, to note the swarm of crawling forms. In that brief instant, the drow saw the distant battlefield, recognized the slope leading to the lip of Keeper's Dale, and knew at once that the dwarves were fiercely fighting.

"What in all the world?" a desperate Innovindil asked again as they touched down on solid ground. "Have they wakened a dragon, then?"

Drizzt had no answers for her, for never in all his life had he witnessed such a blast. His immediate thoughts conjured an image of one Harkle Harpell, a most eccentric and dangerous wizard, and Harkle's family of equally crazy mages. Had the Harpells come to Mithral Hall's aid once again, bearing new and uncontrollable magic?

But none of it made any sense to Drizzt, and he had nothing to answer Innovindil's wide-eyed and desperate stare.

"What have they done?" the elf asked.

Drizzt stammered and shook his head, then just offered, "Let us go and see."

The orc ranks flattened like tall grass before a gale. Those fortunate enough to escape the punch of flying debris went down hard anyway, blown from their feet by a shockwave the likes of which they had never imagined possible.

Urlgen, too, went flying down to the stone, but the proud and strong orc did not cry out in fear, nor did he cower. He climbed right back to his feet against the flush of heat and the last waves of the blast and surveyed the battlefield.

There he saw a squirming mass of stunned orcs and dwarves. The tall orc shook his head in disbelief and confusion. He glanced over at the blasted ridge, to see one giant rushing around to and fro, waving its arms, the whole of it immolated by bright flames.

As life itself seemed to return to the battlefield and to the orcs around Urlgen, he heard terrified cries and shrieks, and only then did he understand the true danger of that horrific blast. He had lost some orcs, to be sure, and his giant flank was no more, but the real danger presented itself far above the orc commander's position, as the dwarves regrouped quickly and began a devastating charge against his confused and scattering forces.

Urlgen shook his head and thought, It isn't supposed to go this way!

The shouts to retreat and run away echoed all around him, and for an instant, Urlgen almost conceded to them, almost ordered his warriors to run away.

Almost, but then he considered the bigger picture and the gains his father would even then be making down in the southwest. Urlgen had planned to soften the dwarves for a bit longer, to use the giants and his original force to shape the battlefield without the possibility of the dwarves escaping. Then he would send in the reinforcements his father had given to him and overwhelm the dwarves.

That had all changed in the instant of that terrible explosion.

With a roar that echoed above the din of scrambling orcs, Urlgen demanded and commanded attention. He ran along parallel to the battlefield, intercepting retreating orcs and turning them around—by sheer will and threat forcing them back into the fight.

And all the while, he shouted out to those reserves he had to that point kept hidden from the dwarves' view, turning loose the whole of his force in one great and sweeping charge.

"Kill them all!" the tall orc commanded.

As the swarm gradually swung around to reengage the charging dwarves, Urlgen lifted his fists, spiked gauntlets high, and for the first time, rushed into battle. It was all-or-nothing for him, he knew. He would win there, decisively, or all would be lost. He would forevermore be crushed under the mantle of his glorious father—if his glorious father even spared his life.

Banak Brawnanvil sucked in his breath when he saw the orc horde pivot and swing around. His boys had fared far better than the orcs in Nanfoodle's blast, and all the lower slopes were littered with orc dead. But his boys were still outnumbered—and outnumbered many times over as a second group charged in from behind the original orc ranks.

Banak growled. Given the effectiveness of the explosion, he had wanted to break out and join the definitive battle that would push the orcs back from Mithral Hall.

"Hit them hard and retreat to hold the line!" Banak called to his nearby commanders.

As he watched the full charge of orcs from below, though, it seemed apparent that there was a different tone to their charge, a different intent and intensity. The veteran dwarf began to understand almost immediately that his enemies did not mean to hit and run again. The old dwarf chewed his lip, considered the strength of his enemies, and considered his options.

"Come on, then," he muttered under his breath.

He set his feet firmly under him, determined to hold strong. That determination shifted none-too-subtly a moment later, though, from sheer dwarf grit to almost desperate need, when scouts out to the west shouted back along the line that there was fighting in the southwest, along the western edge of Keeper's Dale.

Banak found a vantage point and peered into the growing light in the southwest. As he noted the scope of the battle and the size of the opposing orc force, he nearly fell over.

"By Moradin, ye hold them," the old dwarf whispered, barely able to get the words out.

He looked back to the north, where the momentum of the wake of Nanfoodle's blast had played out, where the press of orcs was flowing up at him, driving the dwarves back toward their defensive positions. Then he glanced back to the southwest and the growing sounds of battle.

He surmised at once the orc plan.

He saw at once the danger.

With a determined grunt, the warlord forced himself to look back to the devastation of the western ridge. The orc plan had been a good one, well coordinated to not only win the ground, but to slaughter the dwarves to a warrior as well. Nanfoodle's explosion alone had bought him some breathing room, some time—perhaps enough to escape.

"Moradin be with ye, little one," Banak said, aiming the words at the distant gnome, who was too far away to hear.

The battle sounds to the southwest increased suddenly, dramatically, and Banak glanced back to see that a horde of giants had joined in with his enemies.

"Moradin be with us all," the dwarf mouthed.

The main dwarven line broke and retreated, as ordered, running flat out for their defensive positions atop the slope. Arrows and hammers came out over them in support, slowing the orcs that nipped at their heels every step.

Many of the dwarves were not fast returning, though. More than a few were dead, laid low by orc spears, or by the flying debris of Nanfoodle's momentous blast. Many more, well over a hundred others, lay splayed across the stones, covered in blood.

Not from wounds, though, but from torn waterskins. Thibbledorf Pwent and his Gutbusters, which included more than a few very recent recruits, had used the cover of the explosion to splash themselves with blood and fall "dead" to the ground. Some, like Pwent himself, accentuating the wounds by strategically placing broken weapons against them. Now they lay there, perfectly still as hordes of orcs ran past them, sometimes stepping all over them.

Pwent opened one eye and did well to hide his smile.

He leaped up and punched a spiked gauntlet right through the face of the nearest, surprised orc. He yelled out at the top of his lungs, and up came his Gutbusters as one, right in the middle of the confused enemy.

"Buy 'em time!" the toughened leader cried out, and the Gutbusters did just that, launching into a frenzy, slugging and slashing with abandon, tackling orcs and convulsing atop them, their ridged armor plates gashing their enemies to pulp.

Thibbledorf Pwent stood at their center, directing the battle through example more than words. For there was no overreaching plan. The last thing Pwent wanted was to create an atmosphere of coordination and predictability.

Mayhem.

Simple and beautiful mayhem. The call of the Gutbusters, the joy of the Gutbusters.

THE LAY OF BRUENOR

Watching the countercharge—thousands of orcs streaming up in blood-thirsty rage—Banak Brawnanvil understood that it was over. It would be the last battle on that ground, win or lose, press through or retreat. In realizing the sheer size of that orc force, with so many charging up in reinforcement, the dwarf wasn't thrilled with the prospects.

The sound of fighting behind and below him soon had him rushing back to join some of the others at the cliff ledge.

And there, the old dwarf saw nothing but doom.

The dwarves on the western edge of Keeper's Dale had broken ranks already. And how could they not? For the force arrayed against them was huge, larger than anything Banak had ever seen in all his years.

"How many orcs?" he asked breathlessly, for surely the spectacle of that arrayed force had stolen Banak's strength. "Five thousand? Ten thousand?"

"They'll sweep the dale in short order," Torgar Hammerstriker warned.

And that would be it, Banak knew.

"Get 'em down," Banak ordered, and he had to forcefully spit the dreaded words through his gritted teeth. "All of them. We make for the dale and the halls."

An order to retreat was nothing that the dwarves of Clan Battlehammer, nor of Mirabar, were used to hearing, and for a moment, all the commanders near to Banak stared at him open-mouthed.

"The giants're dead!" one protested. "Gnome blew up the ridge, and . . ."

But as the reality settled upon them, as they all came to see the truth of the orc press from the north and the rout behind them in the dale, that was the only dissenting voice. Before the grumbling dwarf had ever finished the statement, Torgar and Shingles, Ivan and Tred, and all the others were rushing out among their respective groups calling for and organizing a full retreat from the cliff.

The warlord ignored the protestor and turned his attention down the northern slopes, to where Thibbledorf Pwent and his Gutbusters were causing havoc across the center of the orc press. The old dwarf nodded his appreciation—their sacrifice was buying him precious time to get away.

"Fight hard, Pwent," he muttered, as unnecessary a cheer as could be spoken.

"Go! Go! Go!" Banak prodded those dwarves moving to the drop-ropes. "Don't ye slow a bit till ye've hit the floor o' Keeper's Dale!"

Banak watched the dwarves who had met the front end of the orc charge form into tighter squares and begin their pivot back up the slopes.

"We gotta break their front ranks to give them who're coming last time to get over," he heard Tred shout out from somewhere below and to the right.

In response to that call came two familiar forms, Wulfgar and Catti-brie, sprinting down the slope, driving the left flank of the orc line before them.

Banak held his breath. Tred's assessment was on target, he understood. If they could not break the orc momentum, could not turn the front ranks around in at least a short retreat and regroup, then many dwarves would die that day.

Behind him again, he heard several dwarves bickering, arguing that they weren't about to run away while their kin were fighting. Banak turned on them powerfully, eyes blazing with fury.

"Get ye down!" he shouted above the commotion of the argument, and all eyes turned his way.

"Go!" the old dwarf commanded. "Ye dolts, we're all to run, and them behind ye can't start until ye're off!"

One of the group punched another and roughly pushed him toward the edge and one of the drop-ropes.

"Ain't never left a friend," the dwarf continued to grumble, but he did indeed take up the rope in his strong hands and roll off the ledge.

Looking back at the furious battle, then farther down to where Pwent and his boys had been seemingly boxed in, Banak could certainly understand that sentiment.

"Crush them!" King Obould cried to his charges, urging them forward. The orc king didn't stand back and issue the order, but rather charged up toward the front ranks, prodding the orcs on, kicking aside the dead and wounded orcs who had already tried the devastating dwarven defenses.

Obould cursed his luck—his very first assault would have overwhelmed those walls and fortifications, he believed, except that the ground had violently lurched beneath them, followed by a hail of stones from up above. The orc king had no idea what in the world might have happened up there, but just then, it wasn't his concern.

Just then, he was focused on one goal alone.

"Crush them!" he cried again.

The orc king continued to push his way forward, crossing to the leading ranks. He came up against the front dwarven wall, sweeping his greatsword before him to knock aside the many prodding dwarven polearms. A couple avoided his wild parry, though, and the dwarves redirected the weapons quickly to stab at the great orc.

Those weapons of Mithral Hall, fine as they were, barely scratched the orc king's magnificent armor, and he barreled ahead, cutting a downward slash with his sword, igniting its flame as he did. One unfortunate dwarf popped up at that moment and had his head cleaved in half. Obould's sword drove down farther, crashing against the top of the stone wall and knocking out a sizeable chunk of it.

The orc king smashed again and again, sweeping that area clean. He leaped up, clearing the four vertical feet to the wall top.

And there he stood, flaming sword braced against one hip and angled diagonally upward out to the side, his other hand outstretched and clenched.

Arrows and crossbow bolts came at him and bounced away. Nearby dwarves scrambled, bringing their weapons to bear, smacking at the great orc's feet to try to dislodge him.

"Crush them!" Obould screamed, and he didn't budge an inch.

Bolstered by his display, the orcs swarmed the wall, and terrified of the display, the dwarves hesitated. To Obould's far right came a wedge of roaring giants, heaving boulders at the fortifications and charging in with abandon.

Beneath his skull-faced helmet, the orc king grinned wickedly. He had suspected that his bold attack would force Gerti and her reluctant kin into full action.

The front fortifications gave way before the swarm. The dwarves broke

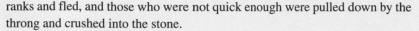

ranks and fled, and those who were not quick enough were pulled down by the throng and crushed into the stone.

Obould held his spot on the high ground, roaring, sword aflame, fist clenched. He glanced back up to the cliff in the northeast and wondered again about that tremendous explosion. But the implications did not hold his attention for long, for he looked back to his own overwhelming force and the growing rout in the west. Even if Urlgen failed him in the north, Obould knew that he would win the day in Keeper's Dale.

Close the door, the orc king mused, and let those dwarves trapped above-ground try to find their way home.

Drizzt couldn't see the front lines of the fighting, but he knew from the logjam of orc warriors in the middle and back of their ranks that the dwarves near to the cliff were putting up strong resistance. He could also see a commotion only a hundred yards or so south of his position, in the middle of the orc horde. As he watched one orc spinning up into the air, blood flying from multiple wounds, the drow figured that Thibbledorf Pwent was likely involved.

Drizzt didn't even allow himself a grin, for he was approaching the rear of the orc line and had drawn the attention of many of the stragglers.

"They will test you," he said to his companion, who stumbled before him, her arms bound behind her. "You must trust in me."

Innovindil tripped and fell, and Drizzt grimaced against his instinctual response, denying even the slightest hint of it, and let her go down hard. He grabbed her by the shoulder and roughly pulled her back to her feet—and again fought against his reflexive urge to wince when he saw the welt on her face.

It was the way it had to be.

Drizzt pushed her ahead, and she nearly stumbled down again, then he prodded her with one of his drawn blades. Orcs came in at the pair, yellow eyes wide, teeth bared, weapons ready. One moved right up before Innovindil, who looked down.

"A prisoner for Urlgen," Drizzt growled in his coarse command of Orcish.

"For Urlgen!" he reiterated powerfully when the orc made a move Innovindil's way.

"A prisoner from Donnia," the drow added, when doubting looks came back at him from many angles.

The orc in front motioned to another, who charged up behind Innovindil and tugged at her arms, checking the bonds. Drizzt slapped him away, after letting him see that the ties were authentic.

"For Urlgen!" he shouted yet again.

Whether in another test or just out of spite, the orc in front stabbed forward suddenly with its spear, right for the surface elf's gut.

Around went Drizzt, rolling around Innovindil's hip, scimitars slashing, taking the spear out wide with three quick hits.

The drow spun again, shouting, "For Urlgen!" with his scimitars working in a circular blur.

The orc flinched again and again, and fell back.

The drow settled before the elf, scimitars at his side.

The orc looked at him, then looked down at its own torso, cut and bleeding in more than a dozen bright and deep lines. Then it fell over.

"Take me to Urlgen!" Drizzt demanded of the others, "Take me!"

The drow moved behind Innovindil, pushing her forward with all speed, and the orc ranks parted before them like the waters of a lake before the prow of a fast sailing ship.

Up the slope they went, drawing stares from all around—but few of those orcs wanted to be anywhere near to them, Drizzt noted hopefully.

His eyes were soon enough drawn forward, up the slope, to the spectacle of one tall orc barking orders and roughly shoving aside any creatures who got too close to him.

The leader. Obviously the leader.

Drizzt began to fall into himself, finding his center, finding his anger, finding the primal creature that resided within his mortal coil, that instinctive Hunter, then moving through the Hunter and into the realm of pure concentration. With the swarm around him, he held little hope that he and Innovindil could get out of it, and given that, the drow had chosen to simply ignore the throng.

He took a quick look at Innovindil, her blue eyes set as if in stone, staring with abject hatred at the orc leader, at the son of the beast who had so brutally taken her Tarathiel from her.

Before they had come in with their ruse, Innovindil had exacted Drizzt's promise that Urlgen, son of Obould, was hers to kill.

The sounds of battle echoed all around them, the cries of the orc leader cut the air, and the orcs pressed on up the slope, where the stubborn dwarves held their ground.

And Drizzt Do'Urden tuned it out, focusing instead on a singular image.

A tower crumbling, burning, falling, and a dwarf rushing around on its tilting top, crying orders to the last.

The Hunter reached for Guenhwyvar.

They knew they had to hold. For the sake of their kin atop the cliffs, the dwarves had to fend the charging hordes. Where would Banak Brawnanvil run if they were forced back into Mithral Hall?

The defenders of western Keeper's Dale knew that truth keenly and used it to bolster their every moment of doubt. There was no choice; they had to hold.

But they could not, and their more immediate choice, up and down the length of their line, quickly became a simple decision to fall back or die where they stood. Many chose the latter, or the latter found them, while others did indeed fall back to the next defensible position. But the orc horde pursued, rolling along, smashing through every wall and swarming around every obstacle.

Like driftwood on an incoming tide, the dwarves fell back.

They sent runners to the base of the northern cliffs, shouting up for Banak to retreat in full, and indeed, their hopes were bolstered in seeing the first dwarves coming down the rope ladders. Immediately, those at the base began setting up a plan for defending the area, waving in the dwarves coming down the ropes to quickly join in.

Other dwarves sprinted farther to the east, shouting out to those guards near to Mithral Hall's doors, warning of the impending disaster.

Soon enough, all the remaining Keeper's Dale defenders were in sight of those great western doors, and every valiant effort to turn and make a stand was overrun, pushing them ever farther to the west.

They were almost level with the drop ropes from above when they made yet another determined stand, knowing that if they were pushed any farther, Banak's retreat would find a swift end.

"The hall's opening!" one dwarf cried, looking back and pointing to the wall.

Every dwarf in the line found a moment to glance back that way, to see indeed the great doors of Mithral Hall opening to their call for help. Out came reinforcements, scores of their kin, many still wearing their blacksmith aprons or still dressed in common clothing instead of battle mail. Out came every remaining dwarf, it seemed, even many of the wounded who should have stayed in bed.

They all came to the call of distress; they all charged forth from the safety of their tunnels to aid in the battle.

Certainly there were not nearly enough reinforcements to win the day, nor even enough, it seemed, to begin to slow the orc rout.

But there was among the ranks of newcomers one dwarf in particular who could not be ignored, and whose presence could not be measured in the form of just another singular warrior.

For a dwarf larger than life centered that reinforcing line.

For Bruenor Battlehammer centered that reinforcing line.

Banak gnashed his teeth as he surveyed the scene below, hardly believing how fast the defenders of Keeper's Dale were being overrun and pushed back, hardly believing the sheer scope and ferocity of the newly arrived orc army.

The old dwarf broke his ranks and sent his charges over the ledge, scrambling like ants down the many rope ladders. It was a decision made on the fly, committed to in the blink of an eye, and when it was done, the order given, Banak could not help but second-guess himself.

For he could see the dark tide flowing west to east across Keeper's Dale. Would any of his fleeing dwarves even reach the floor of the dale before the darkness had crossed by? If they did, would they be able to mount a defense as more and more got down beside them?

The alternative, Banak Brawnanvil knew, would be abject disaster, perhaps a complete slaughter of all those brave souls entrusted to his care.

He continued to shout support at the retreating dwarves. He yelled down to Pwent and his boys to fight their way back up to the cliff, and he personally moved to the escape route of last resort: the drop chute Torgar's engineers had manufactured.

Wulfgar and Catti-brie met him there, just ahead of Torgar, Tred, and Shingles.

"The two of ye be on yer way," Banak instructed the two humans, one of whom was far too large to attempt the narrow chute. "Get to the ropes and get yerselfs down."

"We'll go when Pwent returns," Catti-brie said.

To accentuate her point, she lifted Taulmaril and sent a sizzling arrow sailing away at the orc throng. It disappeared into the morass, but none watching had any doubt that it had to have found a deadly mark on one creature or another.

Wulfgar, meanwhile, pulled two long drop ropes in closer to their position, setting them and looping them over and over to make them impossible to untie and more difficult to cut.

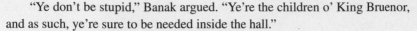

"Ye don't be stupid," Banak argued. "Ye're the children o' King Bruenor, and as such, ye're sure to be needed inside the hall."

"As we're needed up here right now," said Wulfgar.

"We'll go when Pwent returns," Catti-brie reiterated. She let fly again. "And not a moment before."

Banak started to argue but cut himself short, unable to counter the simple logic of it. He, too, would be an important voice in Mithral Hall after that day, of course, and yet he too, had no intention of going anywhere until the Gutbusters began their drop down the escape chute.

He stepped out in front of Catti-brie, Torgar and Shingles on his left, Tred and Ivan Bouldershoulder, who joined in after seeing a reluctant Pikel off along the ropes, on his right.

"Use me head to sight yer bow," Banak said to Catti-brie.

She did just that and cut down the closest of a group of orcs charging their way.

Her movements of grace and fluidity contrasted sharply with Urlgen's sudden, herky-jerky lunges and punches.

Innovindil glided around him, launching a series of thrusts and sweeping sword attacks, most designed merely to set the large orc up for a sudden and devastating finish.

Urlgen turned with her, his heavily armored arms swiping across and picking off each attack, his feet turning and keeping him always on balance as the elf swirled around him, circling continually to his right.

Then she was gone, reversing her movement back to the left, turning a complete circuit to gain momentum, and redirecting that newfound momentum into a single thrust for the orc's heart.

But Urlgen, son of Obould, saw the move coming and had it countered before it ever began. As soon as he lost sight of the elf, the orc turned his hips appropriately and brought his arms swinging down and across his body. That thrust, which would have skewered almost any orc, got nowhere close to hitting.

Innovindil didn't let her surprise show on her face, nor did she relinquish the attack and fall back to regroup. She didn't have the time for that, she knew, for Drizzt Do'Urden was working furiously around her, leaping and spinning, his deadly scimitars slashing down any nearby orcs who dared approach. Across from him, equally effective as she protected Innovindil's other flank, the mighty black panther reared and sprang. She came up before one orc who was scrambling desperately to get away and swiped off its face with one powerful claw, then charged back the other way, bowling over yet another orc.

Those two brave friends were giving her the battle, Innovindil knew, but time was not on their side.

She pressed the attack more furiously, stabbing left, right, and center in rapid succession. Sparks flew as her sword struck hard against one metal bracer, and a second, and again as both bracers crossed over her blade, driving it down and just to the side of Urlgen's left hip.

And the orc countered, not by raising his arms to the offense, but by living up to the reputation of his name, Threefist. He leaned over the blocked sword and snapped his forehead down. Though Innovindil was agile enough to shift her head away from a direct hit, even a glancing blow from the orc's metal head plate had her stumbling backward, dazed.

Instinct alone had her sword flailing before her, fending the heavy punches of the orc's spiked gauntlets. Only gradually did Innovindil collect her wits enough to get her feet firmly under her and solidify both her stance and her defenses. She fought the orc back to even footing.

"Lesson learned," she muttered under her breath, and she vowed that she'd watch for that devastating head-butt more closely.

Upon a stone did Bruenor make his stand.

His legs widespread and planted, his many-notched axe held high, the King of Mithral Hall called for his kin, called for all the Delzoun dwarves, to hold firm. And there did the dwarves of Clan Battlehammer rally. Whether by luck or by the guarding hands of his ancestors and his god, no spear found Bruenor that day.

With the swirling orc sea around him, he stood, a beacon of hope for the dwarves, a testament to sheer determination. Spears thrust and flew his way, orc hands grabbed at his sturdy legs, but none could uproot King Bruenor. A flying club smashed him in the face, opening a long wound, closing one eye.

Bruenor roared through it.

An orc saw the opportunity to get up beside the dwarf, slamming hard with a warhammer.

Bruenor took the hit and didn't flinch, then chopped the orc away with a deadly slash of his axe.

Another orc was up beside him and another and another, and for a moment, it seemed as if the dwarf king would be buried where he stood.

But they went flying away, one after another, thrown by the strength and determination of Bruenor Battlehammer, who would not fall, who would not fail. Blood ran freely from many wounds, some obviously serious. But Bruenor's roar was not in pain nor in fear. It was a denial, stubborn and strong, determined beyond mortal bounds.

Never did Delzoun hearts so swell with pride as on that day, as on that stone, when King Battlehammer cried!

There was no choice before them. To retreat past Bruenor meant to abandon those hundreds of dwarves even then crawling down the cliff face. Better to die, by all measures of dwarven logic, than to forsake kin.

Bruenor reminded them of that. His presence alone, somehow risen from his deathbed, reminded them all of who they were, of what they were, and of what, above all else, mattered: kin and kind.

And so the retreating dwarves did pivot as one, did dig in their heels and press back against the onslaught, matching spear with hammer and axe, matching orc bloodlust with dwarf determination.

And there, around the stone upon which stood the King of Mithral Hall, the orc wave broke and was halted.

Shoulder to shoulder and with Banak Brawnanvil in their middle, the five dwarves met the tip of the orc ranks with sheer fury, leaping in as one and pounding away with hammer and axe. Behind them, Catti-brie worked Taulmaril to devastating effect, coordinating her shots with Wulfgar as he ran back and forth along the short defensive line, preventing any orcs from getting behind the fighting fivesome.

"Pwent, ye hurry! All the boys're down!" Banak shouted to the very depleted group of Gutbusters who were finally making some headway in their desperate attempt to reach him and the drop chute.

Banak couldn't even see if Pwent was alive among that group.

"Girl, ye bring yer fire to bear!" Ivan Bouldershoulder shouted back to Catti-brie.

"Go," Wulfgar bade her, assuring her that he had the situation in hand.

Indeed it seemed as if he did, for no orcs wanted anything to do with the terrible barbarian warrior.

Catti-brie sprinted ahead, coming to a stop right behind Ivan. She took quick note of the situation ahead, of the group of orcs who had turned around in an attempt to seal off the retreat of the bloodied Gutbusters.

Up came Taulmaril, the Heartseeker, and sizzling lines of silver raced out from the line of five dwarves. Catti-brie worked left and right, not daring to shoot straight down the center for fear that her enchanted arrows would blow right through some orcs and into the retreating dwarves. She found her rhythm, swinging left and right, left and right, each shot slicing down to devastating effect. Those orcs in between the continuing lines of deadly arrows found no reinforcements to bolster their barricade against the fury of the Gutbusters, and seeing that reality, the Gutbusters themselves reacted, tightening their ranks and spearheading their way up the slope.

"Now get ye over that cliff!" Banak demanded of Catti-brie and Wulfgar when the line closed. "We got us a faster way down!"

Reluctantly, but unable to argue the logic, Catti-brie ran up to Wulfgar and the pair charged back to the cliff face. They shouldered their weapons, took up their respective ropes, and went over side by side, sliding down the face of the cliff.

They heard the Gutbusters leaping into the drop chute above them and took satisfaction in that. They heard Banak calling frantically for his fellows to go.

And they heard orcs, so many orcs.

Wulfgar's rope jolted suddenly, and again, and Catti-brie reached out for him, and he for her.

His rope fell away, cut from above.

Obould did not see his forces stall around the stone upon which stood King Bruenor, for his attention had been drawn to the side by that point, to the defensive stand in the north, where dwarves were fast descending.

The dwarves were making a stubborn stand, to be sure, but Obould's numbers should have swept them away.

But then a fireball exploded in the midst of his line. And, inexplicably, another charging group ran off to the side and began fighting against . . . against nothing, the orc king realized, or against each other, or against the stones.

A quick scan showed Obould the truth of it, that two others, a human woman and a gnome, had joined in the defensive stand, waggling their fingers and launching their magic. More dwarves came down from above, leaping to the dale floor, pulling free their weapons, and throwing themselves in to bolster the defensive line.

His orcs were going to break ranks!

A bolt of blue lightning flashed through the throng and a dozen orcs fell dead and a score more flopped on the ground, stunned and shocked.

The real beauty of his plan, to not simply push the dwarves into their holes but to slaughter the whole of the force up above, began to unravel before Obould's angry eyes. With a roar, he denied that unacceptable turn. With a growl and a fist clenched so tightly that it would have crushed solid stone, the great orc king began his own charge to that northern wall, determined to turn the tide yet again.

The dwarves were not going to escape his trap. Not again.

Banak went into the hole head first and last, after having forcibly thrown the exhausted and bloody Thibbledorf Pwent in before him. He expected to fall into the steep slide, but he had barely gotten into the hole when he got hung up.

Only then did the old dwarf realize that he had a spear sticking out of his back, and that it was stuck on the stone.

Orcs crowded around the hole above him, whacking at his feet, prodding down with their nasty spears.

Banak kicked furiously, but he knew he was dead, knew that there was no way he could extricate himself.

But then a hand grabbed him by the collar and the smelly Pwent clawed back up before him.

"Come on, ye dolt!" Pwent yelled.

"Spear," Banak tried to explain, but Pwent wasn't even listening, was just tugging.

A searing eruption of fire burned suddenly in poor Banak's back as the spear twisted around, and he gave a howl of agony.

And Pwent tugged all the harder, understanding that there was no choice, no option at all.

The spear shaft snapped and Banak and Pwent fell free, sliding down the steep, turning chute Torgar's engineers had fashioned. They came into a straight descent then and fell through an opening, dropping several feet onto a pile of hay that had been strategically placed in the exit chamber. Of course by that point, most of the hay had been scattered by those coming down earlier, and the two dwarves hit hard and lay there groaning.

Rough hands grabbed them, ignoring their cries of pain. For they had no time to concern themselves over wounds.

"Close the chute!" Pwent cried, but too late, for down dropped a pursuer, a small goblin who had likely been thrown down as leading fodder by the bullying orcs. The creature landed right atop the still prone Banak, who gave another agonized groan.

Pwent rolled back and drove his spiked gauntlet through the stunned goblin's face, and shouted again for the others to close the chute.

Torgar Hammerstriker was already moving. He shoved a lever, releasing a block, then reached up and guided the block plate into position beneath the chute. The top side of the block plate was set with long spikes, and they claimed their first victim almost as soon as the chute was closed, an orc or goblin dropping hard atop it and impaling itself.

The dwarves were too busy to relish in that kill, though, grabbing their two fallen comrades up, ushering Pwent along and carrying the seriously wounded Banak. The escape chamber opened onto a ledge about a quarter of the way down the cliff, where more rope ladders were in place. Many of the Gutbusters were already well on their way down the ladders, rushing to join the critical battle at the base of the cliff.

As soon as he saw that spectacle below, Thibbledorf Pwent shook away his dizziness—or embraced it, for it was often hard to distinguish which with Pwent!—and scrambled over the ledge and down the ropes.

"I got him first," Ivan Bouldershoulder insisted.

He carefully lifted Banak up over his shoulder and moved to the rope ladder. Tred went over the cliff side before him, offering assistance from below.

Torgar and Shingles drew out their weapons and stood guard at the entrance to the escape room, ready to protect their departing friends should the chute's block plate fail and the orcs come down at them. Not until Ivan and the others were far below, moving to the second series of lower rope ladders did the pair from Mirabar turn and flee.

He grabbed for her, instinctively, as she reached out for him. They caught each other by the wrists and held fast as the barbarian fell away, then rolled around, rebounding off the stone of the cliff face. The jolt of his weight almost dislodged the woman from her rope, but she stubbornly held on, grasping with all of her strength and determination.

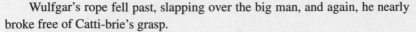

Wulfgar's rope fell past, slapping over the big man, and again, he nearly broke free of Catti-brie's grasp.

But she wouldn't let him go. Her arms stretched, her muscles ached, her shoulders felt as if they would simply pop out of joint.

But she wouldn't let go.

Wulfgar looked up at her, his eyes wide with fear—as much for her, she knew, as for himself, for it seemed that he would indeed dislodge her and drop them both to their deaths.

But she wouldn't let go. For all her life, at the cost of her life, Catti-brie was not going to let her friend fall.

It seemed like minutes, though in truth, it had all occurred in the span of a split second. Finally, Wulfgar caught Catti-brie's rope with his free hand and pulled himself in tight.

"Go!" Catti-brie prompted as soon as she got her wits back about her, as soon as she understood that if his rope had been cut, hers would likely go next.

Wulfgar went down hand-over-hand, verily running down the thick line. He reached a ledge and scrambled onto it, then set himself as solidly as the footing would allow.

Catti-brie came down fast behind, but not fast enough, as her rope, too, came free and she dropped. Wulfgar caught her and pulled her in, and the both of them pressed themselves flat against the cliff.

"Not yet halfway," Wulfgar said a moment later.

He motioned across to the other side of the small ledge, where the next descending ladders were set.

Drizzt double-stabbed, then stepped forward, driving on and forcing the orc to go tumbling backward, thus hindering any approach by those others near it.

The drow turned away immediately, rolling around, scimitars flying widely but not wildly, every strike in complete control, every cut working to fend any interference from the onlookers to the spectacle of Innovindil's battle with their leader.

The drow turned again, taking in the scene across the way, where Guenhwyvar leaped onto an orc and suddenly sprang away to bury another.

Drizzt eyes scanned over to the main fight as he turned to meet the charge of two more, and in that instant scan, he noted that Urlgen was pressing his elf friend hard, that she had stumbled backward. He had to go to her, but he could not as an orc pair pressed in.

"Fall into your anger!" he cried to Innovindil. "Remember Tarathiel! Remember your loss and embrace the pain!"

With every word he cried, the drow had to swipe or parry with his blades, working furiously to keep back the press of increasingly emboldened orcs.

"Find a place of balance," he tried to explain to Innovindil. "A balance between your anger and your determination! Use the pain to focus!"

He was asking her to become the Hunter, he knew. He was asking her to forsake her reason at that moment and fall into a more primal state, a state of feeling, of emotion and fear. As she had worked to coax him from that anger, so he tried to moved her toward it.

Was there any other way?

Drizzt let go of his fears for his friend and let himself fall even more fully into the Hunter. The orcs pressed in, and his scimitars went into a frenzied dance, driving them back, cutting them down.

Despite her suddenly desperate situation, despite the press of that ferocious orc and the tumult of the crowding monsters all around her, Innovindil did hear the words of Drizzt Do'Urden.

Her sword worked furiously, fending blow after blow as the wild orc came at her, his spiked gauntlets swinging wildly. Her feet worked with equal desperation, trying to keep under her as she was forced to dodge and to back away. She tried to find her rhythm, but the orc's fighting style was unconventional at best, with attacks quickly re-angled to punch through any opening she presented. Innovindil had no doubt that she could gradually come to a point of understanding and logical counter, but she knew that she had no such luxury of time.

Thus, she followed the words of Drizzt Do'Urden, who was battling so brilliantly to keep the others away. She allowed her mind to wander the road of memory, to Tarathiel's horrible fall. She felt her anger rising and channeled it into determination.

Out left went her sword, cutting short a hooking right hand, and back fast to center to block a left jab.

Innovindil put her conscious thoughts aside, fell into the flow and the feeling of the fight. Sparks flew as she connected with a fist, and again as the orc blocked her own thrust with a second metal gauntlet.

She worked with sudden intensity, taking the fight back to him, and at last discerned a pattern to his counters and his blocks.

He was setting her up for a head-butt, she realized, looking for that killing opening.

Innovindil rolled with the punches and the continuing flow, fell deeper into her instinctual self, catching herself somewhere between rage and complete concentration.

She ducked one blow and seemed to fall almost completely off her balance, lunging to the side so violently that her free hand slapped against her doeskin boot. In came the orc's counter punch—one that could have truly hurt her. But it was not aimed for her, and she understood that. Rather, Urlgen was going for her sword, striking it hard and knocking it aside.

Presenting him with that opening.

He darted ahead, his strong back snapping his head forward.

Innovindil threw her free hand up across her forehead to block and felt the sudden impact driving down through her hand and smashing against her skull. Back she skittered, trying to hold her balance, but stumbling down to a sitting and vulnerable position.

But Urlgen wasn't pursuing, for he had driven his head down not only onto the elf's blocking hand, but onto the small knife she had cleverly pulled out from her boot, impaling himself up to its crosspiece. The orc staggered back, the hilt of the knife protruding from his forehead like some strange unicorn horn. His black gauntlets waved in the air, and he turned around and around, head thrown back, pommel high in the air.

In that moment of distraction, when all the orcs nearby stared incredulously at their leader, Drizzt Do'Urden rushed to Innovindil and roughly pulled her to her feet, then pushed her ahead, to the north, and took up the run. The drow cut back and forth in front of the stumbling, still-dazed Innovindil, his scimitars clearing the way. When they came upon a particularly dense group of enemies, Guenhwyvar leaped by the pair, launching herself full force into the crowd, scattering them and taking them down.

Drizzt sprinted by, pulling Innovindil behind him. He took out a slender rope and thrust its other end into her hand, and that tactile feel brought her somewhat back to her sensibilities, reminding her of her duties. She urged Drizzt to press on, then brought a free hand to her lips and blew a shrill whistle.

Down they ran, angling to a flat area to the side, and, coming in low under the rising sun, they saw their one hope: a winged horse fast descending.

Sunset touched down and charged across the stone, scattering orcs before his run. Drizzt and Innovindil moved to intercept, one on either side, a rope strung before them. Sunset accepted the hit as he ran into the rope, and both drow and elf used the sudden pull to move them aside the pegasi's flanks, ducking under the high-held wings. Innovindil went up first, Drizzt leaping right behind her, as Sunset never slowed in his run. His wide wings beat the air, and he sprang away, half-running, half-flying, moving out of range of any pursuit.

"Go home, Guenhwyvar!" Drizzt cried out to the panther, who was still scattering orcs, still battling fiercely.

Up into the air they went, climbing fast to the north. Spears reached up at them, but few got close to hitting the mark, and those who did were knocked away by the scimitars of the drow. Finally, they were safely out of range, and Drizzt looked back to the diminishing battle.

The orcs were right up to the cliff, by then, and the drow understood that the dwarves had been pushed over into Keeper's Dale.

Had he gotten up into the sky only a minute before, he might have noted the telltale silver flash of Taulmaril.

Shoudra Stargleam's eyes glowed with determination as she watched her fireball engulf a handful of orcs, sending them scurrying about, all aflame.

The sorceress launched a second strike to devastating effect, a burning bolt of lightning that dropped a line of orcs at the center of their press.

More than one dwarf glanced back her way to nod in appreciation, which only spurred the proud and noble sceptrana on even more. She was a Battlehammer then, by all measure, fighting as fiercely as if Mithral Hall was her home and the dwarves all around her, her kin.

Beside her, little Nanfoodle worked his wonders, confusing an entire company of orcs with an illusion that had them charging face first into the cliff wall.

"Well done," Shoudra congratulated him.

She followed his mind attack with a physical blast of lightning that scattered the confused group and laid many low. Shoudra threw a wink Nanfoodle's way, then glanced up nervously at the cliffs, where dwarves continued their descent. Behind her, she heard those first who had come down forming up the defensive plan that would take them all to Mithral Hall's grand doors.

But they had to hold out until all were down.

The sceptrana turned away and sucked in her breath as one dwarf up ahead of her fell back, a spear deep in his chest. With no reserves immediately available to fill the gap, the sceptrana stepped forward, extending one arm and calling forth a burst of magical missiles that drove the orcs back. So many more came on, though.

Shoudra breathed a sigh of relief as a pair of dwarves scrambled past her, one going to his wounded kin, the other taking the downed dwarf's position at the low stone wall.

The orcs came on.

Looking all around to find the most effective area for her blasts, Shoudra's attention was caught and held by the spectacle of a single orc, a huge, armored creature swinging a sword nearly as tall as she at the end of one strong arm. He waded through his own ranks, orcs scrambling to get out of his way, stalking determinedly for the wall.

A crossbow bolt whistled out and smacked hard against his metal breastplate, but it did not penetrate and did not slow him in the least. In fact, he even sped up his rush, leaping forward into a roaring run.

Shoudra brought forth her magical power and struck him head-on with a lightning bolt, one that lifted him from his feet and threw him back into the throng. Figuring him dead, the sceptrana turned her attention back to the throng pressing the dwarves, and she ignited another fireball just forward of the dwarven line, so close that even the dwarves felt the rush of heat.

Again, flaming orcs scrambled and fell burning to the ground, but through that opening came a familiar figure, that great orc carrying a huge greatsword.

Shoudra's eyes widened when she saw him, for no orc could so readily accept the hit of one of her lightning blasts!

But it was the same orc, she knew, and he came on with fury, plowing over any orcs who could not scramble out of his way, reaching the wall and dwarven line in a rush, his sword slashing across, scattering the dwarves. He dropped his shoulder and plowed on, driving right through the hastily built rock wall, knocking heavy stones aside with ease.

Dwarves went at him, and dwarves went flying away, slashed by the sword, swatted with his free arm, even kicked high into the air.

And all the while, Shoudra suddenly realized, he was looking directly at her.

On came the mighty orc, and Nanfoodle gave a shriek. Shoudra heard the gnome quickly casting, but she knew instinctively that he would not divert that beast. She brought her hands up before her, thumbs touching tip to tip.

"Be gone, little demon," she said, and a wide arc of orange flames erupted from her fingers.

The sceptrana turned, using the distraction to get out of the way, but then she got punched—or thought it was a punch. She tried to move, but her feet skidded on the stone, and she was strangely held in place. She looked back, and she understood, for it was no punch that had hit her, but the thrust of a great-sword. Shoudra looked down to see less than half of that blade remaining before her chest; she knew that it had gone right through her.

Still with only the one mighty hand holding the sword, the orc lifted Shoudra Stargleam up into the air.

She heard Nanfoodle shriek, but it was somehow very far away.

She heard the dwarves cry out and saw them scrambling, in fear, it seemed.

She saw a sudden flash of silver and felt the jerk as the great orc staggered backward.

Her legs looped within the coils of the drop rope, Catti-brie hung upside down, reloading her bow, letting fly another shot at the monstrous beast who held Shoudra aloft. Her first arrow had struck home, right in the thing's chest, and had knocked the orc backward a single step.

But it had not penetrated.

"Get him away!" Catti-brie yelled to Wulfgar.

The barbarian had leaped to the ground and was even then bearing down on the orc. He cried out to Tempus and brought his hammer to bear—brought his whole body to bear—throwing himself at the orc, trying to knock it aside.

Suddenly Wulfgar was flying backward, blocked, stopped and thrown back by a swipe of the great orc's arm. The great barbarian, who had taken hits offered by giants, staggered back and stumbled to the ground.

The orc lifted his arm higher, presented the squirming Shoudra up into the air, and roared. The sword came to fiery life, and Shoudra howled all the louder. The mighty orc jerked his arm side to side.

Shoudra Stargleam fell apart.

Catti-brie hit the beast with another arrow, and a third, but by that last shot, he wasn't even staggering backward from the blows anymore. He turned and started toward Wulfgar.

The spinning Aegis-fang hit him hard. The orc stumbled back a few steps, and almost fell to the ground.

Almost.

On came the beast, charging Wulfgar with abandon.

The barbarian recalled Aegis-fang to his hand and met that charge with another cry to his god, and a great swipe of his mighty hammer. Sword against hammer they battled, two titans standing tall above the onlookers.

Down came Aegis-fang, smashing hard against the orc's shoulder, sending him skidding to the side. Across came the flaming greatsword, and Wulfgar had to throw his hips back, barely getting out of reach.

The orc followed that wide slash by leaping forward even as Wulfgar came forward behind the blade, and the two collided hard, muscle against muscle.

A heavy punch sent Wulfgar flying away, had him staggering on the stones, barely able to keep his feet.

The orc pursued, sword in both hands, leaping in for the killing blow that the barbarian couldn't begin to block.

An arrow hit the orc in the face, spraying sparks across the glassteel, but he came on anyway and cleaved at the barbarian.

At least, the orc thought it was the barbarian, for where force and fire had failed, Nanfoodle had succeeded, misdirecting the blow with an illusionary Wulfgar, to the swift demise of a second orc who happened to be standing too close to King Obould's rage.

Catti-brie leaped down to the stone, caught up Wulfgar under one arm, and shoved him away.

The orc moved to catch them—or tried to, for suddenly the stone around his feet turned to mud, right up to his ankles, then turned back to stone.

"Bad orc!" cried a green-bearded dwarf, and he poked the fingers of his one hand in Obould's direction.

The furious orc king roared and squirmed, then reached down and punched the stone. Then, with strength beyond belief, he tore one foot free.

"Oooo," said the green-bearded dwarf.

Down came more help then, in the form of the Gutbusters, falling all around the pair, leaping into battle. Any who got near to the great orc, though, fell fast and fell hard.

Down came Torgar and Tred, Shingles and Ivan, and the wounded Banak, sweeping up Catti-brie and Wulfgar, the stunned and crying Nanfoodle, and all the others in their wake as they ran flat out across Keeper's Dale, angling for the doors of Mithral Hall.

Only then did Catti-brie notice the pillar of strength that stood supporting the routed dwarves in the wider battle, the indomitable power of her own father, legs planted firmly upon a tall stone, axe sweeping orcs away, dwarves rallying all around him.

"Bruenor," she mouthed, unable to even comprehend how it could be, how her father could have arisen once more.

Out toward the center of the dale, Bruenor marked well the run of Banak's retreat and of his own son and daughter—and glad he was to see them alive.

His forces had held strong, somehow, against the overwhelming odds, had stemmed the undeniable tide.

At great cost, the dwarf king knew, and he knew, too, that that orc sea would not be denied—especially since the giants were fast approaching, bolstering the orc lines.

From up on his rock, the dwarf king called for a retreat, told his boys to turn and run for the doors. But Bruenor didn't move, not an inch, until the others had all broken ranks.

His axe led the way as he chased after them. He felt the spears and swords reaching out for him, but there were no openings within the fury that was Bruenor Battlehammer. He spun and he dodged. He fled for the doors and stopped suddenly, reversing his course and chopping down the closest orc, and sending those others nearby into a terrified retreat.

He ushered all behind him as the doors drew near, refusing to break and flee until all were within. He fought with the strength of ten dwarves and the heart of a thousand, his many notched axe earning more marks that day than in many years previous. He piled orc bodies around him and painted all the ground a bloody red.

And it was time to go, he knew, and those holding the door called out to him. A swipe of his axe drove back the orc wall before him, and Bruenor turned and sprinted.

Or started to, for there behind him stood an orc, spear coming forward at an angle that Bruenor could not hope to fend. Seeing his doom, the dwarf king gave a howl of denial.

The orc lurched over backward and a spike drove out through its chest. A helmet spike, Bruenor realized as Thibbledorf Pwent stood straight behind his attacker, lifting the orc up in the air atop his head.

Before Bruenor could utter a word, Pwent grabbed him by the beard and yanked him into a stumbling charge that brought him into the hall.

And so Thibbledorf Pwent was the last to enter the dwarven stronghold that fateful day, the great doors booming closed behind him, the dead orc still flopping about atop his helmet, impaled by the long spike.

THROUGH THE BODIES

It hadn't been the victory he had hoped to achieve, for most of Clan Battle-hammer's dwarves, even those from atop the cliff, had gotten back into the safety of Mithral Hall. Worse still for King Obould, there could be little doubt of the identity of the dwarf leader who had emerged to bolster the retreat. It had been King Bruenor, thought dead and buried in the rubble of Shallows.

The Battlehammer dwarves had chanted his name when he'd charged from the hall, and the sudden increased ferocity and stubbornness of their defense upon the red-bearded dwarf's arrival left little real doubt for Obould about the authenticity of their leader.

The orc king made a mental note to speak with his son about that curious turn of events.

Despite the unexpected arrival, despite the dwarves' success in retreating from the cliffs, Obould took satisfaction in knowing that the dwarves could not claim a victory there. They had been pushed into their hall, with little chance of getting out anytime soon—even then, Gerti's giants were hard at work seal-ing the hall's western doors. The orc losses in Keeper's Dale had been consid-erable, but there was no shortage of dwarf dead lying among that carnage.

"It was Bruenor!" came the predictable cry of Gerti Orelsdottr, and the giantess stormed up to the orc king. "Bruenor himself! The King of Mithral Hall! You claimed he was dead!"

"As I was told by my son, and your own giants," Obould calmly and quietly reminded her.

"The death of Bruenor was the rallying cry, dog!"

"Lower your voice," Obould told the giantess. "We have won here. This is not the moment to voice our fears."

Gerti narrowed her eyes and issued a low growl.

"You did not lose a single giant," Obould reminded her, and that seemed to take the wind out of Gerti's bluster. "The Battlehammer dwarves are in their hole, their numbers depleted, and you did not lose a single giant."

Still staring hard at the orc king and still snarling, she walked off.

Obould's gaze went up the cliff face, and he thought of the tremendous explosion that had heralded the beginning of the battle and the shower of debris that had followed. He hoped that his claim to Gerti was correct. He hoped that the fight atop the cliff had been a success.

If not, Obould decided, he would murder his son.

Her face wet with sweat and tears, blood and mud, Catti-brie fell to her knees before her father and wrapped him in a tight hug.

Bruenor, his face scarred and bloody, with part of his beard ripped away and one eye swollen and closed, lifted one arm (for the other hung limply at his side) and returned the hug.

"How's it possible?" Banak Brawnanvil asked.

He stood with many others in the entry hall, staring incredulously at their king, returned from death itself, it seemed.

" 'Twas Steward Regis who found the answer," said Stumpet Rakingclaw.

"Was him who showed us the way," agreed Cordio Muffinhead.

He walked over and slapped Regis so hard on the shoulder that the halfling stumbled and nearly dropped from his feet.

All eyes, particularly those of Wulfgar and Catti-brie, fell over Regis, who seemed uncharacteristically embarrassed by all the attention.

"Cordio woke him," he offered sheepishly.

"Bah! Was yer own work with yer ruby," Cordio explained. "Regis called to Bruenor through the gem. 'No real king'd lie there and let his people fight without him,' he said."

"You said the same thing to me some days ago," said Regis.

But Cordio just laughed, slapped him again, and continued, "So he went into that body and found the spark o' Bruenor, the one piece left o' the king keeping his body breathing. And Regis told him what was going on. And when me and Stumpet went back to our healing spells, Bruenor's spirit was back to catch 'em. His spirit heard our call as sure as his body was taking the physical healing. Come straight from Moradin's side, I'm guessing!"

Everyone turned to regard Bruenor, who just shrugged and shook his head. Cordio became suddenly solemn, and he moved up before the dwarf king.

"And so ye returned to us when we were in need," the cleric said quietly. "We pulled ye back for our own needs, and true to yer line, ye answered them. No dwarf can deny yer sacrifice, me king, and no dwarf could ever ask more o' ye. We're in now, and the halls're closed to our enemies. Ye've done yer duty to kin and clan."

All around began to murmur and to look on more closely. They quieted almost immediately, many holding their breath, as Cordio's intent became clearer.

"Ye've come to us, returned from Moradin's own halls," the cleric said to Bruenor, and he brought his hands up before the dwarf king to offer a blessing. "We can'no compel ye to stay. Ye've done yer duty, and so ye've earned yer rest."

Eyes went wide all around. Wulfgar had to grab Catti-brie, who seemed as if she would just fall over. In truth, the barbarian needed the support every bit as much as she.

For it seemed like Cordio's words were affecting Bruenor greatly. His eyes were half-closed, and he leaned forward, shoulders slumped.

"Ye need feel no more pain, me king," Cordio went on, his voice breaking.

He reached up to support Bruenor's shoulder, for indeed it seemed as if the dwarf would tumble face down.

"Moradin's welcomed ye. Ye can go home."

The gasp came from Regis, the sobs from everywhere around.

Bruenor closed his eyes.

Then Bruenor opened his eyes, and wide! And he stood straight and fixed the priest with the most incredulous look any dwarf ever offered.

"Ye dolt!" he bellowed. "I got me home surrounded by stinkin' orcs and giants, and ye're telling me to lie down and die?"

"B-but . . . but . . ." Cordio stammered.

"Bah!" Bruenor snorted. "No more o' the stupid talk. We got work to do!"

For a moment, no one moved or said anything, or even breathed. Then such a cheer went up in Mithral Hall as had not been known since the defeat of the drow those years before. They had been chased in, yes, and could hardly claim victory, but Bruenor was with them again, and he was fighting mad.

"All cheers for Bruenor!" one dwarf cried, and the throng erupted. "Hero of the day!"

"Who fought no more than the rest of ye," Bruenor shouted them down. "Was one of us alone who found the way to call me home."

And his gaze led those of all the others to a particular halfling.

"Then Steward Regis is the hero of the day!" one dwarf cried from the back of the hall.

"One of many," Wulfgar was quick to reply. "Nanfoodle the gnome facilitated our retreat from above."

"And Pikel!" Ivan Bouldershoulder put in.

"And Pwent and his boys," said Banak. "And without Pwent, King Bruenor'd be dead on our doorstep!"

The cheers went up with each proclamation.

Bruenor heard them keenly and let them continue, but he did not join in any longer. He still wasn't quite sure of what had happened to him. He recalled a feeling of bliss, a sense of complete peace, a place he never wanted to leave. But then he had heard a cry of help from afar, from a familiar halfling, and he walked a dark path, back to the realm of the living.

Just in time to jump into the fight with both feet. It would take some time to sort through the fog of the battle and measure their success or failure, Bruenor knew, but one thing was certain at that moment: Clan Battlehammer had been pushed back into Mithral Hall. Whatever the count of the dead, orc and dwarf, it had not been a victory.

Bruenor knew that he and his kin had a lot of work to do.

In the corridor running off the main entry chamber, Nanfoodle sat against the wall and wept.

Wulfgar found him there, among the many wounded and the many dwarves attending to them.

"You did well today," the barbarian said, crouching down beside the gnome.

Nanfoodle looked up at him, his face streaked with tears, and with more still rolling down his cheeks.

"Shoudra," he whispered and he shook his head.

Wulfgar had no answer to that simple remark and the horrific images it conjured, and so he patted the gnome on the head and rose. He brought a hand up tenderly to his ribs, wondering how bad he had been hurt by that tremendous blow the mighty orc had delivered.

But then all thoughts of pain washed away from the barbarian as he spotted a familiar figure rushing down the corridor toward him.

Delly ran up and wrapped her husband in a tight hug, and as soon as they were joined, all strength seemed to leave the woman, and she just melted into Wulfgar's strong chest, her shoulders bobbing with sobs.

Wulfgar held her tight.

From the entrance to the corridor, Catti-brie witnessed the scene and smiled and nodded.

In Keeper's Dale, Obould had lost orcs at somewhere around a four-to-one pace to the dying dwarves, an acceptable ratio indeed against a dug-in and battle-hardened defender. No one could question the cost of that victory, given the gains they had achieved.

Up there, though, without even getting any real body counts, Obould understood that the dwarves had slaughtered Urlgen's orcs at a far higher ratio, perhaps as sorely as twenty-to-one.

The ridge was gone, and all but one of the giants who had been up there were dead, and that one, who had been thrown several hundred feet by the monstrous explosion, would likely soon join his deceased companions.

Obould wanted nothing more than to call his son out for that disaster and to slaughter the fool openly before the entire army, to lay all the blame at Urlgen's deserving feet.

"Go and find my son!" he commanded all of those around him, and his crooked teeth seemed locked together as he spat the words. "Bring Urlgen to me!"

He stormed around, looking for any sign of his son, kicking dead bodies with nearly every stride. Only a few moments later, an orc ran up and nervously bowed over and over again, and explained to the great orc that his son had been found among the dead. Obould grabbed the messenger by the throat and with just that one strong hand, lifted him into the air.

"How do you know this?" he demanded, and he jerked the orc back and forth.

The poor creature tried to answer, brought both of its hands up and tried to break the choking grip. But Obould only squeezed all the harder, and the orc's neck snapped with a sharp retort.

Obould snarled and tossed the dead messenger aside.

His son was dead. His son had failed. The orc king glanced around to measure the reaction of those cowering orcs nearby.

A few images of Urlgen flashed through Obould's thoughts, and a slight wave of regret found its way through the crust of the vicious orc's heart, but all of that quickly passed. All of that was fast buried under the weight of necessity, of the immediate needs of the moment.

Urlgen was dead. Given that, Obould knew that he had to focus on the positive aspects of the day, on the fact that the dwarves had been dislodged from the cliff and forced back into Mithral Hall. It was a critical moment for his forces and the course of their conquest, he understood. He had his kingdom overrun, from the Spine of the World to Mithral Hall, from the Surbrin to Fell Pass. Little resistance remained.

He had to maintain his force's enthusiasm, though, for the inevitable counterstrike. How he wished that Arganth was there, proclaiming him to be Gruumsh.

Soon after, though, Obould learned that Arganth was dead, killed by an elf and a drow.

"This is unacceptable!" Gerti growled at the orc king as night encompassed the land and the weary army continued its work of reorganizing.

"Nineteen of yours fell, but thousands of mine," the orc countered.

"Twenty," said Gerti.

"Then twenty," Obould agreed, as if it didn't matter.

Gerti scowled at him and asked, "What weapon did they use? What magic so sundered that mountain arm? How did your son let this happen?"

Obould didn't blink, didn't shrink in the least under the giantess's imposing stare. He turned and walked away.

He heard the telltale noise of a sword sliding free of its sheath and moved completely on instinct, drawing forth his own greatsword as he swung around, bringing his blade across to parry the swipe of Gerti's huge weapon.

With a roar, the giantess came on, trying to overwhelm the orc king with her sheer size and strength. But Obould brought his sword to flaming life and slashed it across at Gerti's knees. She avoided the cut, turning sidelong and lifting her leg away from the fires.

Obould barreled in, dipping his shoulder against her thigh and driving on with supernatural strength.

To Gerti's complete surprise, to the amazement of all in attendance—orc, goblin, and giant alike—the orc king muscled Gerti right off the ground. With a great heave, he sent her flopping through the air to land hard and unceremoniously on the ground, face down.

She started to rise but wisely stopped short, feeling the heat of a fiery greatsword hovering above the back of her neck.

"All that is left here are the dwarven tunnels," Obould told her. "Go and defend the Surbrin or take your dead and retreat to Shining White." Obould bent low and whispered, so that only Gerti could hear, "But if you forsake our road now, know that I will visit you when Mithral Hall is mine."

He backed away then and allowed Gerti to scramble back to her feet, where she stood staring down at him with open hatred.

"Enough of this foolishness, giantess," Obould said loudly, so that those few astonished onlookers could hear. "We are both angered and sorrowful. My own son lies among the dead.

"But we have won a great victory this day!" the orc king proclaimed to the throng. "The cowardly dwarves have run away and will not soon return!"

That brought cheering.

Obould walked around, his arms raised in victory, his flaming sword serving as a focus of their collective glory. Every so often, though, the orc did glance back at Gerti, letting her alone see the continuing hatred and threat in his jaundiced and bloodshot eyes.

For Gerti, there was only uncertainty.

From a distance, another watched the celebration of the victorious orcs and saw that flaming sword lifted high in glory. Satisfied that he had done his duty well and that his work had been of a great benefit to the retreating dwarves, Nikwillig of Citadel Felbarr settled back against the cold stone and considered the distant glow of the setting sun.

His vantage point had allowed him a view of the general course of the battle not only up there, but down in Keeper's Dale, and he knew that the dwarves had been driven underground.

He knew that he had nowhere to run.

He knew that he would soon have nowhere to hide.

But so be it, the dwarf honestly told himself. He had done his duty. He had helped his kin.

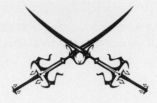

EPILOGUE

"He will know that his son is dead by now," Drizzt remarked.

He was brushing Sunset, paying particular care to the many scratches the pegasus had suffered in the flight from the orc army.

"Then perhaps he will come to us," the elf replied, "and save us the trouble of hunting him down."

Drizzt's concern at Innovindil's grim tone washed away when he considered her wide grin. He watched her walking toward him—he couldn't pull his eyes away. She had taken off her battle gear and was dressed in a simple light blue gown of thin, nearly sheer material that rested smoothly against her every curve. Behind her, the last rays of day leaped forth from the horizon, backlighting the elf in a heavenly glow, surrounding her beautiful hair in soft yellow hues.

"You brought forth my anger," Innovindil reminded him.

"I have found a place of . . . concentration," Drizzt tried to explain, shaking himself from the spectacle of the elf. "A state of mind that is clearer. When I left my homeland, I traveled alone through the dark ways of the Underdark. For ten years, I wandered, mostly alone." He gave a grin and produced the onyx figurine. "Except for Guenhwyvar."

"If the Underdark is as I have heard, then you should not have survived."

"Nor would I have, even with Guen, had I not found the Hunter."

"The Hunter?"

"That place of concentration," Drizzt explained. "A place within my heart and mind where rage transforms into focus."

"Most would argue that rage is blinding."

"And so it can be," Drizzt agreed. "If it is not in control."

"And so you become this creature of focus and rage . . ."

"And the cost is heavy, I have come to know," Drizzt added. "The cost is joy and hope. The cost is . . ."

"Love?"

"I do not know," Drizzt admitted. "Perhaps there is room within for all that I must be."

"Room for Drizzt, and for the Hunter?"

The drow merely shrugged.

"We have much to do," Innovindil told him. "With the dwarves' retreat, all the North is imperiled. Who will rouse the forces of the land against Obould if not Drizzt and Innovindil?"

Drizzt nodded in agreement and added in all seriousness, "Should we rouse the world against him before or after we kill him?"

The thought brought a grim smile to Innovindil's fair face, creating a most amazing paradox to the lavender eyes of the drow. Beautiful and terrible all at once, she seemed, the warmest of friends and the deadliest of enemies.

"We gotta get back," Dagna grumbled. "Them trolls're heading for the halls, not to doubt!"

"We cannot!" Galen Firth shouted. "Not now! My people are nearby—somewhere."

He stopped and looked around, as did many of the others, at the muddy landscape, the few scraggly trees and the ground torn by battle and the march of many great trolls, as Galen Firth had warned upon his arrival to Mithral Hall. The band had been near to the southern tunnel exits when they'd realized the truth of the Nesmé rider's words, when a band of ugly and smelly trolls had struck hard at them.

Quick thinking and quicker feet had gotten the dwarves away, the band scrambling down a tunnel that was too low for the large trolls to pursue. That long tunnel, first completely of stone and rising and turning to stone and earth, had taken them to the edge of the Trollmoors and somewhere to the east of Nesmé, by Galen Firth's reckoning.

Grim-faced, Dagna stared hard at the animated Galen and gradually came to understand the man's point of view. As Dagna felt that his duty was to return to Regis and warn Mithral Hall, so Galen Firth fiercely believed that his course was to search there, to find his people and help them to safety. Dagna couldn't ignore that plea. He had been sent there to help the rider from Nesmé do just that.

"I'll give ye three days o' hunting," Dagna conceded. "After that, me and me boys gotta turn back fast for Mithral Hall. Them trolls didn't keep up the chase—they're heading for me home."

"You do not know that."

"I feel it," Dagna countered. "In me old bones, I can feel the threat to me kinfolk. What're Trollmoors trolls doing in tunnels?"

"Perhaps they chased the folk of Nesmé underground."

Dagna nodded and hoped that Galen Firth was right, that the trolls were not marching on Mithral Hall but were merely finishing their business there.

"Three days," he said to the man.

Galen Firth nodded his agreement, and fifty dwarves gathered up their packs and weapons. They had run flat out for hours, and that after a day of hard marching. The sun was sinking fast in the west, the long shadows reaching out to darken all the land.

But it was not the time for rest.

"The elf's out there," Bruenor muttered over and over.

Gathered beside him, Regis, Catti-brie, Wulfgar, and some of the other leaders just sat quietly and let all the information sink in. They had told him of the flight from Shallows, the fall of Dagnabbit, the unexpected rescue from Mirabar's refugees, and all the fighting that had followed.

"Well, we got to set our defenses all about, above at the gates and below in the tunnels," the dwarf king said at length. "No telling where them pigs'll hit at us."

"Or if they will," put in Regis, and all eyes turned to him. "What is their plan? Do they wish to try to complete their victory? They know the cost will be great."

"Or what else, then?" asked Bruenor.

Regis shook his head, closed his eyes, and let it all settle in his thoughts. The orcs that had driven them into the hall were different, he understood. They had acted cleverly at every turn. They had acted more like an army with a purpose than the typically vicious mob one associated with goblinkin.

"Whether it's the giants," said Regis, "or this orc of renown Obould Many-Arrows. . . ."

"Curse his name!" spat Tred McKnuckles.

"Yerself and yer kin o' Felbarr know him, to be sure," Bruenor said to Tred. "Are ye thinking he's to come crashing in?"

Tred gave a snort and shrugged.

"If he's thinking to, then he's thinking to have all his fellows slaughtered," promised Banak Brawnanvil, who wasn't sitting, but rather lying on a cot set in the side of the room.

Even with all the work Cordio and the others had done on him, the tough old dwarf was far from healed, for the orc spear had bitten him deep indeed. Despite his physical infirmity, there seemed no quit in the old dwarf, though.

Others seconded that sentiment.

"Any word from the south?" Bruenor asked, turning to Regis.

"Not from Dagna, no," the halfling replied, and he glanced around, somewhat sheepishly. It had been his decision to send the dwarves off with Galen Firth, after all. "But there is some fighting in the lower tunnels. Trolls have come forth, and in force."

"We'll hold them," Banak promised. "Pwent and his boys went down to join in the fighting. Pwent likes trolls, he says, because their pieces wiggle even after ye cut 'em off!"

Bruenor nodded, taking it all in. Mithral Hall had held strong against an onslaught of dark elves; he was confident that no orcs, even with the aid of trolls and frost giants, could ever hope to dislodge Clan Battlehammer.

They had much to do in strengthening their defenses, in licking their wounds and organizing their forces, but Bruenor took heart that in his absence, Mithral Hall had been well guided.

But while his confidence in his clan and home held strong, the other issue, that of a lost friend, played heavily on the crusty dwarf's heart.

"The elf's out there," he muttered again, shaking his head. His face brightened as he looked to Catti-brie, Wulfgar, and Regis in turn. "But I'm knowing a way out o' here and a way to get him back in."

"Ye cannot be thinking o' going out there!" Cordio Muffinhead scolded, and he stormed up to Bruenor's side. "Ye just got back to us, and ye're not for wandering—!"

He almost finished the sentence, until Bruenor's backhand sent him stumbling against the wall.

"Ye hear me, and ye hear me good," Bruenor told them all. "I seen the other side now, and I'm back with a mouth full o' spit on this. Ye call me yer king, and yer king I'll be—but I'm a king doing things me own way."

Bruenor looked back to his three dear friends and added, "The elf's still out there."

"Then maybe we should go get him," Regis replied.

Catti-brie and Wulfgar exchanged determined looks, then turned to regard Regis and Bruenor.

So it was agreed.

On a high bluff on a windblown mountainside, the dark elf watched the sunset. He wondered about the personal relevance of that image, of the light sinking behind a dark line. The change of day and, perhaps, of a chapter in the life of Drizzt Do'Urden.

He was an elf, yes, as Innovindil had reminded. He would see many sunsets, unless an enemy blade laid him low.

Merely thinking of that very real possibility forced a resigned grin to the drow's lips. Perhaps it would be such for him, as it had been for his friends, as it had been, before his very eyes, for poor Tarathiel. But it would not happen, he vowed silently then and there, until he had paid back the ugly orc, Obould Many-Arrows.

For all of it.